BLOOD TRAIL

ALSO BY MATT QUERY AND HARRISON QUERY

Wilderness Reform

BLOOD TRAIL

A NOVEL

Matt Query and Harrison Query

EMILY BESTLER BOOKS

ATRIA
NEW YORK   AMSTERDAM/ANTWERP   LONDON
TORONTO   SYDNEY/MELBOURNE   NEW DELHI

ATRIA

An Imprint of Simon & Schuster, LLC
1230 Avenue of the Americas
New York, NY 10020

For more than 100 years, Simon & Schuster has championed authors and the stories they create. By respecting the copyright of an author's intellectual property, you enable Simon & Schuster and the author to continue publishing exceptional books for years to come. We thank you for supporting the author's copyright by purchasing an authorized edition of this book.

No amount of this book may be reproduced or stored in any format, nor may it be uploaded to any website, database, language-learning model, or other repository, retrieval, or artificial intelligence system without express permission. All rights reserved. Inquiries may be directed to Simon & Schuster, 1230 Avenue of the Americas, New York, NY 10020 or permissions@simonandschuster.com.

This book is a work of fiction. Any references to historical events, real people, or real places are used fictitiously. Other names, characters, places, and events are products of the author's imagination, and any resemblance to actual events or places or persons, living or dead, is entirely coincidental.

Copyright © 2026 by Matthew Query and Harrison Query

All rights reserved, including the right to reproduce this book or portions thereof in any form whatsoever. For information, address Atria Books Subsidiary Rights Department, 1230 Avenue of the Americas, New York, NY 10020.

First Emily Bestler Books/Atria Books hardcover edition April 2026

EMILY BESTLER BOOKS/ATRIA BOOKS
and colophon are registered trademarks of Simon & Schuster, LLC

Simon & Schuster strongly believes in freedom of expression and stands against censorship in all its forms. For more information, visit BooksBelong.com.

For information about special discounts for bulk purchases, please contact Simon & Schuster Special Sales at 1-866-506-1949 or business@simonandschuster.com.

The Simon & Schuster Speakers Bureau can bring authors to your live event. For more information or to book an event, contact the Simon & Schuster Speakers Bureau at 1-866-248-3049 or visit our website at www.simonspeakers.com.

Interior design by Davina Mock-Maniscalco

Manufactured in the United States of America

1 3 5 7 9 10 8 6 4 2

Library of Congress Control Number is available.

ISBN 978-1-6680-2423-2
ISBN 978-1-6680-2425-6 (ebook)

Let's stay in touch! Scan here to get book recommendations, exclusive offers, and more delivered to your inbox.

This book is dedicated first and foremost to our parents,
and all others raising their children to love the mountains.
As well as the women we love who keep our feet on the ground
and our heads from ascending into orbit, Sonya and Chelsea.
Lastly, to the next generation for whom these books
will be around long after we're gone, Clark and Quinn.

PROLOGUE

FLANNEL SHIRTS AND NECK TATTOOS.

To Clark Rickert, sometimes it felt as though his entire career had just been a bloody, churning cauldron of flannel shirts and neck tattoos.

Throughout the seventeen years he'd held this job, Clark had encountered many other things far more frequently: guns, violence, screaming packs of hounds, bears, bone saws, gut piles, steep mountain passes, the frosted predawn darkness. Even so, there was something about these two specific things—when adorned by the same person in the specific places Clark worked—that dilated his pupils, quickened his heart rate, and set his teeth to grinding.

Clark owned flannel shirts himself. He'd known people with neck tattoos over the years who were pleasant enough, and assumed that they, likewise, owned a flannel shirt or two. He felt absolutely nothing when he saw someone with a neck tattoo in a flannel at a fly shop or a bar. But whenever he was in the kinds of places his job sent him, and he encountered someone with both these characteristics, he knew it meant things were probably about to go to shit, and fast.

Clark knew this was unfair profiling. He knew this was a flagrant social or implicit bias. He had no doubt about it. All the implicit bias, cultural competency, and scenario-based DEI trainings he'd completed over the years confirmed as much. *He just didn't care.* It was his only organic, unflinching prejudice, and he'd keep space for it with no shame. It set off a red, blinking warning light in the control HUD of whatever part of the brain prepares one for violence.

Clark slowly turned the focus wheel on his Leupold range-finding binoculars. The image clarity of the man across the mountain valley became sharp and distinct, and that warning light began to blink.

Booking photos and social media had confirmed the man Clark hunted had a large neck tattoo, but it was Clark's gut that knew he'd be wearing an old flannel when this day finally came. Yet again, his gut had been right. It felt good seeing this man wear that shirt, the full uniform and livery of his lifelong adversary and foe, here in this wild country where Clark worked. It meant he was officially *one of them*.

Checking the last box in a confirmation bias checklist is undeniably pleasing. This guy's decision to throw on a flannel shirt that morning, before coming to this place, justified everything for Clark. All the time and effort he'd put into making this moment happen, all the disgust and disdain for him he'd let fester and grow unchecked. What he saw was also a vow that a confrontation was forthcoming, one that would balance upon a razor's edge of savagery. This bias was one that had been born of blood and screams.

Six different people who fit this profile had tried to kill Clark over the years. One, in '06, broke Clark's nose with a headbutt then slammed a cheap gas station pocketknife into his scapula. In '09, one put a .380 bullet into his other shoulder. In 2012, one killed his friend Roy Payton, a fellow game warden.

Roy bled to death in sandy, frozen dirt on a sage-covered hillside under the prettiest sunset Clark had ever seen. A frigid, screaming wind blew so hard that evening Clark couldn't hear what Roy whispered as he died. The wind did not obscure Roy's pleading, desperate eyes. Eyes that told Clark the words being whispered, the last words no one would ever hear, were of profound importance to the dying man.

A bark of static hummed through Clark's earpiece before the words came.

"Command for TF Alpha, what's your status? Over."

Clark pressed down on the Push-To-Talk button clipped onto the shoulder strap of his sweat-stained olive-drab plate carrier.

"TF for Command, still at overwatch. Gonna start our creep into staging positions in five. Will report when staged and set to execute the warrant. Out."

He ignored the response as he brought the binoculars back to his eyes. He watched his target take a ravenous drag from his third consecutive cigarette.

He felt all the tension start to ramp up, as it always did. He watched the man flick a cigarette butt onto the steep, rocky two-track he and the other two men stood on. Clark assumed the other two were just a couple of their leader's junkie, booger-eating yes-men.

Elijah Austin Miles was their leader's name. *Elijah.* Clark repressed a scoff as the name echoed in his mind. As a veteran game warden, Clark had busted countless mountain bumpkin tweaker dickheads. However, the criminal act of poaching big game animals was really the only similarity between all those men, and *this one.*

This guy only kept a single canine tooth from each animal he killed, and he'd cobbled together quite the collection over the last few years. He fell far more comfortably into the psych profile of a serial killer than that of any poacher throughout the Rocky Mountain West. This man was thrill-killing. *Collecting souls.*

Clark had spent so many hours burning every word of Elijah's criminal file into his mind he had permanent familiarity with it, like initials carved into an old desk. Over the last few months, Clark had actually started dreaming about this guy, seeing him scream commands at his pack of abused, mangy hounds from an old forest road. A road just like those Elijah had cut his pack of hounds loose from so many times before—a road just like the one he stood on now. He'd never seen this man in person until now, let alone looked him in the eye, but he harbored a boiling hatred for him nonetheless, sight unseen.

Clark had been after Elijah since he'd gotten out of the state penitentiary two years earlier, where he'd done a stint for kidnapping his ex-girlfriend and beating her younger brother half to death. Clark had found fourteen bears, twelve wolves, and six mountain lions he knew this man had illegally killed in that time. Each missing a single canine tooth. Until now, he'd been one step behind Elijah, never catching him in the act, hounds uncaged and gun in hand.

He thought back on the repulsive scene he'd come upon in May, where Elijah had thrown burning Duraflame logs into a wolf den. The desperate, terrified young female wolf and all five of her pups had been riddled with .223 bullets as they scrambled out to escape the flames and noxious chemical smoke. Elijah hung all six dead wolves from a ponderosa near their den with nooses made of 550 paracord. A piece of folded card stock had been stuffed into the mother wolf's mouth, upon which *too late again, Warden* was written with a Sharpie. One canine tooth from each wolf had been sloppily torn from their gums with pliers.

The bays, barks, and howls of Elijah's pack of bear dogs punched out across the valley from the timbered slope that rose above the road where Elijah stood, chain-smoking Pall Mall cigarettes next to his 1997 Toyota T100. He'd kitted the truck out with a three-inch lift, a roof-mounted light bar, and a big dog kennel in the bed. Painfully cliché poacher rig.

"Flannel and fuckin' neck tats."

Clark made the comment to himself, only slightly more than a wheeze.

"What's that, Cap?"

The men standing behind him began to think Clark had not heard the question when he finally responded, not turning to look at them as he did.

"Nothin'."

After another long moment, Clark pulled the binoculars from his eyes, turned, and came down the small rock outcropping to face the five men crouching behind him. One, like Clark, was another game warden for the Law Enforcement Division of the Montana Department of Fish, Wildlife & Parks. The others were two Teton County sheriff's deputies, a trooper from the Montana Highway Patrol, and a special agent with the United States Forest Service. Yet another ragtag task force, staring at him and awaiting orders. Clark let out a long exhale through his nose, then spoke.

"It all comes down to staging positions now, fellas. We can't afford *any fuckups*. This is a high-risk warrant service in a high-risk environment. We can shuck and jive with whatever happens after we make the callout, but only if we nail staging and timing. Screwed-up staging positions means screwed-up containment, and screwed-up containment blows this arrest. Containment is *everything* in country like this. We blow that, and I promise one or all these dickheads'll get away. We're steppin' off *now*, fellas. No such thing as a dumb question at this point, so ask 'em if you got 'em. I need to know you're all crystal fuckin' clear on where your staging position is, and how to get there from here."

All five other men just nodded as Clark looked each of them in the eye.

"Victor, you're with me. JD and Theo, you're staged to move on the back a' the truck while Mark and Lance, playin' blocker, will be set another fifty meters downslope from the county boys. If these guys try to split, they'll either head straight down the road into you guys, or they'll boogie around the truck and up into the timber, toward their dogs. I want a comms check when staged. We good?"

All nodded, tightening grips on rifles or shotguns each held across the olive-green or black plate carriers of their respective agencies. He scanned their features for signs that fear or anxiety had reached the level that gets people killed in situations like this. He was pleased to only find what he considered to be a normal, healthy amount of both.

Anyone who'd worked with Clark, and even those who simply knew his history and reputation, was entitled to such nervousness. Clark had never witnessed it himself, but on dozens of occasions over the last seventeen years, a county, state, or federal law enforcement office had buzzed into a state of excitement whenever they received his request for assistance on a high-risk arrest warrant or raid. They all knew him for the ruthless hunter of men that he was, and how often his operations ended in violence or gunfights. They all knew he only ever asked for assistance to form a task force when he was going after a *real* monster, and they all knew he only ever made a play when these monsters were at their most dangerous; they, themselves, were also hunting.

The USFS special agent in the group, Lance, whom Clark had worked with quite a bit over the years, chuckled as he asked the question the other four men had been wondering since they'd first gotten eyes on their target a half hour earlier.

"*How in the shit* did you know this bastard would be parked *right there*, at this exact moment, *ten days ago*?"

Clark looked back at Lance with no discernible emotion in his features, the expression of someone watching a dull movie in a dark theater. He glanced at the others briefly with his gray-green eyes, one by one, then spoke.

"*Let's move.*"

He took the short-barreled carbine into his hands from where it hung on its sling across his chest, and started moving through the forest toward the echoing, hollow cadence of Elijah's baying hounds.

Clark knew just from the dogs' hunting song that they had not yet actually gotten eyes on or treed a bear or mountain lion, but were still just working a scent. The sounds made by a pack of bear and lion hounds were very different once they actually had one cornered. It was febrile, frantic wailing for their houndsman to come and collect their quarry, to shoot it from the tree and give them the satisfaction of sinking teeth into it.

It took fifteen minutes for the team to creep down the steep, forested slope to the bottom of the valley, cross the trickling creek at the bottom, then stalk up into their staging positions on the slope below the road. Double-clicks in his radio's earpiece told Clark everyone was in position and ready. He was close enough to hear Elijah and his goons laughing. He looked to his fellow game warden, Victor, who stared back at him with wide eyes, rifle shouldered at the low-ready.

Clark nodded at the younger man, and when the gesture was returned, he pressed his radio's PTT button. He hissed the command with his sharp, gravelly voice, sending the message to the other five men on the mountain with him, as well as the command and standby element of Forest Service Rangers and state troopers staged a few miles away.

"*Making arrest.*"

Clark weaved through the last few trees then stepped onto the road about twenty meters uphill from where the three men loitered around Elijah's truck. They stood in a row, staring down the road to their left, away from Clark, toward the area where the two sheriff's deputies were crashing noisily through the rocks and trees toward them. Right as he saw the three men's muscles start to react—fists clenching, hips and shoulders beginning to turn—he barked out his words in a sharp volume, just below a scream.

"Montana FWP enforcement, hands in the air. *Put your hands in the fucking air.*"

All three flinched and whipped their heads in his direction. He moved toward the driver's-side headlight of the truck at jogging speed. Clark's eye never left his rifle's holographic sight as he moved, keeping its illuminated circle-dot reticle steady and centered on Elijah's chest. Muscle memory took over now.

Hips and hands, Clark knew, *they always give themselves away with their hips and their goddamned hands.*

They remained in a line along the driver's side of the truck, stunned as they watched Clark move toward them like a storm. Elijah's 30-30 lever-action rifle was on the hood of his truck, a few feet from his right elbow. The next in line, the guy in the middle, had a .44 Magnum revolver holstered on his belt next to a ridiculously large bowie knife. The third man, the farthest from Clark, stood next to the bed of the truck, holding an old bolt-action rifle in one loose hand. They flinched again and looked toward the sheriff's deputies as they came into view and began moving toward the back corner of the truck bed.

The deputies were now screaming their own commands, demanding weapons be dropped and hands be raised. USFS Ranger Lance and the state trooper Mark were now charging up the middle of the steep road to the deputies' right with weapons raised. *Containment achieved*, Clark noted with relief.

It was a supremely rare thing for someone to try escaping a surprise arrest by sprinting *into* a formation of armed, screaming cops. With his team in position, the only real option of escape remaining was scrambling over the truck, then up the steep, craggy mountainside that rose on the other side of the road. Lance's and Mark's loud voices, and then Victor's off Clark's right shoulder, joined those of the two sheriff's deputies to echo around the valley.

The frantic chorus of law enforcement demands began to compete with the sounds coming down the mountainside where Elijah's bay hounds frothed, yowled, and raged along the scent trail of some bear or cougar.

The man farthest from Clark tossed the rifle forward as though it had grown red-hot and shot his hands into the air. His gaunt, needle-scarred arms shook like river willows. He started crying immediately, shouting at the other two to surrender. The guy in the middle also shook like a twig, but he was locked in place, knees quivering as he stared feverishly at Elijah like one of his half-starved hunting dogs.

Elijah ripped his belligerent gaze between the state trooper and USFS agent coming up the road behind the truck, the sheriff's deputies in front of him to his left, and the two game wardens at his three o'clock. He began bouncing on the balls of his feet, lips pulling back into a snarl to expose a slipshod array of yellow, rotten teeth.

He was working himself up, Clark could see, so he seized the man's complete attention in a way that always seemed to work. He snarled his full name.

"*Elijah Austin Miles*, you are under arrest for the unlawful killing of big game. *Put your hands in the fucking air.*"

All six officers had formed a wide crescent around the trio of men, taking care to close all options of escape and to stay outside one another's shooting lanes. The man who'd tossed away the rifle was on his knees now, pleading for the one with the revolver to do the same. That man remained locked in place, trembling, staring at Elijah with a pure, pants-shitting terror in his eyes. The other five officers were looking between Clark and the three poachers, awaiting his order or move.

The screaming of the five officers and the poacher on his knees blended into a frenzied roar that Clark turned down, intentionally washing the noise away with an exhale.

Clark and Elijah both knew their own, personal business was all that remained relevant here. They both knew this was a proper standoff now, eyes locked like their pupils were connected by a steel fishing line. Neither paid any attention to the tempest of screams, howls, or weeping from the men and dogs raging in the valley around them. Clark's eyes were dark slits under the brim of his old black Stetson hat. Elijah's eyes were widening. Bright red vessels latticed his jaundiced eyeballs like parasitic worms snaking from his brain to feed on his pupils.

The shaking throughout Elijah's body was showcased by the glistening strand of saliva that jittered as it ran from his meth-wrecked teeth, over his chapped bottom lip, to a darkened slick on the T-shirt under his flannel. The large vein beneath the faded mess of a tattoo on his neck pulsed visibly.

A reflection quickly passed through Elijah's mind that he was just like one of the dozens of bears or mountain lions he'd killed: stuck up a tree with starving, furious dogs seething around its trunk.

That thought slipped away as he realized he recognized this game warden. The calm one who'd just shouted his name.

He'd never been able to actually see the face of the dark man from the dreams that had been plaguing him these last months, but this felt like him. All the dreams were a bit different, but in all of them he was paralyzed, unable to move, talk, beg, or scream while he knew this dark man *was coming*. In some of these dreams he'd been stuck in his childhood bedroom, looking out the dirty window to see the dark man pass between trees. In others he'd been frozen in his bunk in his old cell at the Montana state penitentiary in Deer Lodge, the echo of this man's boots growing as he strolled down the row toward him, always whistling that same tune Elijah recognized but could not place.

This was him.

Elijah had never been more certain of anything. The urge to rip out one of this man's canine teeth coursed through his body with more urgency than any craving for opiates or meth he'd ever felt. It was the only thing in the world that mattered anymore. It was the only thing that had ever mattered. A grotesque smile spread across his face as he let his white-knuckled fists open slowly.

No muscles in Clark's body or face moved. This was yet another moment in Clark's life where it seemed as though everything and every person in the world around him had been bogged down into slow motion by some invisible force.

Everything, and every person, *except for him*.

He knew exactly what Elijah was about to do with his head, hands, shoulders, and hips as he turned to reach for the rifle on the hood of his truck. He'd known for some time now.

Flannel and fuckin' neck tats.

Clark also knew he had to let Elijah get far enough into the effort so the other officers, in their keyed-up states of adrenaline, would also be able to clearly perceive what Elijah was attempting to do. He'd learned long ago that all the after-action investigation and fuss was considerably easier if he waited just long enough for a few other witnesses to see, in real time, that which he somehow managed to see ahead of time.

So Clark waited, very patiently, for that precise moment.

And when Elijah made the long-anticipated move for his gun—just as his hips rotated and his hands extended upward, away from his body and toward the rifle—Clark shot him in the face.

The 62-grain 5.56 hollow-point bullet struck Elijah Miles in the tear duct.

The bullet blossomed like a rose as it passed through Elijah's brain—a considerable portion of which followed it through the baseball-sized hole it punched out the back of his skull—then cracked into the windshield of that man's beloved truck, splintering the glass into a white spiderweb.

The crack of the rifle shot stunned everyone else into silence as it echoed in a static roar across the mountain valley.

Elijah's body toppled over, lifeless as though all his tendons had just ceased to be. His face slammed into the hood of his truck above the wheel well. It connected with enough force to splash a pint of blood onto the hood and redirect the course of his fall, which crumpled back-first onto the rocky road and kicked up a halo of dust around his body.

Clark had busted hundreds of poachers and other violent criminals throughout his career. He'd killed three other men before today, and maimed or hurt many times that number. None of those men, or his efforts to stop them, had mattered at all. They were all nameless now. Meaningless. Because he'd never felt *this*. He'd never felt as fulfilled as he did the moment that bullet tore through the brain of Elijah Austin Miles.

The sensation became physical as a heavy weight lifted from Clark's hips and shoulders. A pulsing ring of furious dark red around his vision and a piercing tinnitus screaming in his ears all vanished in an instant. He hadn't even noticed any of it until the moment it washed away. He'd never felt anything like it before. Nothing even close. But he did not reflect on its uniqueness, or his having just experienced a psychosomatic shock wave caused by another's death. He just shivered, blinked hard, and chalked it up to adrenaline.

Before anyone had taken their eyes from Elijah's body—before it had even come fully to rest—Clark's rifle was aimed at the man who remained standing with the holstered pistol, shaking and stunned as he stared down at his dead friend. Eyes like a loyal dog's that whined and paced around the old man who'd just collapsed on their morning walk, anxious for him to stir and rise while knowing he never would, capable of feeling death, yet unable to grasp its permanence.

Again, Clark saw clearly how this guy was about to draw down on him. He saw how his shoulders would tense and hips would turn as he dropped his trembling hand to his revolver. He saw how his eyes would narrow in agitation as he yanked on the pistol's battered grip, then open wide in dread as he realized the gun was still button-strapped into the holster on his belt. He saw how that dread would curdle into a tragic humiliation that can only be found in the face of a man—one who's spent a lifetime idolizing fabled cowboys of the old West—realizing his final act in life was giving himself a wedgie instead of drawing his gun.

Clark's gift of violence-induced foresight was not necessary now, however. Plain old experience rendered everything about a guy and situation like this down into a cashable certainty. The outcome was already set.

This was a twitchy, pinned-out Narcan mascot who'd just been caught dead to rights in the commission of a felony now refusing to move his hand away from his gun: a situational recipe justifying lethal use of force in virtually any jurisdiction in America. On top of that, Clark sensed the other five officers' adrenaline was about to start blistering their skin. He knew this dude was a sudden fart away from getting himself a toe tag and a body bag.

Clark also knew, however, that this guy wasn't an inherently evil man. He hadn't forfeited his right to life long before today—as the dead monster at his feet most certainly fucking had. This was the walking, talking sociological afterbirth of bad luck, worse decisions, and not enough hugs. The type who'd gone all in on every busted flush he'd ever seen, yet still blamed every slight in life on the dealer for a bad hand. The type whose judgment calculus defaulted toward throwing most things into the old *fuck-it bucket*. This was a stupid man who'd only ever had stupid, shitty friends.

And Clark Rickert had a soft spot for such men. These were his people. Those of his tribe.

So when the dumbass finally went for his gun, Clark didn't shoot him. Instead, he flipped the safety on his weapon and exploded forward in such a sudden eruption of speed it made his deputy flinch.

By the time the terrified simpleton even registered the shadowy mass blitzing toward him, it was too late. Clark had already closed the distance and speared the heavy, steel flash hider on the muzzle of his rifle into the man's chest.

The strike connected like a snakebite with brutal, rough-hewn precision, fracturing the man's sternum. Both local deputies and the younger game warden winced as a sickening, wet crack punched into the still mountain air.

The man's body bent around the rifle as air and spit blasted from his mouth. Before his lungs had emptied, Clark had already dropped his rifle to hang on its sling, clamped one viselike grip onto the guy's shoulder, and another onto the wrist of his gun hand. As he collapsed forward, Clark spun around him like a wraith. In what looked like a single, fluid movement, Clark arrested the guy's collapse, set him down almost gently, then pinned him with a knee to his upper arm and an oaken forearm to the back of his head.

The others cast quick glances at one another, then moved toward the last poacher. He was still on his knees, but silent now, all his screeching panic replaced by a look of dumb wonder. He didn't resist the officers as they cuffed him. He barely registered it. He just stared at the man who'd just hit his buddy like a truck. The man who then rolled his buddy onto his side and began patting his back as his friend gagged and hacked bile into the dirt. The man he'd just seen move faster than he thought men could.

Two and a half hours later, the assistant chief of Montana Fish, Wildlife & Parks Law Enforcement Division, Leonard Price, arrived at the scene.

Elijah's body and the two living poachers had been taken to the little town of Choteau an hour earlier, once the state and county detectives finished their primary investigation. Those detectives plus around twenty other personnel from USFS, Montana State Police, Teton County Sheriff's Office, and FWP were still at the scene wrapping up their respective after-action duties.

Price looked around until he spotted Clark, alone, leaning on the hood of one of the trucks now choking the steep forest road. The county and state detectives approached him, both mentioning their confidence in the lawfulness of his warden's use of lethal force, as well as how downright impressed they were by it. Price shook hands and thanked both, then made his way up to Clark. Neither man spoke as Price leaned his elbows on the hood next to Clark's and took in the same view of the ridge across the valley.

Not much needed to be said.

They'd worked together at FWP since Clark graduated from the police academy seventeen years earlier and started his career as a game warden. While twelve years Clark's senior, Price had treated him as an equal since the start. Today, each man privately figured he was the other's best friend. Of the 108 commissioned FWP law enforcement officers throughout the state of Montana, there were only two who had been on the job longer than Clark: the division chief, behind a desk in Helena, and Leonard Price himself, the chief's second in command. After a full minute of silence, Price shifted his weight onto one elbow to face Clark.

"Gettin' soft, *eh*?"

Clark didn't look his old friend in the eye, but turned his head a few degrees toward Price and lifted his eyebrows. Price spoke through a grin.

"The county and statie detectives said that after you smoked the ringleader, another one a' them sons a' bitches made a move for his gun. But, instead a' just shootin' him, too, they said you went 'n beat the brakes off that poor little tweaker so bad *he'll wake up on Christmas achin' from it*."

Clark couldn't help but snort in amusement at Price's prose. Both men spoke in the old Western *Montana patois*.

It wasn't a distinct accent like those found in the South, Midwest, or Northeast. It was just *Western*, still heard throughout rural stretches of Montana, Wyoming, and the Dakotas, a laconic rhythm with flat, clipped vowels, hard *R*s, and an occasional, almost bashful twang. It's a deliberate parlance, one annealed in terse exchanges about hunting, ranching, weather, and Indians. It's a speech pattern that was left rough and unfinished by a need for it to be easily shouted outdoors in country where wasting time can be deadly. Extra consonants or words easily replaced by a single letter were discarded. Words like *or* and *than* were replaced by slapping an *R* or *N* onto the front of any word requiring the services of a conjunction. *G*s were amputated from the *-ing* at the end of a word, leaving an unsanded *N* for a stump.

Clark took off his Stetson hat, ran his arm across his eyes and forehead, then put the hat back on. He glanced at Price with an unamused, bored expression, then back at the ridgeline across the valley. It was illuminated in the deep yellow light of an afternoon starting to turn toward evening.

"Been here all goddamn day, Price. You better be tellin' me we're rigged to flip and that you're my ride. Finished all my AAR stuff two hours ago. So, can we jet?"

Price nodded.

"*Yeah* . . . yeah, I 'spose we're all squared away here. Same as before, though, gonna have to put you on administrative leave for a bit, shootin' protocol 'n all. C'mon, I'll bring you back to your rig."

Clark put on his pack, slipped his rifle sling over his shoulder, and the two men walked down the forest road through the mess of trucks.

Clark whistled the tune softly as they went, the only one he ever whistled. The only one he knew how to whistle, Price suspected, if such a thing were possible. It was the sad, lonely theme song to his favorite Western, *High Plains Drifter*. Over the years, Price had challenged Clark on many occasions to whistle something else, literally any other song, just to prove he possessed the ability. Clark had responded to each with a mumbled suggestion that Price *kiss his ass* or some other such thing, but never had.

Elijah's pack of hounds had been rounded up throughout the day and put into a kennel in the back of an FWP truck. They'd been barking and yowling nonstop, increasing in anger and volume whenever one of the officials on the scene got within a few meters of the truck bed. Clark walked by the kennel, close enough to touch the dogs' noses, and glanced into the eyes of the closest one.

All six dogs' tails dropped as their ears went back. They backpedaled—a few letting out quick whines as unkempt toenails clicked on the bed of the truck—until they were huddled together along the far side of the kennel, shivering visibly in their lean, muscular shoulders.

For the first time that day, all six dogs went completely silent.

CHAPTER 1

DEPRESSION.

It's the fourth stage of grief, at least according to the 1969 Kübler-Ross model. *The stage of lonely, hopeless, sad, and despairing reflection as an individual comes to realize the magnitude of their loss.*

It was visible in the eyes and posture of almost everyone in the room, and audible from the few who'd begun to softly cry or mutter prayers. They weren't dealing with the death of a loved one, but they'd all just witnessed the death of something equally precious: their grasp on the natural order of the world.

Their conceptions of what fell within the realm of *reality*, and what was supposed to be relegated to the leagues of fiction, fable, and fantastical impossibility. This understanding had been there for them all since they were children, hearts pounding in their little ears as they fought the dread of what might dwell under their beds, or charge from a dark basement as soon as they turned their backs on it. These were inveterate, foundational notions of understanding everyone developed, honed, and relied upon throughout an entire lifetime. The nameless program within everyone's mind that ran the profoundly important yet simple calculation: *what's real, what's not, what's possible, what's impossible.*

This conception, understanding, program, whatever it was, was something almost everyone filling the Situation Room in the West Wing of the White House had taken for granted, and now they knew it. None of them had realized how important and precious it was until they'd just watched it die.

They'd watched it *murdered*, kicking and writhing as its face was held into the mud. And they grieved its death like they'd grieve an older sibling.

They'd torn through the first three stages of grief pretty quickly.

Denial, the first stage, really only lasted a minute or so. The distant, confirming expressions on the faces of several in the room—the president, the secretary of defense, the director of national intelligence, the director and deputy director for operations of the CIA, and officers from the CIA's Special Activities Center—told them all that denial was futile.

Anger came next, demands to know *why the hell* they hadn't been briefed on this situation until now, or *how the hell* those few who'd known didn't understand it better.

Then came the *negotiation* phase. This is when things started getting a bit hysterical. The president's advisers, members of his cabinet, Joint Chiefs of Staff, a few senior legislators, they all began shouting over one another. Suggestions flew with unfounded confidence, growing in both volume and absurdity.

We need the British Royal Household, the Israelis, and the Vatican on the phone immediately. We should nuke the threat. No, we should reason with it, cut a deal. No, let's find it and sink it to the bottom of the ocean in a titanium cage or send it into space.

Malcolm Thorn, the man who'd just shattered all these people's minds, stared at the president sitting at the far end of the massive mahogany table. Thorn had spent the last twenty-one years playing this moment over in his mind: who'd be here, what they'd say, and how they'd react when it all really began.

Between the retirement of the man who'd been on duty during the *last event* in 1909 and Thorn's first day on the job ninety-four years later, six other men had held Thorn's title and position. Five of those had gone through their entire careers fully aware of how unlikely it would be for them to be activated to carry out the duties of their position, almost certain they'd never be in this situation. They'd each held their post with faithful dedication all the same, marshaling information and resources to improve the effectiveness of their successor, and all who'd follow. The sixth of those men, however, Thorn's predecessor, thought he *might* be on the clock when it all went down. Toward the end of his career, however, Thorn's predecessor had confidence that his successor would certainly be on station *when it happened*. As such, he'd recruited, trained, and advised his replacement with that in mind, and had done well.

Standing here, now, staring at the president, Thorn thought about those men. He wondered how they'd critique his execution of the job thus far. He barely heard one of the president's senior advisers shouting about the Navy's *direct energy weapons and surface warfare lasers*, or the vice chairman of the Joint Chiefs' insistence that *martial law be declared and the DHS and FCC shut down the internet immediately*. Thorn tuned it all out and just watched the president. He saw the large man's jaw and fists clench and assumed, correctly, this meant that his deep well of patience and control had finally run dry.

The president launched up from his chair and slammed a heavy briefing binder onto the table. A shock wave of pens, papers, tablets, mugs, glasses, coffee, and water jumped, clattered, and spilled away from the binder's impact. He paid zero attention to the yelps and gasps as everyone flinched away from the crash. He just slowly planted his massive fists into the mess he'd made, leaned forward, and cast his gaze down the long table. He did not look at the CIA director, but locked eyes with the head of the CIA's Directorate of Operations, DDO David Benson. He asked his question in the salty, calm, and threatening timbre he was so famous for.

"Benson, ETA on standing up a task force and workup for your direct-action operation?"

Benson responded immediately.

"Five days."

The president flicked his eyes onto the man sitting next to Benson, chief of the Special Operations Group, Harry Jacobson. The SOG element of the CIA's Special Activities Center was the most terrifyingly effective direct-action paramilitary force within the Directorate of Operations, or, arguably, within all of humanity's history. Jacobson had started running the SOG three presidents earlier.

"Your assets ready for that kind of turnaround, Harry? You good with this?"

Jacobson held the president's gaze as he took a deep, long breath. He knew well that the president, his old friend, was asking him for *far more* than a simple yes or no in this moment.

"Yes. Most of my Ground Branch operators, aviation personnel, and tech and surveillance teams are stateside. All REDCON-1 and combat ready. When it comes to workup, we don't have much time, or much need. We've only got one target location flagged with any confidence. All we know about enemy force profile is that it's increasing by the second, so no matter what, we're going into this with an incomplete target package, and with speed of action as our top priority. Assignment of additional JSOC elements to the task force will only take a day, and with how patchy and thin our intel is, unless we stumble upon a gold mine of information, I can't see how targeting and mission prep could take more than five days."

Jacobson leaned forward, glancing at his deputy chief, Charlotte Bishop, as he rested his elbows on the table. Each saw the thoughts of the other in that glance. Charlotte had been his deputy at the SAC for over six years. They'd both grown fluent in the kind of silent, professional, shorthand language only born from long hours, profound stress, and extreme consequences. Harry looked back up at the president with narrow eyes as he answered the silent question he knew had actually been asked.

"This isn't going to be like anything we've ever done, for more than the obvious reasons. There's no playbook here, and no time. We know little about this enemy, but enough to clarify a few mission parameters I need to make clear, *right now*. The first has to do with risk tolerance. To do our job—to interrupt and get inside this particular enemy's decision loop—we'll need to move, pivot, act, *and react* faster than we've ever had to. Targeting, op planning, intel collection, we have to do it all ad hoc, make calls on a dime and on the fly, *while already engaged*. As such, straight out the gate we need to accept a baseline of elevated risk of fuckups that *we have never* considered acceptable. The second parameter has to do with *loss tolerance*. The monumental severity of this threat, by itself, imposes a new rule of gameplay. A new minimum standard of uncompromising dedication to mission success, one *that will* frighten us all. A condition that we accept certain . . . *utilitarian tenets*. I'm not talking about running probability models or acknowledging potential for collateral damage, incidental loss, or spilling American blood in American streets. I'm talking about making a commitment, *right now*, that no matter what kind of bump we feel under the tires, we cannot, *we must not*, hit the brakes and look in the rearview mirror until this is done."

The president held his old friend's gaze. He saw the warning it carried. A few, those who grasped what Jacobson had just said, stared blankly at the table. All the others looked between the president and Jacobson, fear and concern growing in their eyes. After several long moments, the president looked across the table to Vice Admiral Francis Rourke, commander of Joint Special Operations Command.

"Admiral?"

The head of JSOC nodded at the president then gestured toward Jacobson.

"I've already re-tasked elements from CAG, DEVGRU, 24th STS, the 160th, and army ISI to high-ready standby for assignment, and set all special operations assets in JSOC's stable to critical readiness posture. So far as I'm concerned, until this operation's over, the entirety of JSOC will effectively serve as their QRF, or on standby for direct action, as needed. Day or night, Benson and Jacobson get whoever and whatever they need."

The president looked back at DDO Benson.

"What's cover and concealment strategy, Dave? What's OpSec look like for this?"

Benson, again, responded immediately.

"Special Activities Center's in full swing. Political Action Group's propo, media, and covert influence teams will have a full report for operational security, cover and concealment plans, and contingencies done by this evening. I'll sit down with AG Cooper here when we're done to make sure we've got full cover at the DOJ. Also, as usual, the PAG and the SAC at large are ready to activate the full suite of joint-op capabilities with our counterparts at the NSA, DHS, FCC, and the rest. I also have a list of names of those at the state and private level who I'd suggest we read into this operation, as well as a list of our own officers and assets embedded in those and other private institutions. Obviously, keeping this operation under wraps from the public and media will depend on flash and volume of kinetic engagements: what happens, where, and who's around when it does. As Harry said, we'll be doing it all live. From what little we know, the target seems keen on staying isolated in rural places, which should make things easy once we brief the governor, but only so long as it stays rural. If we end up going loud and banging it out in downtown Bozeman, we'll have to adapt."

Benson moved forward in his chair and linked his fingers on top of the table.

"To be frank, Mr. President, the spectrum of consequences of this operation becoming public grow quite insignificant when compared to the . . . *cataclysmic* nature of the threat we're facing. OpSec and containment will certainly remain a critical priority, but we're going to be on the ground, rather noisily turning over stones. Harry's spot-on in this being something completely new on the ground side, so we're going to have to move and shoot with respect to OpSec, as well. The nature of this operation necessitates OpSec and concealment taking a second chair, given how little time we'll have to be preemptive with such efforts. As Harry said, we simply don't have the luxury of hesitation or taking our eyes off the road on this one, so I just want to be clear that we'll be sweeping our tracks as we go here. All that being said, for now, every OpSec duck I've got is already in a row on this."

The president nodded, then looked down the row of Joint Chiefs on the right side of the table.

"I want all assets in the western eleven states, the Dakotas, Nebraska, Kansas, Oklahoma, and Texas standing at FPCON Delta within the hour. I want Alaska, Hawaii, and all other CONUS assets, personnel, and facilities in critical readiness posture. This will obviously leak, so, Benson, get the PAG on it. Blame it on a terrorist threat, whatever you think's best. Get with Hammond and get him set up to hold a presser on whatever story you cook up."

Benson, FBI Director Chris Hammond, and all the Joint Chiefs nodded gravely in response, the weight and historic significance of what had just been ordered clear on their faces.

After a long moment the president hung his large, shaved head and stared down at his fists, planted into the tabletop, knuckles still sporting scars from boxing at the Naval Academy, and other much nastier fights that had followed. Of those few sitting close enough to actually hear some of what the president whispered to himself, only one had sufficient acuity and familiarity with the Bible to place it somewhere toward the top of Chapter 3, Second Thessalonians.

This is right around when the *depression* stage of most of their grief kicked in.

The attorney general had swiveled his chair away from the table to stare blankly at the ground, elbows on his knees. The director of national intelligence pointed at some spot above the table with a pen in his hand, lips pursed, eyes narrowed as though preparing to speak, but he hadn't moved in two minutes.

The secretary of state cupped a palm over her mouth and wept softly. Several others did the same. No one would hold it against them. Not now.

Many would never reach the fifth and final stage. *Acceptance.*

For most in the room, *acceptance*—coming to terms with the loss of what was now their dead, bloated, and rotting conception of what was real and what was fantasy—would never be achieved. At least not in a way that involved moving past the fourth stage. Under these circumstances, the best most of those present in this infamous, hallowed room could hope for was a state of depressing, hopeless acceptance.

Some of those present, however—those who'd never put much faith in what the world told them was real or impossible, or those who just didn't really give a shit—would move on, accepting these new conditions in stride. The president had a bit of both these qualities, as well as an immovable resolve that intimidated allies and adversaries alike across the world. He looked up at Thorn and found the short, pudgy older man staring back at him with no discernible emotion.

He'd only met this strange little man once before. In this very room, in fact, a few days after his inauguration. About a year and a half earlier in a prescheduled briefing only including himself, the secretary of defense, the director of national intelligence, his national security adviser, and the chairman of the Joint Chiefs. Thorn had introduced himself, told them his classified title and position within the government, and then briefed them on this situation and what it was he did.

They'd all thought it was a joke. Thorn had anticipated this.

He'd pointed to a remote on the table and then toward the array of large digital monitors on the wall behind him. Looking at Thorn now, the president recalled the apologetic, almost parental sympathy in his face as he'd done so. He'd told the president that there were several people standing by on a secure video connection to corroborate the validity of what he'd just told them. The president turned on the monitors, and to all their surprise—and bone-chilling dread—those people were two former American presidents, the prime minister of Israel, the president of France, the king of England, and the pope. He'd also given the president an envelope for his eyes only, which described a secret location within the White House where he later found several letters from former presidents, addressed to their successors, on this particular issue. He'd read them all several times, but had read those from Jefferson, Lincoln, and Teddy Roosevelt dozens of times over the last eighteen months in his rare moments of privacy.

He'd come close to calling Thorn on several occasions to order him to return and provide more information, but never had. It had been a profoundly busy time, one that'd flown by, so he'd just prayed to never look into Thorn's calm, calculating eyes ever again.

The president, and those four other men who'd been at the initial briefing, were also the only people who'd been read in on the details of Thorn's *other duty*, the duty that came after confirming *the event* was beginning, informing them immediately, and briefing them on what it all meant. Thorn had just met with those same five men in the Oval Office an hour before this briefing began, and assured them he was well underway in carrying out this other duty, even going so far as to claim that he was very close to completing it.

The president, to his own surprise and without any real basis, felt confidence and faith that Thorn would succeed.

Perhaps it wasn't confidence, but just hope. The president, unlike most other living humans, actually knew how important it was for Thorn to succeed in this other duty, and how desperately all those others depended on it now.

CHAPTER
2

"**EXCUSE ME, CAPTAIN** Rickert..."

Clark looked up from his computer to find his administrative assistant and secretary, Lucy Westerna, in the doorway to his office, rapping her knuckles lightly on his doorframe. Clark raised his eyebrows and nodded at her, putting on his best version of a smile. He could always tell she was a bit nervous around him, even now. While it certainly did not seem to work with everyone, his forced smile was the only way he knew how to try to palliate the anxiety he so often perceived in those who had no choice but to interact with him.

"Assistant Chief Price is here. I know you were expecting him. He's still on the phone in the lobby; I just wanted to give you a heads-up."

Clark nodded.

"Thank you, Miss Lucy. Send him on back when he's ready."

Lucy turned from the office doorway and walked back toward her desk. Clark saved a draft of the email he'd been working on and leaned back in his chair, closing his eyes, giving himself a moment to relish the day's first respite from the torture of drafting reports and lengthy emails. In a moment of slight panic, he leaned back down and saved the email again, twice in a row.

A year back, the whole division got brand-new computers and for some sadistic reason was forced to embrace a new email system. Lucy had shown him how Outlook autosaves drafts of emails every few seconds, but Clark did not trust the feature. Not one damn bit. Computers were one of the very few things in this world capable of cracking his composure and sending him into a public display of anger. It was an unreasonable hatred, bordering on something pathological.

Software programs and operating systems were screeds of chaos to

Clark, always one click or swipe away from mutiny and sabotage. Something in his brain prevented him from developing any kind of working fluency with them. He felt they were expressions of complexity for complexity's sake, fun house mirror rooms, double-dealing boxes of shit and treachery.

God preserve Miss Lucy, Clark often thought. If it weren't for her amused patience and hand-holding, he might've walked off the job a few times due to his computer-related rage. On several occasions, infuriated by his own technological illiteracy, he'd begun indulging rage-baked fantasies about driving to Helena and smashing the computer onto the floor of the governor's office. *Fuck the twenty-year pension*, he'd snarl as he spiked his badge onto the floor. *One more minute is unbearable, let alone another year.*

The fast-approaching twenty-year pension had been building itself up into a separate source of anxiety and frustration for Clark, one that had been spitefully amplified by the dizzying complexity of new software programs he'd been forced to use. In reality, Clark's rage at new technology was almost entirely a manifestation of his anxiety associated with retirement.

The twenty-year pension.

A sociocultural Americana tradition of one's solemn, graceful drift from a life of government service into a life of reading, fly-fishing, and training a hunting dog. As a physically and mentally youthful forty-three-year-old, it felt downright punitive to Clark. He loved reading, fly-fishing, and bird hunting. On a Saturday, maybe, to clear the mind before another week of hard work. *Not on some goddamned Tuesday.* The prospect of retirement had felt less optional the closer it crept, shedding all the luster of a reward. At this point, it felt like something externally imposed, an *expectation* that he move out of the damn way and out to pasture.

The Montana state legislature hadn't been helping, either, with their initiation of an audit on the entire Law Enforcement Division of FWP several months earlier. As game warden captain of Region 4—an area spanning twenty million acres across twelve counties, with only thirteen wardens under him—he'd felt abused by the tedium of the audit, emailing random stats and figures, answering questionnaires, and other bullshit that kept him indoors instead of outdoors.

He'd always been treated with complete deference and respect by his current and former bosses, and all the chiefs of the state Law Enforcement Division he'd worked under. The current governor, like the three before him, loved Clark, albeit in the way a Saudi prince or Russian oligarch loves a pet tiger. Even so, the timing of the audit felt like punishment. Clark sensed that when one finally hit the twenty-year pension mark, no matter who they were or how relatively young they may be, something deep within the steam, boilers, and cogs of state government just wanted them gone.

This office, which he hated so deeply, was something of a tabernacle for Clark. Something about it pushed his emotional baggage to the surface. Perhaps it was just what he considered the stunningly depressing aesthetic of all government offices, or his general disdain for being indoors at all.

A sinister energy roiled around this room, one he felt staring back at him every time he looked up from his computer. Like the ambient static hum that dances menacingly around an alpine ridge above the tree line just before a summer lightning storm. Clark suffered here in this room. But he felt there was a contemplative purpose to that suffering, a meaning that underlay the room's tyrannical effect on his emotions, so much so that he'd actually added things that increased his discomfort.

He opened his eyes to stare up at the wall across from his desk, where two things, both deeply sacred to him in their own way, were hung, one above the other. Clark did not have artwork or anything decorative in his home. He did not have cherished photo albums, keepsakes, or any real treasures beyond the collection of arrowheads and spear points he'd found over the years that sat on the windowsill in his bathroom. The only things he owned that could reasonably be described as *art*—important belongings one felt compelled to display in positions of visual prominence—were those two things on the wall of this office, this room he put such strenuous effort into avoiding at all costs.

The first of these items was the skull of a mule deer buck, mounted on a walnut plaque he'd cut, sanded, and stained himself. He'd killed that deer in 2004, just a few months before starting this job. He'd tracked and stalked it for three days before shooting it. Legally, of course. This buck netted a Boone & Crockett score of just over 198 points, landing the animal and his own name in the Montana record book as one of the largest mule deer ever harvested in state history. However, it symbolized something far more sanctified and profound than a state hunting record. He'd never tried putting it into words, but it served as a totem for new beginnings, of starting again, a reminder of the new quarry he now hunted.

Poachers.

Between 1998 and 2004, a restless and eventually rather famous poacher operated throughout Montana. He'd shot two mule deer bucks even larger than the one on Clark's wall, three of equal size, and had illegally *guided clients* who'd killed quite a few that came close. Those deer, however, *were not* in the state record books. And this poacher had taken great care to ensure they never would be, as he'd done with the trophy elk, bighorn sheep, mountain goats, moose, and grizzlies he'd killed, which would've also netted top-ten spots within state and even world record books.

Many of these trophies were found throughout what turned into a national investigation and effort to identify and arrest the poacher, and the poacher's string of hunting records had been begrudgingly confirmed by hunting associations. Pictures of several of these trophies were still easily found online. Shoulder mounts of colossal deer, elk, moose, and bighorn sheep held aloft by grinning state and federal law enforcement officers outside mansions in Florida, Texas, and Michigan; mansions owned by those the poacher sold them to for outrageous sums. These photos had been attached to articles about the Ghost Hunter of the Bitterroots, as the *Idaho Statesman* had described him, or Montana's Phantom King Slayer, a name given to him by the *Houston Chronicle*.

Like every Montana game warden who'd been on the job between 1998 and 2004—and many others from a score of other law enforcement agencies who'd pursued him—Clark still thought about that poacher. Unlike those people, however, Clark had missed the poacher's shadowy reign over the mountains, foothills, and prairies of Montana by only a few months. Even so, Clark had immediately dedicated himself to the case. He'd spent countless long nights those first years on the job scouring every investigative record he could find. He spent his own off time at the state archives and county sheriff's offices around Montana looking for a shred of evidence that could help identify the poacher. And he never found one. Like so many others who'd worn the badge Clark now wore, as well as the badges of the dozens of other state and federal law enforcement agencies who'd joined the hunt, Clark eventually gave up.

Given the abrupt end to his crime streak, some thought the old poacher must've died alone somewhere out in the backcountry. Killed slowly by hypothermia or starvation after breaking a leg. Others say he died sobbing, shrieking at the horrid sound of his own bones crunching and skin tearing, pinned to the forest floor while flayed alive by a grizzly. Some figure he just knew illegal trophy hunting was a young man's game, and that he'd taken it far enough.

The most prolific poacher of trophy game animals in the Rocky Mountain West.

They never learned his name, of course, so that's how one journalist at the *Billings Gazette* had described the poacher in November of 2004, an autumn that represented both the crescendo and final act of that poacher's career.

A Montana game warden by the name of Frank Farrington was the only man who'd ever come close to catching him.

Frank had been a good Baptist, but an even better woodsman, hunter, and detective. His wife and sons, if asked today, would recall the only time they'd ever heard Frank use profanity was during his brief retirement, sitting on his porch staring out into the sage and the hazy mountains beyond, grumbling quietly to himself about *that slippery goddamned wraith bastard of a son of a bitch.*

Frank Farrington had been considered the best game warden of his time. And he had been outstanding, but those who'd overlapped with both him and Clark knew, within a shockingly short time, that the younger man was simply on a different level, if not the best game warden to ever hold the job. Many had said as much to Clark, while even more had silently concluded it, but this praise did nothing for him. He just wanted to know how he would've stacked up against this famous, nameless poacher had they both been at the peaks of their diametrically opposed careers at the same time. Over the nineteen years of Clark's career, this hypothetical quandary had actually played a big role in how Clark assessed his own vocational aptitude. He felt confident he'd have been able to catch the old rogue, but he'd never know.

What Clark did know was that legendary trophy poacher would've certainly deemed the buck on his office wall worthy of pursuit. But Clark had killed it, and legally. While the old phantom was still out there in the last few months of his criminal career, no less. So Clark saw it as a kind of motivating symbol, a totem of remembrance that, while he'd never have a chance to go toe-to-toe with the fabled poacher, in a way, he kind of already had. *And he'd won.*

These last few years, late at night, Clark would find himself hoping someone as skilled and prolific would start poaching again.

There just weren't any professionals out there anymore.

It was getting so stale, chasing down impulsive morons. Idiot kids, drunk on Keystone Light and that bloodlust only a group of young men can gin up, blasting away at a herd of elk or pronghorn with an AR-15 from the back of a truck. In addition to the armed, impulsive assholes, there were other kinds of common poacher. Most poachers in America were just folks who lived out in the country who'd shoot an elk or a deer a few times a year to fill their freezer. Very few of these ever even got suspected of the felony, let alone caught. Another common group were those just too lazy or stupid to apply for hunting tags, but with the gumption to hunt anyway.

Then there were the rare ones. Those with actual skill, who'd spent years in the field studying migration patterns and seasonal habitats of trophy animals. A game animal reaches trophy size because of their cunning, and outwitting one requires true skill in the art of locating, tracking, and stalking. These poachers were usually in it for money. Trophy-scoring deer, elk, moose, and bighorn mounts are sold every day right in the open on Facebook, eBay, and Craigslist, with no one ever asking for proof of lawful harvest. Even more can be made through the $20-billion-a-year illegal wildlife market, which is mostly centered on African big game, but hundreds of millions a year are exchanged for North American animal parts. Claws, teeth, gallbladders, hearts, livers, pelts, and pretty much any other thing that can be carved from a dead bear or mountain lion can fetch a high sum on the Chinese or Korean black markets. However, in America at least, these types of *professional poachers* were going extinct just as fast as the white rhino.

Quietly, deep in Clark's mind, this depressed him a bit. Of course, his entire career was dedicated to undermining all poachers, whether it was the impulsive dipshits, the rural landowners, the sly trophy hunters, or sadists like Elijah Austin Miles. Even so, he felt he was entitled to privately enshrine a truly gifted poacher. He reckoned doing so was at least less egregious than how fabled gunslingers from the old West are revered today, despite their bloody wakes of murder, rape, and orphans.

He thought, as he did almost every day, about Elijah Austin Miles. It felt like he'd been the pinnacle of Clark's career, everything he'd been working toward. Nothing he'd done before, or since, had even come close. Thinking back on the moment he'd cornered that twisted shithead, the moment he'd felt him die, it had an almost religious profundity for Clark.

Clark let his eyes fall to the second and final item of meaningful decor in his life, mounted to the wall just below the record buck's skull.

It was a framed photograph taken in the summer of 2003. He'd had a framing shop in Bozeman put it together. In the photo was a younger Clark and his wife, Mary, each smiling as though caught laughing at a joke no one else alive could possibly understand. Each stood on either side of Clark's beloved chestnut American quarter horse, Quincey. By a mile, Quincey had been the best friend Clark Rickert ever had. In Quincey's saddle was Clark and Mary's only child, a two-year-old boy named Ben with a beaming smile.

A violent cocktail of guilt, shame, grief, and rage boiled into Clark whenever he looked at the photograph. He kept this picture in its prominent place all the same. He'd make himself look at it throughout the day, force himself to hold his gaze on each smiling face, letting the terrorizing emotion course through him until his jaw was clenched and white noise roared in his ears.

That photograph, under that buck's skull, formed a sort of altar of atonement for Clark, a flesh-biting cilice, a bladed steel instrument of penance he forced upon himself.

Clark had never been a member of any self-flagellating Christian sect, but he'd read about such things, and had quietly reflected upon the similarity between those nutjobs' use of whips and chains to flay their backs into bloody tatters, and his use of this photograph. The main difference between those crazy assholes and himself, he'd once mused, was that he didn't think his version of self-abuse provided expiation of sin. It would not put an end to his suffering or give him peace.

Only death could do that. This Clark knew.

Clark saw evil everywhere in the world. He thought of it as some invisible, acrid, roiling electrical storm that was ageless and immortal, all around everyone all the time, filling any empty space it found.

To Clark, evil was like bad weather: an abjectly invincible foe. One can avoid it with some success, going about life trying to stay out of its way. One can keep a brave face while inside the shelters of wood and rock and steel man depends upon to survive bad weather's passing wrath. But everyone has that moment—glancing at the ceiling or out a window toward blistering hail, screaming wind, and rock-splitting lightning—when the truth becomes crystal clear. Eventually, everyone knows the score. Eventually, everyone knows it'll win in the end.

The only evil in the world one could truly vanquish in a stand-up fight, Clark believed, was one's own. That little ball of black, jibbering, shrieking malice he knew was inside him. The evil he kept like a prisoner, chained to a radiator in a soundproofed crawl space deep in his soul. Everyone had one, Clark knew. It didn't need to be fed, or given light and exercise. It also couldn't be killed by will, God, blades, or fire. Many try to eradicate their little ball of evil with a bullet in their mouth, but that's no different from just surrendering to it and setting it free. Suicide might mean fewer people get hurt by one's evil in the short term, but it still allows it to escape, to writhe and giggle and dance and add its schemes and hate to that invincible mass outside.

It can only perish along with its host, and only so long as it's still in the dungeon when that day finally comes. Clark *knew this*. He could feel it.

This photograph, for Clark, was a reminder. An elegy to evil. A sticky note on the fridge, imploring him to never forget what he had chained up in the basement. In Clark's mind, should a day come when he lacked the strength to stare into this photograph and hold a meaningful gaze upon each smiling face within—when the pain and guilt and rage were just too much—it would all be over. If he lost that strength, it would be the same as dropping a ladder down into the rank, black pit where he'd kept his evil starved and shackled for so long.

Heart pounding in his ears, pressure building in his tear ducts, Clark had reached his limit and looked away from the photograph.

Leonard Price walked into his office seconds later, and Clark did not look at his old friend until several moments after he'd planted himself into one of the chairs facing his desk. Price gave him a tight-lipped smile before speaking.

"*Welp* . . . shall we?"

Clark responded with a long exhale through his nose before standing. He adjusted the holstered Glock 20 and the heavy magazines of 10mm rounds on his belt, then held an open hand toward the door with a tight-lipped smile of his own. He told Price he had to check in with Jay Hart, his second-in-command, and peeled away.

Clark was heading into the mountains alone the next morning on horseback to follow up on a few reports of some redneck shooting a moose from his ATV, so he wanted to make sure Jay had gotten his email detailing the plan. Clark, a sound woodsman and mountaineer, strictly adhered to the rule about making sure someone knew where he'd be and when to expect him back whenever heading into the backcountry. It didn't matter that he always had a radio and satellite messenger—this was a rule one simply did not break. Clark didn't have family, or any real friends he saw more than once a month, so Jay was who he relayed that information to. Jay was a former Marine infantryman with several tours in Afghanistan under his belt and a subtle but sharp intelligence, and a damn fine warden Clark was grateful to have on his team. He was a passionate Mormon, so Clark found the two often had very little to discuss beyond the job, but he was as reliable as men came. Jay had received the email, recited the key facts from it in ten seconds, told Clark to be careful, then looked back into his monitor as Clark turned back toward the lobby.

He slapped Price on the back as he reached Lucy's desk. His old friend was leaned over, watching a video on Lucy's phone of her son's baseball game. Price smiled at her.

"*Gah-lee*, Luce, that boy's growin' like a weed."

Clark touched his hat as he passed by Lucy's desk.

"Headed to Helena, Miss Lucy. I'll be in the field tomorrow and Friday, so enjoy your weekend."

Lucy smiled at him as he turned and went out into the glaring summer afternoon. When the doors shut behind the two men, Lucy welcomed the familiar, physical sensation of relief and safety she knew was about to shudder through her. The one she always enjoyed whenever the distance increased between herself and Clark Rickert.

CHAPTER 3

CLARK AND PRICE were greeted by the hot Montana sun and the hum and chug of the great Missouri River across the street from the FWP's Region 4 headquarters. Both men silently pulled themselves into Leonard Price's truck, and neither spoke until several minutes into their ninety-minute drive to Helena.

There was a slight strain between the two, one that had never been there. Clark never had a dad or big brother, and Price never had a son or little brother, so they filled each other's respective vacancies and argued with a venom most colleagues never would use. But Clark's angst about the state audit and other agency changes had boiled over several times in the last months, enough to kick off some fiery arguments. Clark didn't want to add to that, though the bizarre secrecy of this meeting had pissed him off. He did not look over at his old friend and boss as he blurted out new iterations of the same questions he'd asked several times over the last two days.

"*What the hell* is this meeting about? Why the damn secrecy? Is it about the legislature's audit?"

Price chuckled as he responded.

"Still don't know anythin' about it, Rickert. All Chief said is he wants you there this afternoon to go over somethin'."

Clark's bad feeling about this meeting had evolved from a rash into boils over the last two days, and they ruptured at Price's nonchalance. He responded with more consternation in his voice than he'd usually allow when talking to this man.

"For fuck's sake, don't pull your *gee, gosh* bullshit with me, old man. What the hell do you *think* it's about, then? *Christ almighty*, you and division have me at my wits' fuckin' end."

Never one to resist consternation threading into his own words, Price's voice went up an octave as he responded in kind, flicking his eyes between Clark's and the road.

"*Christ's golden fuckin' throne*, son. I've told you ten cocksuckin' times I don't know what it's about. You think I'm lyin'? You know as good as me it ain't disciplinary, so cinch your fuckin' britches before you go blowin' a gasket 'n shittin' yourself. *Lord above*, boy, you've had extra mustard in your shit sandwich for *months now*. The hell's goin' on with you?"

Clark rolled his eyes and shook his head, unable to hide a grin at Price's capacity for colorful, high-speed verbal abuse.

"*Never mind*. It's just fuckin' weird, is all."

Price let out a quick bark of laughter.

"Yeah, well . . . weird world fulla weird fuckin' things, Rickert. You've seen enough of it to not go lettin' yourself get all shook up by a damn *meeting*. Cool down, slick. *Seriously*. Elizabeth'll be there. She's your guardian angel, but you know damn well if you walk in there wound tighter 'n a steer's ass in fly season and get all lippy, she'll rip your tiny little pecker off, so stow your shit. I'm tellin' ya, son, if this meeting was about some ground-shakin' stuff, you and I'd both fuckin' know."

Clark believed him. He knew he wasn't getting fired, all too familiar with the painstaking bureaucratic procedures something like that would require, and he had too many acquaintances in the state government who owed him too many favors for something like that to go under his radar. Even so, the vast majority of professional minutiae he'd ever had to deal with in his career could be handled over the phone or via email, so these circumstances were unusual.

He also couldn't help but laugh at more of Price's guff. That was another thing about the old Western patois they both spoke with. For being inherently concise, it was often weighted down with expressions, but ones developed honestly by those like Price's kin, who'd settled in this area before the Civil War. Folks like his fourth great-grandma, who was *tougher 'n boiled owl* because her kids were hungry and that's all she had. Folks like his fourth great-granddad who'd learned there *ain't no sense standin' around jawin'* because he smelled winter on the wind, had other children the last one hadn't killed, and a lot of things to finish before it got here. Things he'd promised God he'd never let go unfinished before winter again as his tears froze and he hacked that tiny grave into the rocky, frigid prairie only about forty miles from where his fourth great-grandson was driving now.

Ten minutes passed as neither man interrupted the steady croon of the diesel engine, the rubber on the asphalt, and the blasting AC; a curtain of sound occasionally penetrated by a high note from Hank Williams's voice or steel guitar from his 1952 song "You Win Again" playing quietly on the stereo.

"What're you thinkin' about?"

After several seconds, Clark turned to look at Price, adjusting his body in the passenger seat to stare more directly at his friend. Twice as much time passed before he responded.

"Have you ever asked me that before?"

Price raised his large, graying eyebrows and pursed his lips, seriously considering the question.

"Once, yeah. I've asked you that once before."

A *hmm* was the only noise Clark made as he nodded slowly a few times—the same way he'd respond had Price shared some mundane factoid about one of the mountains in the Lewis Range looming to the west. Several long moments passed before he spoke, never looking away from Price's face.

"What was my answer?"

Price responded without looking from the highway.

"Said you were thinkin' about ol' Frank Farrington and that poacher who kept givin' him the slip."

Clark's only response was a single bark of amused laughter through his nose. Price looked over at him.

"Your *old hero and his arch nemesis*. 'Member how much you used to ask me about them? How smitten with that case you were your first years on the job?"

Clark shook his head a few times as he adjusted his ass in the seat and looked forward again.

"Frank crossed my mind just this mornin', as it happens."

Price glanced at Clark over his big right arm, which reached out to grip the top of the steering wheel.

"You ever meet him, in person? I know you were comin' in the door pretty much right as he was walkin' out, but I can't remember if you ever actually met him, officially."

Clark stared ahead as he responded.

"Not officially."

Clark worked under Price when he'd first started, who'd worked under Frank when he'd first started. Price felt obliged to share the magic of

Frank's lore with the young, angry, heartbroken Clark Rickert, who'd been eager to hear it. In the way colleagues and old friends do, they'd discussed everything about the legendary man. Several times over, and with all the same mysticism about *the old days and ways*, knowing full well a story had already been thoroughly covered, excusing that fact, and rehashing it anyway with the same detail and enthusiasm. In those first few years of Clark's career, the only questions he'd ever asked Price had been about Frank Farrington or the fabled poacher that Frank, Price, and all the other agency silverbacks had spent the late '90s and early 2000s trying to catch.

Price told Clark all about how Frank had been the only man who'd come close to catching the sly trophy hunter. Frank stayed on him for years, and Price regaled Clark with all the details of the investigation. Frank never got far enough to identify the poacher, his cancer forcing him into retirement, but he'd been closer than any other.

Frank eventually figured out that the poacher had been paying off managers of the many private ranches around Montana owned by wealthy people who'd only visit twice a year. He was paying for access and discretion so he could take other rich East Coasters into these pristine game sanctuaries to kill trophy deer, elk, antelope, moose, bear, wolves, even a few of the buffalo that would wander from Yellowstone. Frank eventually busted the guy who handled the poacher's freight, shipping trophies from Montana to clients' homes. He'd even teamed up with the US Marshals, serving almost a dozen warrants on the poacher's former clients or those he sold trophies to in Delaware, Florida, Texas, Michigan, California, and Louisiana. None of them had an existing phone number, address, or a name. None could even say specifically *where* they'd gone hunting. They'd all been driven to the hunting areas in the predawn darkness by that quiet, nondescript young man in his old truck. None of them had pictures that showed the poacher or any identifiable landmarks either. Their "guide" had a strict rule, insisting on carrying any camera they'd brought and taking all photos himself. Frank had seen hundreds of photos the poacher had taken, and not a single one showed any kind of discernible landmark. Every lead Frank followed dried up with some shit-heel local swearing they had *no idea who that could be.*

The poacher had covered his tracks with masterful precision.

Be that as it may, in a certain sense, one unworthy of too many words, that poacher still ended up changing his ways because of Frank Farrington. Price could never tell Clark about that fact, however. The poacher got away, so there were just certain things about him neither Price nor anyone else in the world knew. Certain things Clark would never find in Price's history lessons on Frank and the poacher, or in the investigative records he'd pored over for years.

One such fact was that, on four separate occasions, that poacher found himself humbled, staring in awe through binoculars at Farrington from the other side of a valley or across some alpine expanse above tree line, following the poacher's hours-old trail. This meant that Frank had not only encountered the poacher's intentionally deceptive fake trails, but that he'd been good enough to see them for the bullshit they were. The poacher found himself elated and reinvigorated in these moments, finally having to change his tactics and up his game. Frank made him smarter. Frank made him *better*.

"So, what're you thinkin' about?"

Clark glanced at Price with almost imperceptible traces of a grin at the corners of his mouth, held his gaze for a moment, then looked forward.

"*Nothin'*."

Price chuckled and shook his head at how well Clark's nonanswer was explained by all the years and experiences the two had shared.

The drive to Helena down I-15 along the meandering Missouri River was one both men had done thousands of times, and went by quickly in the way a familiar drive often does. They pulled into the state headquarters of Montana Fish, Wildlife & Parks and silently walked into the lobby. The receptionist, expecting them, stood when they arrived and greeted both by name. She ushered them toward the conference room where Clark could see several people already seated at one end of the large table through the office-facing windows.

One of those was Elizabeth Lobdell, the agency's chief legal counsel. On several occasions over the eleven years Liz had been in her position, she had described Clark Rickert to a colleague, friend, or her husband as the primary source of her insomnia and graying hair. Even so, they were undeniably dear friends at this point, at least in the way two concise, mostly affectionless people can have a dear friend.

Clark was a magnet for the kind of violence that kicks off a frenzy of media coverage and investigations, more so than anyone else in the agency, or perhaps any law enforcement agency in the state.

Be that as it may, he always played by the book, or was careful to never leave anything in his wake that would suggest otherwise, and Liz greatly appreciated either and both traits. Over the years, at the end of many fourteen-hour days dealing with fallout from Clark's antics, she'd leaned back in her chair and felt sincerely grateful that she was just dealing with optics, instead of civil rights violations. Liz had come to know what anyone who'd worked with Clark Rickert long enough had: He was a reckless, violent, quietly tortured man, but overall, a good one. She'd lived long and hard enough herself to know Clark's mixture of churlish honesty and live-edge decency was a rare thing, and she respected him for it.

Another person in the room was chief of law enforcement Marcus Albee, Montana's head game warden. Albee and Clark had butted heads many times. Clark had vocally opposed Albee's leadership decisions on several occasions, flat-out ignored ten times as many, but he'd had Albee's back a few times when it had really, really mattered. So they got along well enough.

Marcus Albee and his two brothers ran their family's sixth-generation, forty-four-thousand-acre ranch and had a locally royal name that was synonymous with the state of Montana itself. Clark Rickert, on the other hand, had spent his first twelve years in a drug-ridden trailer on the outskirts of Miles City and the next four bouncing between the Watson Children's Shelter in Missoula and a string of foster homes. Despite this profound difference in pedigree, Albee still felt as though he owed his job to Clark. All four governors to hold office since Clark's career began had offered him the appointment to chief. He'd sat in the same chair, at the same table, in the same room in the east wing of the state capitol, and rejected them all. At the most recent of these meetings, however, Clark had recommended Albee for the job instead.

Clark did not recognize the third person in the room. He wore a sharp navy suit, leaned back in his chair with a leg over one knee, and looked to be around Clark's age, early to mid-forties. To Clark, he had the vibe of a lawyer. With a honed experience, he repressed the impulse to dislike the guy right away.

Like many working-class Montanans, Clark harbored some implicit suspicion and contempt for anyone who owned land in Montana, traveled by private jet, and spent most of the year east of the Rockies or west of the Cascades. However, he neither understood nor cared enough about the world outside Montana to develop a real working bias against any one race or creed. Truth be told, those who'd cut Clark deepest in life shared his own mongreled ethnic provenance, that special blend of western and northern European bloodlines that gave the world big, strong white guys prone to ingenuity, discipline, grit, alcoholism, rage, and violence. He'd never known which part of the old country his ancestors had called home. He'd never cared. Such things were nonsense to him. Useless detail. A primal mistrust of claims and assurances made by others had been forced upon Clark early in life, resulting in a social judgment calculus based entirely on another's deeds, never mere words. As such—except for assholes with neck tattoos in flannels in the backcountry, a bias he'd die with—Clark gave everyone he met a fair shake up front. He'd grown to dislike most of those people, but never because of anything biographical that could help him pick them out of a crowd.

All three stood when the captain of Region 4 and assistant chief of the agency followed the receptionist into the room. Albee's deep voice welcomed them by name before introducing the unknown man in the suit.

"Gentlemen, this is Special Agent in Charge Colin Larson, runs the Homeland Security Investigations office in Billings."

Handshakes and brief nods were exchanged before all five sat around the end of the large table. Clark touched the brim of his hat and settled into his chair as he winked at Liz, who responded with a dry, unamused grin. Albee looked between the two newcomers as he spoke, then at the outsider sitting across from Clark.

"Clark, I reckon you're wondering why I dragged you to the capital for this instead of just sending an email, so I'll have Mr. Larson here explain why."

Larson nodded at the chief before looking across the table at Clark.

"Captain Rickert, you've been selected as a good fit for a federal law enforcement task force that's being put together by several three-letter agencies back east."

Clark blinked slowly then turned a flat gaze toward Albee, who held up his hands, palms facing Clark.

"Don't look at me, Rickert. I didn't put your name in any hats. First I heard a' this was two days ago, in an email sent by Mr. Larson here."

Larson's voice pulled Clark's attention back to him.

"That's correct, Mr. Rickert, though I don't know either why your name came out of the hat. All I know is what's in your file, which is quite illustrious. It says you've got one of the highest case resolution rates out of all law enforcement offices in the entire state, even better than most detectives with the state police. It says you've carried out a staggering number of high-risk warrant service operations. It also says you've been on quite a few federal task forces over the years with the Forest Service, BLM, FWS, Customs and Border Protection, the ATF, US Marshals, and even the FBI. So, could be they just want someone who's got a record of playing nice with the feds. You're also known to be something of a gunfighter, familiar with kinetic operations and whatnot, which could be what they're after, but your guess is as good as mine. You'll have to find out when you get out there."

Larson shrugged as he spoke the last words then let the silence stretch on, clearly waiting for Clark to respond. Price smirked a bit as he watched his old friend, knowing he would not. Clark held Larson's gaze, unblinking, until the man coughed once into a closed fist then continued speaking.

"Unfortunately, that's all I have for you. The circumstances behind the formation of this task force are classified even above my clearance, which is why even the few details we're discussing here today had to be shared in person."

He leaned forward and slid the large manila envelope that had been on the table in front of him toward Clark.

"That's from the desk of Floyd Jorgenson, the deputy secretary of the Department of Defense. It's a request for you to be in Virginia on Friday, day after tomorrow, to receive your federal security clearance and then meet the rest of this new task force. In the envelope you'll find a schedule, tickets from Bozeman tomorrow morning and your return trip, as well as the information regarding your rental car, lodging, and all the necessary site credentials."

Clark made no effort to reach for the envelope, knowing Liz would want to review everything first. She leaned forward and snatched it as she put her glasses on. Larson shrugged again and leaned back in his chair.

"I apologize for the imprecision here, but that's honestly everything I know. I'm not a part of this task force; my bosses in DC just wanted me to be the one to brief you on its formation and their selection of you, in person. First time they've ever had me do something like this. So, can I tell them you'll be there on Friday?"

Clark remained silent, so Larson glanced at Albee, who was reading the letter Liz had handed to him. When he finished, he glanced at Liz with surprise in his expression, then looked at Clark.

"Your senior warden, that's Jay Hart, right? He's done a good job of covering for you in the past. So, do you have any real, serious reasons not to go, Captain?"

Clark cast a side-eyed glance at his longtime colleague-turned-boss.

FWP law enforcement got considerable funding and material through federal grants, and Albee had always been an enthusiastic participant in any multi-agency law enforcement effort. On top of that, no matter who the chief of the agency had been, whenever such a task force had been brought up, Clark was assigned to it without any say in the matter. Thus, he knew that he'd be going to Virginia, regardless of his preference. Clark had grown bored of the monotony of most federally managed operations, and disliked the deprivation of the professional autonomy he'd worked so hard to create for himself.

Clark acknowledged his lack of any *real, serious reasons not to go* by shrugging, shaking his head once, and exhaling audibly through his nose.

"Ain't much worth seein' east of I-25 . . ."

Albee and Price laughed. Liz smiled and shook her head. The chief tapped on the letter from the DOD with a big finger and looked over at Larson.

"Tell your folks upstairs Captain Rickert will be on that plane tomorrow and at the briefing the next morning, *with bells on.*"

The regional DHS director left, and the other four remained in the conference room for a few more minutes, speculating as to the purpose of the task force. Everyone concluded, predictably and in short order, that they had absolutely no idea. They discussed the ongoing agency audit for a bit, then Price and Clark showed themselves out.

Back in the truck they began their return journey, both silently ruminating on subjects discussed at this meeting.

Clark had, indeed, served on quite a few federal and multistate law enforcement task forces throughout his career, as the DHS man had mentioned. Most of these related to illegal poaching rings or illegal trafficking of endangered animal parts, a few focused on rural trafficking of drugs, guns, and people across the Montana-Canada border, and even several federal warrant fugitive teams.

However, none of these task forces had involved top secret security clearances. None had involved the Department of Defense.

And certainly, none had ever involved *going to the Pentagon.*

CHAPTER

4

BETWEEN THE CONTINENTAL breakfast at his hotel and the large room where he now sat, Clark's first morning in the state of Virginia had been a bizarre and frustrating sequence of shitty instant coffee, fluorescent-lit hallways, and jarringly oppressive heat.

He'd never been fond of humidity. Hated it, really. Reminded him of a fever. It felt dirty, the way it got into one's clothes. Neither breeze nor shade provided relief.

He'd begun the morning by going through multiple layers of security and credential checks as he made his way to the nondescript office at the Pentagon where he'd been instructed to be. He'd arrived twenty minutes early, but the only purpose of this effort, it seemed, had been to receive his security clearance from a young DOD staffer. He was given a piece of paper with a new set of instructions for the morning's meeting schedule, conspicuously missing the locations thereof. He was then ushered away by a different DOD staffer back outside to a town car waiting to take him to another location. While confused by the fact that the briefing was not taking place at the Pentagon, he was grateful to find the town car as mercifully air-conditioned as the driver was mercifully taciturn. Although, after the driver told him where he was being taken, he felt the urge to ask a flurry of questions—a very rare sensation for Clark, but one he did not surrender to. He reckoned this guy knew as little as he did, but would remain reticent either way.

They drove through a nexus of highways and morning rush-hour traffic. Clark was a casual, self-taught student of American history, and knew this particular tidal region of Virginia was the site of so much of the history that fascinated him. He knew how close he was to Washington's and

Jefferson's homes, and great battlefields of the Revolution and the Civil War he'd read about over the years.

But here, now, looking out at it all, it disgusted him. Roads, suburbs, commercial development, strip malls, office parks, concrete, power lines. Everywhere, stretching to the horizon in every direction. People, asphalt, machines, lighting, all crammed together without any real, open, wild country for hundreds of miles in any direction. He couldn't fathom how anyone could tolerate living within or even near such a repulsive mess.

They finally arrived at another government complex, passing through multiple security layers just to get to the main visitor entrance. Clark's name was on some list that opened gates and disarmed guards.

Clark paused as he exited the vehicle, standing with one hand on the open door and looking up at the large, underwhelmingly bland building. He'd only ever heard it called *Langley* in movies, and hadn't known, until this moment, it was officially called the *George Bush Center for Intelligence*. The driver cleared his throat, snapping Clark out of his reverence for this structure and its intimidating history. Clark nodded to the man, closed the door, and began working his way toward the entrance.

Clark had stared down grizzlies, black bears, mountain lions, and junkie poachers clutching AK-47s in sweaty, shaking hands. Smugglers who ran guns, money, and people. Skinhead militia leaders, their febrile, sycophantic, idiotic followers, and other intimidating beasts. In all these encounters, he'd held his ground, kept his breathing steady, and let the potential outcomes and consequences slip from his mind to focus on the present moment.

Walking into this building was something else entirely. A feeling of helpless foreboding crept into him. Something powerful and nameless began constricting his lungs and bladder. He slowed his stride, forced himself to take a deep breath, wiped his sweaty palms on his jeans, then made his way inside.

Clark was greeted by another young government staffer after checking in and being issued a visitor badge. This one, like all the others thus far, looked him up and down, amused, as though he was in costume. Looking around throughout the day at all the primly clad professionals in their suits and other trappings of the modern, professional gentry—and seeing their appraisals of *him*—Clark began to feel as though he actually were in costume. It might've been the first time in Clark's life when he'd felt any level of concern about being underdressed.

To put it mildly, he stood out in worn flat-toe western boots, Stetson hat, FWP game warden badge emblazoned on the shoulder of the white button-down tucked into his old jeans. It didn't help having a fretwork of scars across his tanned face that was hard to miss even under his three days' stubble and large mustache. For twenty years, he'd shave his face every few days with an electric razor, and shave off his mustache every two or three months then let it grow back in. It was something he never deviated from.

He was led through more security checks, more ID scans, and even more fluorescent-lit hallways, until he was finally dropped off at the entrance to a large room that reminded him of a movie theater. Well over one hundred chairs faced a low stage with massive monitors above it and on its flanks. A young woman at the door took his name, and his phone, which Clark watched her put a sticker on before dropping it into a thick gray bag. She assured him he'd get his phone back when he left the room, then directed him inside.

It was packed. It looked like hundreds of people were already there. So many that Clark checked his watch to confirm he was still early, which he was.

Many were in suits, quite a few others wore fatigues or military dress uniforms, but one large cluster of thirty-five to forty men seated around the center of the room stood out immediately. They were dressed casually in a combination of athletic, hiking, and street clothes. Clark took these men in first. Their Salomon shoes, beards, large digital watches, the scars on their hands, necks, or scalps were all more than enough to give them up for what they were. But before he noticed any of those cosmetic attributes, he saw their posture, the way they held themselves, and how they studied the room.

These were the dangerous ones. These were Uncle Sam's beast hunters.

Two men, both older than Clark, approached him shortly after he entered. The first and older of the two introduced himself by stating only his name, *Harry Jacobson*. Clark responded in kind, and noted the strength and saddle leather texture of his hand. He was a hard-looking guy with dark eyes and a scar running from his jaw down under his shirt collar. He could've passed as a chiseled fifty-year-old, but Clark suspected he was actually in his late sixties or early seventies. The next man was unmistakably in his mid-fifties, with a hawkish face, piercing blue eyes, and soft hands that suggested having lived a very different life than Harry Jacobson had.

"Captain Rickert. Welcome to Langley. Thank you for making the trip out. I'm David Benson, deputy director for CIA operations. I lead things best I can here at the Special Activities Center. My colleague here Mr. Jacobson runs the Special Operations Group and Ground Branch operations here at the SAC. We were very impressed by your personnel file and think you'll be a great fit for this task force. I trust, based on your presence and timing, you got your clearance and made it here from Arlington without too much trouble."

Benson handed Clark a thick, stapled paper packet.

"Your briefing materials. We'll be starting up here soon, Captain, so please help yourself to some coffee or water and find a seat."

As he'd done when seeing the DHS stooge in Helena the day before, and with the same ease, he stifled the judgment of this David Benson's character he felt welling up. Even if Clark's social appraisal metrics focused solely on others' actions, he was still a rash, judgmental grump with arbitrary, even unfair standards. There were just things a man should never do, even once. Send an entrée back to the kitchen, bring Bluetooth speakers on a hike, pay someone else to train their hunting dog, put a Tom Thumb bit in a finished bridle horse, take a cell phone from a pocket in a social setting for any reason other than calling 911, and many other things. In Clark's mind, these were obscene things no spoken word or earthly circumstance could excuse. Until he saw it, he'd ignore his sense that Benson was prone to something on that long list.

Clark skipped the offered coffee and found a seat in the back row and took in more of the people around the room, head beginning to spin again as the gravity of where he was, and who these people were, began to sink in even deeper.

He tried to not let himself be overwhelmed by having just met *the guy who ran the SOG's Ground Branch*, which Clark had read about over the years. He knew Ground Branch fell somewhere under the nebulous umbrella of the SAC, and that it was effectively the most selective special operations military force on the planet.

The meat and potatoes of Ground Branch was its direct-action combat element, which was a unit of only around two hundred Paramilitary Operations and Specialized Skills Officers. These guys were all handpicked, the most experienced operators from Combat Applications Group or Delta Force, DEVGRU or SEAL Team Six, other SEAL teams, Green Berets, the

75th Ranger Regiment, Marine Recon or Special Operations Command, and other elite special missions units.

As if that baseline experience weren't stunningly deadly enough, upon selection, each operator was trained as an independent clandestine intelligence operative. Clandestine operative training rounded these guys' skill base out so that they could perform at the highest level either working alone or as a combat-hardened special missions unit. This was the farthest end of the killer spectrum, Clark knew. The world's most extraordinarily dangerous gunfighters.

He glanced back at them, the three dozen or so casually attired men seated in the middle of the room.

He was amused by how bored they appeared. Some chatted, picked at fingernails, or sipped coffee. At least two wore flip-flops, and two others were playing pass with a can of Copenhagen over the heads of the others. One was fast asleep, arms crossed over a Vans hoodie, head lolled back, snoring audibly at the ceiling.

Looking at them, Clark realized the collective vibe of this group of men was strikingly similar to most of the countless wildland fire hotshot crews he'd worked with over the years.

There were some differences, of course. The average wildland firefighter was about a decade younger than most of these men. The casual gaze of the average wildland firefighter carried far less calculated wrath. And, despite all their hard work, wildland firefighters did not dwell in the shadows of the margins of modern history.

This particular group of men, here, very much fucking did.

CHAPTER 5

CHARLOTTE BISHOP WATCHED Benson and Jacobson approach and shake hands with the man she assumed must certainly be the Montana FWP law enforcement investigator, Captain Clark Rickert. She waited for them to finish speaking, then rose from her chair along the back wall of the room.

Charlotte had been looking forward to meeting this man since she'd first reviewed his file. Not only because of his rather colorful career, but also because of the strange circumstances surrounding her finding his file at all.

It had been sitting on top of her keyboard, in her highly secure office deep in the bowels of CIA headquarters, at 5:45 a.m., the morning after she'd been explicitly tasked with finding a local law enforcement liaison for this task force. That surprise, and no one in her staff taking credit for having put his file there, had been unusual. But Charlotte had grown accustomed to the unusual throughout her twelve-year career at the CIA.

She'd been recruited while still an undergrad at Georgetown. This came as no surprise to anyone, including Charlotte herself, given her esteemed ninth-generation Virginia family, her success as a student and a D1 athlete, and her fluency in four languages. In the years since, she'd become fluent in one more, and conversational in another five. She'd gone straight to the CIA's infamous training facility, the Farm, only days after graduating summa cum laude. She spent the next four years in the field as a case officer, recruiting and handling high-level assets in South Africa, France, and Israel, followed by two more years doing the same in Iraq and Syria. She stood out because of her tenacity and freakish record of mission success, so was tapped by Jacobson to come work for him at the Special Operations Group. She'd spent the last six years here, coordinating global deployments of Ground Branch's kill-capture rendition squads. Until two weeks ago, she'd felt there was very little mystery left in this world.

Thus, any significance of the strange appearance of Clark Rickert's file on her desk was easily shrugged away. This was made even easier after reading the file and finding that he was, indeed, a perfect fit for this particular operation. Although neither she, nor anyone else alive, could honestly say they'd ever worked on an operation like this one.

Clark looked up as Charlotte approached him. She wore a navy pantsuit and a white blouse, blazer hung over her left arm as she extended her right toward him. She was of average height and obviously an athlete, but her eyes and smile blindsided him. He stood, flustered by her easy confidence, and her beauty, in the same way most men were when meeting her.

"You must be Captain Rickert. I'm Charlotte Bishop. I work here in the Special Activities Center under Mr. Jacobson to help run SOG and Ground Branch operations. I'm part of the team that stood up this task force. I was also the one who suggested you as a good fit after reviewing your file."

Clark nodded.

"Pleasure to meet you, Charlotte."

Her smile, as relaxed and confident as it was strikingly beautiful, caused something of a logjam in Clark's mind. Charlotte saw this, even as all the wild, violent, and tragic anecdotes from this man's file tumbled through her mind.

Charlotte had spent her entire career briefing, instructing, leading, and otherwise being a handler of dangerous men, men not only capable of carrying out acts of extreme violence with casual detachment, but also of falling victim to it with the same ease and familiarity. Men who could not count the times they'd clamped another person's mouth shut while whispering *shhh* directly into their ear. Men who never failed to find that sweet spot along the left side of a sternum where a blade can slip directly into someone's heart. Men whose resting heart rate hadn't exceeded 60 bpm at any point during weeks spent while dehydrated, starving, concussed, half blind, and internally bleeding in hiding or captivity. Men who'd seen their target's spouse or children in the apartment or car with them, categorized them as *acceptable collateral loss*, then unflinchingly detonated the hidden explosive anyway. Men who'd poisoned a village's only well or launched AGM-114 Hellfire missiles into crowded weddings and funerals just to kill a single target.

The eyes she was looking into now were those of a violent man, undoubtedly, but this one was different.

Charlotte was very good at reading people through casual conversation. She didn't need more than a few minutes of small talk to effectively categorize someone by intelligence, motivations, and desires. Indeed, very few people on earth were better at this than her, and this aptitude saw her excel faster than most ever had in this professional realm. This man, however, made her feel as though she were staring at a tree.

She had no existing category to file him into—and she was trying quite hard to think of one. The eyes are where the real substance of a person is offered up, she'd always known. The eyes are where someone like Charlotte can do some real prospecting. Eyes betrayed good, evil, desire, stupidity, intelligence, rage, instability, insignificance, and any mixture thereof. But this man's eyes were like none she'd ever seen. The guy himself appeared to be in his late thirties or early forties, but something about his eyes felt ancient. They were more gray than green. They brought the word *merciless* to her mind, but what she saw wasn't the human incapacity for mercy she'd seen in the eyes of so many throughout her career in the SOG. It was similar, but entirely different at the same time. It wasn't *human* mercy, or a *human* lack thereof. What she saw now was closer to the unappeasable nature of a storm, or the dispassion of a heat-shimmering salt flat.

All of this churned through her mind in a second.

After being briefed at the White House on the purpose for this task force and mission, she didn't imagine anything in the world would ever be able to surprise, frighten, or truly perplex her again. Yet here she stood, staring into this man's eyes.

She felt the sudden urge to step away from him, but suppressed the sensation as quickly as it came. Grasping the improbability that he would say anything more than the five words he'd just spoken, she flipped a strand of chestnut-brown hair away from her face, and forced herself to smile.

"Well, I just wanted to say that I sincerely appreciate you helping us out and making the trip to be here today."

Something indescribable changed in his face as she said this, something that even her keen eye almost missed. Some subtle thread of what might've been disappointment tinged his expression. She felt, for the first time in a very long time, that she'd been seen—*truly seen*—in the way she was able to see others.

"All right, then, Charlotte."

He offered a tight-lipped smile and a nod, then took his seat again. Charlotte stood locked in place, staring down at him, when Harry Jacobson's voice punched across the room.

"All right, everyone, grab a seat. Let's get started."

CHAPTER 6

THE HEAD OF SOG and Ground Branch operations, Harry Jacobson, stepped onto the stage at the front of the room and began controlling the large monitors with a remote. His voice was somehow both deep and sharp in pitch. There was a conclusive finality in his tone, the kind that foreclosed any response other than *yes, sir*.

Former infantry officer, then, Clark assumed. It was the voice one must develop to keep men focused while in situations that jeopardize sanity. The kind of voice one needs to cut through air that's boiling with fire and steel and screams.

The muffled conversations around the room quickly tamped down until replaced by the scuffling cadence of people dropping into chairs. The first slide of a PowerPoint presentation opened onto the large screens behind Jacobson. He glanced up at three words that filled the slide—*Operation Red Castle*—then turned around to face the room.

"Some of you have worked together before, some of you have not, so I'm going to quickly run through the team..."

Jacobson gestured with a flat, open hand toward the back of the room, where dozens of men and women remained standing behind the arranged chairs. Most wore suits, but several standing on the fringe of the group wore camouflage fatigues and dark red berets.

"In the back we've got the Special Operations Group's control team, our living command center for Ground Branch and the central nervous system of this task force. Also back there are a few of the aviators, controllers, and other officers from SOG's own aviation and armor branches, as well as a few from the 160th Special Operations Aviation Regiment we're going to be borrowing from the army."

A few of them nodded, and all maintained serious expressions and a general air of casual familiarity with what was happening. This gave the impression that it was certainly not their first top secret task force briefing, more strongly even than the Special Activities Division badges hanging from lanyards around most of their necks.

Jacobson gestured toward a cluster of people a few rows in front of Clark, set aside from the rest by a few empty seats.

"Here, we've got one of the FBI's Hostage Rescue Teams headed up by Special Agent Dwight DuBroux, as well as some support staff from their Critical Incident Response Group. The Bureau has been kind enough to lend us some of their best shooters and intel wizards for the operation. They've brought a few sniper teams and others that will be rolling with and supporting the core Ground Branch element, as we've done in the past, and their intelligence officers will integrate with ops control."

Dwight DuBroux, a lean, balding man in jeans and a white button-down shirt under a blue blazer, stood, looked around the room, nodded once, then sat again. Clark had worked with FBI agents in the past, but never the HRT, which he knew was composed of some of the best shooters in the world, and who he knew often deployed to war zones with various Tier-1 special operations units. To the untrained eye, this man Dwight DuBroux could look like a banker or accountant, but Clark could see something coiled in his posture that suggested this man was fast, very fast, if he wanted to be.

Jacobson gestured toward the largest identifiable group present, the several dozen men in the middle of the room whom Clark had pegged as the Ground Branch operators.

"Here we've got the core of the task force's Ground Branch door-kicker element, headed up by Paramilitary Operations Officer and former DEVGRU commander Jackson Nowell. For now, this combat arms complement will be broken into six assault teams plus several smaller recon elements, in addition to supporting air from the 160th and SOG's own aviation branch, our FBI assets, and others. So we've got our own little army of glass-eating ground-pounders for this one."

A muscular man in the front row with a thick, trimmed beard half stood, gave a quick two-fingered salute to the room, then sat back down again. He wore a Stihl chain saw baseball hat, and his left ear was a mess of cauliflower damage Clark assumed had come from wrestling, Brazilian jujitsu, or some other kind of grappling training.

Jacobson shot another openhanded point toward a cluster of around twenty men and women to Clark's right, sitting in the back two rows, all wearing either camouflage fatigues or dress blue uniforms.

"Here we've got our Tactical Air Control Party, plus a detachment from the Twenty-Fourth Special Tactics Squadron under Captain Tucker Reichman that Air Force Special Operations Command has loaned us for a bit."

Captain Reichman, who appeared to be in his early thirties and held a striking and somewhat obnoxious resemblance to a Ken doll, nodded and raised his hand as his name was mentioned.

"The TACP will obviously be embedded with operations, and we'll have the commandos from the Twenty-Fourth wearing a few different hats—running some recon and rolling with the ground teams as needed, staging as our quick reaction force, and of course manning rotations of pararescue and CASEVAC, should necessity arise. Let's all hope for our own sakes that these sons of bitches have a *very boring time* here on this task force."

This drew a wave of laughs from the people around the room. Jacobson now pointed toward the back corner of the room where Clark sat.

"Back there is Montana game warden and investigator Captain Clark Rickert. He will be the task force's local law enforcement and regional liaison, but don't let that role or his cute hat fool you. This guy's been in the stack, he's a land-nav wizard, he's served more high-risk warrants than most of the FBI guys here, and he's been in as many gunfights and put as many bad guys in the dirt as a Marine Corps fire team. He'll be an asset to ops planning and the ground teams."

Clark looked across the room, tipped the brim of his Stetson hat with an index finger, then looked back at Jacobson. Almost every one of the Ground Branch operators was staring back at him, with looks of amusement or cold appraisal. He felt his cheeks burn a bit under the attention, a long-forgotten, boyish sensation that was immediately frustrating.

Jacobson introduced several others with titles Clark did not recognize from agency branches he'd never heard of, then turned to face the large monitor behind him, pointing up at the words on the first page on the screen.

"Operation Red Castle. As I'm sure most of you have noticed, this task force and mission were slapped together in what has truly been *record time*, and as I'm sure many of you have gathered, that means the matter is urgent. As such, I'm going to cut right to the chase here and take questions at the end."

He clicked the remote and a strange symbol in dark red on a white background filled the screens. A pang of recognition or even déjà vu had Clark lean forward in his chair. There was something globally familiar about the symbol, like the Nike swoosh or the Olympic rings, but he couldn't place it.

"This is the symbol of an organization that, to be frank, we don't actually have an official title for. That is to say, the members of this organization do not refer to themselves by any name, nor do they even really refer to themselves as any distinct organization at all. This is the only unifying symbol any of them ever employ to which they signify any membership or allegiance. In a way, this symbol *is their name*. As such, we've given them our own moniker based on some of the cryptic subject matter they discuss. We'll be calling their organization *Red Castle*."

Jacobson clicked to the next page, which was a bullet-point list of dates.

"Domestic federal intelligence first picked up on the existence of Red Castle back in 2018, when twelve members of the group in seven different states individually but, within the same week, made notably large purchases of weapons, ammunition, and ammunition reloading materials. These twelve individuals spent between $56,000 and $94,000 *each*, purchasing collectively hundreds of AR-15 or AK-style carbines, semiautomatic handguns, longer-range bolt-action rifles, optics for everything, hundreds of thousands of rounds of ammunition, and enough gunpowder, primers, and casings to make even more. At that time in 2018, there was no known association between these individuals, and none of them pinged any red flags in federal systems. But one real go-getter analyst at the DHS started doing some digging and found all twelve of these people were actually in contact via a chat room only accessible through a Tor browser. Using means not worth diving into, she confirmed all twelve purchasers were regular participants in this chat room, and that there were thirty-eight *other members* of this chat room who participated just as frequently. Digging even further, she was able to positively identify eleven more of them. They, likewise, made significant purchases in that same week in 2018 in the $4,000 to $18,000 range, but these hadn't set off any NSA flags."

Jacobson clicked on his remote to jump to the next page, continuing the bullet-pointed timeline.

"In the years since, these individuals continued purchasing a smattering of other survivalist-type prepper shit and sharing contents of and discussing their *stockpile* in the chat room. One of the more concerning red flags about this group was their relatively rigorous operational security. These weird fuckers run a very tight ship when it comes to OpSec and have gone to great lengths to keep their identities shrouded. This situation was run up the line, and eventually the FBI, NSA, and ATF were able to positively identify an additional sixteen of the members of this chat room, giving us the identities of thirty-nine of the fifty members, all of whom are equally active, daily participants. A FISA warrant was obtained in late 2019, and a domestic surveillance operation was initiated to keep an eye on these individuals and whatever it was they were up to, which has been maintained over the last several years."

The PowerPoint page switched to show surveillance photographs of a dozen different people engaged in the minutiae of daily life. Some of them were walking down a sidewalk, several were talking on cell phones, one was taking her toddler out of a car seat, another was working behind the bar at what looked like an expensive restaurant.

"These thirty-nine members of the chat room have proven to be almost *more* confusing to us than enlightening. There is no demographic link between them that we can identify, whatsoever. The oldest is sixty-eight, the youngest is twenty-four, and every age between. All are citizens, but six of them were born abroad. They are of all races, all major religions, some are atheists, some are Republicans, Democrats, activists, meat eaters, vegans, parents, socialites, loners, some of them make minimum wage, some of them make six-figure salaries. One of them speaks three languages; quite a few speak two. They're teachers, bankers, nurses, lawyers, teamsters, an electrician, a janitor, a personal trainer, a fireman, one loads trucks at a lumber yard, one owns a 1,200-acre farm, and one's a wealth manager bringing in over a half million a year. They're basically a random representation of any group of thirty-nine American citizens. The only thing tying these people together is their daily participation in this chat room, their fluency in the strange subject matter discussed therein, and, thus, their membership in the organization we're calling *Red Castle*."

Jacobson clicked his remote and what appeared to be a Realtor's high-resolution photograph of a picturesque ranch somewhere in the American West popped onto the screen.

"All members of Red Castle have long referred to something, likely some*place*, called the *Homestead*. It was never clear where this Homestead was, but it was made clear through their communications over the years that, at some very distinct point in the future, they would receive what they referred to as the *assembly call*. When this assembly call was issued, they were to all drop whatever they were doing in their lives, no matter what it was, and immediately make their way to this Homestead so they could finally carry out what they've simply referred to as the *Awakening*."

Scowls and confused expressions began to spread on the faces around the room.

"Despite our best efforts early on, we were not able to ascertain where this Homestead was, or whether it even really existed at all. Between 2020 and several weeks ago, our surveillance operation on Red Castle kept fairly close tabs on the chat room, the thirty-nine known members, and everything else possible, and nothing really changed or developed at all. They kept discussing the same cryptic stuff without ever divulging anything useful. It started to seem more like some fantasy role-playing community than anything else."

The next page of the PowerPoint was an image of some chat room with a single message in the discussion field. Everyone in the room seemed to lean forward together to try to read it just as Jacobson clicked to the next page showing a zoomed-in screen grab of the single message.

"Eleven days, twelve hours, and about twenty minutes ago, every one of the fifty members of the Red Castle chat room was removed from the group, the years of chat log archive were entirely deleted, and the only thing remaining was a message from a nameless admin of the board who'd never commented once before. This admin posted a single, final comment in the chat room: *Assemble, Those Who Crave the Blood, at the Homestead. The Awakening Is Nigh.*"

The next page of the presentation was another collage of surveillance photographs like before, but in these images, it appeared as though all twelve were carrying bags or luggage of some kind, instead of going about their daily routines.

"Eleven days and about *four hours* ago, all thirty-nine known members of Red Castle, well, they all just *disappeared*."

Jacobson looked around the silent room with an almost apologetic expression before going on.

"All of them employed a concerningly high level of tradecraft in their efforts to do so, as well. I'm talking advanced, professional clandestine shit here, folks. They ran comprehensive and, to be frank, *upsettingly effective* security detection routes, like they'd been trained, and well."

Jacobson began clicking through slides showing pictures corresponding with the narratives he began to share.

"One of them, a homemaker from Minneapolis, took a bus to Chicago, a flight from Midway to Baltimore where she rented a car that was found abandoned in a parking lot without cameras in West Virginia. This one, a banker from Lexington, Kentucky, rented a U-Haul, which he drove to Little Rock, where he took a bus *back east* to North Carolina, then took a two-connection flight to Los Angeles, but he never boarded his second flight, and was last seen on security footage walking away from the airport in Kansas City. This one left her one-year-old twin boys at home alone in their crib for six hours before their father got home from work. This one, a lawyer from Lubbock, stood up and walked out of a deposition without a word. Another, a third-grade teacher in San Diego, left her classroom. This one was driving to a dressage competition, towing her beloved competition horse she'd owned *for sixteen years* in a trailer. She just left it at a truck stop on I-76 outside Denver, got an Uber to the airport, where she rented a car we found abandoned two miles away from a used car lot in Cheyenne, where she'd walked and bought an old T100. The same story goes for all the other known members."

Jacobson clicked to the next slides quickly, all showing some kind of police record.

"Thirty were filed within the first two days, but as of yesterday morning, missing person reports have now officially been filed by husbands, wives, children, parents, friends, or colleagues of all thirty-nine known members. We were able to positively ID two additional Red Castle chat room members via missing person reports filed around the same time, but we still lack conclusive ID for the nine remaining members. Regardless, not a single one of them made any contact with their families or loved ones before disappearing. Not a single note left or final text sent, no mapping history in any of their phones or browser data, zero indication of their destination or expected return was given by any of them. These sons of bitches dropped everything and just . . . *vanished*, and wherever they went, it seems they'd committed plans on how to get there to memory long ago. Furthermore, we haven't found a single trace of any of the guns or ammunition or other prepper gear they all bought in 2018 in any of their homes, or any records to suggest they shipped it anywhere."

Everyone in the room now had some expression of confusion, disbelief, or concern. The PowerPoint changed to the picture of the charming ranch home at the foot of the mountains that had been shown earlier.

"This, we believe, is the *Homestead* they all referred to, and where we believe all fifty members of the chat room are currently assembled. We're not one hundred percent certain of this, but without getting into all the details, our intel wizards have a high degree of confidence this is it. For several days we've maintained constant thermal, FLIR, and other ISR on the location, but it hasn't shown us anything other than the day-to-day operations of a normal, active cattle ranch. This ranch is located . . ."

Jacobson looked across the room, nodded toward Clark, them aimed the remote at the monitor and changed to the next slide.

". . . about thirty miles east-southeast of Havre, Montana, in the foothills of the Bears Paw Mountains. We've had two undercover operatives attempt to gain entry into the ranch, but they have guards, who style themselves *ranch hands*, stationed at all vehicular entry points during the day, one roving at night, and they refuse entry to any and all attempted visitors. In our case, one operative posed as a UPS driver, and the other posed as a veterinary pathologist with the Montana Department of Livestock tracking the spread of brucellosis through cattle in the area. But again, neither had any luck. We've had a surveillance and observation ground team set up in the mountains above the ranch for the last couple of days, as well, who have likewise not seen a thing to confirm the presence of the fifty members of the Red Castle chat room. However, our operative posing as the veterinarian did end up with some good photos from her hidden cameras of one of the ranch hands guarding the gate to the property, and we found this . . ."

The next image in the presentation was a collage of five pictures of a younger man standing next to a gate crossing a dirt road, appearing to have been taken while the guy was in the middle of speaking, arm raised and finger pointing behind the photographer. The man himself did not look familiar to Clark, but he knew the type all too well. A shit-heel cowboy, the quintessential seasonal ranch hand. The type who've been turning up on and lighting out from big ranches all around the West for going on 175 years.

The presentation went on, and the next page was a close-up of each of the five pictures, zoomed in, showing something like a scar or a tattoo on the man's inner forearm. Everyone in the room, again, leaned forward in their chairs, until the next slide showed the symbol of the organization that had been displayed earlier in the presentation imposed next to the image of the tattoo or brand on the man's arm. It appeared identical, and when enhanced, it became clear the symbol had not been tattooed, but carved or burned into the man's forearm. Jacobson's voice startled many in the room as it cut through their silent focus.

"As you can see, the symbol of this organization we're calling Red Castle, the one so often shared in the chat room, is burned or carved into the skin of that man's inner forearm. Our operative confirmed it was on the inner arm of the second man guarding the gate, as well, but was unable to get a photograph. Thus, despite the lack of additional actionable intel, and to just skip ahead a bit, this is where our own and sister agency analysts feel confident that the missing members of Red Castle are hiding out, and that this is the place they've referred to as their *Homestead*. This is where we think they've gathered to initiate whatever they've been obsessively referring to as the impending *Awakening* for over half a decade."

Everyone was silent as they looked back at Jacobson.

"So, the reason we've gathered this team, the reason we've initiated Operation Red Castle, is to conduct a raid on this location to capture members of this organization for questioning. The operational briefings will contain detailed individual and team reports on the raid plan we've put together, but to sum it all up right now, that's what we're going to be doing, and we're executing the raid in three days, this coming Monday morning. So, after this we'll be loading up and moving everyone to our forward operating base and tactical command center on US Forest Service land a few miles from the target location. We've already got an advanced team on the ground there running security, setting up the TCC, and standing everything up."

"Sorry, Skip . . ."

The head of the Ground Branch paramilitary element, Commander Jackson Nowell, put his hand in the air and rose to his feet as he spoke. He was silent for a few seconds, shaking his head in some display of confusion, then went on in a subtle accent that betrayed his provenance as somewhere between the Texas-Louisiana state line and the Florida Panhandle.

"Some of us have sat through countless briefings for an SAC operation before, but never one that was going to take place inside the continental United States, never with this short of a workup, and never one that was, well, expected to be done with such a flagrant lack of intelligence. This all seems *paper fucking thin*, Skip. It seems like we know next to nothing about who these dickheads are or what they're up to. On top of that, again, this is here, *within the United States*. Why is this not just a state or federal issue? How and why are we involved? I've never gone in *this blind* in any country I've operated in, and you've put together a massive ground and control team for this. You have got to give us something more, Harry. I mean . . . who the hell are they? *What the hell is this?* We've all got the clearance; why are we not being read in?"

Jacobson betrayed no emotion as he held Commander Nowell's gaze for a long moment. From this look—as well as Nowell's casual use of profanity while addressing the older man by his first name as well as a shortened version of the title *Skipper*—it was easy to gather these two men had worked together quite a bit over the years. Dwight DuBroux, the head of the FBI HRT, leaned forward in his chair and linked his fingers under his chin, appearing eager for whatever answer was to come.

Jacobson shifted his posture as he cast a quick glance toward the back of the room without moving his head. Clark was the only one who turned to follow the line of his gaze, and found a portly, middle-aged man in a suit sitting in a chair against the far wall. The man stood out as notably unathletic and professorial in this group. He sat with a hunched-over posture, fingers linked in his lap, and one leg over a knee. Clark watched as this strange little man almost imperceptibly shook his head, then continued to watch him for several long moments after Jacobson began responding to Commander Nowell.

"Unfortunately, Commander, I cannot give you every bit of intel here. What I can tell you is that Havre, Montana, sits in Hill County, with Liberty County to the west and Blaine County to the east. Over the last two months, as of a few hours ago, five hundred ninety-one people have been reported missing, almost all of whom are from those three counties. Entire families, entire staffs of businesses in several instances. Those three counties I named have a collective year-round population of around twenty-four thousand people, making this the most prolific missing person case in the history of the United States. A larger percentage of the population of those three counties has gone missing in the last sixty days than the percentage of Americans who died in World War II. A dozen federal agencies have leveraged every available asset and put considerable effort into preventing this crisis from exploding in the public sphere. We've undertaken that effort to get an operation underway before it becomes national and, certainly, international news, as it definitely will eventually."

It sounded as though half the people in the room let out a collective exhale in disbelief.

Dwight DuBroux, the head of the FBI HRT, stood. He stared at his feet with unfocused eyes as he slowly clasped the top button of his blazer, then looked up at Jacobson and spoke. His voice, surprisingly sharp and raspy, felt completely at odds with the domesticated country-club-dad vibe he put off.

"Mr. Jacobson, is there reason to believe this could be a human trafficking operation, or, perhaps, some kind of serial murder spree of a magnitude we've simply never encountered before?"

Without moving his head, Jacobson quickly glanced again to the back of the room, then back at DuBroux.

"Special Agent DuBroux, all I can say right now is that we believe it is incredibly unlikely that any one of the five hundred ninety-one missing persons is still living."

Another stunned silence enveloped the room. DuBroux nodded, eyes narrowing but never leaving Jacobson's.

"I would assume everyone here maintains the appropriate clearance to be read in on the intel provided thus far, so, respectfully, I'm just curious why, or perhaps even *how*, this situation warrants the involvement and domestic deployment of assets and special military units that operate under the purview of the Central Intelligence Agency, Joint Special Operations Command, and the Department of Defense at large. I can honestly say this is the first mission briefing I've ever been a part of where, at the end of it, the legality thereof remains entirely unclear to me."

Jacobson's head dropped a bit as he sighed and nodded slowly. His body language suggested he'd not only anticipated DuBroux's comment, but also the strong voice from the back of the room that addressed it. Everyone turned in their seats to look at the speaker. Clark had seen this man before. He'd watched his Senate confirmation hearing on C-SPAN a year and a half earlier. He stepped forward from where he'd been standing in the back of the large room.

"Special Agent DuBroux, I know we only met in passing, but I am Michael Flood, director of the Central Intelligence Agency. David Benson over there, deputy director of operations, reports directly to me, and

I report directly to the president. Standing across the room over there is Ronald Comley, the undersecretary of defense for intelligence and security. He reports directly to the secretary of defense, who reports directly to the president. From this moment until the conclusion of this operation, Undersecretary Comley and Deputy Director Benson will be giving myself, the SecDef, and the Joint Chiefs of Staff a briefing on mission status every three hours. The president has tasked the SecDef, the Joint Chiefs, and myself to brief *him* every *six hours* until the operation is concluded."

The man who was presumably Ronald Comley, standing against the wall to Clark's left, stepped forward a few feet and nodded with a grave expression on his face.

"The president personally green-lit this operation, under the counsel of the heads of all pertinent intelligence agencies and the unanimous encouragement of the Joint Chiefs of Staff, as well as the attorney general, who's also here and can corroborate the lawful authorization of this operation. Speaking frankly—and Mr. Benson, Mr. Comley, Ms. Bishop, Mr. Jacobson, and anyone else who was at the full briefing at the White House last week can back me up on this here . . ."

Flood removed his eyeglasses and rubbed his eyes with the back of a hand as he walked down the aisle between the seated crowd. Clark glanced behind Flood to find a man he immediately recognized: Attorney General Howard Cooper. Clark had seen the large, boisterous Texan prosecutor on TV hundreds of times, but he'd never seen him look as he did now. *Scared.* Flood reached a spot in the center of the large room, put his glasses back on, but continued staring at the floor, considering his next words carefully. After a long moment, he looked back up.

"Speaking frankly, Special Agent DuBroux, this operation feels strange to you because it is strange. I've never been a part of anything like this either. Truth be told, I can say confidently that no living person ever has. It's almost hard to believe it's even happening, but a full suite of military assets has been green-lit for this operation, no holds barred. The collective national intelligence agencies, the Joint Chiefs of our military, and the president of the United States himself all unanimously agree that this Red Castle group, Mr. DuBroux . . ."

Flood removed his glasses and used them to point at the screens where the PowerPoint presentation had been given. He held them there, turned to make eye contact with someone in every corner of the room, then looked back at DuBroux as he finished his point.

"We believe that this group poses a more imminent and potentially catastrophic national security threat to the United States than any we've ever faced in the history of this republic."

CHAPTER 7

CLARK LANDED IN Bozeman Saturday morning and felt like he was on autopilot the entire drive back toward Great Falls. He wasn't expected at the task force FOB outside Havre until the next morning. So he'd go home, pack his gear, catch a bit of sleep, then get wheels up before sunrise. He felt some urge or need to go to his office, but could not figure out why. It had been the first thing he'd felt when he woke up in the hotel that morning, and he'd felt it throughout the flight home. When he flipped on the blinker to exit the highway toward home, he felt something almost like muscle memory trying to override him to commit to staying on Highway 87 and continuing on to Great Falls, but he shook his head and ignored the strange impulse.

Clark lived in rural Cascade County, not far from the small town of Belt, Montana. Foothill country, that part of Montana where the mountains start to break, roll, and apron out, spilling the prairie badlands into the east.

Clark's home was at the end of a rural county road. Between the turnoff from the quiet state highway and its dead end at the gate across Clark's driveway, the road provided access to only three other private properties. All four properties were on the floor of a wide, shallow valley, lush from the creek that had carved it into being and still flowed through it today among the thick band of cottonwoods and willows that marked its winding course. The other three properties were cattle ranches at least four times the size of Clark's seventy-four-acre parcel. Each was owned by a married couple in their early seventies to early eighties, all of whom had been here since before Clark bought the undeveloped property at the end of the county road twenty-three years earlier. The Lees, the Yockims, and the Tulls.

They were all still here. Alive and well, too, as a result of the ranching lifestyle that keeps one sore, exhausted, grumpy, quietly fulfilled, and healthy. All of them still worked their land, running cattle on large BLM grazing leases that surrounded the little valley and beyond. The Lees and Yockims each had five children. The Tulls had six. When he bought his property at the end of the county road, Clark was actually younger than some of their kids, only a few years older than the rest. At least two children from each household had built their own homes on the family land in the last decade, while most of the rest lived relatively close. So, he'd known them all for decades, and every member of the families' growing horde of grandchildren since birth.

One of the neighbors, who owned the property adjacent to Clark's, was out in his 5065E John Deere tractor, the one he'd spent four years saving for. He was riding parallel to the creek that ran through the valley. His pair of border collies, Hank and Hondo, were caked in mud, bounding along the flanks of the machine. The two men waved at each other as Clark drove by. Mike, a diesel mechanic by trade and former PBR champion roper, was as good as neighbors came in every way that mattered. What stood out most, to Clark, was how much love and care the older man had given Clark's horse, Quincey. During the months Quincey was nearing the end, while Clark was on his long shifts, Mike spent hours with the old horse, every single day.

That horse's death had broken both men's hearts. A flare of that heartbreak burned as Clark stared at the animal's gravestone under the big cottonwood tree in his front pasture, waiting as his gate noisily swung aside under the power of the haggard old motor.

He drove down his long driveway and parked where he always did, in the weed-ridden gravel expanse within the vague horseshoe formed by the house, the garage and shop, and the large red barn. The barn had been red, at least, but had been faded dull and flat by sun and thrashed by weather. The elements gave it far more attention now than the man who'd built and once devotedly maintained it. Clark had needed some help from a few buddies who were electricians, plumbers, and general contractors, but he'd built the house, the garage and shop, and the barn, mostly on his own.

It had truly startled him on occasion, back then, how much he'd loved it here. He hadn't thought anyone, let alone himself, capable of loving any one place or piece of land that much.

He went inside through the kitchen door and got straight to packing, which did not take long. It never did. His day pack, camping gear, spare boots, batteries, ten gallons of extra diesel, extra water, radio equipment, and other supplies were already in his truck, as they always were. He had no indoor plants. No pets. Mike and his wife had a spare key and kept an eye on the place for him. He could leave it for months at the drop of a hat without any fuss at all beyond a quick text to Mike.

He filled up two five-gallon jerricans with water, grabbed two weeks' worth of freeze-dried food, his 3000W solar generator, and a pillow from his bed, and stuffed a small duffel with spare clothes. He grabbed the large duffel that lived permanently on the floor in the corner of his bedroom where he stowed his duty gear. He grabbed a full case of Four Roses bourbon and two cartons of Marlboro Golds from his abundant and diligently maintained stashes of both. Finally, he grabbed a few Pelican cases and went to his safe.

The duty weapons his agency provided were fine, *good* even, but he'd be taking his personal weapons on this outing. He loaded a range bag with a dozen magazines and a few bricks of ammunition for each rifle he'd be taking. He threw a Sig 365 9mm with some extra magazines in as well, which would live in his truck, then some boxes of 200-grain 10mm ammo for the reliable Glock 20 he carried every day.

He loaded the first Pelican case with his Geissele Super Duty MOD1 short-barreled rifle, on which he'd put an EOTECH holographic sight and a paired magnifier. It was like any other AR-15 chambered in 5.56, but because of its 11.5-inch barrel, foregrip, and stock, it fell into the ATF's nebulous *SBR* category. Into the second hard case went his LWRC REPR MKII rifle, an AR-10 variant chambered in the beefier 7.62x51mm or .308 round, on which he'd mounted a Nightforce low-power variable optic. He grabbed his SureFire RC2 suppressor for the SBR and his SilencerCo 36M suppressor for the MKII.

Both were reliable weapons of fine quality, but neither wildly over the top. The Nightforce optic was worth more than both guns combined. He kept both meticulously oiled and clean. Every weekend he checked their zeros before running shooting and manipulation drills at the little range he'd built at the base of the ridge on the southern edge of his land, and then again afterward. His proficiency with handguns and rifles had saved his life several times, and this was a skill set he had no interest in letting diminish. These shooting drills—along with working out in the makeshift boxing gym in his garage, and eating dinner alone at his counter—were some of the only routines he had left.

He loaded the last of the gear into the truck. A quiet desire to lock the house and get the hell away from this place guided him toward the front door. Once there, acknowledgment that he didn't have anywhere to be until the next morning guided him down onto the old glider bench on the front porch—the porch Mary had described on their first date, the one she wanted to wrap around her dream home.

Clark rested one knee atop the other, removed his old Stetson, and dropped it onto his suspended toe in one familiar movement. He glanced down at his other boot, then wiped a skid through the film of dust and pollen caking the old decking. He used to power-wash it twice a year, but hadn't once in the last ten.

Through the balustrades of the porch was a sea of the rigid green leaves of tulips, daffodils, and irises. They'd bloomed earlier in the season. The few irises that remained were dropping petals, close to joining all the others in their leafy summer form.

A deep swath of all three flowers mixed together skirted three sides of the house at the base of the wraparound porch. Thick belts of the floral trifecta also flanked the flagstone walkway from the porch to the area between barn and garage, where they opened into deep, lush drifts that enveloped both buildings.

Every spring—somehow, all these years later—there was even more of each flower than the last. The daffodils were all yellow, as the originals had been, but there were somehow new colors of tulips and irises, colors Clark would bet good money hadn't ever been present until the last few years. The flowers had spread out from these original, intentional beds, as well. Considerably. Like a fungus. Now pairs, clusters, strips, and individual flowers carpeted the pasture over a hundred meters out in every direction from the homestead.

Not being much of a gardener, Clark wasn't sure how it was possible, given how all three flowers were perennial. *Must be the goddamned squirrels*, he'd reckoned while scowling at the breathtakingly beautiful scene five or six years earlier.

It was that same spring when people somehow found out about Clark's flowers. People neither Clark nor any of his neighbors knew, and who all seemed to be from out of state. Mike had blamed it on *internet nonsense*. On four different occasions within a three-week period, Clark had gotten home in the evening to find a car parked near his gate, the driver and passengers all leaning on his fence and taking photos of his home and the extraordinary botanical chaos surrounding it.

The neighboring families had seen several times that number of flower peepers during the long days or weekends Clark spent in the field, and had banded together to enthusiastically encourage the outsiders to fuck off. All three families were fiercely protective of Clark Rickert, but they did this for their own reasons, as well. Flower photography may be as benign and charming a hobby as any that exists, but this was a country road, in a rural corner of a rural Montana county bigger than Delaware but with less than one-tenth Delaware's population. The safeguarding of privacy in a place like this was something profound and sacred. In a place like this, taking photographs of another person's home, without permission, no less, was unacceptable. Grounds for violence, even, as the county sheriff and prosecutor would quietly agree, so long as it didn't get caught on camera or leave any scars.

The efforts of the neighbors worked, as he hadn't seen any of these photographers for several years. While they'd disappeared, the flowers kept coming, more every year.

Stubborn and relentless, fighting their way up through the weeds and long grass until thousands upon thousands of flowers bloomed in unkempt, vibrant, wild triumph over neglect. It felt spiteful to Clark. An annual torture, this ever-growing horde of feral, untamed descendants of the few hundred Mary had planted over two decades ago. Every year, the true end of winter was kicked off by this stunning, cruel act of nature.

The simple routine of daily existence has endless ways of torturing someone with subtle yet excruciating reminders of what they've lost, and how much shittier life is as a result. It does this through small objects, mundane sensations, little things one never imagined capable of harboring such potent, malevolent power. Her favorite clay mug in the gloom at the back of the cupboard where it'd sat since she'd last put it there. The smell rain coaxes out of lilacs and warm asphalt she never failed to proclaim her affection for. A small two-year-old's handprint, now faded almost flush into the concrete at the base of the porch. The rope hanging from the cottonwood in front of the house that swayed solemnly in the breeze—stiffened, frayed, and taskless—as it had for twelve years since the windstorm that'd finally ripped a beloved tire swing away. The quiet from the house itself, the crushing portent and sorrow cooked into that absence of sound. Little things like these are what the horrible force of grief finds most delicious, where it can nest with the most torturous, nauseatingly resonant effect.

The flowers, though, were somehow worse than all the rest. To Clark, there was something uniquely fucking miserable about encountering these reminders of loss in expressions of nature. He could smash that clay mug, rip up the concrete, tear down that rope, burn the house down, and sell the land. He'd considered it, many times, and while he wouldn't do those things, they remained options. He could methodically scour all physical, man-made remnants of their lives from his own.

Nature, however, would not accommodate such emotional decluttering when it came to these flowers. Indeed, nature seemed dead set on fostering them.

To Clark, being able to see, feel, and smell another person's impact on the natural world—one that would remain even if they and everyone else who knew them were dead and gone—nurtured an exquisite misery. One orders of magnitude worse than the mug, handprint, tire swing, or silence.

Clark looked beyond the pasture toward the band of cottonwoods and willows that lined both sides of the creek's meandering course through the valley. He could hear the frigid water babbling somewhere in their shade, fighting to be heard over the metallic drone of grasshoppers and red-winged blackbirds. His son, Ben, had loved that creek as much as he'd loved anything. He'd spend all day there with Ben, catching frogs, building forts, throwing rocks. Sitting here, even after all the years and chaos that'd filled them, Clark could still see Ben's smile, smell his hair, and hear the patter of his little feet on the old wooden floors with a clarity that was stunningly brutal.

The light started to warm and darken. Shadows began to reach. It was getting close to Clark's favorite time of day on this land. The most painful time of day. He squinted into the west. The bees, dragonflies, and frantic clusters of gnats were seared into blazing gold by the blades of light that cut through the leaves of the giant cottonwood.

The thought of the *new moon* popped into his head. Again, as it had several times over the last few days. Moon phases weren't something he usually thought about until September, when elk started piercing the mountain air with the stentorian bugling of their rut, the only time Clark ever paid attention to moon phases, given their influence over the animals' behavior.

Before he thought about what he was doing, he'd already risen from the chair, locked up the house, and was pulling out of his driveway. *There's something I need at the office*, Clark thought. He didn't know what it was, but he'd stop there before driving straight to the FOB. He'd rather sleep there in his truck than in that relentlessly quiet house.

The last place he'd ever feel drawn toward was his office, especially on a day off, but he let his subconscious take the wheel, vaguely aware of something he had to do or get or finish. However, when he got out of his truck in the mostly empty parking lot, he still had no idea what that was.

CHAPTER 8

LUCY WESTERNA HAD worked for Captain Clark Rickert for just over five years. The job itself was all right, but she figured Clark was as good as bosses got. This was not because of wisdom he imparted or creativity he inspired. Her first year there, at a retirement party for one of the wardens, the half-drunk staff rallied together to insist that Clark give them all just one piece of advice, and it was the only advice she'd ever heard him give.

Never miss an opportunity to shut your fuckin' mouth.

He almost never overreacted or betrayed elevated emotion. The rare exception was a brief jet of exasperated rage associated with some computer program.

He made big decisions quickly with what she alone knew was zero input from anyone else, and as far as she could tell, they all seemed to be the right calls. He was always curt, often awkwardly distant and detached, but he'd only ever been kind to her. He interacted with all those below him in the agency hierarchy with the same dry tact and brusque courtesy he used with those very few above him. From the janitorial staff to the governor, it did not change.

He's a man of tragic, contradictory balance, she'd read in some book a few years earlier, and thought the words described him perfectly.

His bearing felt as unshakably steady as it did explosively volatile, but these attributes were not in conflict. In him, they braided together into some distinct quality, rare and yet to be named. Like sticks of old dynamite fused together by time, filth, and the rot-hued crystals of unstable nitroglycerin— inside a felt-lined, masterfully handcrafted antique wooden chest. It was as hard to look away from as it was to be around.

She knew beyond any doubt that if she died on her way to work tomorrow, Clark would not shed a tear. She was equally certain that if she or her six-year-old son were in real danger, and the only way to help them required walking through fire and killing men with his teeth, he'd do it. The likelihood of him ever causing her harm felt as improbable as him ever making some gesture of platonic or paternal affection. Lucy knew all about Clark's superlative professional reputation and everything he'd done to earn it. She knew fact from fiction within the glittering lore that surrounded him. She knew all about the tragedy and loss he'd suffered. And while neither Lucy nor Clark was aware of this, there were only five or six people who knew him better than she did, yet she still didn't really know him at all.

Two of those were the twins, Hank and Pete, who'd grown up with Clark in the trailer park outside Miles City until he fell into state care. Since she'd been here, the twins would drive from Miles City every July to take Clark fishing for a weekend. To the best of her relatively considerable knowledge of his life, this annual weekend was the complete extent of the relationship between Clark Rickert and the only two people alive who'd known him as a boy.

As peculiar a man as he was, he'd given her a chance. Only one who ever had. Lucy had bad habits and a criminal record that read like a love letter to recidivism, but he'd picked her application out of the stack. At the end of their interview, her heart stopped when he pulled her state police file from a drawer and tossed it onto the desk in front of her. He leaned back, rested one knee on top of his other, and raised his eyebrows. She almost broke down sobbing right then and there, but didn't. Something in his eyes forbade it. Her tears spilled free, but her words came measured and firm. She promised she'd work hard, listen, and never lie or steal. He nodded slowly, then spoke the words she immediately understood would bind her soul to an unbreakable vow, should she agree.

You'll put your little boy first and raise him right. That starts by makin' goddamn sure your name ain't in a whispered prayer or a police report ever again.

She made that vow, and he told her she'd start Monday. A deeper pact was made in that moment, as well. A mutual one. They'd used each other in that moment to quietly satisfy some ridiculous, self-imposed debt each had felt crushing them, but neither could explain.

Despite all that, despite harboring more trust and loyalty for Clark than any man she'd known, there was still something distinctly unpleasant and afflictive about being anywhere within thirty or forty feet of him, and something unmistakably relieving whenever her distance from him increased. Being near him felt like standing a few inches from an exposed 120-volt wire you know is live, or that moment you feel your car lose traction and start to fishtail on black ice. Moving away from him was like escaping the orbit of some static, inert danger. The sensation carried some inexplicable hint that he, himself, wasn't actually the source of the danger. Like when you were close to him, some primordial, formless thing was now *watching you too*.

The sensation was very subtle and brief, insignificant enough to forget as soon as it faded, but still real enough to be vaguely grateful for. So, while Lucy would miss his presence in the coming weeks, she was also relieved when she read the emails from Price and Jay Hart informing the office that Clark would be working on some task force for the next several weeks.

This electric, feverish sensation of his presence amplified the surprise when she heard someone walk into the lobby of the headquarters on a Saturday—when few were ever in the office—and saw who it was.

"Hey, Captain Rickert."

Lucy's voice, and the questioning smile on her face, were the first things to startle Clark out of the trance state he'd been in since walking out of that briefing in the bowels of Langley the day before.

"Hey there, Miss Lucy. Hell you doin' here?"

She gestured toward her computer with her head.

"I'm taking Monday and Tuesday off, and Jay just got saddled with your task list for this state audit, so I'm organizing some things to help get his head around the reports he'll need to finish. Mostly payroll and grant compliance stuff."

Clark nodded slowly, grinning a bit.

"Poor fella, hope he'll find it in his heart to forgive me."

Lucy shrugged and smiled back.

"Perks of being the boss. What're you doing back here, though? I thought you were off in Maryland or something and would be out for a few weeks."

Confronted with the fact that he had no real idea why he'd come back here, he felt a flush of embarrassment.

"I am gonna be out for the next few weeks, just gotta grab somethin' I left in the office."

He gestured down the hall with a thumb as he turned. When he reached the open door, he stopped and scanned the room with narrow eyes. He instinctively patted his pockets to confirm the presence of his phone, keys, and wallet. He just knew, deep in his mind, there was something he needed in this room. Something important he couldn't go into the coming weeks without.

In a semi-daze, he went around to his desk and pulled open the second drawer down on the left. Only slightly curious about why he was doing it, he grabbed all the filing folders within and dropped them on his desk, then pulled up the thin rubber liner that covered the bottom of the drawer.

Seeing it, he bumped into his chair as he recoiled and took a quick step back. His heart skipped a beat. Adrenaline flooded his face and hands.

It had been here. It had been right here this whole time.

It was a small, thin bracelet that had been smashed into a flattened knot. So small it would barely fit over two of his fingers. It had a simple braided pattern of blue and white cotton string, though so old now the blue was bleached, the white dirty and grayed. He squinted, rubbed his eyes furiously, then looked back at it blinking in disbelief. His hand shook as he reached into the drawer and took it into his fingers.

It had been nine years since he lost it.

He'd spent a full weekend on his horse, Quincey, combing the mountain trail he was sure he'd dropped it on. He'd been on the trail the day earlier, checking bow hunters' licenses during the first days of archery season. For two straight days he'd gone up and down that trail from before sunrise until after sunset, at which point he'd gotten down on all fours, using a headlamp and leading an irritated Quincey by his reins. He checked under every rock and tuft of grass. He could still remember making deals with God as he went, promising every kind of positive change if he found it. He could remember frantically scanning the sky for a star that second night, feeling that if he could just see one star, it would be a sign that he'd find it.

There were no stars, just bruise-colored clouds pulsed by heat lightning.

That Sunday night, after two days of searching, he got home and spent all night tearing his house to pieces. As the first light of dawn crept into the air that following Monday morning, he called in sick for the first time in his career. He spent the next six hours sitting on the kitchen floor amid the mess—every item from every drawer and cabinet having been thrown down in his increasingly desperate search—weeping like a child. After smoking a pack of cigarettes and drinking half a bottle of Four Roses, he passed out among the pots, pans, silverware, cereal boxes, and cheap tubes of spices.

He stared down at the little bracelet in disbelief, then brought it up to his lips, then to his nose. He prayed to a God he had not trusted in a very long time that there would just be one faint wisp of his smell, one trace of him left within the frayed cotton strings.

It smelled like his office, like the rubber liner at the bottom of the drawer. He choked back a sob as he looked up at the picture under the deer skull, his shrine of anguish and torment. The little bracelet, the one his mother had made him, could be seen clearly in the photo around his son Ben's tanned, strong little wrist just above where his hand gripped Quincey's reins.

Clark stared into the picture until tears blurred his vision and blood roared in his ears, submitting himself to the urgent, tyrannical power he'd bestowed upon the photograph.

Clark had spent what he felt was an embarrassing amount of time privately, silently pondering this twisted ritual he felt was an inexorable part of his struggle over the evil within himself. He had neither the vocabulary nor education to do this with ease, so his mind always looped him back to the same inescapable bumper-sticker conclusion: good can be, but *evil just fucking is*. Evil's inevitable triumph over good was something he felt a dire need to remind himself of, daily. He didn't know why. He just knew it's why he prostrated himself before the haunting photograph he held in a place of such emotional and spiritual reverence.

He wanted to look away, but as usual, that faceless, irrational, yet very real thing reminded Clark that if he did so too early, the evil within himself—which spent all day and night thrashing against whatever it was that contained one's soul—would breach the wall and hoist its black flag.

He let out a shuddering breath when he couldn't take any more, looking down at the bracelet in his hand. He looked up into the hall, remembering Lucy was there, anxious he'd been seen having this strange moment. He cleared his throat and wiped his eyes on the sleeve of the shirt he'd worn for three straight days, pulled out his wallet, and tucked the little bracelet deep into a card pocket. He took a few deep breaths then went to leave his office, but stopped, turning to look back into the room with narrowed eyes.

How the hell did I know to just waltz in here and look right there? Clark wondered.

Maybe the brain cells storing a trace recollection of where he'd actually seen the bracelet last had fired off one final salvo of electricity before finally dying. He ran his hand over his wallet as he realized that the bracelet was exactly why he'd indulged the manic urge to stop at his office. He knew, as well as he'd ever known anything, that this little bracelet was what he could not go into the coming weeks without. He felt the dull, excited anxiety that accompanies creepy, inexplicable things, then shook his head and strolled back toward the lobby.

A long hallway ran toward reception, lined with portraits of a dozen former FWP game wardens. There was no official rubric for making it onto this wall. Some had had uniquely successful careers. A couple had been killed on the job, one by a man and the other by a mountain. The photos were of them posing in dress uniforms before the American and Montanan flags, or in their duty gear somewhere in the wilderness.

The picture at the far end of the row showed an older man above a steep mountain valley, sitting on horseback at the head of a mule train that snaked out behind him, all the animals loaded down with pannier bags and other gear.

That man's name was Frank Farrington.

The fabled game warden who, along with the infamous poacher he'd pursued so relentlessly, Clark had held himself up against throughout his career. He'd made it a hobby those first few years on the job, poring over the state and federal investigative records and interviewing Price and dozens of other law enforcement officers who'd pursued the poacher, hunting for any shred of a lead they or Frank might've missed. He was the greenhorn. It was natural, even a bit endearing, for a new guy to be enchanted by the unsolvable case and uncatchable villain. No one suspected anything.

There was another part of Frank and the poacher's story, however, that no one alive could learn by scrutinizing the official investigation records or questioning those who'd made them.

At the end of Frank's life—which was less than a year into his retirement—the poacher heard the warden's cancer had gone terminal and landed him in hospice. A few days later, Frank received a letter, wherein the author claimed to be the fabled poacher and recalled several instances when Frank had been close to catching him, with details and times only Frank and this poacher could possibly know about. The letter also affirmed to the dying man that his relentless pursuit is what had motivated the poacher to quit, once and for all, and begin a new life as a law-abiding, working man. The author advised Frank, if he wished, to leave a return letter on a particular fence post on a tract of BLM land about twelve miles from Frank's home. Frank died three days after reading that letter, before he could write one in return. Unaware of that, the poacher checked that fence post every day. Finally, a week after Frank's funeral, the poacher found Frank's old black Stetson hat resting on the fence post.

It was a fine hat, but a plain and common one. Even so, standing in the windswept prairie—imagining that old man in his last hours of life instructing his wife or sons to leave his old Stetson on the fence post, wondering what they must've thought about such a request—that poacher cuffed tears from his eyes. That same thought brought tears to his eyes several other times in the almost two decades that'd passed since that day, as well.

Walking by his photograph now, Clark reached up, gripped the brim of Frank Farrington's old Stetson, and tipped it in respect.

Lucy was still typing at her desk and felt the familiar, lukewarm angst when she heard Clark approaching down the hall. She smiled at him as he knocked lightly on her desk a few times.

"I'm off. They said two weeks, but I dunno. Got a feelin' it may be longer. Not sure I'll have my phone, but Price and Albee can contact the task force leadership if there're any real fires. I know the place is in good hands with Jay at the helm."

She nodded.

"Where are you going? What's the deal with this task force? I didn't get any overtime forms or releases or anything sent to me by other agencies like usual. Is it like the CBP one last summer, up on the border?"

Clark grinned and cocked his head a bit.

"For the first time in my life I can honestly say: *That's classified.*"

Lucy raised her eyebrows and lifted her palms toward him.

"*Well, excuse me*, Cap. Out there on top secret missions now, huh?"

Clark looked down at her desk with his subtle grin and let out a few short bursts of air through his nose. This, Lucy knew, was almost as hard as anyone would ever see him laugh. He looked back up at her, raised his eyebrows quickly, then knocked on her desk again as he turned.

"Take care, Miss Lucy."

She stared at his back, feeling the twinge of electric discomfort begin to ebb as he walked away.

"Be safe, Captain."

As he strolled into the evening light, Lucy enjoyed the feeling of warm relief that always came when he got too far away to see, the sensation of escaping the sinister, scheming gaze of whatever always seemed to be watching him.

CHAPTER 9

EVERYONE STOOD AROUND the table in silence, awkwardly staring at the maps, digital display monitors flanking them, or one another. The screaming roar of the ascending UH-60 Black Hawk helicopter had forced them into silence.

It felt to Clark as though they'd been over these minutiae a dozen times in the two days they'd been living at this pop-up forward operating base, prepping for the raid that was set to take place the next morning at 0400. DDO David Benson, Harry Jacobson, and Charlotte Bishop insisted all "team leads" participate in these operational development meetings. Clark, to his surprise and distaste, was deemed to be among the group. The others were Commander Nowell, the head of the Ground Branch operators; Special Agent DuBroux, the head of the FBI HRT element; Captain Reichman, leading the Air Force Special Operations Command team; several subordinate operators or agents from each of those groups; and a few others from the operations control side who would be coordinating surveillance and air assets. Occasionally, suits from Langley or the Pentagon would show up for a meeting or two, then disappear to be replaced by new ones.

Every time they did a run-through of the newest situational report and plan, either Commander Nowell, Special Agent DuBroux, Captain Reichman, or someone else would ask a new question, instigating a new half-hour deliberation about something that, to them, seemed mission critical.

Once the helicopter had gotten far enough away, Jacobson coughed loudly, testing the volume of his own voice, before carrying on.

"As I was saying, we've got the six known residents of the ranch patterned. Again, that's Mr. and Mrs. Brookings, their son, and the three ranch hands. The ranch hands shift between the two gates during daylight hours; Brookings Jr. is usually with or near cattle spread throughout the southern pastures, and the Brookings couple take care of things around the homestead."

Clark kept one ear open for the rest of this meeting, but tuned most of it out as he continued to take stock of the personnel coming and going on the steady traffic of helicopters that flew in and out of the FOB.

When Clark had driven his truck into the base several days earlier, he noted the presence of the quiet, portly man from the back of the briefing room at Langley—the one Jacobson seemed to look to for authorization to tell the group more, and who appeared to refuse the Ground Branch chief's silent request. Within an hour of arriving, Clark was surprised as he watched this man walk over to Jacobson and Bishop and point in his direction. Seconds later, Charlotte came over and informed Clark that he was considered a team lead, and needed to attend all these meetings.

Clark had seen this man again several times throughout the last few days. He'd turn up for a few hours on one of the helicopters, then disappear on another. It was subtle, but Clark saw the way that Harry Jacobson, Charlotte Bishop, and DDO Benson seemed bothered by his presence. It was as though he radiated something foul or tragic no one wanted to confront. This was the first time that this quiet man had actually sat in on one of these meetings, though Clark had lost interest in him by the time he spoke.

"Captain Rickert."

The strange voice surprised everyone. Pronouncing the name as *Rick-et* suggested he'd been reared in whatever part of Massachusetts sent its children into the world with the strongest version of its accent.

Clark's eyes narrowed as he looked back at the man. This would be his only acknowledgment. Clark had always enjoyed letting silence stretch to an awkward duration. The little man eventually smiled a bit, then stepped forward toward the table.

"Captain Rickert, is there anything you would like to add? Any thoughts on the plan for tomorrow?"

Everyone present looked from the short man to Clark's face, which did not change.

"Nope."

The man's expression grew serious. He tilted his head to the side as he spoke.

"Nothing at all? Are you certain you have nothing to add?"

Clark remained a statue.

"*Yep.*"

The strange man held Clark's gaze. Eventually, he nodded, patted Jacobson on the elbow a few times as though permitting the much larger man to continue, then turned and walked away.

Everyone stared, enchanted by his peculiarity. The briefing ended shortly thereafter without any meaningful change to the operational plan for the next morning's raid. The leadership disbanded to trudge back to their team's respective nucleus, composed of trailers, tents, storage containers, and satellite communication equipment. Clark decided to walk the perimeter of the FOB by himself, as he had several times a day since arriving.

At this point, on the eve of the raid, there were over 150 people stationed, sleeping, and working here. The US Forest Service—which had closed all the roads and national forest around the FOB—told the local community via newspaper articles and a press release this was a training operation for federal wildland firefighters. This was an excuse Clark knew would only hold water for a week or so, until the local volunteer crews began poking around, wondering why they weren't invited to participate as they normally would've been.

No new intelligence of real substance had been gleaned over the last few days. Nothing that even began to answer the question of why this situation, and whatever was going on at this ranch, had been described as such a cataclysmic threat to national security. Likewise, Clark had not been able to gather any real, substantive purpose for involving him in these meetings beyond some notion of procedural deference to local law enforcement.

What he did know was that six assault teams of Ground Branch operators would creep into the ranch early in the morning. The large tractor garage and barn and stables nearby, the bunkhouse, and the ranch hand on security duty were each assigned to a team, while two would hit the big ranch house, and another would play flex. At the same time, the FBI HRT element would move in with the rest to sweep the grounds while three sniper teams and drones would provide overwatch, with the Air Force TACP and PJs and an additional quick reaction force on standby. Clark would be shadowing the team hitting the bunkhouse, a task they'd briefed him on extensively over the last two days.

Clark could not deny the growing anxiety he felt. Something had motivated the American government to hastily assemble a Tier-1 capture-kill team to operate within the continental United States. He had gotten to know several of the SOG Ground Branch operators over the last few days. Most had either come from "the Unit," DEVGRU, the Rangers, Green Berets, or the Marine Raider Regiment. He knew these were the guys sent to the most dangerous corners of the world to kill or kidnap dictators, warlords, terrorists, or anyone else deemed to be a "high-value target."

However, there was a goddamned Wendy's only six miles away, a local football team doing summer training just down the road from that, and a 4-H competition later tonight at the county fairgrounds.

This was America, and their deployment here created an anxiety he could read in others too. This was amplified by the infuriatingly cryptic nature of the scant, meticulously trimmed-down intelligence provided to the task force members. Clark had watched DuBroux, Nowell, and others grow increasingly frustrated by the curated ignorance imposed by whoever was calling the shots.

Clark made it back to his truck and the camp he'd set up on the fringe of the base after declining the rack he was offered in one of the air-conditioned travel trailers. Clark had spent hundreds of nights somewhere in the sprawling landscape of Montana sleeping in the bed of his truck under the old, rusting topper. Whether he was in his bed at home, on a pad in his truck bed, or on the ground in the backcountry under the open sky, Clark's quality of sleep did not change.

He lowered himself into the old camping chair next to his truck's tailgate, took a small nip from the flask of bourbon he'd left in the chair's cup holder, then lit a cigarette.

Clark was not a smoker, but he wasn't *not* a smoker either. He never craved them in the morning. Sometimes he would smoke half a pack a day, sometimes he'd forget about them for a week. He just never thought to light one up until he felt the pack of Marlboro Golds in the breast pocket where he always kept them, while also somewhere it was appropriate to smoke.

A bountiful hour of solitude and two cigarettes later, Clark was startled by a foreign sensation. It was similar to exhaustion, but also nothing like it. His chest started to hum with an electric anticipation of *something*, but instead of tensing up, his body's instinct wanted him to relax, be still, and let it happen. His mind rebelled against this, which resulted in a mild dose of adrenaline.

He sat up straight, made himself take a deep breath, then lit another cigarette. He leaned back again, wondering whether this was what the onset of a panic attack felt like. Unlikely, he figured. His heart rate was barely elevated. The buzz and thrill of anticipation humming under his skin seemed to be increasing, but he had no real urge to resist it. Whatever the sensation was felt too similar to fatigue to warrant panic. Like anesthesia setting in before surgery, or the last thirty seconds of semi-lucid thought right before sleep. So, vaguely assuming he was about to simply fall asleep, he let it slide over him.

CHAPTER 10

A MAN RECLINED on the ground, legs crossed and resting on his elbows. He stared out at a band of sage-carpeted hills that rolled into mountains beyond, squinting against a steady breeze and the hard, flat rays of a setting sun. The satisfaction in his features was so genuine it was infectious. Clark could sense the man's gratefulness to feel the sun on his face and bare feet, the pleasure and relief that accompanied every breath, the comfort of digging fingers into the warm dirt, gravel, and duff. A giant, gnarled cottonwood tree rose up behind him, its shadow seeming to reach eastward into the prairie for miles.

Clark was off to the man's side about thirty feet away, but also nowhere at all. He'd been here for a while now, waiting for something he had no words for but knew was getting closer. Clark's dreams always seemed to begin halfway through whatever bizarre narrative his mind had cooked up, equipped with a vague awareness of what had already gone down but no operative memory of it.

Clark realized he knew this guy. Quite well, actually. Maybe better than anyone he'd ever known. Clark didn't have a brother, so far as he knew. If he did, this would be him. He felt a deep familiarity with every feature in his face. Every physical mannerism. He knew exactly how the man smiled, the sound of his nervous laughter, his genuine laughter, and his weeping. The way he'd chew on the inside of his cheek and drum a thumb on his thigh when exhausted and stressed.

He knew exactly how this man sounded as he screamed in a battle rage. The tenor and pitch of his snarl as he slammed the blade of a basket-hilted broadsword inside an enemy's pauldron, through his collarbone, and deep into his chest cavity. He knew the vindictive, sneering smile he'd have on his face as he'd plant his boot into that convulsing enemy's belly to kick him away. How his eyes would roll back as he'd shudder in ecstasy when that sound hit his ears—the hollow slurp of his blade coming free from meat and wet, splintered bone.

The deep, almost fraternal familiarity was quickly drowned away by a crashing awareness of how vile and wicked this man was. Every kind of contempt, loathing, and hostility flooded through Clark, braiding together into an exquisite kind of malice. It was a pure, uncompromising, and righteous hatred. Now he could see how viscerally pathetic the man looked when he begged and pleaded, his revolting lack of dignity as he'd shake with sobs and piss himself. Clark was overwhelmed by a burning desire to cause this man that same misery and dread. He was ravenous for it; he needed to hear this man scream and beg and weep. Again. He needed to behold that, *again*.

Clark had no distinct memory to explain his familiarity with the images of this man. It was just that kind of vague, jumbled, dream-sphere recollection or awareness, the kind a dreaming mind accepts as truth despite a complete lack of context or reasonableness. That unfounded, baseless certainty about particular things one is born into a dream with. A series of events, circumstances, or conditions that make zero goddamn sense at all, but the dreaming mind automatically accepts just to maintain some intelligible storyline, to prevent the architecture of a dream from unraveling into formless, untethered chaos.

Clark had no clue when or where he'd terrorized this man into such a state of pitiful, horrified desperation, and certainly no idea why he'd done so. He just knew that he had, that he'd loved doing it, and that he desperately wanted to do it again. *Needed to do it again.*

The man glanced toward something on Clark's left, or his right. It wasn't clear. He nodded, then said something. The man spoke in a strange language, belching out a medley of glottal consonants. It was an old language, and Clark's mind reacted to it with nostalgia, like hearing the name of a long-forgotten kindergarten classmate. It was classical Latin, Clark knew, but made vulgar by the thick accent it was spoken in, a lilt his dreaming mind also somehow knew was either Vandalic or Illyrian.

Clark had never heard it actually spoken before, but he knew the Latin language existed. Vandalic and Illyrian, on the other hand, were two words—and apparently entire languages—he'd never even heard of, let alone how they would've infected their native speakers' words in another tongue.

Clark tried to turn, to see who the man was talking to, but couldn't. It felt like he was buried in sand. He settled his gaze back on the man relaxing in the sun. He noticed his clothes for the first time. He wore a beige, pearl-buttoned long-sleeve shirt under a black jean jacket that perfectly matched the black, washed-denim jeans his shirt was tucked into. He had expensive-looking ostrich leather roping boots sitting next to him, and a belt that matched the boots, both gaudy with burnished silver. He was a big guy, lean, muscled, and tall. He looked to be around thirty-five years old, or sixty-five years old, or any age between. There was no way to tell.

The man suddenly whipped his head around.

A lot happened in that instant. The wind ratcheted from the casual sailing breeze into the furious, bursting gusts of Montana's early winter. Clark's throat closed and stomach dropped. The terrible noise Clark had, but also hadn't noticed until now—jittery screaming, the hammering of railroad spikes, the throaty chanting of nauseating and profane verses— it all immediately ceased.

Startled urgency was visible in the man's eyes as he scrambled to his knees, then to his feet. He was looking toward Clark, not directly at him but near him, as though trying to find something hidden in the flotsam of dust and parched summer grass the wind had kicked aloft. He looked over Clark's shoulder, then somewhere near his forehead or scalp, then at the ground in front of him. Clark felt, *he knew*, he had to leave now. He tried to scream to wake himself up, but his throat was sealed shut. He tried to thrash against the invisible mass holding him in place, but couldn't budge. After a few seconds whatever had been working against him began to give. He saw the man lean forward a bit as his eyes began to narrow and focus somewhere near his own. Then, like light from an explosion, a flash of blackness consumed the world.

CHAPTER
11

THE SENSATION OF being in complete free fall woke Clark up with a gasp. He coughed into a closed fist a few times then looked around, checking self-consciously if anyone had witnessed the embarrassing spectacle of him awaking from a nightmare. No one had. He leaned back into the camping chair and took a deep breath.

He flinched when he felt the cigarette he held between the scars inside his index and middle fingers—scars from multiple burns earned falling asleep holding a cigarette. He began the motion of flicking it away but stopped and stared. His eyes narrowed as he brought the cigarette closer to them.

He knew he'd lit the cigarette right before falling asleep, and could clearly recall only taking that single drag to ignite it. He wasn't usually aware of details from moments that immediately precede sleep, but he was this time.

It was still lit, the tip nice and flush, burning fully. It hadn't been lit then snuffed by neglect, nor had it burned down or run along a side. Clark took a deep drag from it, then inspected it closely again and saw the obvious, distinct progression of the burn. He snuffed it out on a rock at the base of his chair.

The dream kitchen or whatever part of the brain cooks up dreams is a peculiar fucking thing, Clark mused. Twenty real-world seconds is all the real estate it needs to build out a ten- or fifteen-minute experience.

This reflection is not one he'd normally engage in, but whatever that dream had been felt nothing like any he'd ever had before. It left a stain behind like a sunspot. Like a cigarette burn.

As peculiar as it may have been, he'd been plagued by a pretty diverse and vivid lineup of recurring nightmares for decades. This one had been bizarre, but it hadn't filled him with rage and grief as the others would. Well-versed, if not downright masterful when it came to ignoring manifestations of internal turmoil, he took a deep breath, then a small pull of bourbon from his flask.

Only two minutes had passed when he heard someone approaching, though Clark was unable to discern which one of the three men he surmised it must be based on the sound and length of the stride.

"Taking the edge off, eh?"

Clark did not look up at who he now knew to be the Ground Branch team leader, Commander Jackson Nowell.

"*Whaddaya say, Nowell*. One to cut the dust?"

Clark held up his flask without looking at the newcomer. It was taken from his hand, which he then used to reach for the other camping chair leaning against his bumper. He popped it open and set it next to him. After he heard a few bubbles thrum past the bourbon being poured from the flask, he held up his hand again. When the flask was placed back into it, he turned to face the man lowering himself into the chair.

For the purposes of this particular mission, Commander Nowell was Clark's boss, and as such, Clark had taken care to give him deference and respect over the last few days. Although Clark had not felt the need to say much of anything at all, let alone anything antagonistic, and they genuinely enjoyed each other's company. Clark had learned that Nowell had spent fourteen years as an enlisted man and then an officer in the SEAL teams, the latter half of which had been spent as an O-5 Commander in DEVGRU, before moving onward, into the life of a Ground Branch paramilitary officer. The two men sat in silence for a minute before Nowell spoke.

"You ready for tomorrow, game warden?"

Clark did not take his gaze from the mountains to the south.

"Not much for me to do other than stick behind your boys, right?"

Nowell issued a snort of laughter but did not speak. Clark turned to face him.

"I'll be on the heels of the team hitting the bunkhouse, which your man Jake will be leading. I know to stay outta their way and which end of my rifle's dangerous. But I'll tell you what, Nowell, I still can't make heads or tails of what *the hell* is goin' on here, or what we'll find down on that ranch tomorrow."

Nowell looked over at the game warden. He could not remember Clark's year of birth from his CIA file, but based on the timeline of the career described therein, he'd figured Clark to be around his own age, somewhere between forty and forty-five. To a certain platonic extent, he'd also grown to trust this strange man over the past few days. This Clark character was the no-complaint, no-bullshit type. Never said anything that wasn't worth saying. Furthermore, based on his file, Clark was a guy who stayed cool when things got loud and violent. In the weird limbo state of this FOB—so profoundly dissimilar to any of the others Nowell had spent so much time in throughout his career—Clark was a genuinely intriguing distraction for Nowell from his leadership role in such an excruciatingly awkward assignment. Nowell felt something else while talking with Clark, something he had no memory of encountering before. To Nowell, it was like there was an electricity beneath this strange man's skin, some kind of loosely corked potential energy, like a boulder teetering on the edge of an eroding cliff.

"Full disclosure, Rickert, I can't make sense of it either."

Clark did not take his gaze from the operator's face, silently encouraging him to expand on his thoughts, which seemed, eventually, to work.

"I've done certain things, in certain places, to certain people that I'll take to my grave because that's what I took an oath to do, and frankly, few would believe me even if I told them. Never anything like this, though. Never anything *here*, at home."

Nowell exhaled through his nose before looking southward, toward the mountains glowing pink and orange in the evening light.

"I'd say there's a fifty percent chance we don't find those people at that ranch tomorrow. Total dry hole. But if we do find 'em, I've got a bad feeling that there'll be something very, *very* strange going on. They wouldn't be running a show like this if we were going after missiles, chemical weapons, or even a damn nuke. We'd have been briefed, *extensively*, on things like handling hazmat or sensitive weapon systems. *Nah* . . . whatever they think we're going after tomorrow, whether it's there or not, it's something we haven't dealt with. Something new. Something fucked up. There isn't much left behind door number three capable of really knockin' my socks off, and Harry Jacobson's been in this game even longer, and whatever this is has him shook. It's something, well . . . something that definitely shouldn't be here, at home."

Clark leaned back in his chair, took another sip from his flask, then offered it to Commander Nowell, who obliged. A minute of silence passed before Nowell spoke.

"So, how's one end up as a game warden?"

Clark glanced at the officer, wondering just how much information there really was in the CIA's personnel file on him, which, it seemed, damn near everyone on this task force had been given a copy of. In Clark's mind, there were four reasons he'd become a game warden.

First and foremost, his soul had just been crushed, his life turned upside down, so a dramatic lifestyle change was natural. Second, the monetary reward of poaching had never properly reflected the endless hours spent tracking trophy animals or soundly navigating the illegal market of wildlife articles, not to mention the serious risks of injury or prosecution. Third, consistently and often comically outmaneuvering law enforcement not only required spending a profound amount of time thinking the way a game warden thinks, but, eventually, it became tragically boring. One can only scoff at the flat-footed zeal and dim creativity of those opposing them for so long before identifying a skills gap and, thus, an opportunity.

In Clark's mind, hunting poachers—and getting a salary, benefits, and pension package to do it—was the only natural progression left for a disillusioned poacher with no record of ever having actually been one. However, hearing Nowell ask him this question, he now wondered how well he really had covered his old tracks. Perhaps the CIA's file on him did contain some evidence of his former criminal life. Maybe there was something in there that the state and federal background checks he'd passed decades earlier, before admission to the police academy, failed to find.

Nah, Clark silently concluded. *Not even these spooks would've caught me.*

So Clark decided he would now try to find the words to describe his *fourth* reason for becoming a game warden, something he'd never actually attempted. He looked away, and enough silence passed for Nowell to assume he'd considered the question until concluding it was not actually worth acknowledging at all. This was an amusing gimmick Nowell had seen Clark use several times over the last few days.

"You ever hunt coyote, Commander?"

The question was surprising enough for Nowell to look over at Clark, unsure he'd heard him correctly, and saw he still gazed to the south, the setting sun igniting the leathered skin of his face and the small caddis flies, gnats, and mosquitoes dancing in the air around him.

"No, I haven't."

Clark nodded slowly for a moment before responding.

"Used to hate 'em. Before I got into law enforcement, I spent years gettin' paid by ranch managers all over Montana to shoot 'em, mostly in the spring, when stock starts calving and lambing. Lord knows how many I've killed. I remember shooting eleven one night, and dozens of other nights I'd shoot four, five, *fuckin' nine*. Hundreds of 'em over the years, to be sure. Money was okay, but not nearly good enough to warrant spendin' all damn night tryin to call the tricky little bastards in, huddled up against a hay bale in some frigid, windy pasture with a rifle and a spotlight. No, I got into the coyote-killin' business because, well . . . *I just hated the bastards*. Reckon I hated 'em more than I've ever hated anything."

Nowell watched Clark shake his head and shrug, take another sip from the flask, and hold it out to him. Nowell declined with a wave, and Clark went on.

"When I was eight or nine, Mom drove us out to Dodson, little town not that far east from where we sit. Not sure why, but we stayed with her friends for a few weeks, nice young couple, had a little ranch outside of town, little cow-calf operation. One mornin' the grown-ups went into town for somethin', made me promise I wouldn't leave the yard where I was playin'. Not long after they left, I hear this ruckus in the pasture. A heifer just started bullin' like crazy. I stand up and see the whole herd was clustered together in a tight group, shoulder to shoulder, staring at another cow about fifty meters away along the fence line, the one makin' all the commotion. I make my way over there and eventually could see that she was in the process of having her calf, saw its slimy little front legs stickin' out. Then I saw the coyotes . . ."

Nowell grinned, amused by how this man pronounced the animal's name as a two-syllable word, *kai-yuts*.

"Two of the coyotes were latched onto that calf's legs, one on each. Another three or four were yippin' around the heifer, jumpin' in to land a bite on her neck or flanks as she kept on bullin' and screamin', spinnin' around to get away from the dogs as she tried to push her calf out. She was frantic, eyes huge. I watched as that calf's head popped out and it saw the world for the first time, watched as those two coyotes pulled it out into the mud and slush, then as the whole pack set in on it. They devoured that little thing alive, right there where it spent its whole terrible life. The heifer spent a little while tryin' to scare 'em away from her baby, even after the little thing was thoroughly fuckin' dead. Kickin', lungin' at 'em, slippin' in the mud, umbilical cord still hangin' out of her. Eventually, she kinda just gave up and trundled off toward the rest of the herd, which was still bunched together around the calves they'd already had, just watchin' the madness."

The jarring detail of the story left the Navy man speechless, unsure how to respond. He imagined his own eight-year-old son, alone, watching such a brutal scene. That terrible excerpt from Clark's personnel file flashed into his mind, the one outlining the deaths of his son and wife. But Nowell knew damn well one was never to knock at such a door; prior invitation was the only circumstance to warrant a stroll into the dark, poisoned corners of another man's mind. Clark looked over at him.

"That was the day my personal war against the coyote began, Commander. *Smoke a pack a day* wasn't just a bumper-sticker slogan for me. *It was my creed*, the reason I was here, my solemn vow to God Almighty. Those coyotes, on behalf of their entire species, crossed some sacred boundary that day. They violated some rule. I could neither put this rule into words, nor understand why it was so important to me, but it was sacred, and they broke the hell out of it."

Nowell took a deep breath, held it in for a second, then let it out noisily as he shook his head. Clark looked back toward the Bears Paw Mountains to the south and went on.

"But, over time—many years, hundreds a' dead coyotes, and thousands of lessons schooled into me by these mountains and the wild things that call 'em home—I realized somethin'. I realized I'd been angry at the wrong beast. Some animals can't survive on what grows outta the ground. Some, to survive, to follow the most base, primal instinct, gotta rip and tear the life out of something as it bleeds and screams. I guess I eventually realized there's natural brutality, and unnatural brutality. Animals killin' to survive is just as natural as a blooming flower, a spring rainstorm, aspens turnin' yellow in September. I guess what I realized is that this world is just chock fulla the pain, blood, shrieks, and screams of the innocent. We're surrounded by it. All day long. So, on nights like this—nights before I confront a violent man or go door-kickin' into some militia's meth house—I just try to remind myself..."

Clark held the flask up as though making a toast, took a sip, then stretched his legs out, resting one large boot heel on the toe of the other.

"*A coyote's just a damn dog*. A dog tryin' to get by on a mean fuckin' block with mean fuckin' rules. There's nothin' sacred about a baby calf or a coyote. That calf could've grown into a fat 'n happy cow that died quick one day. But it got yanked out its momma into this world by beasts. Only thing it ever heard was snarls. Only thing it ever felt was pain and rotten teeth. Those dogs ate well that mornin', but let's say that heifer ran those coyotes off. Maybe that afternoon one of 'em, so riddled with parasites and weakened by starvation, just lay down in a prairie. Alone, scared, panting, and drooling, listening to the wind and the birds until he finally died. Which one's worse? Who am I to get involved? Who am I to hold a grudge about such things? Yotes and calves, hawks and hares, cats and mice, trout and mayflies, all that killin'. Guess I just realized some brutality is natural, and some *fucking ain't*."

Nowell watched Clark as he chewed on the inside of his cheek for a moment.

"Man, though . . . Man is liable to act that same way against fellow man and animals alike, killin' in anger or for sport. But, unlike the yote, hawk, cat, and trout, our butchery doesn't have any real point to it lotta the time. Bad men doin' bad shit for bad reasons, Commander. That is somethin' I simply cannot abide. Setting a vendetta against coyotes for preying on the innocent is no different from gettin' angry at a tree. Setting out to stop man from doin' bad shit, *unnatural shit*, that's worth everything I've got to give, Nowell."

Commander Jackson Nowell closed his eyes and shook his head, then wheezed out a barely audible "Jesus fuckin' Christ" as he stood from his chair, then spoke.

"Well, I guess I understand that part. Bit of a rambling, roundabout way to not even answer my question though, you dismal fuck."

Nowell looked back at the game warden, who spoke through a grin, eyes barely visible under the brim of his battered old Stetson hat.

"I knew early on I loved to hunt. First thing I ever liked doin'. I heard game wardens got to *hunt hunters*, and stop bad men from doin' bad shit. So I joined up, and turned out I wasn't wrong."

The operator smiled despite himself, then spoke as he pinched the bridge of his nose between a thumb and index finger.

"Well, next time someone asks you that, maybe skip the whole country wisdom bit, and just fucking say that part. Consider saving that winded lead-in and the details about your fucked-up childhood for your therapist, eh?"

Clark snorted in amusement as he looked back at the mountains.

"You went 'n missed the whole damn point, Nowell; them coyotes *were my therapists*."

Nowell laughed and shook his head, cast a thumbs-up toward the game warden, and walked away.

CHAPTER

12

THE CAMP CRACKED into a frenzy at 0130 hours. After the Ground Branch teams ate a quick meal and ruthlessly caffeinated themselves, they piled into blacked-out, armored M-ATV vehicles to get into positions around the Brookings ranch. Clark was attached to the assault team tasked with hitting the bunkhouse, where two of the six inhabitants known to be present on the ranch slept. The surveillance teams had kept locations on all of them for days, and confirmed one of the ranch hands as being on the usual night-watch shift, while the two others were sleeping in the bunkhouse.

After Clark's team and another were dropped off by the transport vehicles, they moved about a mile on foot until they were in position at the base of a dried-up arroyo, a few hundred meters behind the barn and stables. Clark looked around as they crouched there in silence, thinking vaguely about how this would be a great spot to find arrowheads, and how impressive night vision technology was.

He'd been fitted with a ballistic helmet with a set of mounted white phosphor night vision goggles. He used either handheld or weapon-mounted night vision and thermal optics quite a bit, but had only ever worked with it mounted on a helmet while running shoot-house training events with the state police. This set of night vision was far superior, however. He'd been able to see individual crickets jump from their route through the prairie, and a mouse that'd just scurried through the ditch over forty meters away. He fiddled with the mount on his helmet, trying to familiarize himself with the button that allowed him to lift the heavy tubes up and away from his eyes.

Everyone was connected through radio comms via speakers in the Peltor ear protection and PTT-activated mic booms mounted to their helmets. Clark listened as one of the overwatch elements confirmed the single ranch hand on night watch was still in the Chevy parked inside the ranch's main gate. The teams were now minutes away from the 0400 mark when they would move into their final staging positions, or *phase line alpha*, as they called it, from where they would initiate the coordinated raid.

When the moment finally came, all six assault teams plus the HRT guys, almost forty people, began silently moving in toward the ranch from every direction. Clark followed the guys he was attached to and was impressed by their ability to navigate the rugged terrain with sure-footed swiftness, and in near silence. The man at the rear of his team regularly glanced over his shoulder to check if Clark was still with them, and always found the game warden right on his heels. A few minutes passed at their final phase line position before the order was issued to breach.

Clark's team entered the barn and stables on the heels of another team that was tasked to clear and hold it, but passed through the massive old structure toward the bunkhouse.

He watched as the other team cleared the large structure, infrared lasers lancing into every corner and doorway as they went. They moved at a speed, with a level of efficiency, Clark would never have imagined possible. He was transfixed by it, and how much repetition and training such a skill set must require. Every inch of the large space seemed to be covered by one of them at any given time. As they passed through the big doors of the barn and crossed the open ground toward the bunkhouse, Clark heard the faint song of a yellow-breasted chat somewhere off in the prairie, a bird with a night song he'd long enshrined as a good omen.

Through the night vision optics, he saw a rave of infrared strobes, lasers, and weapon lights lancing around the dark, silent ranch from all the different teams moving toward their respective targets. He shuddered as he thought about what anyone without night vision would be seeing right now, if they were looking at what he was. All they'd see was quiet, still darkness. They would not hear or see *anything at all*.

Operators chimed into comms with technical jargon and unfamiliar acronyms every few seconds. Clark listened, understanding only half of what was being said. He knelt at the corner of the bunkhouse as his team stacked up outside the side door behind the team leader Clark knew only as Jake. Jake had briefed him extensively on where he expected Clark to be throughout every step of the raid, instructions he knew were specifically designed so that he'd stay out of these combat operators' way.

Clark was fine with that. Watching them move now, he wouldn't want it any other way.

He heard the muffled *pop* of a breaching charge somewhere beyond the bunkhouse, then it was drowned out by a louder, much closer charge that blew the bunkhouse door inward in a cloud of dust and splinters. It hadn't even finished its swing as the assault team surged into the house, peeling into singles and pairs as they went about clearing the building.

Clark followed them into the room behind the destroyed door and stopped, as previously instructed. He could see his hands shaking through the reticle of his rifle's optic, which skittered and jumped as he aimed it around the room, checking corners and hiding places his team had already cleared.

He looked ahead down a long, dark hallway, over the shoulders of two operators stalking down it. They moved like sharks, forward but appearing completely still, rifles shouldered and aimed ahead. The sound of an old, iron doorknob and creaking hinges came from down the corridor ahead of them. A second later, a young, shirtless man came out of a doorway on the left, about forty feet ahead of the two operators.

He wheeled into the hallway, a cheap AR-15 held loosely in one hand at his waist, and stopped. Clark could tell this guy didn't actually see the two men stalking toward him through the darkness. He squinted past and beyond them with a delirious, angry expression toward Clark and the room where the crash of the breaching charge had come from.

The operators opened up with their suppressed M4s. Clark saw a dozen dark holes stitch up the man's exposed skin—beginning right above his beltline, working up his breast until the final bullets struck the man in the cheek and forehead, whipping his head back into the doorframe before he crumpled to the old floorboards in a lifeless heap. Most of the bullets went through the guy's body into the wall and doorframe behind him, kicking a cloud of splinters and dust into the air.

The instantaneous eruption of shooting startled Clark. He flinched and took an unintentional step backward, then steeled himself and took a knee, rifle shouldered and ready but aimed at the floor.

He saw the two operators suddenly stop advancing and rapidly exchange hand signals. The one on the left aimed his rifle at the wall that ran from their position to the doorway and the growing slick of dark, arterial blood still visibly glugging from holes in the guy's body.

While Clark was still trying to discern what had been communicated via the operator's hand signals, the one on the left began firing. His first shot went into the wall a few feet in front of his left knee, and his next eight or ten inches beyond that. He shot fast, about twice a second, putting bullets through the wall in a jagged course away from himself. At the same time, the operator on the right bounded forward until he reached a spot a few feet from the doorway. He crouched in a low firing position, rifle aimed into the empty space above the dead body.

Several of the operator's bullets tore into an old piano set against the other side of the wall, snapping long-untuned wires in loud, thrumming twangs.

Clark heard thumps and shuffling on the other side of the wall being blasted through, and an unmistakable "son of a bitch" growled in a man's voice. Another shirtless young man half crawled, half stumbled into the hallway over the body of his fellow ranch hand. He'd only made it a few feet into the open area, using one hand to brace himself on the shoulder blade of his dead buddy, when the second operator put three bullets into the confused man at point-blank range.

The last bullet went through the bridge of his nose. Every muscle in his body slackened. He fell hard, face crunching into the floorboards. His lower half came to rest on top of the first man's shoulders and head as the black pistol he'd been carrying clattered across the hallway.

Before the handgun had even come to rest, both operators had dropped the depleted magazines in their rifles to the floor, yanked new ones from their chest rigs, slammed them into the magwells of their rifles, then released the bolts. They'd completed their reloads in the time it would've taken Clark to bring his hand up and snap his fingers.

In a flash, Clark imagined the man who was just killed in the seconds before his death, frantically scrambling away from the furious line of bullets tearing through the wall behind his hiding spot—a hiding spot these operators had somehow discerned in complete silence and darkness. Watching these guys was like watching a pair of veteran hunting dogs work a covey of quail.

As Clark grasped the shocking efficiency they'd employed to locate, flush out, then kill the second man, both operators were already moving into the room the ranch hands had come from. At the same instant, another pair of operators emerged from a door farther down the hallway on the right, then stalked down its length to clear the next room.

A few seconds later, Jake sent an all clear over his team's comm channel and lights began getting flipped on. He winced at the lights' blinding effect through the night vision tubes, then mashed the mount on his helmet until he found the button allowing him to lift the unit up and away from his eyes. He walked to the bodies of the two young men, saw the pistol was a Glock 17, slid it out of their reach with his boot, then gripped the second man's upper arms and dragged him off the first. He removed the rifle from the first man's still-warm hands and let the magazine drop to the floor, then ripped the charging handle back, sending a bullet spinning from the chamber into the air to clatter down the hallway.

Clark had leaned the empty rifle against the wall then stared at the operators moving around him as they secured the scene. Jake and another operator approached the bodies and nodded at Clark as though excusing him. They rolled them both onto their backs and began searching them with the indifference of looking through a backpack.

Clark walked back into the room they'd first entered when chatter started coming through operation-wide and command channels. What he gathered was that the ranch hand on guard duty in the Chevy had been apprehended, alive, and he heard Jake mention both ranch hands in the bunkhouse had been killed. A few moments later, someone else confirmed one of the three members of the Brookings family within the main house had been killed, although it was unclear whether it was the son, mother, or father.

Clark felt along the wall for a light switch until he found it, then looked around the room. It was the common area of a ranch's bunkhouse, a predictable one he'd seen many versions of. There was a whitetail buck mounted on one wall above an old TV, a coffee table covered in rodeo and gun magazines, but the symbol painted on the far, bare wall caught his attention. He stared at it as he thumbed his radio's PTT button, then spoke into the boom mic mounted to his helmet.

"Warden for Jake."

One second went by before the team leader responded.

"Go, Warden."

Clark cleared his throat before speaking.

"Those two dead fellas got anything carved into their forearms?"

Several seconds passed before Jake responded.

"A-firm. They've both got the cult symbol we saw in the briefing; looks like it was burned instead of carved. I dunno. Can't say."

Clark grunted an acknowledgment.

"Do the burns look recent? Fresh?"

Another several seconds passed before Jake responded.

"Looks pretty fresh. One's still a bit open, infected maybe."

Clark did not respond. He approached the symbol on the wall, which appeared to have somehow been painted, carved, and burned into the bare Sheetrock. Curious, he removed the glove on his right hand and reached up to feel it.

When his bare fingers touched it, he shuddered as gorge rose in his throat. He could hear his son laughing. Then he heard him crying. These noises came to mind the way a song does—heard, but not with the ears, a different part of the brain playing the record. He stepped away from the symbol and swallowed the stomach acid, sending him into a coughing fit. He looked up at the symbol, then down at his hand, just as he heard the hum of diesel engines.

He looked out the destroyed door into the darkness to see lights ripping across the landscape. He assumed this meant the rest of the task force was now entering the property in armored MRAP vehicles to begin the real, comprehensive search and investigation of the place, as planned.

He glanced back at the symbol, shuddered, then flipped the night vision back down over his face and walked toward the door where Jake had tasked him to hold after securing the target.

He felt a childish terror coil in his muscles as he walked away from it, as though it had been waiting for him to turn his back to make its move. He did not let himself turn around, and was embarrassed by the sensation of relief and escape that hit him once he crossed the threshold into the cool morning air.

The wolf light of dawn was starting to creep over the vista of rolling plains to the east, which was a welcome sight; the sooner the light of morning arrived, the sooner he could remove the godforsaken helmet. The whole contraption was heavy enough to score aching lines where the chin strap contacted his skin.

Until the arrival of the rest of the task force in the vehicles, and other than the occasional comment made across the general command channel of the radios, virtually everything had been carried out in complete silence. Clark glanced around the homestead at the other operators holding security or moving around their respective target areas, finding every one of them with their weapon stocks glued to their shoulders, eyes locked down the length of their barrels, as though their rifles were fifth limbs, something they'd been born with.

This morning he'd just been a tourist. A useless appendage dangling alongside the body that was this team of special operators. Watching them kill those two men was astounding, but simply watching them move was one of the most violent spectacles Clark had ever beheld.

Wolves coordinating an attack on a herd of bedded elk was nothing remotely close to the level of ruthless, calm, silent lethality exhibited by this team. But they did look like wolves, especially as they moved in the light of an almost-full moon. *Almost full*, thought Clark, and was surprised again by his own attempt to calculate precisely when the next new moon was.

Eventually, an all clear was announced for all the target areas except the main ranch house. Several of his assault team members broke away to assist, while Jake instructed him and one other operator to remain in their respective security positions at each entrance to the bunkhouse.

Clark ground his teeth, resisting the building urge to lean over so he could glance at the symbol etched into the wall. Over the last five minutes, he felt its desire for attention evolve from a manipulative plea into a screaming demand. The impulse to get away from the symbol grew in unison with his need to look at it again. He finally gave in and leaned over to look at it, just to prove to himself it was nothing more than the deranged scribblings of some cult-smitten lunatics.

As soon as he let his eyes fall upon the symbol, several things happened at once.

His heart started pounding in his ears and face. The image blurred away as his mind conjured a reel of memories that pulsed in vivid, excruciating detail. The image of his son Ben's laughing face. Giving him a bath in the kitchen sink. Wrestling with the little boy in his bed. The wonder in his eyes as he stared down at the frog Clark had put into his hands. Sitting on the glider bench on the front porch, holding Ben as he napped, knowing the boy slept from the cadence of his breathing. Feeling Ben's face smushed into his chest and his little head of blond hair under Clark's whiskered chin.

He could smell the stale air of the old chapel as he stared down at Ben's little coffin. He saw the exhausted, resigned despair in his wife's face as she stared down at it too. He felt the same helpless fear her expression of detached anguish had filled him with that day.

It was the same expression she had that morning a week later when she'd walked outside to get something from her car. The last one he'd ever seen on her face.

He could hear the gunshot, the blast awkwardly dull, flat, and muffled as it passed through the walls of their barn, the screaming blizzard, and then the walls of their house. He'd still known immediately what that noise was. What that noise meant. He could feel the bite of ice and snow on his bare feet and bare chest as he sprinted out of the house to the barn, toward the spot he knew the gunshot had come from, where he knew he'd find her.

He tore his gaze from the symbol and forced himself to take slow breaths, the same way he always did. Clark relived this same sequence of terrible memories on a fairly regular basis. It cut into his thoughts like some ritual dagger. A diseased, corrupted blade incapable of growing dull no matter how many times it was slammed into a skull and ripped free. Many years earlier Clark had accepted the abject impossibility of avoiding this blade of wicked memories and the pain it caused, but he'd also learned that it wasn't actually lethal. The pain it was capable of could only ever last a minute, and could always be remedied by some deep breaths. Clark knew this. Mary had not.

So he took his deep breaths and drew comfort from his familiarity with the temporary nature of this grim routine. He also worked very hard to ignore the overwhelming sensation that this symbol—this *thing* hacked into a wall—had needled its way into that dark corner of his mind *and pressed play*.

A frenzy of excited comments pulsed over the radios. One came through distinct and clear, and without any obfuscation of the obnoxious military acronyms. It stopped his breathing.

"AT 1 for Command. Behind the main house, they . . . they're here. There are at least forty, maybe forty-five people here, at the big tree. They're . . . dead, I think. Confirm one's alive and ambulatory, for sure. Only one. Unsure on any ID yet, but we think most of them are dead."

CHAPTER 13

BEFORE THE TRANSMISSION even ended, Clark was up and preparing to fall into a sprint toward the massive cottonwood behind the main ranch house. He stopped himself, startled by his own impulse to get there, or maybe just away from the symbol on the wall behind him. He had an assignment, and it was to stay here until told otherwise. Despite how unimportant this task felt now, he'd see it through. He stared over at the crown of the huge tree visible above the house, increasingly distinct in the growing light.

He glanced around the bunkhouse toward the operator tasked with security at the other entrance. He knew this man's first name was Kyle, and that he'd grown up in a suburb outside Detroit. Kyle betrayed no emotion or sign he'd even heard the sinister news regarding dead people behind the ranch house.

He was glued into his position, scanning the sector before him. He was just like the red-tailed hawk on the telephone pole running along the county road a half mile behind him, scouring the pastures, ditches, and prairie for rodents.

The radio was going wild with commands. Outlines of people could be seen running toward the main ranch house from all around the property in the predawn light.

Several minutes passed until the rising sun shot expanding spears of red-golden light up and away from the eastern horizon. More vehicles had arrived in that time, plus a helicopter that came roaring into the silent morning. It landed in front of the ranch house, dropping off several people Clark could not identify, then peeled away again. Jake sent a command over the team channel, but Clark only made out a few unfamiliar acronyms. Kyle jogged up to Clark's position seconds later. He didn't slow as he passed, just glanced at Clark and cocked his head toward the ranch house as he spoke.

"We're moving."

Clark followed Kyle toward the sizable crowd growing on one side of the ranch house and spilling into the area behind it where the large cottonwood tree stood.

He slowed a bit when he saw Captain Reichman and five of his guys from the Air Force's 24th STS carrying something large, covered by a tarp, toward one of the armored vehicles parked out front. Clark assumed it must be the body of whichever one of the three Brookingses had been killed.

This group on the side of the house was made up of Ground Branch operators and FBI HRT agents that had comprised the assault teams, some members of the control and support element that had come in sometime over the last fifteen minutes on the armored vehicles or the helicopter, and even several people in suits.

One of the FBI HRT guys was set apart from the group, hands on his knees, spitting out the last bit of vomit coating his mouth. Another operator was a few feet away, holding the hair of a young woman from the support team who was heaving vomit into the gravel between her feet. A mixture of disgust and fear was visible on most faces.

Clark saw Charlotte Bishop and Harry Jacobson, who'd come in on the helicopter, directing personnel on-site. Jacobson held a grave expression as he switched his focus between one of the assault team leaders facing him and a large radio in his hand. Charlotte gave another woman from her staff some directive, then walked slowly away from the group to face the mountains to the west. She had one hand on her chest as her shoulders began to rise and fall. Clark could not see her face, but from behind it looked as though she was trying to ward off an asthma attack. He began walking toward her when "all clear" was shouted from somewhere behind the house.

It came from a group huddled around several ruggedized laptops controlling an equal number of small tracked ground drones used by the explosive ordnance disposal team. They looked like large RC cars as they hummed away from the tree in the backyard.

Clark looked toward the massive cottonwood tree to find a solitary figure standing at the base of its large, gnarled trunk. He narrowed his eyes, straining against the fussy light of dawn to pick up more detail.

Four pairs of operators surged toward the base of the tree from different sides, weapons shouldered and aimed at the person Clark slowly began seeing in better detail.

It was a woman. Completely naked. She had long, tangled black hair rolling over her shoulders, down her back, and over her breasts. She was covered in dried blood, wounds, and cuts from head to toe. All of this was taken in at a glance by those watching the scene, because her face commanded the most attention.

She was *smiling*.

It was a grotesque smile, stretching from ear to ear. Her teeth glistened in the growing light, contrasting sharply with the dark red of the cuts and dried blood caking her face. She held her arms out, palms toward the sky, mumbling through her smile and giggling before and after she jabbered out each phrase.

Clark, like everyone else present, felt locked in place, speechless, as the operators took her by the elbows and shoulders and led her through the group toward one of the armored vehicles idling in front of the house. The rumble of their large diesel engines was the only audible noise until the woman got closer. As she was hauled through the aisle formed by the silent parting of everyone present, all could now see that she was covered—from her scalp to the tips of her toes—in what must have been *thousands* of small glyphs, runes, and symbols. They'd been meticulously carved into her skin with a small blade. One large symbol—the one on the wall in the bunkhouse, the one they'd all first seen at the briefing at Langley—was deep and dark in the flesh of her chest. What she was mumbling could finally be heard, repeated over and over.

"You're too late. He has been awoken. You're too late. He has been awoken."

Clark watched as she was led around the house, then turned back to the group, many of whom were still transfixed by the tree she'd been standing under, while others slowly, as though in a trance, walked toward it. Clark followed their gaze up to the tree. What he saw made him recoil a step before slowly approaching the tree with widening eyes.

There were seven or eight massive branches that reached up and away from their junction with the main trunk of the tree.

Up and down their entire lengths were *people*.

All were naked, motionless, covered in blood, and somehow connected to the tree. Some were upside down, some were straddling the branches, some facing into the tree and others out at the landscape. Dark blood with a sap-like hue had channeled through the rough bark to where it pooled into the dirt, gravel, and dry grass at its base.

Orders were being shouted that Clark disregarded as he approached the tree. He stopped when he got within a few feet. He saw what appeared to be railroad spikes in the shoulders, hands, elbows, knees, and feet of every one of these people, driven through flesh and bone to secure them into the soft timber of the cottonwood. Dozens of people were staked into the tree, the closest of which were just a few feet above his head, the farthest fifty feet up, where the large branches began to narrow.

Charlotte watched Clark as he stared up into the tree. One of the FBI HRT guys began pulling gently on his elbow, and he allowed himself to be directed away but walked backward as he went, not breaking eye contact with the mutilated corpses stapled up and down the tree's length. Members of the control and support elements were around him, moving toward the silent carnage, some with large cameras who began taking photos of the tree and the victims tangled into it. Clark turned and shrugged away the hand but didn't look at whoever'd been pulling him from what was now effectively a crime scene, and Charlotte saw what she assumed was a rare expression for him: shock. She saw him stare around at the others nearby, as though seeking to validate they also saw what he had. He looked at Jacobson, then Nowell, then DuBroux, each for several long moments, none of whom noticed as they talked into radios or to their teams.

Clark appeared to give up looking for whatever he'd sought in the others' faces, then made his way to the outer limits of the crowd. From there, he began walking slowly, very slowly, in a wide arc around the tree. Charlotte watched him until he came to a stop, then knelt down to take a closer look at something on the ground.

A helicopter came roaring into the landing area established in front of the main ranch house. Several more people disembarked from the aircraft, jogging away from the rotor wash of the screaming machine with hands shading their eyes. The helicopter then ripped up and out into the morning sky. Among the new arrivals were David Benson, the deputy director of operations for the CIA, and Ronald Comley, undersecretary of defense for intelligence and security. They were the executive administration's eyes and ears for the operation.

They walked around the house and stopped, staring up at the tree. Comley removed a handkerchief from his inside jacket pocket and held it to his nose. Jacobson briefed the two men on the few details of the situation they didn't already know. Both had been in constant communication with the ground team, and indeed actually watching the operation unfold from the control center all morning via live streamed feeds from dozens of weapon and body-mounted cameras worn by the operators on the various raid teams.

Benson took a few steps toward the three surviving members of the wicked little family band that were known to inhabit the ranch up until this morning: the ranch hand who'd been nabbed from his truck early in the raid and the old Brookings couple. All were now flex-cuffed, sitting in a row along the side of the house. Not far from them were three body bags, two of which contained the ranch hands killed in the bunkhouse and the third containing the Brookingses' son, killed during the raid on the main home. Benson took in a breath as though preparing to ask them something, held it in for a moment, then let it out slowly as he turned away and walked back toward the others.

Several dozen people from the control and support elements were beginning the meticulous search and documentation of the homestead's structures, and an equal number of operators were sent to maintain a security perimeter throughout the area. That left the rest of the unassigned ground guys to loiter uncomfortably around the command staff, as Benson's level of agitation grew until his anger was hard to ignore for anyone within earshot.

There was a frenzy of activity behind the group that cut through Benson's invective. Urgent voices were screaming, *"Grab him, grab him."*

The surviving ranch hand was sprinting away from where he'd been seated next to the older Brookings couple, albeit awkwardly, with his hands flex-cuffed behind him. His blond hair was caked with a streak of drying blood where he'd been struck during his apprehension. As startling as his sudden movement and speed was his smile. He was beaming a severe mix of boyish elation and madness.

He was headed toward a cluster of old horse-drawn farm equipment of the kind not uncommon throughout the rural American West, buried in weeds wherever it'd been abandoned, or set along a driveway as decorative aesthetic. An old plow and tiller were visible, and an old spike-toothed harrow that'd been flipped up on top of them.

A group of assaulters and support personnel sprinted after the guy. Their commands for him to stop or be stopped were not easily heard over the maniacal, shrieking laughter coming from the young man himself. Just before it looked like he was about to connect with the old tiller, he dropped his speed with quick, arresting steps.

When he was within a foot of the old harrow resting atop the other equipment, he began slamming his face into its dense row of two-foot-long, rusted blades pointing into the morning sky, scream-laughing as he did.

He grunted a bit at the first impact. He put his entire body into the second, and a few of the spikes appeared to go several inches into his face. His shrieking laughter was interrupted by a choking, squealing gasp, that sound of being shocked by pain. Several of those who'd chased him finally got their hands on his shoulders, but not until a split second after he'd already put all his remaining strength into one forward motion. He bent his knees, cocked his head up toward the sky, then blasted forward at the waist, smashing his face down onto the spikes one final time.

His laughing ended immediately, as did all control over his body, and a wheezing moan was the last sound he ever made.

Three rusted spikes were visible, glistening in the morning light where they peeked through his mess of blond hair on the back of his skull—a skull now thoroughly stuck to the old farming device that hadn't been moved in seventy-four years.

Commander Nowell and others were screaming about securing the prisoners as a cluster of task force personnel scrambled around the now obviously dead ranch hand. Benson and Jacobson had both watched the chaotic scene unfold but still demanded to be told "what in the fuck just happened," almost in unison.

Everyone's attention, eventually, and perhaps naturally, fell upon the old Brookings couple, the two remaining, living prisoners. Both stared with faint, prideful smiles at the young ranch hand's body as several operators lifted his legs and trunk into the air while several more gripped the shoulders and head to pull his skull up and away from where it was skewered onto the old harrow.

A wet, sucking noise cut through the air as his head was yanked from the harrow's maw of spikes, prompting a chorus of nauseated groans and one distinct "fuck me" from the group watching. Blood poured freely from the holes in the dead man's limp head as he was rotated then placed on the ground. A seemingly hopeless but pro forma effort was now being undertaken by a couple of Ground Branch medics to find a pulse and check for any vital signs.

Verne and Grace Brookings slowly looked away from the dead man up at the group that had formed around them. Everyone stared back, disgusted at the horrendous suicide they'd just witnessed and edgy with the collective expectation that these two would now try to do the same.

The old couple had genuine smiles on their faces, as though they'd just watched a beloved grandson graduate from high school. As they began to speak in almost perfect unison, their smiles grew, and they giggled through their words.

"You're too late. He has been awoken."

Benson, Jacobson, and Nowell dominated the atmosphere over the next minutes with furious indignation, demanding answers and scolding those tasked with prisoner security. At the same time, the older couple was escorted into one of the large vehicles idling in front of the ranch house while the suicidal ranch hand's corpse was rolled into a body bag. The bag was zipped up, then carried over to be laid alongside the other three.

Clark looked at the row of four body bags from where he stood on the other side of the tree. He then looked around for Air Force Captain Tucker Reichman or any of his guys from the 24th STS. He'd assumed they'd been removing a body from the house when he'd seen them earlier, but all four who'd been killed were bagged up right here. He was curious what, if not a body, they'd carried from the house and loaded into the back of that MRAP, and dropped his eyes to the ground and continued cutting for sign.

Charlotte Bishop lost focus on the voices around her for a moment as the game warden caught her attention again. She saw that he had gone back to walking slowly in a wide circle around the tree of carnage, hands still on his hips, focused on the ground around his feet. She watched as he stopped and took a knee in the dirt, then gently pushed some grass to the side before leaning in to get a closer look at something beneath it.

Her attention went back to Jacobson as he turned away from some of the support team conducting the investigation at the base of the tree, then spoke to all the senior task force personnel standing in a crescent around him.

"There are forty-nine people up in that tree. The living woman makes fifty. She was one from the chat room we'd had under surveillance. Her name is Courtney Putnam of Santa Fe, thirty-seven years old, mother of three. So, yes, we have good reason to believe that every one of the fifty members of the Red Castle chat room are all now accounted for, but we'll confirm shortly after we get the bodies taken down and go through biometrics and identification procedures. What we know at this point is that, based on the specialists' initial review of the blood, skin dexterity, coagulation levels, they think that, well, *this . . .*"

Jacobson gestured up toward the tree without turning all the way to look at it.

"*. . . this* must have taken place sometime in the last few hours, early this morning or sometime late last night. They aren't sure about anything yet, but they're fairly confident that these people cannot have been dead for any longer than about six hours."

Everyone remained silent until Benson snarled out a string of profanities. He stomped past Jacobson, several meters toward the large tree, extended his arms up at its branches, then turned back to his team.

"So, *how the fuck* did we not catch this happening last night on the thermal or aerial FLIR we've had aimed at this place for weeks now? That little hundred-pound witch back there didn't do all of this on her own—*that's not fucking possible*, Jacobson, not even with the help of those ranch hands and the Brookings family, who we've been watching on live feeds for days now. This would've required a *goddamned crane* to carry out, or even *several goddamned cranes*, and hammering all those hundreds of spikes into them would've been as loud as fucking *gunfire*. So if *all this* was done in the last twelve hours, how in God's *good fucking name* did we miss it? How did *whoever else* helped do all this get away sometime in the last few hours? *Where the fuck did they go?*"

"That way."

The gravelly voice surprised all those watching Benson's diatribe, even Benson himself. Everyone looked over to see it had come from the game warden, Clark Rickert, who stood about twenty meters from the tree, one hand at his waist, thumb hooked into a belt loop, and the other pointing toward the western mountains. Clark turned a few degrees toward the others after a moment but kept his gaze and finger pointing westward as he spoke.

"He went that way."

CHAPTER 14

BENSON'S EYES NARROWED. He put his hands on his hips, stared at Clark for a few breaths, then leaned forward as he responded.

"Fucking . . . *who*? *Who* went that way?"

Clark turned to face the suited man, who appeared so out of place in a rural setting, and among dozens of combat operators adorned in full tactical battle rattle.

"Couldn't give you a name, sir. What I can tell you is that a man around two hundred and forty pounds, barefooted, with at least size-thirteen feet, went out that way sometime around . . ."

Clark looked at his watch, then over toward the sun rising in the east, then down toward something near his feet, and finally back up at Benson.

"Sometime between 0200 and 0330."

Benson, Jacobson, Bishop, and a half dozen others were immediately power walking toward Clark, issuing demands over one another that he show them "what the hell" he was basing this claim on. Clark pointed at the ground near his feet, then slowly lifted the same finger toward the mountains in the west, tracing the course of the alleged trail that, it seemed, he was the only one capable of seeing. He turned from the group forming around him, ignoring their storm of questions, staring at the ground as he went. After several steps he knelt, glanced over at the others, and gestured with his head that they come to him.

They did, several placing hands on knees and leaning down closer. Clark used two fingers to move a tuft of long, yellow prairie grass to the side. Underneath was a distinct human footprint impressed into the fine, gray, silty dirt. Clark picked up a long twig and reached forward several feet, moving another tuft of grass to expose another clear human footprint in the dusty topsoil. Charlotte Bishop asked the first question.

"How do you know these tracks are from this morning? How can you be sure they're from between 0200 and 0330, just a few hours ago?"

Clark remained kneeling but looked up at her as he spoke.

"Weather data from the NWS gauge few miles south, checked it this mornin' before we lit out. Rained a bit here last evening between 1900 and 2300 hours, while there was a steady southeast breeze with gusts around thirty that held till around 0130 when it died down to almost nothin'. Would've dried quick, especially with wind. Sign like this, in country like this, it doesn't look like it does now after drizzle and wind. No, ma'am. These tracks are from early this mornin' after the wind died, and I take it none of us saw the son of a bitch once we had three dozen sets of eyes on this area around 0330 when we were staged within view. So this fella here must've strolled off yonder sometime after the drizzle and wind, and before we had the place surrounded."

Benson looked from the bare footprints in the dirt and into the faces of the others around him, then strode several paces along the mysterious trail. He began speaking while still facing away from them.

"So, the one who did all this—or, rather, the one who helped that psycho we found under the tree, the Brookings family, and their little band of henchmen do all this—ran off into the mountains this morning and our drones, our ground tech, our sniper teams, even the goddamned *satellites*, it all just . . . completely failed? We had full system failure? Not a single tool in our imaging suite or array of ISR tech saw this bastard running away from the target area? Is that what you're fucking telling me?"

"No, sir."

Benson turned to face Clark. The unexpected answer to the series of scolding rhetorical questions seemed to push a bit of anger and even amusement into his expression. Clark used the twig he still held in his hand to gesture at the footprints as he stood and looked Benson in the eye.

"He didn't run anywhere, sir. Not these tracks. This fella here was just walkin'."

No one spoke. None could have if they tried.

Something new happened then. Something that broke all the rules. No one present had known these rules existed, but as they stared along the trail this barefooted man had not run, but *walked*, all could feel them being broken. None could have easily explained this feeling either. No existing human language contained the necessary words to describe such a concept.

A rough approximation would be that it felt, vaguely, as though something nameless and ancient had finally decided it simply could not wait any longer.

This feeling came from the way the light fell on the rocks and dirt, the way the air felt static against the skin, some silent code hidden in the way the sage scrub and tall summer grass creaked and bent in the breeze.

It all told of water breaking, the first small cracks that crept along the surface of an eggshell, something horrible and filthy slithering into the world and gratefully stretching skinless, bloody limbs. Heart rates spiked and mouths went dry as adrenaline dumped into everyone's hands and feet.

Every one of the members of the Ground Branch team, the FBI HRT, and even many in the support and leadership side of this task force had encountered considerably more teeth-grinding danger, human wickedness, and shrieking chaos than most other adults throughout the developed world. Yet, despite this group's individual and collective exposure to extreme stress and trauma, all fifteen or twenty people within earshot of the game warden's last words experienced a sensation so entirely new and foreign—so sickening and heinous in nature—it numbed them all into astonished silence.

At that precise moment—as the game warden explained how the barefooted man had not run, but had merely walked into the mountains, walked away from this miserable scene of impossible butchery—everyone privately experienced a jarring sensation of broiling, bone-deep dread. Pure somatic horror. A kind of terror that blinded and paralyzed.

This revolting sensation only lasted one crushingly abusive instant, then reality shifted. Everyone found themselves ripped back in time and abrasively smashed into their own little bodies, looking through their own innocent eyes. It wasn't right, though. They didn't fit there anymore. *They weren't supposed to be here.* And they all knew precisely where *here* was— the exact spot where they'd all experienced the most terrible, traumatic moments of their respective childhoods.

Several, in this moment from their past, could only see stars bursting in their vision, but they could feel what they knew to be the calloused fists of a father or mother's boyfriend cracking bones in their face.

Ground Branch operator Kyle Brown found the world sideways, watching that man pull his older sister into the back bedroom, his little cheek stuck to the adhesive film of grease and blood on that filthy kitchen floor. For HRT Special Agent Brett Chandler, it was the view down the hallway toward the front door where his father rocked back and forth, weeping into his hands, where he'd just seen his mother for the last time as she stormed out of the house. For Ground Branch operator and combat medic Mike Fraser, it was the bookshelf in Uncle Edwin's guest room—in shocking, impossibly precise detail—the only thing he could really see in that moment twenty-seven years earlier when his capacity for trust and innocence had been murdered. For Charlotte Bishop, it was her cousin and her friends holding her down in that muddy soccer field, slapping her, tearing her clothes, smearing gravelly mud into her mouth and eyes as she wept and screamed.

These visions of the past were ripped away as suddenly and violently as they came on, like a bag yanked off one's head. Most stood in astonished silence, staring at the game warden and the mountains that rose up beyond him. Several of the operators glanced around at others nearby, blinking in shock and disbelief, unsure whether anyone else had seen them experience this panic attack or whatever kind of mental break it had been. As soon as most saw others looking back at them, they cleared throats and shook heads, doing their best to appear unmoved, as though nothing at all had just happened. They were good at this, very good. They had to be.

These people were experts at expeditiously repressing, shrouding, and stowing away any signs of cognitive, behavioral, or emotional issues, or even just the more basic symptoms of overly frayed nerves. They might've been better at it than anyone alive. Anyone who sought to maintain active employment within a top echelon of combat operations had to be.

This was different, though. They were all exhausted. It felt as though they'd been standing here for weeks, or as though they'd been chained to a truck and dragged back through time from that horrible moment. Joints ached, ears rang, eyeballs throbbed. Within a few seconds, however, most felt the shock and adrenaline ebb until they just stared silently at the mountains a barefooted man had walked into, now blazing in the brilliant palette of a Montana sunrise.

Clark remained standing ahead of the rest, also staring into the mountains. He was unaware he was being scrutinized by every one of those behind him for some sign, any suggestion, that he'd just experienced something like they had. He betrayed none of this, because he'd felt nothing close to what they had.

If anyone had been in a position to see Clark's face, they'd have known right away that what he was experiencing now had to be a considerably different sensation.

Clark Rickert felt, perhaps, as good as he ever had in his entire life. As good as his wedding day, or the day his son was born. Killing Elijah Austin Miles had come close—it had been similar in a way, but not nearly as jarringly profound as this.

He felt purpose in his soul, a level of motivation he'd never known, and, to his own surprise, a sense of gratitude and faith that was almost religious in its conviction.

He'd had no idea until now, but he'd been waiting for this moment his entire life. Everything he'd been through had led to this. Everything anyone had ever been through had led to this.

There was no question anymore. Clark Rickert hadn't been born to hunt. He'd been born for *this hunt*, the one that had officially just begun.

CHAPTER

15

WHEN IT BEGAN almost two weeks earlier, the trees could feel it. Not all trees, certainly, but a few.

One was a 4,856-year-old bristlecone pine in the mountains of Nevada. Another was a 5,100-year-old yew in Wales. A 3,100-year-old sequoia in the Sierras, a 4,500-year-old cypress in Iran, and a 3,300-year-old olive in Portugal.

It would be marked in their rings as the others had been. A tiny burst or blip, almost too small to see, but identical to the one they boasted from 1909, and all the others before.

They felt it starting again.

Trees couldn't *know* things, not in the way those who created the word can *know* things. They did in their way, though. In the way they know it's time to draw nutrients from the branches to the trunk a bit early before what they know will be a long, dark winter.

They'd been through it before. Dozens of times, for some. More than any other individual, living things.

Other living things that hadn't experienced the event before could also feel it begin. Most were animals, but there were a very small number of people who could, as well.

One hundred forty-four people, to be precise. The fated ones. The exemplars. Those born manifest and bound to a lifetime upon the path of the dove, or the path of the raven. Each path was a distinct moiety, and each was pledged a constant retinue of seventy-two souls who'd bear the ancient word of their distinct and diametrically opposed creeds. Elijah Austin Miles had been one. He'd have felt it begin again, too, if he weren't dead beyond rot in the sad little state cemetery along Highway 89. The Chilean boy who'd replaced him—born eleven minutes and six seconds after Elijah was shot in the brain—smiled when he felt it.

But again, the vast majority of things that could feel it, despite never having felt it before, were animals. This was not strange. The moon influences innumerable natural systems, so most animals have an acuity with lunar phases humans not only lack, but can hardly even conceptualize. It's like trying to imagine a new color.

The sensation, the warning that it was beginning again, was tethered to a precise moment in a lunar cycle. Beings that feel it are those that still depend on their grasp of natural systems, whose survival is still tethered to their sense of it. Unlike people, who'd disconnected from it all so enthusiastically and entirely. Humans think of something like a full moon as a condition that lingers for a day, not as something that actually only happens in a single, flashing instant. Humans are even less attuned to its opposite: *a new moon*. The darkest night in the cycle, that moment when, like a lantern, the moon just *goes out*. And that's when it happened. That's precisely when they felt it.

A steelhead felt it as it made its final journey up the Columbia to that particular patch of gravel hundreds of miles upstream where it was born. It was a slight shift in the water chemistry, but one that meant so much. It stopped abruptly, letting the massive river's current have it for a moment until its nose pointed back downstream toward the seals, sharks, and poisons of the Pacific.

An old axis deer buck in the Sundarbans felt it under its hooves, just a minor shift in magnetism. He'd grown wise by respecting minor shifts. They'd led him through a lifetime of deceiving the tigers, leopards, and beasts that'd tried so hard to eat him alive. He lifted his head up, stared eastward, flicked his ears once, then disappeared into the humid mangroves in a silent, explosive blur.

A wolf in Kamchatka turned toward the faint rumble of the waves beyond the old trees when she felt it, an acute change to reverb in her ear canal. She growled deep and low in her chest, then turned to nose and prod her cubs back into their den.

None of these creatures could've explained it, obviously. They didn't know about the two men, or how unlike men they really were. They didn't know what their conflict was about, or any details from the previous iterations of the ancient duel. But they'd certainly felt it, and knew it was cyclical; not just beginning, but *beginning again*.

Like songbirds in the Everglades that stop, look south, tilt their heads, then shoot up to flit northward. They're completely unaware of how or why the warm waters of the Gulf occasionally churn a regular storm into a monstrous tempest of broiling violence. That didn't matter, though. They'd felt it, whatever it was that carried the urgent suggestion that it was time to get out of the fucking way, and trusted it.

So while animals didn't bear the experience or scars of time the old trees did, they still felt this cycle begin. They knew that the coming storm would fall within the boundaries of the lunar cycle that'd just begun, this new moon to next new moon. They knew that this storm would push everything to the brink of annihilation, that this conflict promised either ruin or continuity.

The battle that He forced man to have every now and again. *The weaver.* The trial He made men pass to determine their worthiness, or the need to cleanse their mark on His creation. If any of these creatures had the faculty for abstract thought, they might find themselves aggrieved by His decision to stake their well-being on the impulsive, savage passions of man and their two monstrous champions, angry at the injustice of it.

But they didn't. Their own futures falling subject to the whim and caprice of man was something they'd been dealing with since man left the caves. This was just another severe consequence of man's existence. It wasn't all that different from chain saws screaming through their ancient trunks, arrows or bullets punching holes through their lungs, or chemicals poisoning their food. These were constants they lived with every day, grim potentialities they went through life trying to avoid. The only real difference was that now, by the end of this lunar cycle, there was a chance all those terrible things would sweep the entire world in a shock wave of fire, poison, and pain.

If the one they'd just felt open his eyes and take his first breath was victorious, the dangers of men would no longer be avoidable. There would be nowhere to hide.

Then, several days after feeling it all begin on the new moon, they felt something else awaken. This was different, though. When it had begun, it'd carried the warning like those whispered by changes in air chemistry or pressure before a wildfire or hurricane, or in microseismic waves or infrasound before an eruption or earthquake. This was more subtle, less jarring. It didn't set off their sensitive alarm systems. It was related, though. It told them whatever else had just awoken was on their side, standing against that horrible force.

He felt it too: the one whose return had sent a shock wave of dread across the earth. It stopped him in his tracks. He wanted to turn around, to look behind him, but wouldn't let himself. He'd felt this sensation many times, and had been waiting for it since he'd awoken. It was no less infuriating, however. No less terrifying, and just as dreadful as it always had been.

He dug his bare toes into the grass and dirt, took a deep breath, and stretched his arms out to the sides, centering himself by enjoying the simple, mundane sensations he'd gone so long without. He turned his head toward the sky and exhaled, watching the bloom of smoke, ash, and rippling heat distortion from his lungs dissipate into the mountain air.

He had to master himself and accept the unavoidable reality that he'd be feeling this—he'd be *feeling him*—for the rest of his time here. But that was all right, because this time he'd beat the wretched beast he'd just felt awaken behind him. This time, that pest would lose. This time, he really was going to finish it. It felt more certain than it ever had before.

He closed his eyes and smiled into the sky as the grass, moss, and insects at his feet curdled and died.

CHAPTER 16

SHORTLY AFTER THE task force's local law enforcement liaison, game warden Captain Clark Rickert, identified the barefooted human trail that morning, two Ground Branch teams and an FBI HRT element were sent off with Rickert to track and apprehend the mysterious person. DuBroux was put in command, and several drones and helicopters equipped with FLIR thermal imaging optics assisted. As the tracking team was getting ready to set off, Clark had insisted upon exchanging all the heavy tactical gear he'd worn on the raid for his usual duty kit.

Clark Rickert, as well as two SOG K9 units that had been assigned to the ground pursuit team, had naturally fallen into the lead positions. The going was slow, as the team directed air assets to conduct scans and sent out flanking elements on the ground around any feature in the landscape where an ambush could be staged. There were many such features in these mountains.

It was all standard practice for K9 operator Jordan Quinn and his Belgian Malinois, Reggie, who had deployed all over the world together, tracking and apprehending dozens whom Uncle Sam or his allies had deemed worthy of their relentless pursuit. They'd done this together in the jungles of Colombia and the Philippines, snowy farmland in eastern Europe, arid flats or mountains throughout Iraq and Syria, and most other earthly biomes. It was as though Quinn and Reggie were a single being, extensions of each other, and their reputation was impeccable. Whenever they were set upon a fleeing target, no matter the circumstances, mission success was effectively guaranteed. In the four years man and dog had deployed together, hundreds of American and allied special operations personnel had worked with or adjacent to them while tracking down an enemy, and all had been impressed. The other K9 handler on this team was just as experienced.

However, for Quinn, something was happening that he'd never seen before. An hour into the tracking effort through the foothills and into the increasingly steep Bears Paw Mountains, Quinn looked yet again, with even wider eyes, between Reggie and the game warden, Clark. Quinn had been watching his dog, Reggie, look up at Clark in the same way he'd seen so many others *look at his dog* over the years—as though *the dog* sought *the man's* concurrence that they were still on the right trail.

Whenever the team would reach a new drainage, ridgeline, or other geographic feature where the barefooted man could've gone in several different directions, Quinn would slow the dog to make him focus on maintaining the correct trail. In the thousands of previous instances Quinn and Reggie had done their slow-down-and-make-sure procedure, Reggie would almost immediately indicate the correct course by orienting his body along it and pulling against the lead in Quinn's hand. Today, however, the dog would look up at Clark and cock his head to the side as though awaiting the man's confirmation. Clark would cast a quick glance at Reggie, nod, then set off again.

After maintaining the trail westward for around six miles, they were working up a long, steep spur that led to the peak of a mountain that the operators' Foretrex GPS devices told them was called Big John Butte. The heat of the summer day had fully set in. On this hot, dusty mountainside, Clark felt very glad he had taken the time to get his normal day pack and ditch the heavy plate carrier and battle belt with all the extra ammunition and accoutrements attached to both.

None of the Ground Branch or FBI HRT guys had changed their gear, however, and it seemed to Clark as though they'd been born in these heavy load-outs. The Ground Branch operators had chased men throughout far larger mountains in much hotter parts of the world, and the special agents of the HRT element were so obscenely well-conditioned they could've kept the tracking up for days.

Everyone was fanned out through the grass and sage as they worked up the open ridge. When Clark, several meters ahead of the rest, halted abruptly, everyone else did the same. Reggie leaned forward in a point, muscles coiled, tightening the lead in Quinn's grasp. Clark turned toward them, extending one open palm as though signaling them to hold up.

He had just begun to say something when an eruption of noise and movement exploded directly up the slope from where Clark stood. The noise was abrupt and jarring, an instantaneous chorus of rapid drumming that cut through the quiet mountain air in the same second everyone registered the large blur of movement. Every member of the team immediately shouldered their rifles and crouched or dropped to a knee as they all fell into shooting positions.

Everyone except for Clark, who stood ahead of the rest and stared back at them with a little smile, cradling his heavy MKII rifle in an elbow, barrel out like some pheasant hunter with an over-under shotgun on the cover of Filson's fall catalog. The tension in the group uncoiled a bit as they all stared past Clark and registered what had just screamed out of the grass with the same abrupt speed and noise of a land mine detonating—a small cloud of plump, gray birds flying off toward the fold of the ridgeline. Clark was the first to speak.

"A covey of Huns is all. *Gray partridge.* Sons a' bitches can be awfully startling. I was turnin' around to tell y'all we were about to flush 'em so I didn't get shot in the ass, but they beat me to it."

The team relaxed. Some laughed; others cursed the upland game birds with the colorful profanity of career infantrymen. About five minutes later, they reached the summit of Big John Butte. The others watched Clark and the dogs slow down to a stalking pace, focused on the ground.

Clark stopped entirely when he'd reached a spot just a few feet away from the apex of the mountain's summit—a large circle of very fine gravel, sand, and topsoil almost entirely devoid of grass. Quinn and Reggie were on his right, while Special Agent DuBroux and the other K9 unit were on his left. All three men followed the gazes of the dogs and the game warden down to where the clear tracks of a barefooted human could be seen. There were seven or eight distinct footprints showing this person had walked into the center of this sandy area, then stopped.

The person's last forward step had been with the left foot, and then they had planted their right foot next to it. It did not take tracking experience to see the person had come to a complete stop, feet shoulder width apart, standing there and facing the vista of rolling mountains and plains beyond. The two side-by-side footprints were sharply defined in the fine dirt and gravel, clear and unmistakable. One could almost imagine the mysterious barefooted man crossing his arms and taking in the strikingly beautiful view.

Dwight DuBroux was certainly no wilderness tracker by trade, but he was a career investigator, and had a keen enough eye to clearly see what had frozen Clark Rickert in place for the first time since they'd set out that morning. Without taking his eyes from the tracks, DuBroux issued sharp orders for everyone to get away from this open circle at the summit of the mountain, disperse, and establish a security perimeter. Several of the operators who'd been closest to the team leader and who'd also seen the final visible tracks backed away slowly, eyes narrowed, one muttering a soft "what the fuck" to himself.

Surrounding the two side-by-side footprints—where it appeared this man had come to a stop and just stood there—was a complete ring of the same fine, sandy topsoil extending at least forty feet away in every direction. What had them all silently staring at the area was the complete absence of any *other* tracks. There were the seven or eight made as the person walked to the center of the circle at the mountain's peak, the two where they'd come to a stop, and nothing else. Clark took a wide, arcing route to the opposite side of the open area, then knelt to stare toward the toes of the footprints.

Neither Jordan Quinn nor the other K9 handler needed orders to split up and begin working their dogs around the perimeter of the open area to try to pick up the trail where the man had, somehow, walked out of it. DuBroux followed Quinn and Reggie, then stopped and knelt next to Clark as the dogs and handlers passed one another behind him. Neither man said anything as both K9 teams completed their first loop around the area, and remained silent as they did it again. The dog handlers set themselves twenty meters out from their original starting points and ran a wider circle around the first. After they'd finished a third and even wider loop without picking up any scent at all, Quinn looked over at DuBroux with an expression of confusion and almost boyish wonder. He shook his head slowly and shrugged his shoulders as he shouted over to them.

"Dog's not pickin' up a fuckin' thing. I mean, *nothing*. His last hot scent, the *only* scent he's still picking up, is the trail this guy took into the circle. We'll backtrack and run the dogs back over the route we took up here, see if we can't pick up something behind us to affirm this trail was a fake, a misdirection. I'll tell you what, though, if this dude *somehow* doubled back from where he stopped there, then snuck off on a different route, that'd be the first time Reggie's nose has ever missed that stupid old trick, and trust me, we've gone after *many* that've tried it."

DuBroux keyed his radio's PTT button and ordered several of the other operators to accompany the K9 teams as they went back down the slope. Clark hung his head and stared blankly at the dirt a few inches ahead of where his knee was planted. DuBroux glanced at him as he spoke in his sharp, raspy voice.

"Could he have brushed them over, or done something to cover over his tracks out of . . ."

Clark had been shaking his head as soon as DuBroux started the question, then cut him off before he could finish it.

"*Nah*. I mean, it's possible, but I don't see any sign of it, nor, more importantly, any reason for it. Let's say he lit out around 0330, just as we staged for the raid. At a steady walkin' pace, he'd have made it up here no later than 0630. That's an hour before anyone was even tailin' him. Plus, he left distinct tracks through a thousand stretches of ground between that tree of death and this spot here, but he didn't bother coverin' any a' them up. Moreover, he passed right by just as many far superior spots to try to lose us by settin' a fake trail, backtrackin', then coverin' up his real one, but didn't bother. But more than anything else, those two Belgians are the best trackin' dogs I've ever seen. Honestly didn't even know they made 'em that good. They've been wired to the trail all damn day. I didn't see one of 'em miss a single track over six miles."

Clark pointed at the two bare footprints in the sand ahead of them.

"Plus, *just look*. If someone covered up a trail in this kinda ground, we're talkin' about a truly masterful bit of work. It's all uniform and undisturbed, they'd have needed to use a trapping sifter to set a base over the whole area, not just the tracks themselves. Then they'd have needed to go about dustin' it all over again with the bigger gravel on top without leavin' any signs of impact. It's doable, but would've taken a whole lotta time to pull off. But again, all that aside, those trackin' dogs are tellin' us his trail ends *right here*. Waste of time tryin' to argue with a good hound. They're smellin' more than a man can even see. I've been runnin' hounds through this country over twenty years now, after men, cougar, bear, wolves, you name it. Some good hounds, too, *real* good. But I've *never* seen a dog work a scent like that Reggie. Doubt there's a man alive who could fool a dog that good."

DuBroux, with the sharp edge of agitation in his voice, gestured around the area with both hands as he spoke.

"Well, he *went somewhere*, Captain Rickert, unless you're suggesting this cocksucker *can fly*. I assume if a helicopter came in to pick him up from this exact spot this morning we would have heard it, plus our surveillance or control assets certainly would've picked it up, and the rotor wash would've obscured his tracks in this fine dirt, or at least left them far less distinct than they are now. So *where in the hell* did he go?"

Clark's mind was plagued by this same question as he rode in the helicopter back to the FOB. He hadn't been able to consider anything else in the two hours that'd passed as they combed the area until the trio of UH-60s had roared in to pick them all up from the mountain. He felt angst and rage build at his inability to even begin answering the question. So, as he felt his mind start to slacken and empty, he welcomed it. For a moment.

That was until he felt something strange and nameless, but familiar. All his anguish over his inability to answer DuBroux's question, his own desire to know *where the hell he'd gone*, flushed out of his mind entirely.

He felt the electric anticipation begin to hum under his skin, and the blanket of vague, anesthesia-like fatigue roll through his body. As he had the evening before while sitting in the camping chair next to his truck, he let the dream take him.

CHAPTER 17

WHERE IN THE *hell did he go?* is effectively the same question that David Benson, the CIA's highest-ranking employee in the after-action briefing taking place in the large command tent at the FOB, had just asked for the tenth time since the meeting had begun.

It was also exactly what Clark had been asking himself as he'd been overcome with another dreamlike vision in the helicopter. What traumatized Clark more than falling victim to another delusional episode was the fact that what he'd seen answered that exact question. He'd thought about nothing else since.

This meeting—the debrief of the morning's raid—had begun almost two hours earlier, shortly after everyone who'd been assigned to pursue the barefooted man had returned to the FOB, and should've ended some time ago. It hadn't taken long to run the AAR, and Jacobson had only needed five minutes to brief them in on what they'd learned since.

All fifty members of the Red Castle chat room who'd disappeared two weeks earlier were now accounted for. Forty-nine had all been positively identified after their bodies were removed from the tree on the Brookings ranch. The one surviving member of the original chat room, Courtney Putnam of Santa Fe, was undergoing a combined interrogation and psych evaluation off-site. Nothing useful had been gleaned by this effort in the eighteen hours since she was found naked, jabbering incoherently amid the carnage of her comrades. Indeed, Jacobson told them how the only thing she'd said since being apprehended was the same sinister phrase: *You're too late. He has been awoken.*

All those present had been going full steam since 0130 that morning and were exhausted. However, Special Agent Dwight DuBroux, Clark Rickert, and seventeen operators who'd been assigned to that ground pursuit team were far filthier, and perhaps even more deeply troubled, than all the rest.

None would have guessed there could've been something else to make that day even more bizarre than the glyphs and symbols carved into the skin of the woman stammering under that bloody, corpse-filled tree.

Yet, here they were, confounded by another disturbing impossibility.

The tension had risen steadily throughout the last hour, which had been spent focused on the failed effort to apprehend the person who'd left the target area on foot. It seemed as though everyone—from the military and agency leadership to the ground team operators and support and control element staff—was growing increasingly angsty and defensive. The repeated explanations of what they'd found at the end of the trail, and the abject lack of any sane explanation for it, increased the collective agitation.

Clark had been more than happy to let DuBroux field the majority of the questions regarding the immensely disappointing and seemingly impossible conclusion of the ground pursuit of the barefooted man. After all, DuBroux had been assigned as the official leader of that ground team. Likewise, Clark had no idea what the hell to say. It was possible he felt more disturbed and perplexed in this moment than he ever had. The combination of emotions and exhaustion, and the comedown from his elation earlier in the day, when he first found the tracks, was mind-numbing. All his discomfort and anxiety were amplified by what had happened in the helicopter on the flight back to the FOB.

Benson's repeated question now, however, was expressly directed toward Clark, whom he prodded after a long stretch of silence.

"Well, Captain Rickert? I was led to believe you're one of the best trackers in America, and you have *no theories at all* about where this guy went after stopping on the top of that mountain?"

Clark slowly looked up from the spot on the ground he'd been staring at for an hour. He locked his eyes onto Benson's, who was standing next to an array of monitors showing images of the footprints on the mountaintop taken by the ground team as well as drones.

"No theories, Mr. Benson. Haven't got a clue where he went from there. Trail just went totally cold, and the dogs confirmed as much."

Benson used a hand to whip one front of his blazer aside before planting it on his hip. It was obvious he was as exhausted as all the rest. With his other hand, in which a small stack of paper was gripped, he gestured toward the monitors behind him.

"So, he just *teleported* away, then? Are you telling me we're going after a man capable of *teleportation*?"

Clark responded in a flat, monotone voice.

"I've gone through life with the understanding that teleportation is fictional, Deputy Director. So, no. I highly doubt that."

Several people around the room snorted in amusement as many looked over toward the game warden. Benson's expression did not change, but there was a bit more ice in his voice as he responded.

"Are you unfamiliar with what a rhetorical question is, Captain Rickert?"

Clark nodded a few times, letting awkwardness compound until he eventually leaned back, crossed his arms, and spoke.

"I'm familiar with the concept of rhetorical questions. Over the last few days I've gathered that you, sir, are actually quite fond of 'em. Myself, well . . . *I fuckin' ain't*. Whatever could compel a man to say somethin' intentionally pointless is a far greater mystery to me than any of the weird shit I seen today. Yet you just *keep on askin' 'em*. So, reckoned if I started answerin' 'em as though they weren't the waste of time and air they damn well are, you might just go ahead and *stop fuckin' askin' 'em*."

Everyone in the large tent turned to stare at both men. A few even stood to get a clear view. Someone whistled a long, curved note. Nowell and several other Ground Branch operators openly smiled in tired amusement as they leaned back or crossed their arms. Jacobson and Charlotte looked at each other with raised eyebrows.

Benson's eyes narrowed as he took several steps in Clark's direction. Both men held the other's gaze for a long moment, until Benson looked at the ground. He took two deep breaths before speaking in a measured tone none had yet heard this evening.

"I apologize to you, Captain Rickert, and to everyone else here, if I've come across as facetious or disrespectful. As many here know quite well, this kind of investigative dead end, this collection of unanswered questions, these gaps in our intelligence, they're things that we at the Special Activities Center are as unaccustomed to as we are frustrated by. We're all exhausted, but everyone here did an outstanding job today, that's the truth. I'm going to let Mr. Jacobson wrap this AAR up, but before we do, Captain Rickert, respectfully, do you have any theory, no matter how improbable, about where this man could have gone or how he just seemed to disappear from the top of that mountain?"

Of course I know how he disappeared, Clark thought silently. This thought, this *knowledge*—a detailed answer to Benson's repeated question—was all Clark could think about since the helicopter ride back to the FOB. Since it had boiled up from the corner of his mind in another bizarre nap dream that'd only seemed to last for fifteen real seconds. The problem, however, was that Clark knew his answer to this question of the day was completely impossible. *It was insane.* An unhinged fiction. Not only that, but he had no way of explaining *how* he knew the ridiculous answer.

It's goddamned impossible, Clark thought to himself. *It was just a dream. Humans are incapable of such things; that's just pure, window-licking insanity. I must have heat exhaustion, maybe some parasite in my brain. It was just a dream. It was just a fucking dream.*

Some version of this had been on repeat in Clark's mind since stepping off the helicopter. However, he felt this explanation for the dream or delusion growing weak. Now, it felt like an excuse, or even a lie, a cruel one, as though something in his soul was offended that what it'd shared in the vision was being questioned.

Clark squeezed his eyes shut and swallowed, then leaned forward in his chair to rest his elbows on his knees. He took a deep breath, cleared his throat, and stood.

"I, likewise, apologize for my rude comment just now. Long day, but that don't warrant bein' an asshole. And no, Deputy Director, unfortunately I do not have any theory as to where that guy went. Never seen anything like it. Just like them trackin' dogs we were runnin', I just lost all scent of his trail on top of that mountain. Trail just went cold. I'm, well . . . I'm sorry."

Benson looked Clark in the eye and nodded.

"There's no reason to apologize, Captain Rickert, and I was kind of asking for it just then anyway. It's been one hell of a day, and when I say that you exceeded your duty and our expectations of you out there today, I do so with sincerity."

Clark nodded, then sat back down in his chair. He felt a very familiar but exceedingly brief pang of guilt for having been directly and publicly scornful toward a professional counterpart, but it had worked. It always seemed to.

If the one doing the shaming was on good ground, it was an incredibly effective way to shock someone back into the present, force them to look around and take stock of just how much attention, time, and respect they were wasting. If there was a better way to do that, Clark was not aware of it.

He reached into his pack for a canteen and drank half of it as Jacobson went about concluding the meeting, not hearing a word.

Clark was now coming to terms with the fact that he'd had his mind seized by some kind of hallucination, delusion, or vision. He was unsure which word fit best to describe having his mind involuntarily dominated by a dynamic, vivid, and completely fucking ridiculous experience. What terrified him even more was his own primal instinct to trust it as something real.

Clark did not nap. He sure as hell didn't let himself fall asleep around other people, either, and never had. Yet he had twice now, two days in a row, and both had been to accommodate dreamlike moments that had been centered on the same thing.

The same man.

In Clark's most recent dream experience he'd seen exactly what the barefooted man had done to escape, in the exact way Clark's dreaming mind already knew he was going to, as well. He could hear the man's voice too. He could still hear it, even lucid, in this very tent.

It felt like it came from mental archives, the cognitive source of memory, wherever that was. He felt panic building as the man's name came close to mind. *All his names.* Strange, old names he knew he'd never read or heard spoken in his life. Names he knew with deep familiarity. He felt something within, also entirely separate and distinct from himself, begin thrashing against whatever contained it. The same *thing* he felt growing angry at his effort to ignore the dreams and chalk them up to exhaustion or insanity or both. It had begun silently screaming the barefooted man's names.

Clark felt air slip from his lungs and his lips start to move as it began *trying to make him whisper one of them.*

He leaned forward abruptly and rubbed both eyes with his palms, hard, as though trying to scrub these insane thoughts from his mind. He leaned back in his chair and tried to concentrate on breathing as he blinked focus back into his eyes. When focus returned, the first thing he saw was that short, chubby man across the room in the black suit he always wore, seated behind and off to the right of where Charlotte Bishop stood.

He was leaning forward in his chair, burning holes into Clark with wide, intensely focused eyes. Clark looked to his right, then his left, finding nothing else that could have grabbed the guy's feverish attention. He looked back at the strange little man, welcoming any distraction from what he was coming close to accepting was some kind of real mental break. Clark cocked his head up and shrugged at the man, hoping to elicit some response. The only one he got was the man slowly removing the glasses without looking away. Clark felt his panic begin to amp up again as he considered whether this guy had somehow been able to see the fiery anxiety that had just been churning through him.

Jacobson ended the meeting, directing everyone to eat, hydrate, stretch, rest, and be ready to go in the morning.

Clark stood, hoisted his pack onto a shoulder, and made his way toward the entrance to the large tent as others rose to their feet and conversations began breaking out. He clocked two men in his periphery approaching from the left. A quick glance showed one to be the K9 handler, Jordan Quinn, while the other was an operator who was also on the ground pursuit team with Clark all day. Both were smiling broadly and chuckling. Jordan extended a closed fist in Clark's direction, and the one whose name he couldn't remember started saying something to him. The guy had just finished describing something about his harsh words for Benson as "fucking epic" when Clark spoke a single word.

"*Tomorrow.*"

Both fell silent as Clark passed, and he immediately felt better when he left the stale, hot tent. As the cool night air hit his face and flowed into his shirt, his heart rate stabilized. The manic collage of images of the barefooted man that had been pulsing behind his eyes immediately began to dull and fade. It felt so good Clark actually smiled into the darkness as he walked toward his truck.

When he reached it, he threw his pack into the back bench and quickly removed his boots. He turned on the fan set into the window of the topper, set his boots next to each other in the dirt below the tailgate, hung his Stetson from a bolt on the outside of the topper, then closed it all up. He grabbed a camping chair and his flask, and walked briskly, barefooted, into the darkest reach along the boundary of the FOB. He set his chair down facing his truck and fell into it.

Over the next half hour, he quietly sipped Four Roses bourbon as he watched his ruse effectively deter anyone from trying to talk with him, assuming he was already asleep inside the enclosed truck bed. Nowell and

DuBroux were the first to come by, and a few minutes later it was Jake and Kyle, both of whom were on the team he'd run with early that morning during the raid. Both pairs of men stopped several feet away from his closed-up truck bed, one would point at his boots and hat, then they would leave.

The last to stop by was Charlotte Bishop. She also paused, looked at the boots and hat, then up at the truck, but instead of leaving like the others, she took a few steps toward it. Clark narrowed his eyes when she raised a fist as though she was preparing to knock on the old topper covering the bed of his truck, but she hesitated, then turned and quickly walked away into the muffled hum of generators and engines throughout the large encampment.

Clark felt briefly offended by her gumption—the *audacity* to even think about waking him up after a day like today—as though he were actually sleeping in the truck about to be woken up.

He checked his watch two cigarettes later and saw it was almost midnight. Helicopter traffic seemed to have ceased, and a nice blanket of quiet had fallen over the base. Feeling it was unlikely many remained successful in warding off the exhaustion of the day, he walked back to his truck.

Clark stripped his filthy clothes off and climbed into his bed in the back of his truck. Staring up into the darkness, for the first time since leaving the meeting, he allowed himself to think of the barefooted man, something he'd been exerting significant effort to avoid doing.

No emotional conflagration accompanied the thought. No fevered visions of the barefooted man thrummed behind his eyes. No wheel turned in his mind of old, cryptic names in forgotten languages. Overwhelmingly relieved—and eager to categorize the earlier experience as mere symptoms of heat exhaustion—Clark quickly fell asleep.

Somewhere down the slope in the heavily timbered valley below the FOB, coyotes began to howl.

CHAPTER 18

THE AIR FELT unusually warm to Clark. He'd expected it to be somewhat chilly as they screamed across the calm surface of a lake at fifty-five knots in an open-air, rigid-hull inflatable boat in the predawn darkness. Clark squinted toward the pair of what he assumed must be at least 250-horsepower motors powering the blacked-out boat, but could not tell what kind of motors they were. The only light came from the blade cast by the setting moon, shimmering on the water they shot across. Whatever model or make, they seemed impossibly quiet for their power output, giving off nothing more than a dull hum.

He wanted one for work. His agency patrolled lakes during the summer in Boston Whalers with 225 Mercury outboard motors that were noisy as hell. Most assholes fishing without angling licenses could reel in and hide their gear as soon as they heard one. With one of these stealthy bastards, however, Clark thought his guys could make it rain citations all summer long. He had patrolled this same lake in his career, and knew it quite well, but he was not looking for people fishing illegally today. Having ever done so felt small and insignificant as the boat slowed, the shoreline loomed closer, and the gravity of what he was about to do began to sink in.

Fort Peck Lake—the fifth-largest reservoir in the United States—was, to an extent, shaped like a giant upside-down V. The task force's current target location was another cattle ranch in the middle of the rugged chunk of land that jutted northward between the two massive fingers of the lake, forming a sort of broad peninsula within the crescent of water.

In the fifty minutes it took his team to work silently inland from the beach toward a position that had been deemed *phase line alpha* during their mission planning, the wind had picked up significantly. It moaned and howled through the sage and juniper and rock outcroppings they crept through, setting aloft an aerial flotsam of dust, dry leaves, and bits of straw. This obstructed the white phosphor view of the world through the night vision tubes dropped over Clark's eyes.

Clark was attached to the assault team led by Jake again, which was set to approach the ranch from the east. Two assault teams, including his, had set off in these fast boats from Spring Creek Bay, which cut into the eastern shore of Fort Peck Lake. Two other teams had set off across the lake from the Sixth Coulee, a name given to another large bay that cut into the western shore. Once they reached predetermined locations along the muddy beaches of the large peninsula, all four teams moved slowly inland through steep drainages thick with juniper and sage scrub.

Clark knew how many goddamned rattlesnakes called this area home, and was grateful to be creeping through the landscape in the dark before they slithered into the world to bask on warm rocks.

They designated team names based on their positions around a clock, the center of which was the ranch, and each time corresponding with final staging positions referred to as *phase line bravo*. Jake's and the other team assaulting the target from the east were staging at the two- and three-o'clock positions. Two other teams had moved in from the south, making their way overland so that they'd be staged at five and seven, while the two other teams that had come over the lake from the west staged at nine and ten.

All teams were in position after two long hours, and Clark's heart began beating fast when he could actually see his team's particular raid target—the eastern entrance to a massive tractor garage. When he heard Nowell's calm voice issue the final command for teams to initiate the coordinated raid, everything started happening very fast.

Clark followed his team as they streamed out of the rocks to the northeast of their large target building. Once again, looking across the expanse of the ranch, Clark was momentarily stunned by the effusion of infrared lights and lasers coming from the weapons and helmets of the almost forty Ground Branch operators streaming into the area.

He knew, from the mission briefings, that a large group of forearm-branded cultists were living here and that several of them ran security patrols throughout the night and early morning. He also knew that right now, all those poor bastards could see was pitch darkness, and all they could hear was howling wind. None of them had any clue they were about to be set upon by such a deadly, terrifyingly efficient force moving at an almost inhuman level of speed.

Clark's team hit the flat area leading toward the tractor garage and fell into a sprint. He did everything he could to keep up. He saw the other team that'd come in from the east off to his left clearly now. He watched as one of them in the lead slowed almost imperceptibly and took four shots with his suppressed rifle. The muzzle flashes and soft *thwap* of the gunfire came without any warning. None of the operators reacted at all.

Movement in front of the assault team grabbed Clark's attention. A young man in jeans and a white T-shirt crumpled to the ground ahead of him, falling into the dirt on top of some kind of long gun. Clark had completely failed to see the man where he'd been leaning against a split-rail fence surrounding a horse corral before the operator killed him. Clark flinched as an assaulter on his own team shot twice, putting two bullets into the head of the young man in the dirt as he ran by.

Clark sped up again to catch up with the rest of his team. Like in the raid on the Brookings ranch two days earlier, he took a knee in a security position as his team stacked up on the entrance to the large tractor garage, preparing to breach.

The two lead breachers checked the door to determine how entry would need to be made, and found it was actually unlocked and open, which they indicated with hand signals. Clark had barely registered Jake's announcement over the comms in his helmet that his team was making entry when they began flowing into the large, dark building.

In the same instant, the staccato of shooting from suppressed rifles punched through the howling wind somewhere to Clark's left, then more issued from several different locations up ahead within the tangle of trailers, barns, and outbuildings that made up the homestead. At the same time, a feral scream came from somewhere in the middle of the ranch. The scream was followed by six or seven shots from what Clark knew from its distinctive bark to be an unsuppressed semiautomatic pistol. It was not a weapon anyone on the task force would be using. *This is now officially a gunfight*, he thought.

A muffled rattle of gunfire punched out of the doorway his own team had just entered. Clark cursed as he pushed himself up and through the doorway to fulfill his next breaching assignment by holding a security position just inside the structure.

When he entered, he saw the body of a young shirtless man lying on his back next to a Remington 870 shotgun. It looked as though he had ten different gunshot wounds. A garbled moaning and blood poured from his mouth and nose as his left knee contracted in a spasm of small kicks. The guy's forehead ruptured abruptly—jetting a slick of blood, brain, hair, and skull fragments several feet across the floor—as an operator ahead of Clark shot him, immediately ending his convulsions.

Clark glanced toward movement on his left where two operators were working their way around a large stack of four-by-six hay bales that reached up to the ceiling. The operator who'd put the final bullet into the corpse and one other moved slowly down the corridor between the massive stacks of hay directly ahead of Clark. At the end of this corridor, ahead of the two operators, there was an open space among the canyon of hay bales. Light from a fire or a lantern somewhere out of view flickered aggressively off every surface, enhanced by its washing effect on the night vision. Clark settled into a crouched position and flexed a sweaty grip on his rifle.

"What tha hell was that, Pete? Tha fuck is going on out there?"

The deep, rage-edged voice came from where the light and shadows danced in the center of the building directly ahead. A massive man came around the corner of the hay bales from the obscured, open area. He looked to be over six and a half feet tall and at least 350 pounds. His jeans were tucked into size 14 roping boots, which sent deep clunks echoing off the walls. He carried an AK-style rifle by its grip in one hand, muzzle almost dragging along the cracked cement floor.

The first bullets stitched into the man's giant gut and solar plexus. He dropped the gun and grunted as he bent forward at the waist and planted both hands on his stomach. The two operators ahead of Clark squeezed off another storm of bullets that lanced into his shoulders and the top of his head. He was dead and limp before he smashed onto the floor. The two operators killed him while moving at the same steady pace they'd maintained since entering the building, knees bent, leaning forward, eyes never leaving their optics.

Clark felt his brain and lungs scream a silent demand for air and he sucked in a breath, realizing he hadn't in some time.

Lightning flashes of gunfire jumped off the walls and ceiling of the aluminum building somewhere ahead and to the right. The shooters were obscured from view by stacks of hay and pallets loaded with dusty, rusted farm and ranch supplies. Clark assumed the suppressed shots came from the operators who must've moved around the wall of hay bales to his right before he entered the building.

A loud metallic crash rang out from somewhere in the center of the large room. A few seconds later, three people came jogging into view right where the huge man had. It was one man and two women. They wore tank tops or T-shirts and either jeans or just underwear. None were wearing shoes, but all carried rifles. They screamed and began shooting before they'd even wheeled around the enormous corpse who'd come this way seconds earlier.

Leading the trio was a young woman wearing an XXL men's T-shirt that almost reached her knees. Her long blond hair was a wild mess. She'd started shrieking like a banshee before she even came around the corner, an inhuman noise that dropped into a jittery snarl through clenched teeth as she saw the large man's body. She started shooting a Ruger Mini-14 rifle from the hip before she'd even seen the operators, her shots wide, punching into the hay bales ahead to Clark's left and sending tufts of dust and straw into the air.

Her demeanor was so jarring Clark could not make out any details of the two others behind her. But that didn't matter.

The two operators Clark had seen go around the wall of hay bales to his left, and the pair directly ahead of him, crushed the trio in an L-shaped wall of fire and lead.

All three cultists began jerking and shuddering in brutal spasms as their bodies were shredded by the eruption of accurate, close-range gunfire.

As the snarling woman stepped over her dead comrade, her upper body snapped to the right with such speed and force it was as if her skull were tied to a truck speeding in that direction. Her wild hair and large T-shirt jumped and puffed where bullets were punching exit wounds through her head and torso. She stumbled over the massive dead man and collapsed in a heap.

In the span of just about three seconds, the four operators fired ninety-one bullets into the cluster of armed cultists, seventy-nine of which tore through some part of their three bodies. Before the last spent brass casings had finished skittering along the cement floor, all four operators had replaced their spent magazines and released their bolts to rearm their weapons.

They're like synchronized swimmers, Clark was surprised to find himself thinking. *They're just astoundingly silent, calm, and ferocious synchronized swimmers.*

As the operators rushed off to finish clearing the structure, Clark watched them cut and weave in singles and pairs throughout the hay and machinery that filled the cavernous building. He heard a distinct "motherfucker" shouted in a young man's voice from somewhere on the opposite side of the structure, immediately followed by a single shotgun blast then another fusillade of suppressed gunfire. A few moments later, Jake's voice came over the comms to announce an all clear.

As Jake began flipping on lights, the team went about securing and searching the bodies of the cultists whom they'd killed in as many seconds. Fluorescent lights flickered and buzzed into life overhead. Clark flipped his rifle's safety and quickly lifted the night vision unit away from his eyes. As soon as he did this, he noticed the bursts and flurries of gunfire outside from other parts of the ranch.

Disregarding these other gunfights—which he assumed were likely playing out in the same ruthless, one-sided manner this one just had—he rose and moved quickly toward the body of the mostly headless young man the team had first encountered.

Using his boot, he rolled the man's forearm until the sinister symbol of Red Castle could be seen, appearing infected and raw in the flat, electric light. He advanced toward the dead giant and the other corpses and checked each of their forearms as well, finding the same symbol, all of which appeared to have been both carved and burned into their forearms somewhat recently. Chatter was picking up over the radio from the other teams, and Jacobson's voice announced the rest of the ground elements were advancing into the ranch on armored M-ATV vehicles and UH-60 helicopters.

Clark could actually hear Jake's voice echoing off the aluminum walls of the structure at the same time he heard it come through the radio.

"We've got an entrance to a basement over here."

CHAPTER
19

CLARK FOLLOWED JAKE'S voice toward the open area at the center of the building. An oil lantern burned on a small camping table surrounded by folding chairs. A few feet away was a large set of steel doors set into an angled cement housing, like an entrance to a cellar or storm shelter. The doors were closed, but it was clear they opened out and away from each other and, presumably, covered a staircase or ladder that went to some subterranean chamber below.

Jake and two of the other operators were kneeling ten to fifteen meters away from the doors, aiming rifles at them. Clark stood there staring as he felt a hand tug on the shoulder strap of his plate carrier. It was Kyle, hauling him to a safer position a few meters away outside the shooting lanes of the others. Here, Kyle took a knee and aimed his rifle at the doors, patting Clark on the back in a silent suggestion that the game warden do the same. He did.

Several minutes passed, and chatter across the team and command radio channels suggested another entrance to a basement had been found in the large barn located directly next door to the tractor garage. Most agreed that both were likely different entrances to the same underground structure. Eventually, Clark heard the metallic thrum of the big armored vehicles' engines as they pulled up outside the tractor garage. Seconds later, the large doors of the building were opened from the outside and another assault team—Commander Nowell and Harry Jacobson himself with several members of the control groups—entered the tractor garage.

The newly arrived assault team fell into security positions around the underground entrance as Clark's team was called toward the open garage doors where everyone stood in a cluster around one of the 24th STS operators holding a ruggedized laptop.

Clark stood on the edge of the group and looked out into the predawn scene of the ranch. Several other armored vehicles made their way around the homestead. A UH-60 helicopter dropped down to an open area several hundred meters to the south. The rotor wash from the helicopter joined forces with the natural wind itself to amplify the roaring wall of dust in the growing morning light.

This was the first time Clark had seen Harry Jacobson wearing a plate carrier and a battle belt, where a Browning Hi-Power pistol was holstered. *Nice taste*, Clark mused, as Jacobson's strong voice grabbed everyone's attention.

"All right, our R2TD got solid, high-res imagery of the underground structure. The staircase under this set of doors and the one in the barn next door each lead down to a small room. Both small rooms appear identical, and about three hundred square feet, and both open into opposite sides of the same, much larger room, about twenty-five hundred square feet, which comprises the rest of the underground complex. So, we stagger breaches at both points of entry. We're getting wonky readings on human form and vitals down there, but Jake clocked at least three or four that came up from downstairs here. So, breaching teams need to assume there's going to be contact, and that there're some assholes down there prepping to oppose one or both breaches. Remember, *we need more prisoners*, so do what you can in that regard, but obviously shoot if you've got to shoot. Nowell, set the teams and let's get this going, I need full control of this AO five fuckin' minutes ago."

Nowell did not acknowledge the order, he just immediately turned to Jake. He gave the team leader some directive, then hit the PTT button on his shoulder and began rattling more orders into the mic mounted to his helmet.

Clark stayed out of everyone's way, and while he silently appreciated Jake approaching him to let him know he would "not be needed" to help their team breach through this set of trapdoors, he already knew that. Within ninety seconds of Jacobson issuing his order, both teams were in place and ready to make entry.

Clark stood outside, attaching himself to another assault team that was on standby to follow the first down to help secure the underground area. From here, he watched Jake's team throw flash-bang grenades through the large doors then crash down as soon as they detonated. A few seconds later, he heard the muffled clatter and bangs of the other team making entry in the adjacent barn.

Jacobson and a dozen others watched live feeds of the basement-clearing operation via gun and helmet cams. The crash of grenades and the subsequent staccato of gunfire were muffled by the earth. Not knowing exactly what was going on down there made the passing of time, somehow, even more gut-wrenching.

Sixty long seconds after Clark watched the last operator on Jake's team disappear into the hole in the ground, he heard Jake's voice come into his ear.

"All clear, all clear. But, uh . . . standby teams, go ahead and make entry now, we need a hand, we . . . well, we've got a lot of . . ."

Nowell's voice came over the command channel before the end of Jake's transmission.

"Jacobson, get down here. *Now*."

Clark was, yet again, startled by the prompt movement of these men. Before Nowell even finished his call for Jacobson, the standby team was already flowing through the trapdoors and down the cement staircase. Clark ran to catch up with them.

On the floor of the small room at the base of the stairs, there was a body between the pair of bunk beds that were pushed up against each wall. It was another twentysomething male with a patchy beard and greasy hair in a ponytail, staring up at the ceiling with dead, unfocused eyes. His left forearm was mostly severed from his body, connected only by a few strips of skin and tendons around his elbow. He had several other visible gunshot wounds to his stomach and chest, as well as a mustache of dark blood channeling from his nostrils down the sides of his face.

Once the team stepped over the body and through the small room, the imposing size of the large area beyond could be seen, all cast in a warm, sickly yellow glow coming from strands of Edison bulbs strung between the rows. If diseased, malarial humidity had a color, this would be it.

A voice echoed off the stout, dank walls of the large room.

"Get these prisoners topside right fucking now, let's go, *let's go*."

Nowell and Jake were in the center of the room, while other operators moved around them. Two of them, to Clark's left, struggled with a young woman who was shrieking and snarling as she kicked out with both legs and spasmed against their control. She shot her head toward one of the operators trying to control her, mouth wide, trying to bite him straight on the face. He leaned out of her reach and cracked his elbow into her nose. Two other guys from the breaching teams came toward Clark with another prisoner.

These two led another shirtless mountain tweaker by the elbows, his hands flex-cuffed behind him. As he got closer, Clark could see the operators were mostly just dragging the poor kid, who could only make feeble attempts at planting his limp feet. His eyes were barely open, and Clark could see a film of blood coating his teeth and dribbling down his chin. He'd been shot in the left side of his stomach. On the right side, a bulging cluster of intestines ballooned out from the big, lipless exit wound below his bottom rib where blood flowed down to a darkened slick that covered the hip and crotch of his filthy sweatpants.

Clark barely registered any of this, however. As he saw what sat under the lights, all he could hear was his heart thundering in his ears, each fierce beat making his vision jump. His mind went slack and grayed out for a few moments, as though a defense mechanism had activated. His mind resisted against putting what he saw into translatable language, and worked to override its automated task of collating something into a memory, screaming at him to look away before it was too late, before he was stuck with it forever.

He let out a shaky breath and forced himself to walk deeper into the large room, among several of the other operators, who moved silently around him from body to body.

A sudden and desperate impulse told him that his ability to breathe depended upon immediately removing his helmet. He let his rifle fall on its sling so he could use both hands to frantically unbuckle the chin strap. It felt like his fingers were the size of bricks, and panic started to course through him. When he finally got it off, he dropped it to the floor as he tried to control his breathing for a moment.

Filling the room, from wall to wall, were *people*.

They were all naked, seated in a random assortment of camping chairs, lawn furniture, and even some higher-quality wooden dining room chairs. They were spaced neatly apart, forming a perfect grid across the large space. Clark stepped toward the two people closest to him.

One was an old man, likely in his eighties, while the other was a woman in her thirties. Both had ashen, gray skin. Their ankles and wrists were bound to their chairs with a mess of chains and fencing wire secured to a big steel eyebolt sunken into the concrete. Every person in the room was restrained in such a manner.

Clark tore his buckskin shooting gloves off and replaced them with a pair of nitrile gloves he yanked from his drop pouch. He took a knee in front of the woman and felt for a pulse on her wrist, then her neck. Her skin was cold and stiff, hugging her bones unnaturally. Feeling nothing but a lack of life, he lowered her head down, and saw something small drop from her face onto her thigh. He carefully picked up the small object, then turned on the compact Fenix tac-light he always clipped onto his plate carrier, and inspected it under the bright, concentrated beam.

It was a coin. An old one. It was a flat, drab gray with very worn markings. Clark used a thumb to brush away a few specks of what looked like soot or dried blood and brought it closer to his eyes. A man's head and shoulders were in the center, surrounded by a laurel of letters entirely foreign to Clark. On the other side, there were more strange characters surrounding the faded profile of someone standing, possibly naked, holding a shield and a spear.

As Clark stood, the strong beam of his vest's tac-light illuminated the woman's body. When he finally looked up from the coin, he noticed two things that hadn't stood out in the languid, dingy glow of the ceiling lights.

First, he saw some kind of black crust on her lips and around her mouth. He leaned closer. It did not look like dried blood. He ran a thumb over the crust below her mouth. It was completely dried, caked firmly to her skin. The other thing he noticed was some kind of flower crown on her head, the kind little girls made in the summertime. He looked around and saw the same laurel circlet on every lolled head in the room. He thought he recognized the tubular, hollow stem that led to a wilted puff of tiny pinkish-white flowers. He pinched a few of the stems, rubbed them between a thumb and finger, then smelled it.

He knelt before the older man next to her, checked his pulse, and found him equally lifeless. He adjusted his light toward his mouth and saw the same ring of black crust. He reached up, hesitated for a moment, then used one hand to grip the man's face and the other to open his stiff jaw and mouth. As soon as his teeth parted, another small coin came tumbling into his lap. Clark picked it up and inspected it. This one looked just as old and faded. One side had only a vague rectangle stamped into it, while the other showed the side profile of a man in a crown with a bow in one hand and a clutch of arrows in the other.

Clark checked the vitals of the next three bodies. Each had the flower crown, the black crust around their mouth, and a small, old coin inside it. Staring up from what appeared to be an owl with huge eyes stamped onto one of the old coins, Clark noticed the machines for the first time. They were a bit larger than a desktop printer, but with big touch screens above a few buttons and dials. There were quite a few of them spaced throughout the room.

He recognized them, narrowed his eyes, then went back down the row of bodies, checking every arm. Until now, he'd failed to notice the irritated, dirty strip where IV tape had been torn off all their forearms. He turned and stared down the row, using his light to scan the ground, and saw what he was looking for coiled around the base of a chair several bodies back.

He quickly checked the vitals of those he passed, then knelt and gently picked up the IV tube hanging from the dead man's forearm. He peeled the tape away slowly and saw the unique catheter underneath.

Clark stood as he traced the clear tube from the catheter to its end, which he brought close to his eyes. It had been connected to something, and flecks of dried blood showed on the half inch of stretched, cracked clear tubing where it'd been yanked away.

Clark knelt before the body and took a stiff hand into his own. He pinched the tips of several fingers. Turning the hand over, he pressed his thumb hard into the skin above the wrist, then stared at the spot for a few seconds.

A commotion came from an operator whom Clark knew only as Mike, who'd been checking vitals ahead of him along the same row of bodies. Mike had picked up one of the little machines, spun, and smashed it into the wall. The shock and volume of the device exploding against the concrete made everyone in the room flinch, many bringing their weapons up as they wheeled toward the noise, scanning for threats.

Mike began screaming the word *fuck* repeatedly as he tore his helmet off and spiked it into the grimy floor. Pieces of the night vision tubes, ear protection, IR light, and comms system on the helmet—which altogether cost more than Clark's truck—showered and skittered in every direction.

Several operators were jogging toward Mike's outburst, one unintentionally checking Clark to the side as he ran down the row of bodies.

Commander Nowell got to Mike first. He grabbed the taller man by the shoulder straps of his plate carrier and shook him once, hard, then pulled Mike's face into his own. Nowell barked his words with an edge on every consonant sharp enough to cut steel.

"Mike, look at me. *Fucking look at me, Mike.* You needa lock it up, brother, you hear me? Stow that shit up and deal with it later—now is *not the fucking time*, you copy?"

Mike's tirade of profanity ended, but his jaw twitched as he glared back at his commander through murderous slits of eyes. Mike spoke through clenched teeth in a low, growling voice.

"Skip. It's . . . *That's a little girl.* She can't be more than ten *fuckin' years old. What* . . . what the fuck is going on here, Skip? *What the fuck is this?*"

Mike was gesturing at the body behind Nowell, which, like all the rest, was slumped forward in the chair where it had been arrested in this final, awkward position by the nexus of chains and wire. Unlike the rest, however, was the small size of this body. Nowell didn't take his eyes from Mike's as he gave the big man another vicious shake to get his full attention.

"Go upstairs and take five. Mike, no. *Go upstairs*, drink some water, and take fuckin' five. Right now, brother, *right fuckin' now.*"

Mike did not take his eyes from his commander's for several long, tense seconds, but then his rage began to ebb. The tension cooked out from his shoulders and back with an audible exhale, and he stared down at his feet, nodding. He unclenched a fist and patted Nowell where his plate carrier's cummerbund wrapped his ribs.

Nowell nodded at this wordless communication, then released the man's shoulder straps. He put his hand on the side of Mike's head and lifted his face so he could look for something in Mike's eyes. Nowell nodded when he saw whatever he'd wanted to, then cocked his chin toward the exit.

Nowell watched Mike until he disappeared up the stairs, then looked at the other men around him, snapping out a command that startled everyone. His Louisiana or Mississippi accent was stronger than normal.

"Let's fuckin' go, boys. I need vital checks on every one of these people. Move."

Nowell slapped Jake on the shoulder and pointed across the room toward another operator standing motionless. Unlike everyone else, he hadn't gone back to the revolting task at hand, but just stared with wide eyes down at one of the bodies. It also looked smaller than most of the rest.

"Go check on Porter. Get him topside."

Jake nodded and jogged over to the man who, Clark assumed, had succumbed to the same traumatic shock he could feel snaking through his own mind and coiling around his muscles.

Nowell stared over at the small body that'd set Mike off. Clark saw Nowell's jaw was also clenched into a twitching rictus of rage, just as Mike's had been. He turned away eventually, wiped a palm across his mouth, then looked up to find Clark staring at him.

Jacobson and several others came down the stairs. As soon as they'd made it through the small room to the threshold leading into the charnel house, the newcomers stopped moving and bunched up as though realizing they were about to walk off a cliff. Jacobson waved a hand back toward the stairs without looking away from the bodies, ordering them all to go back up and to hold all personnel topside.

He walked slowly over to where Nowell and Clark stood unmoving, silently staring at each other. Jacobson looked up from the bodies when Nowell spoke in a low, dangerous voice, each word gnarled by rage.

"You got something to say, fucking *game warden*?"

Nowell was suddenly overcome with a sense of violent fury toward Clark Rickert. He knew it wasn't justified; he knew his anger came from the scene of brutality around him and the monstrous fucks who'd perpetrated it.

Be that as it may, Clark had just stood witness to a very rare moment—one of Nowell's men cracking at the seams a bit, displaying emotional vulnerability, and that was something very few living people had ever beheld. Then, Clark had watched as they'd shared a brief moment of fraternal intimacy when he helped calm Mike down, the kind that can only be shared between battle brothers who'd won, lost, killed, and bled together around the world, as Nowell and Mike had.

Clark was an outsider. He hadn't earned the right to bear witness to such things. Now, this outsider was staring Nowell down, showing no discernible emotion. That, in this moment, in this setting, was more than enough for Nowell to nominate Clark as a suitable target for his rage.

He stepped toward Clark as he took in a sharp breath—just enough air to fuel a command that this game warden "either get the hell out or cast that motherfucking gaze elsewhere"—just as Clark spoke.

"It's their blood."

Nowell, disarmed by the unexpected words, let the air out of his nose and squinted at Clark. Jacobson looked at him with the same confusion. Clark reached down to the arm of the body closest to him, found the IV line, traced four feet of it through his fingers until he found its terminus, then held it up to eye level for them to inspect.

"Sucked all these poor people dry. Those things . . ."

Clark pointed at one of the small machines on a table nearby with his free hand, then at the ruins of the one Mike had smashed against the wall.

"They're dialysis machines, portable kind designed for dyin' at home. The kind of catheters used for dialysis are the kind this fella here's still got in his arm. They got big ol' needles on 'em, and then this splitter, here. Problem is, for this fella, the only tube's runnin' from the outflow valve, and the factory cap's still on the inflow."

Clark had lifted the man's arm up and removed the tape so he could show them the catheter, which the other men kept staring at as he gently lowered the arm and continued.

"So, looks like they used 'em to pull all the blood out, but obviously didn't bother puttin' any back in, defeating the purpose of a dialysis rig. So, only reason I can figure they'd used 'em at all is so they could bag it all up, nice and easy. Pretty slick system, if you're lookin' for a nice and easy way to bag a bunch a' blood and you lack affection for the donors. If keepin' someone outta hypovolemic shock ain't a priority, you can skip all the pint-by-pint fuss of a blood draw. Just fire up the pump, crank up the outflow setting, and drain 'em in one go."

As Clark explained what he saw going on here, he'd carefully watched both men's faces as they stared around the room. He'd not missed their expressions darkening with surprise, disgust, and anger.

"The cultists Jake and his boys smoked upstairs I saw, that one back there at the bottom of the stairs, and those two prisoners y'all hauled outta here a minute ago, they all had that symbol carved into their arms. But, haven't seen the brand on any of these folks down here."

Clark looked at Jacobson as he leaned down to inspect the forearms of the closest bodies.

"What's the number of missing Montanans we're dealin' with again, five hundred somethin'?"

Jacobson looked up at Clark, blinked several times, then shook his head before answering.

"*Uh* . . . Most recent count is five hundred ninety-one."

Clark nodded then turned to look around the room.

"Well, once you ID these poor folks, I'd wager the title to my truck that list shrinks to four hundred eighty-nine."

Jacobson and Nowell both looked around the room, the implications of Clark's words slowly sinking in as they stared out at the 102 slumped, ashen bodies. Nowell spoke first.

"I suspect that you're right, game warden."

Clark extended an open hand toward the men, who looked down at the ancient coins in his palm. He pulled a small four-by-six-inch evidence bag from the pouch he always kept a few in, and carefully began dropping the coins in as he spoke.

"Old coins, not sure what kind, but there's one in each of their mouths. Those little crowns they're all wearin', they're garlic flowers, and garlic starts getting harvested right about now, so they're probably local. There's also somethin' crusted around each of their mouths, but it ain't blood. Seems like some kinda wax or ash. Gonna wanna get some good samples to test, among countless other things down here. So, *Commander* . . ."

Both men had been switching their gaze between everything Clark mentioned, then back at him when he addressed Nowell. Clark held Nowell's gaze as he offered the baggie to Jacobson. When he took it, Clark held his gloved hand up to eye level and spoke in a quiet, flat tone.

"Please have your boys put on sterile gloves before they contaminate every fuckin' inch a' this crime scene."

Nowell held Clark's gaze as he let out a long exhale that carried a soft growl. Amid this carnage, Clark's cold, calm demeanor was jarring, and when men like Nowell got jarred, they got violent. However, this game warden was absolutely right, and that suppressed his frustration. He and Jacobson began barking orders across the large room for men to stop what they were doing and put on sterile gloves before touching anything else.

As everyone started digging into pouches and med kits, Clark walked over to where he'd dropped his ballistic helmet on the floor, tucked it under an arm, and walked slowly back down the row of bodies. Nowell and Jacobson watched him as he went, both feeling the electricity of something left unsaid. Clark stopped as he passed them, stared at his feet for a moment, then turned his head and locked eyes with Jacobson. For the first time, both men heard a current of rage in Clark's voice.

"Blood is what these sons a' bitches are after, but unlike most murderers, *they ain't just tryin' to spill it*. They coulda used a knife and some buckets, but they rigged up quite the little system down here, lotta effort to avoid loss or waste. Gotta suppose, then, they got some kinda plan for it, one that requires movin' it elsewhere. This place, what they're doin' here, it's a *step* for a group workin' like this. A node of logistics. An intermediate target, like a chop shop, a weapons cache, a cut house, a dope kitchen. It's in the middle a' the chain. What's goin' on here's only *the means*. A decent target, but only if ya hit it in a way and at a time that actually deprives shitheads of somethin' they're after, which we certainly fuckin' didn't here. I really hope there's someone back east callin' the shots who knew all a' that already, because you fellas got looks on your faces sayin' you fuckin' didn't. Guess what I'm sayin' here is that if I'm really the first asshole to put all this together, well . . . may God preserve all those other missing folks, because that'd mean this was one sorry-assed, witless outfit that sure as shit won't."

Clark turned and walked.

CHAPTER 20

THE FORENSIC TEAMS identified most of the dead within a few hours. Clark had been correct regarding the likelihood that the victims would be found within the existing list of missing persons. Most were, and those few that weren't just hadn't been reported as missing yet. They'd also identified quite a few of the cultists they'd killed and several they'd taken alive, and it turned out most of them were as well.

Clark had also been right about garlic flowers, the coins being in the mouths of all 102 victims, the substance crusting their mouths being something other than blood, and the grim purpose of the dialysis machines. Charlotte Bishop approached Clark to tell him as much.

She leaned next to him on the split-rail fence surrounding an empty corral where she'd seen him standing, motionless, for the last hour. She went through it all, and her optimism that something valuable would be uncovered once they began digging into and contrasting the backgrounds of the cultists and the victims.

He turned his head toward her as she spoke, but not his eyes. They stayed fixed on something in the distance. This, she gathered, would likely be his only acknowledgment of having heard her.

Until this morning, Charlotte had only once seen a Ground Branch operator express the kind of unrestrained rage and raw emotion she'd now seen from several of those who'd gone into that basement. It was understandable, as there were children down there. She'd long known that victimized kids were one of the very few things left in this world capable of piercing the veil of discipline to rattle the kind of man who made it to Ground Branch.

From the IC's file on Clark Rickert, she knew fate had been cruel to him from a young age, and that his nineteen-year career had been full of exposure to violence and other terrible things, but nothing like this, nothing like what they'd found in that basement. The sun made the scars on his forehead, eyebrow, nose, and cheek stand out, and she wondered about those that people couldn't see. Not truly knowing him at all, she worried now whether this was too much for the state law enforcement officer to handle or come back from whole.

Unsure where this man's head was, she wanted to offer a bit of levity and tried to ask the question with some humor in her voice.

"So, Captain Rickert, have you done a lap around the AO and found us another set of the cult leader's tracks?"

She also couldn't help herself when it came to conducting a little push and prod, being the career intelligence officer that she was. That is to say, she enjoyed and found utility in gauging what others did with just a bit of information presented in just the right way.

Over the last two days since the raid on the Brookings ranch, interrogators and psych analysts had been working with the three cult members they'd managed to apprehend alive: the woman from the base of that gore-festooned cottonwood tree who'd been one of the original fifty members of the Red Castle chat room and the old Brookings couple themselves. They'd come to a rough conclusion that whoever had walked away from that scene, leaving the barefooted trail this game warden had found, was—in the broken minds of these three cultists, at least—the nameless leader of what the government had branded as the Red Castle organization. So she was curious how he'd respond to her describing the barefooted man as the leader of the cult.

She couldn't read anything in his features. He just squinted into the sun, now rising over the shimmering water of the large reservoir's finger to their east. Almost a full minute passed before he responded.

"He's never been here, Miss Charlotte."

So it seemed he'd either already concluded on his own that the barefooted man was the cult leader, or was entirely unmoved by her suggestion he was. Neither surprised her.

What did surprise her was his assertion regarding where that man had never been, and the dispositive confidence he stated it with. She tucked a strand of hair behind her ear and turned to face him more directly.

"Are you saying that the man who left the tracks leading away from the Brookings ranch has never—"

Clark abruptly pushed himself away from the fence and turned to face her, staring down into her eyes.

"Yes, Miss Charlotte. The branded ones are his followers, clearly here on his orders, but he's never been here himself. We might pick up his scent again at the next blood farm, but that's assuming you and your spook colleagues have found one yet, which they better do quick if they haven't. *Time* is the most precious thing for the other victims now, time we've been wastin' standin' around here twiddlin' our dicks all mornin'."

Charlotte's eyes narrowed, a demand that he immediately reveal *who told him about the other target locations* dancing at the tip of her tongue. This man's presumption regarding their existence rattled her. Over the last thirty-six hours, there had been several intelligence breakthroughs that tipped the agencies off to the location of the cult stronghold on Fort Peck Lake, where they now stood, as well as others. To her knowledge, which was comprehensive, there was no way he could possibly know about them. None of it had been shared with the vast majority of personnel in the task force, let alone Clark.

However, she didn't make the demand. Her mind engaged in its usual lightning-fast deductions. One conclusion was that this was actually a fairly reasonable inference to make for a career investigator who'd proven himself at this point to be skilled at his job. It was an explainable inference to assume there were more targets of this kind, but she was still curious.

"What do you mean by *the next blood farm*?"

She was immediately frustrated by the shallowness of her question, then angry as she gathered that Clark was as well. He let out a short breath through his nose. This sound he made came dangerously close to one of contempt, one that carried a subtle accusation of stupidity.

Anger helped Charlotte focus. It always had. She'd shaken and humbled countless hardheaded men before, and it seemed she needed to again. She crossed her arms and shifted her weight as the words all came to mind and fell into perfect order. She'd now calmly deliver an exquisite, balanced, soul-destroying invective of scorn and abuse that few on earth were as artful at crafting as her.

Clark spoke just as she was about to, something Charlotte figured he'd meant to do.

"Obviously, this isn't the only blood mill these dickheads are runnin'. It's too tidy. This place had a fixed capacity before they brought anyone here. This ain't the only cache. There are others. I told you the boss man hasn't been to this one. Maybe he hasn't been to any, but the best spot to start cuttin' for his sign is wherever he's got his groupies bunched up like they were here. If I knew where that was, I'd already be on my way, but I don't. That's *your job*, so fuckin' do it, because people are gettin' trussed up right now to be bled like hogs, if they haven't been already."

Charlotte heard anger in his voice for the first time since she'd met the man. He turned and began walking back toward the bustling activity in the center of the ranch. Charlotte narrowed her eyes and began to ask a question somewhere along the lines of *how the hell can you substantiate a conclusion that he's never been here*, but all she got out was *how* when he stopped, turned, and cut her off again.

"Don't bother askin', Bishop. I don't know how I know; I just do. You certainly don't have to take my word for it. I wouldn't if it were you. I'm just tellin' ya; the sooner we un-ass this spot and get to the next, the better, because we ain't wasting *our time* anymore; it belongs to others without *any to fuckin' spare*. I don't have the resources to find the other spots, but *you do*. So call who you gotta call, do what you gotta do, *and fuckin' find 'em*."

Clark turned and walked.

As he did, he was surprised to find himself thinking of his assistant, Lucy Westerna. This was strange on its own, but an even more unfamiliar sensation accompanied the thought—an urge to call her, to check in on things, check on her and her son. A preposterous impulse, Clark felt, one he quickly shook from his mind.

CHAPTER 21

ABOUT 220 MILES away, Lucy Westerna was thinking about Clark in that same moment, but she often thought about her boss. She was about halfway into the Taft Hill Loop, a trail in a state park near Great Falls that she ran several times a week in the summer. She loved the trail, the view from the top of the butte and cliffs, and the history of the place. She'd been running there since she was in high school.

There were many confirmed buffalo jump sites around the United States, but this was a protected site, officially known as the *First People's Buffalo Jump*. For thousands of years, native hunters relied on locations like this one. A band of hunters would slowly encircle a herd of buffalo, not stalking or hiding as they approached, but actually making sure they were seen by the animals. They were playing the role of sheepdogs, to an extent, slowly tightening their formation, herding the beasts toward the edge. When they were close enough, other hunters would spring from hiding places near the edges of the cliff where they'd remained concealed for hours, sometimes days. When they jumped out, screaming and flailing, the others who'd been herding them all fell into a charge toward the panicked animals. The herd would spook into a stampede and plunge over the edge of the cliffs in great numbers.

At the base of the cliffs were others from the tribe, waiting for the storm of two-thousand-pound beasts to smash into the rocks and scree, shattering legs and spines but rarely dying outright, not at this one at least, as the cliff was only around forty to fifty feet high. Those waiting below then began the process of putting the stricken, broken, roaring beasts out of their misery, then the real work began. Butchering and dressing the large animals. Men, women, children, and the elderly all had a job. It was a sacred process. A time for thanks and celebration. They'd get firepits burning, cooking and drying some of the meat, then others would start pulverizing it with dried berries and fat to make pemmican. Others went to work on the hides, stretching them out onto willow racks and using the animals' brains to tan and preserve the robes.

Lucy always slowed her pace at the top of the cliff, imagining the chaotic scene. The hunters, the panicked animals, the jarring image of them kicking at the air as they fell then smashed into the rocks below.

She saw a man up ahead leaning against a large boulder a few meters off the trail. He turned his head toward her when she got closer and smiled. He was breathtakingly gorgeous, with a thick head of black hair and a lean, muscular build. He had a tanned face and a few lines of age around what were perhaps the kindest eyes she'd ever seen. He was dressed like some wealthy cattleman going out for a night of line dancing: a white gambler-style hat, a pearl-buttoned shirt, a silver-traced belt, black jeans, and immaculately clean and expensive-looking roping boots. Lucy couldn't help but blush and slow her pace as she smiled back awkwardly. When she was only a few feet away, he waved and spoke. His voice was somehow as striking as his smile and eyes.

"Hey there. You know what this place is, what the natives used to do here?"

She stopped and put her hands on her hips, smiling and nodding for a moment as she caught her breath.

"Yeah, it's a buffalo run. Indians used to run 'em off the cliffs here. Used to be some old cairns up the trail, ones they built long ago to mark the spot on the cliff they'd try to herd them toward, but some asshole kicked 'em over a few years back."

The man laughed, and became even more attractive as he did. He pushed himself away from the boulder he'd been leaning on, and pointed to something on its lichen-covered face.

"You ever see the petroglyphs on this boulder?"

Lucy cocked her head, then shook it as she began walking toward him. He stepped away from the boulder and continued pointing at it.

"Check it out, pretty neat."

She came around the boulder and saw a large symbol carved into the stone. It was intricate, stunning, and beautiful. Her eyes went wide, and she glanced over at the man.

"Wow, no, I've never seen this. I've run by this rock probably ten thousand times but haven't ever noticed it."

She stepped closer, tracing her fingers along the lines and curves of the symbol. She felt a strange sensation as she touched it. Her heart quickened a bit. She felt both angry at it, and also a nostalgic fondness for it at the same time, like seeing a once-beloved picture book decades after having forgotten about it. She felt a bolt of fear and excitement. Loneliness and love. They all happened at once in a flashing instant, balancing one another out in a wash that saw the sensations flood away just as fast. She shivered and glanced over at the man again, finding him staring toward the edge of the cliff and the sprawling, heat-shimmering vista beyond, thumbs hooked into his belt loops. He didn't look at her as he spoke.

"Smart way to hunt, you know? Before they had horses to ride them down. Pretty ingenious. Requires some real patience too. It sure is a dramatic spectacle to behold, all those creatures getting herded off a cliff. The sound of it is just as memorable."

He had a subtle accent Lucy couldn't place, but she felt confident was not one picked up anywhere on this continent. She spoke through a smile.

"Are you saying you've actually seen Indians herd buffalo off a cliff?"

He looked over at her, a sly, tired grin on his face, then let his head hang to stare at the ground. His smile changed a bit as he began to nod, in the detached way one might smile at a memory.

"Well, I've never seen *that*, but I have seen the Sami people herd reindeer off cliffs in Scandinavia. Same principle, and I assume it has a similar sound."

Lucy smiled and crossed her arms.

"When'd you see *that*?"

He took in a long, deep breath, and spoke as he looked out at the view.

"A long, *long time ago.*"

He appeared distant in thought for a moment, then reached into his pocket and took out what looked like a slender piece of dark stone. He smiled as he walked toward her, holding it out for her to take.

"Found this down the trail a ways."

She saw now it was a large spear tip of mirror-black obsidian. She'd seen ones like it in museums. She looked at him with wonder as she stepped toward him and took it from his hand.

"Are you serious? You found that here, today?"

He nodded as she turned it over in her hands.

"Sure did, and check this out . . ."

He reached for the spear tip, but didn't take it from her. Instead, he gently closed her palm around it, and even more gently closed his palm around her fist. He looked into her eyes, smiling.

"*You feel that?*"

She looked at him, then down at their hands. With his other hand, he gracefully ran his finger in a slow circle on the inside of her right forearm. He leaned in until his mouth was only an inch from hers, looking deep into her eyes.

"*Do you feel that, Lucy?*"

She very much did, but before she could scream, her world went black.

CHAPTER 22

FORTY-EIGHT HOURS AFTER assaulting the ranch on the south side of Fort Peck Lake, the task force raided their next target.

Another location that intelligence flagged as a Red Castle stronghold. Another blood mill, as some had started calling them. Another cattle ranch in rural Montana, as well.

This one was north of Winifred, Montana, nestled up against the steep valleys, bluffs, and coulees that characterize the Upper Missouri River Breaks region. Though this rugged stretch of badlands had been known more simply as just *the Breaks* for over two hundred years, at least by those English speakers who really knew it.

As had been the case at the Brookings ranch target four days earlier, then again at the Fort Peck Lake target two days after that, the entire band of cultists stationed at this location was taken by complete surprise. Five of them were visible outside at 0400 hours, when all elements of the assault were staged and set to initiate.

A pair of them patrolled around the property, while two others loitered in static guard positions near each gated entrance to the main homestead area. All four of them carried some AR-15 variant, and all four mumbled grotesque vows and observances to their leader in a rhythmic cadence that rolled between a whisper and a shriek.

The fifth stood above the dead body of another cultist, whom the task force would ID later that day. She had disappeared from work two weeks earlier and, based on the diabetic ketoacidosis that'd shut her organs down and killed her a few hours before the assault, hadn't thought to bring along her insulin. She'd collapsed into the dirt and weeds next to a shed and started seizing as the still-living cultist stared down at her, rocking back and forth and mumbling as he did now. When she'd gone still, or still enough for his needs, he'd opened her belly up with his cheap pocketknife, and since then had used her blood to slowly paint the cult's symbol onto the side of the shed.

When Commander Nowell gave the order, all five of them had their lights turned off.

The skulls of the two cultists patrolling around the property appeared to rupture simultaneously, as though small explosive charges implanted within both had detonated. In reality, each had been hit by a single 175-grain OMT 7.62x51mm bullet, one in the center of his eyebrow and the other at the top of her ear, fired by the M110 rifles of the two Ground Branch operators in overwatch positions only 180 meters away. The two cultists holding security positions at each gate were both ripped from their feet, and very much killed, as 250-grain OMT .338 Lapua bullets tore through their ribs, lungs, hearts, and spines. Through the optics of their AXSR rifles, it appeared to both FBI HRT snipers over 400 meters away as though their respective targets disappeared in clouds of blood and dust.

The fifth cultist never saw the final flourish on his revolting work of graffiti: the small hole in the center of the symbol he drew onto the shed's wall made by the 62-grain EPR 5.56 bullet or the burst of his own blood, brain, skull fragments, and hair that followed close behind.

The shooters put on a master's clinic of coordinated sniper fire, killing all five of their targets with single, lethal shots in just under two seconds.

Fourteen other cultists remained alive, sleeping or moving around within the main house or other structures on the property. A few had heard the snaps of the snipers' shots, or the louder wet smacks of their bullets hitting bodies. One sat up in his bed, another turned to look out a cracked window into the darkness, one shouted the name of a comrade he didn't know had just died outside. It was all too late, though. By the time the first of them even noticed the assault teams materializing from the darkness at a full sprint, they were already dying or being apprehended with vicious, methodical efficiency.

Five minutes after securing the last cultist, one of the Ground Branch operators keyed his PTT button and spoke to the rest of the assault teams on the broad channel. As soon as they heard the tone in his voice, most knew what he'd just encountered.

Seventy-eight more victims were found exactly where the task force command had suspected they were being held. They'd discussed the strange structure and reviewed extensive imagery of it during the briefing a few hours earlier. Its existence and presence on the property was actually one of the reasons the location had been flagged by intelligence.

There was just no intelligible reason why six Corten steel shipping containers had been set end to end to form a long, aboveground tunnel. These particular containers were the relatively rare kind with doors on both ends, unique in purpose and function. But there was no clear purpose or function for such containers at a place like this, let alone six of them used to form a long, completely unventilated tunnel.

Intelligence and command had unfortunately been correct. The victims had been spaced neatly throughout the entire length of the hot, rank corridor from end to end. Under the pulse and twinkle of the schizophrenic assortment of cheap Christmas lights that had been lazily strung throughout the long tunnel, it looked a bit like the gray, naked bodies were all spasming.

They were not.

All of them were dead. They'd been secured to chairs with chains and steel wire, and all had been drained of their blood. As had also been the case at the target ranch on Fort Peck Lake, quite a few bodies showed bruising on ankles and wrists, evidence of having struggled fiercely against their sharp bonds. As though telling the sadistic story without words, all of those with signs of having struggled against their bonds also showed signs of having been beaten with clubs or pipes.

Until sunrise, the only light source within the dark tunnel of steel was the mishmash collection of Christmas lights. Some strands were the standard kind; assorted colors set to a fixed brightness. Others were the soft yellow ones that dimmed and brightened in a slow, hypnotic cadence. A few were those of a sickly, metallic blue set to a seizure-inducing twinkle. They failed to provide a sufficient light to read anything under, yet were still harsh and abrasive.

As had been the case at the previous two target locations, the command and after-action elements of the task force had been flown in from the FOB or staging positions to begin site remediation as soon as the ground teams had secured the target area. The entire AO was searched and sanitized, and forensic teams went about the grim task of identifying the bodies of the victims and the cultists killed during the raid.

Light grew in the east until bright morning sun broke and spilled over the bluffs and coulees to illuminate the depressing scenery. It had many of the ubiquitous traits of a cattle ranch, but unlike the first two targets, this one was no longer active. Indeed, all the trappings of neglect present suggested it had turned out its last steer long, long ago.

The condition of cattle fencing is most informative as to how much time has passed since someone ran stock on a piece of land, and the fencing here suggested it had been decades. Much of it lay slack and drooping, or was just missing entirely between naked T-posts. In those places where barbed wire remained taut, decades' worth of tumbleweeds had formed massive drifts thirty meters deep on their windward sides. Corrals and pens were half standing. Roofs over the barns, stables, and haylofts were sagging or caved in. There wasn't a pane of glass in sight that remained unshattered. Patches and tufts of goat heads, cheatgrass, and rough fescue had conquered areas they'd once been held at bay by boot, hoof, or tire traffic.

As heat from the rising sun awoke a hot, dusty breeze, an old windmill with only three remaining blades began to spin with a clicking squeal, just as it had for years. It made everyone want to grind their teeth.

In the same way he had after the last two raids, game warden Clark Rickert replaced his ballistic helmet with his battered old Stetson hat and then loitered, taskless, around the periphery of the target area while everyone else carried out their respective site exploitation duties. He did this largely in the same manner he carried himself during the loud, fast, violent assaults themselves: always somewhere close but never inconvenient, always scanning the ground or the distance as though searching for some tiny, priceless thing he'd lost there years earlier.

Jacobson, Bishop, Nowell, DuBroux, and Reichman eyed him as he strolled his little circuit around that old ranch up in the Breaks. Despite it only being the task force's third target, it already seemed to be a familiar routine, one he felt was important to complete. They were all vaguely annoyed by it. It seemed as though he felt all the people around him—the world-leading experts in realms of sensitive site exploitation, remediation, and forensics—were wasting their time, but were just too cute and amusing to interrupt.

None of this was discernible from his facial expressions, his conversation, or anywhere else hubris and vanity might normally be spotted. The impression came more from the way he looked at the horizon or down at a rock he rolled between his fingers. This didn't make any sense, and that's really what annoyed them. They were all hawk-eyed profilers, masters of behavioral cartography, but they couldn't figure out where the hell his arrogance came from, or if it was really even there at all.

Each of them knew how unlikely it was that anyone else on the task force would've found that barefooted trail away from the Brookings ranch four days earlier, as Clark had. Even more, none of them thought any living person was capable of tracking such a faint trail for miles through rugged country, until he had a few mornings earlier. Then they'd watched him piece together several critical conclusions about the cult's actions within minutes of walking into the room of death at Fort Peck Lake, ones their intelligence apparatus had failed to glean. As a result, none of them had hesitated to grant him some serious professional respect.

That respect had suffered two days later. The night after the raid on the ranch along Fort Peck Lake, Bishop told them about his baseless yet absolute certainty that the cult leader had never set foot there before. They'd all shaken heads or rolled their eyes in response, unwilling to grace such a ridiculous assertion with the presumptive curiosity or validation a verbal response can carry.

However, privately, it intrigued them. They'd already developed a respect for his ability to perceive certain things most would miss. What he'd said to Bishop planted a tiny seed in their minds that'd sprouted into a dull, quiet, yet nagging curiosity regarding this asshole's ears and eyes, whether they might actually be picking up a few extra frequencies and colors.

Whatever it was, something had to explain why he occupied a bit more real estate in their respective minds than they'd normally allow any one person to fill. Something dwelling in the way he looked at things, moved, held conversation, and whatever other qualities the mind collates so messily as it builds a working impression of another's outward bearing.

He had that rare charm that grabs attention without seeking it, but it had some kind of isotopic half-life or other property that ate itself alive before it could be remembered. His relaxed demeanor and effortless ease had an immediate calming effect on people, but nothing about it was contagious. It was proprietary, *it was his*, and he left none behind when he walked away. He always found the right words to briefly but genuinely engage someone, but strung between those lines was a razor-wired social boundary that he'd kill you for crossing.

He'd intrigued them. Not enough to give him the credit of asking him what he saw or thought that they hadn't or couldn't. But certainly enough to check the strange bastard's eyes from time to time, looking for whatever the hell he was looking for. He'd become a peculiar, amusing distraction from the fiercely disturbing operational situation, and the increasingly horrific scenes the task force uncovered.

Not enough of a distraction, unfortunately. His vaguely amusing mountain-man countenance was no longer something that stood out against all the rest.

Like a sunspot you can't blink away, that image—the corridor of steel filled with dead bodies under the sickly, manic spectrum of those Christmas lights—had been burned behind the eyes of all those on the task force who'd seen it. Very few thought it was possible to lay eyes on anything more disturbing. No act of man could be more perversely sadistic or depraved.

This collective notion—*I've just seen the most evil thing I'll ever see, and I saw it here, at home*—could be felt among the task force personnel at that decrepit old ranch up in the Breaks.

Less chatter as assignments were carried out. More long stares into the dirt or the distance. All the leadership and most of the others present had felt the oppressive despair that hung over certain places, sites like those of ISIS's mass killings in northern Iraq and Syria, among others.

This was different. Very different, and the leadership cadre was starting to realize everyone could feel it, including themselves.

What they didn't know, what they couldn't know, is that what they were feeling *was him*.

CHAPTER 23

IT WAS HIM they felt. The one they hunted.

His stain of gleeful malevolence and corruption, the mark of blight and rot he always left behind in a place of sacred harvest. Even if he wasn't present as his disciples gathered and blessed the sacred blood, his bane and taint would still befoul the place. They *were him*, after all, those who wore his mark.

They were his fingers and his tongues.

Between the new moons, throughout his holy month of observance as the darkest night grew near, convenience and security were really all a location needed for his marked disciples to deem it worthy ground for their preparatory bloodletting. Just so long as it was quiet and secure enough to ritually prepare the lambs for slaughter, set far and away from the eyes and ears of the Unawakened.

Some slightly different but equally profane version of the Unawakened was always there as soon as he arrived, always working to prevent his final ritual from taking place. They'd spend his absence ruthlessly butchering and enslaving one another, yet always seemed to unify to thwart his efforts. It enraged him now as it had every time before. The sun dancers, stargazers, fetishists, idolaters, or Abrahamics like the wicked little Christlings. The Unawakened foolishly thought they were different or unique, but they were all the same. They'd carried different banners, snarled different gods' names from their filthy, frothing mouths as they'd hunted him. But their blades, torches, ignorance, and dedication to thwarting his ritual always remained the same, as had their infuriatingly perfect record of success in doing so. Every cycle.

Thus the need for precaution and effort to avoid them by carrying out his preparations in quiet, remote places. Whether that meant herding his flocks of lambs deep into jungles, mountains, woodlands, dunes, deserts, or steppes, it didn't matter. He knew how almost every earthly environment carried the echo of the lambs' begging, weeping, and screaming, and had danced to that beautiful, devotional music wherever it had pierced the night.

However, when it was finally time, when all was prepared and his disciples began to giggle, drool, and chant his sacred liturgies, when the lambs' blood began to flow and their last screaming was heard, all the different places did gain a new, unifying characteristic.

His stain. His corruption would drip and slosh into the dirt, rocks, and roots of a place, leaving behind a blighting smirch that would linger for thousands of years to come. It didn't kill or degrade rocks or trees or rivers. It just imbued them with his memory. Standing in a place marked by his bane, one would see nothing, have no awareness of what had once happened there. *But one could feel it.*

It was the memory of a feeling, like the faint words of a familiar song on the wind. It was a formless, untextualized blast of what the lambs who'd died there had felt in the end. No narrative, no color or sounds, just what that kind of fear did to a human mind and body.

How a victim would've felt watching him dance, frolic, and shiver in perverse ecstasy as his disciples chanted and butchered their way down the row of lambs writhing against their bonds.

It was the psychophysiological effect of that poor lamb's final, horrible moment boiled down into a single stench or noise; the sensation that kind of hopeless, pitiful terror punches into the gut, teeth, and soul.

He'd left these stains all over the world.

Most animals avoided them on instinct. Some people too; those blessed seventy-two souls set upon his holy path of the raven, those wretched seventy-two set upon the fetid path of the dove, or just those other rare few born with the special sense for such evil. Most, however, had to feel it at least once as they passed near or through one of these places, the old sites of his past sacraments. After that, once they'd felt it, they would live the rest of their lives knowing to avoid it, but not knowing why.

The people at that old ranch up in the Breaks, the task force—those who pursued him during this sacred month, who'd try to stop him from holding the ritual on the fast-approaching darkest night of the lunar cycle, those Unawakened he hated most—they felt it.

He could feel them feeling it. He'd make them feel far worse too.

This new age was strange. Man had jumped so very far ahead. Their toys, machines, gadgets—it all presented challenges of a kind he'd never faced. But that was all right. It presented opportunities, as well.

More than anything else, the *music*. This new music was so very diverse and wonderful. Especially this genre they called honky-tonk, country, or western swing. It awoke something within him, something that wanted to dance and laugh *and feast*.

This time, really for the first time, *he felt like he was going to win.*

CHAPTER 24

LATER THAT NIGHT, Jacobson, Bishop, and Nowell felt the full weight of the palpable lowering of morale they'd seen, and privately felt, at the target location. They discussed it quietly in Harry's trailer over lukewarm beers and the rumble and hum of generators and air conditioners.

The problem, they agreed after about an hour of discussing it, was how difficult improving morale would be *without understanding an enemy's motive*.

At its core, this problem began with the blood, which was still nowhere to be found. There were a few drops on the floor below bodies. A few splashes around one of the dialysis machines used to extract it. But *hundreds of gallons* of blood had been drained from these people, so the prevailing assumption was that the blood was being moved off-site somewhere as soon as it was taken from the victims.

Jacobson and Bishop had interrogated Benson, Comley, and others up the command chain, colleagues back at Langley, and connections at other agencies. No one had the faintest clue why this cult was collecting blood, where it was, or what purpose it could serve, and these were very important things to understand. Not just from an operational standpoint either.

Obviously, answers to questions like these helped explain the intent, objectives, and economy of any organization, and it was easier to destroy something when working from a good target profile. But understanding *why* they were doing it had a human, emotional importance. A need to understand this burned hotter in more members of the task force every day.

Not many had discussed it openly, but throughout the last week a collective dread that all this brutality had no real purpose—that it was just evil for evil's sake—had begun to grow. Jacobson, Bishop, and Nowell all admitted to one another even feeling it grow in themselves.

They'd need to ascribe a motive eventually, and would as soon as any shred of evidence was found to suggest one. However, economic motivations, religious motivations, the drive to conquer resources and land, none of the old boots fit, and the personnel on this task force were too smart to be convinced otherwise.

Pure, unfiltered wickedness, at this scale, was a truly terrifying concept.

Many on the task force had spent years fighting ISIS throughout Syria, Iraq, and Kurdistan—religious fanatics who blew up schools and openly maintained harems of sex slaves. Guys who crucified, stoned, buried, and burned people alive for no more than the blasphemous crime of owning a Disney movie or the adulterous crime of *being raped while married*. This was all true evil, but evil caused by a wicked interpretation of a theology that's shaped the world for almost two millennia. The whole doctrine of ISIS, ISIS itself, was an overdramatized, unauthorized spin-off. *Fan fiction.* Truly evil, without any doubt, but ruthlessly cruel and violent victimization of others in the name of religion is almost as human as dancing around a bonfire. Go far enough up a family tree, and every living person will find someone who did some truly horrifying shit *they just knew* their God would be psyched about.

The cultists' behavior was so jarring to behold that the concepts of mind control or feverish religious conviction were really the only explanations that even remotely fit, but not very well and not for very long.

Mind control was easily eliminated as an explanation. To the extent such an instrument exists, it remains in its infancy, and could very well never leave the crib, or just die there. It's a flaccid, passive, laughably impotent tool. Especially so when compared to the volcanic, tried-and-true power of fundamentalist religious conviction.

Religion itself isn't the poison. Quite the opposite. Like fire, it guides, warms, provides, and fends off the darkness. But whether a peaceful village is set upon by the excruciating horror and pain brought about by an accidentally tipped-over candle—or by the torches of snarling religious fanatics—the screaming has always sounded the same.

Like fire, religion has an awesome power, and when it comes to instilling unshakable devotion and brain-scraped lunacy, at scale, there's really no better tool. So maybe that's what explained what was happening here, some had considered. It's a religion. These are religious fanatics.

Most cults baked in the key ingredients: divine prophecy, revealed truth, worship of the sacred. This one probably had, as well. These cultists proudly declared their own rabid fealty to some venerated guru, whoever the hell he was. Every disgusting thing they did was not only done in obedience to some commandment set forth by their lionized master, but done with giddy, vulgar delight. Their fanatical, masochistic zeal for their leader's carnal edicts certainly had a martyrish *I'll be rewarded after death* zest to it, as well.

So, as a motive, religion had been a better fit than mind control for those who'd considered it, but it eventually fell apart as well, failing to provide the bizarre comfort that knowing an enemy's motive somehow can.

On paper, maybe Red Castle did qualify as a religion, but it still lacked that *human* element of theologically motivated evil. It didn't help anyone digest the horror they'd been exposed to over the last week. Old religions, big religions, they'd always just been here. It was as if they all had some inherent, canonical entitlement to a few centuries of obscene wickedness that no one liked, but everyone begrudgingly understood. It had shaped anthropology and geography. It was part of history, part of the human story. This cult, what these maniacs were doing here, it just failed to qualify. The gut rejected it.

Many quietly, but passionately, hoped it would be discovered that the cult or its leader had a financial incentive. Some black market for twisted, occultist, voodoo fuckery where the blood was being peddled to other lunatics. That would at least feel tragically human.

After what they'd found reeking in shipping containers under those Christmas lights at that ranch up in the Breaks, however, those hopes had mostly begun to die.

But again, most had accepted that what they'd found was *as bad* as anything could be. They'd reached absolute bedrock, as deep as evil could dig, and there was a strange comfort in that, as well. *It can't possibly get any worse.* This was the last point Jacobson had made before telling Bishop and Nowell to fuck off and get some sleep.

A hundred meters away, Clark sat in the back of his truck. He tried to take a sip from his Nalgene bottle without spilling water all over himself and his sleeping bag. He gave up, started to screw the cap back on, then tried again. He was unsuccessful.

His hands were shaking too badly. His heart hammered as though he'd just done sprints. He rubbed each hand with the other, then his eyes with his palms. He marshaled all his willpower against spending the next hour or hours rehashing every moment of it, every single detail from the delusional vision he'd just awoken from.

Don't. Just fucking ignore it. Don't. Just fucking forget it.

This had become Clark's first mantra. An admittedly very shitty one, Clark had conceded to himself, based on its perfect record of failure after each of the six or seven instances he'd relied on it over the last two days. *He had* rehashed every moment of each, every little detail he'd seen, for hours and hours.

But he'd try it again, and did. He punctuated every word of it in his mind like a liturgical chant. Just as he had leading up to and following the prayer he'd hissed out six or seven times in the last two days.

It wasn't as much a prayer as a panicked, whimpered plea. A teary-eyed, pathetic request for the delusions, visions, or whatever the hell they were, to *just fucking stop*. A desperate entreaty to the God he'd once loved and feared, or any others within earshot, to punish him with lightning, a bullet, a freak accident, *anything instead of this.*

The prayers had evolved a bit, though. The requests had gotten more specific and disturbing. He still prayed for the delusions or visions to stop, but their stopping had become less important with each one. Now he prayed with a distinct, burning fervor for them to have *no bearing on reality, no connection to what was going on here.*

Now, this time, Clark prayed for something far more simple. Clark prayed that he was actually losing his mind. He prayed for his own insanity to be the culprit.

Neither Jacobson, Bishop, Nowell, nor anyone else in the task force had any idea or sense of what Clark was going through, the reason for his new mantra, or his decision to dust off the long-abandoned discipline of praying several times a day. Indeed, the way his *affliction* manifested externally was telling a profoundly different, even contradictory, tale of his emotional condition from the one he actually felt.

Most of them were far too laden down with their own heavy thoughts, and the strange sensation of optimism and pessimism fighting each other for supremacy over the same reflection: *I've just encountered the worst thing I've ever seen, the deepest spectacle of evil it is possible for man to behold. However, by necessary extension, everything I will encounter in life from here on will be less evil.*

Unfortunately for everyone who'd found comfort in their own versions of this strange quandary, just about forty-eight hours after finding the bodies in the shipping containers, and in the same silver light of dawn, they were proven very, *very wrong.*

CHAPTER 25

FORTY-EIGHT HOURS AFTER the assault teams stormed the deserted ranch in the Breaks, the task force hit their next target.

This target location was a chicken farm situated in the open prairie country along the winding Musselshell River, about halfway between the small towns of Melstone and Mosby, Montana.

Here, they all learned, it did get worse. After this morning, most could feel now that this was officially something rare, something beyond human sadism. Most could sense they were making first contact with an exquisite, raw, off-the-vine evil. Most of those on the ground teams would be haunted by what they'd found. Several would think of it every day for the rest of their lives.

None were aware of this as they stalked through the darkness toward their staging positions, warmed by the familiar electric thrill that always preceded a gunfight, the one they'd chased up the professional ladder of special operations. That pre-battle zing that activated an almost inhuman sensory acuity, slowed time, and just felt fucking right.

They were also unaware of Francis Bingham and his strange, sad story.

Frank had been one of the four cultists who'd been spotted and tagged by Captain Reichman and his team from the 24th STS using FLIR reconnaissance drones and thermal optics from the advanced overwatch positions they'd stalked into several hours earlier. All four lurked around the property in static guard positions. Frank was the one standing next to a fire burning in a fifty-five-gallon steel drum alongside one of the large henhouses.

Later that evening, during the after-action briefing, the task force would learn that Frank had been named as the primary and only suspect in a double homicide opened by the Roosevelt County Sheriff's Office about a week before the task force had been assembled in Virginia. His wife and son had been found shot dead in their home on the outskirts of Wolf Point, Montana. His seven-year-old daughter had awoken to the raised voices of her mother and older brother, both demanding to know what her dad was doing leaving the house with a backpack and a shotgun in the middle of the night. When she heard the front door open and close a few seconds after the shotgun blasts had crashed through their small home, she jumped out of bed and hid in her closet. She'd stayed hidden in the same spot for the next nine hours until a family friend had stopped by.

At the conclusion of the anecdote of Frank Bingham's ruthless murder of his wife and son, Ground Branch assault team leader Zach Moritz snorted in derision.

This was far more emotion than any Moritz had shown or felt when he'd killed this man about eighteen hours earlier.

The family-murdering cultist, Frank, on the other hand, was only aware of the operator who killed him for just under four seconds—the span of time that passed between first registering movement and his last heartbeat. His final living act was snarling incoherently as he swung a Winchester pump-action toward the team of predators. Both shots of 00 buck he managed to get off missed by several meters, while he was hit by eight of the ten 5.56 bullets fired at him by the operator sprinting toward him.

His left calf fell to rest on the seven-hundred-degree steel drum as he crumpled, lifeless, into the weeds, garbage, and dust at the base of the firepit. As the last air in his body wheezed out of bloody nostrils and perforated lungs, the skin on his calf began to sizzle and hiss.

Clark Rickert would've been able to hear this buzzing whine coming from the corpse as he ran by it, but in his effort to keep up with the speed of the assault team he was attached to, he did not.

As was the case with the previous three raids, the task force surprised and steamrolled the cultists, killing most of those who shot at them or moved in a way they didn't appreciate, and tackling then flex-cuffing any they decided to overpower.

Within a few minutes, more of the cult's victims were found in the last structure to be cleared on the property.

They'd been chained and wired to chairs in the aisle that ran through the center of one of the massive, cavernous aluminum henhouses. A digital climate-control monitor inside the entrance reported it was 103 degrees.

The smell.

The smell was something those who'd entered the building would never forget. It managed to hit all the senses at the same time. The stench from metric tons of chicken shit woven together with the gases seeping from decaying humans and poultry in the unventilated, stagnant heat. It was a humid, tactile aroma that punched one in the back of the throat and behind the eyes.

The sound was just as bad.

A good number of the hens were dead, but thousands of the desperate, panicked, half-starved animals remained. They squawked, screeched, and jittered from their cages, which ran the length of both walls, forming a canyon around the row of dead, still bodies.

Commander Nowell ordered the assault team who'd breached the building to leave it as soon as they'd cleared it for threats, before they'd even begun checking vitals on all the ashen, still bodies. Orders came over the command channel that no one was to be allowed back inside to conduct this grim task until support elements arrived with full-face chemical respirators and nitrile elbow gauntlets.

Even if they had not been drained of blood, it seemed the hurricane of stench and heat could kill a healthy man within an hour inside that hellscape. Clark had stood outside the henhouse with others and, not having seen or felt the biological wreckage inside, wondered why such an ominous order had been issued.

He approached Nowell, nodded respectfully as he reached the commander, then asked if he could go in to check vitals to see if anyone in there was alive.

Clark made an effort to not put Nowell on the spot by publicly challenging an order, making the request quietly, man-to-man, while covering his mic boom with a hand.

Nowell saw this effort for what it was, but made no indication of responding. Clark leaned in closer, speaking just above a whisper.

"Commander, I'm only here as the *local liaison* to provide legal cover for this task force. *I'm easily replaceable.* But this task force is here, *I think*, to try to save innocent people. Based on how those boys who made entry are describing the conditions in there, I reckon there's a slim chance any one inside's got a ticker that's still tickin', but every second matters right now. *Every single second. Please,* Commander Nowell, I'm askin' you, please let me go in and check 'em, or at least pretend you don't see me goin' in."

Nowell stared back into Clark's eyes with no emotion until he nodded, then began striding like a storm back toward the henhouse. He shouted an order into the command channel for two assault teams to follow him "and Captain Rickert" back inside. His decision to place Captain Rickert in a position of authority beside himself—even if just rhetorically, as a brief, passing reference—was one that Clark did not fail to notice.

Clark heard Jacobson and Benson questioning what he was doing, going back inside without the hazmat gear, and nodded to himself as Nowell responded with, almost verbatim, Clark's same words from moments before.

All of them were dead, and had been for at least a day. All had been secured to an eclectic assortment of chairs, many appearing to have been beaten, and all drained of their blood.

So now, for the fourth time in just over a week, the task force went about the grim procedures of site remediation at yet another target location. Yet another scene of unspeakably cruel slaughter of civilians—people, Americans, they'd been too late to save. Yet another eerily remote place where screams would've been mistaken for a prairie wind from the closest road or property, but likely hadn't been heard at all.

All the leadership, and several others, felt it themselves. They saw it in the faces and posture of their teammates as they milled around outside that henhouse. The same heavy air, the same invisible, infectious dread they'd felt at the last location, and the one before.

Very few, this time, had the mental bandwidth to pay Clark any attention. His strange behavior was no longer annoying, or intriguing.

None had noticed him head toward the stables near the homestead. None saw him emerge and make his way toward a dirty trough near a round pen. None heard him ask God for mercy as he stared at the ancient hand pitcher pump nearby, or noticed him begin cranking on it, his movements relentlessly mechanical like the rusted-out pump derricks that heaved mindlessly throughout the western landscape.

When the first chug of water splashed into the dust, he began ferrying water to the trough in the round pen, bucket by bucket, then hauled over an eighty-pound bag of sprout feed he'd seen in the stable. A few had noticed Clark by the time he finally led the horse, a bay gelding, to the round pen. A few minutes later, after the horse had slaked its thirst and begun grazing on feed pellets as Clark brushed the animal and spoke softly to it, quite a few more were openly staring at him.

Clark had seen the well-kept arena at first light. An hour later, when he noticed the five rotting horses that'd been shot outside the stable, he went to it.

As he did, he reflected on how this was the first time he'd acted upon one of his visions. The first time he was testing something he'd seen during one of the deluded, frantic scenes that'd been seizing his mind.

He had to at least check.

He confirmed his grim hunch when he found the young, quivering horse in a rank, dusty stall inside. The only water left in the trough had been greened by piss and shit and time. The static roar of thousands of flies made him begin to tremble a bit as well. He bridled the animal slowly, but found the horse too weak and terrified to do anything but just hope this man wasn't going to hurt it. Its eyes, a bit dull and sunken with dehydration, still had some focus, and while lethargic from hunger, the gelding kept its head up. He led the twitchy horse to the trough, then felt a physical relief in his own body as he watched it drink and eat. He inspected the gelding closer as he brushed out its bay coat. It was half-starved and filthy, but a fine animal. Finer the closer he looked. A calm alertness began returning to its eyes. It had good muscle tone in its straight legs and shoulders, a strong back and chest, and balanced hooves without any cracks or chips. It was big, at least sixteen hands at its well-defined withers.

This gelding had been ridden and loved. Someone had taken great care of it until not all that long ago. Someone Clark assumed was rotting in the house beyond the stables, or in one of those rancid henhouses.

At this point, many had noticed the game warden and what he was doing. Some had just stopped to stare. It felt abrupt and alien to them, Clark's care for this horse, given what was happening, what was in that henhouse, what had happened over the last week.

Some wanted to be annoyed by the guy's antics, but couldn't. This man didn't have any responsibilities when it came to after-action damage assessment, forensic analysis, or clearance and sanitization of an area of operation. He wasn't shirking duties. This was just a quiet Montanan staying out of everyone's way as he went about quiet Montanan things.

If he weren't doing this, he'd be strolling on the fringes of the AO somewhere, staying out of everyone's way as he waited for a ride back to the FOB to continue his vague, nebulous role of *local law enforcement liaison* on the periphery of the task force.

He hadn't found any obscure tracks since the first raid on the Brookings ranch, which remained to many as his largest contribution to the operation thus far. This time, however, it would seem he'd done something useful again. Something useful for a horse, at least, and for him, and uplifting for those who watched, as well.

Eventually, the assault teams began boarding UH-60s to return to the FOB, and Jacobson strolled down toward Clark.

"Found yourself a friend."

Clark nodded but did not look at Harry when he leaned up next to him on the panel of the round pen.

"He's a fine horse, well trained."

Harry took his word for it, not knowing how to appraise such an animal.

"We've got about a half hour until last of us are wheels up back to the FOB. We'll run a site security team here until the op is wrapped up, like the others. Already made a call to have all those chickens killed, but I'll make another to ensure someone's taking care of the horse."

Clark looked over at him then, an almost boyish mistrust in his hard face, gauging Harry for a few moments before looking back at the horse.

"That'd be good of ya."

Harry watched the game warden. Remembering what he'd seen at a glance in the subterranean charnel house after the raid near Fort Peck Lake, what he'd said to Charlotte a few hours later, he felt an urge to ask him if he, the leader, had been here before. He shook the ridiculous thought away. It was nonsense, and Harry knew it. Rickert was a stark contrast to the usual profile of someone on a task force like this, but that's really all that was special about him. He'd found some footprints, could track well, had a knack for crime scene deduction, seemed to have an unshakable demeanor no matter how much chaos he'd been exposed to, and displayed a rustic charm and vibe that—evinced by his little horse rehab showcase—had a positive effect on morale. But that was it.

It had been a very long time since Harry Jacobson had been smitten with or intimidated by another man. It unsettled him, and he welcomed a swell of confidence that this guy was just an amusing but genuinely ignorant person, not some goddamned soothsayer. He was about to turn and head back to his staff when Clark spoke.

"Can I ask you something, Harry?"

Harry raised his eyebrows, a bit surprised, then nodded.

"Go for it."

Clark looked over, then gestured at the land around them lazily with an open hand.

"Why was I put onto the task force leadership team? And please don't tell me it's just *protocol* to include a local law enforcement liaison among the command, because I know it isn't. I understand why the lawyers would want me on the ground, rolling with the assault teams. That makes sense, but the command element? With you, Benson, Bishop, Nowell, and the rest? It just doesn't track. And it may well be that you don't know why, and if you honestly don't, at least tell me who ordered you to do it. From day one I could tell you all thought it was as strange as I did. I could tell it hadn't been your call. So, just help me understand, that's all I'm askin' here."

Harry held Clark's gaze as he took in a deep breath. The leadership team had, indeed, been confused, even troubled, by the CIA director, the secretary of defense, and then the president himself insisting that the mysterious Malcolm Thorn be placed among the command element of the task force. Several days later, shortly after the task force was assembled and briefed at Langley, Thorn—for the first and only time since—exercised his bizarre authority to make things even weirder by insisting that Clark be included in the command element as well.

Now, the unsettling game warden stood here and proclaimed his awareness of this already troubling pile of peculiar bullshit, decorating it with yet another layer of tinsel and trim. Even a career clandestine officer like Harry Jacobson had limits to their weird shit bandwidth, and he was reaching his.

It made him frustrated. It awoke the remorseless infantry officer mindset he'd never been able to shake. The battle-honed ability to smother speculation, doubt, and fear in the minds of other men with a few sharp, barbed words.

"You're simply wrong on that front, Rickert. Including local law enforcement liaisons in the leadership cadre *is protocol*, and it *always fucking has been*. You got a problem with your role and place here, *then walk*. Any other paranoid questions?"

Clark took in a breath, held it as he looked at Harry with an expression of tired disappointment, then dropped his head and let it out noisily. Harry felt a brief pang of guilt for addressing this guy so aggressively.

He watched Clark push himself from the fence panel, throw on his backpack, then sling his rifle over a shoulder. Clark stood there for a moment, then spoke as he stared at the horse, his words a command as quietly fierce as any Harry could issue.

"You see this horse is taken care of properly, Harry."

Clark turned to look at him.

It took some longer than others to finally see that thing living in Clark's eyes, that pledge, the oath that not even death could stop him. Harry finally saw it as Clark spoke just above a whisper.

"Because I'll know if it ain't."

As Clark walked toward the landing zone, Harry believed him.

CHAPTER 26

THE NEW FORWARD operating base—where they'd been flown to from the chicken farm, which looked like a wartime FOB one would find in the mountains of Afghanistan—was on isolated federal land in the Bull Mountains, just over an hour outside Billings. The abnormal traffic of armored vehicles and aircraft was being explained online and in the *Billings Gazette* as a National Guard exercise. Given all the traffic, noise, and frenzy of the place, many had begun to wonder just how long the public would buy it.

Almost eleven hours had passed since the operators, support, control, and forensic personnel had removed the last body from the henhouse. As soon as they stepped off the UH-60s at the FOB, anyone who'd set foot inside that rancid structure was ordered straight to the camp showers. Orders weren't necessary, as all who'd been inside eagerly took their turn under the lukewarm water in the shower stalls buzzing and humming from the generators and pump motors powering them.

The after-action briefing had ended an hour ago, and what followed was a rundown on the findings from the interrogations of the cultists taken alive at all four targets so far. The most notable takeaway from the interrogations and psych analyses was that the cultists had undergone the most comprehensive conditioning or mind control effort anyone in the academy of sciences had ever encountered.

Not a single one of the prisoners deviated from their sinister whispers or shrieks about *his awakening* or *his blood rite* or *him—the great one*. The federal staffers and contractors running the interrogations at government facilities and university hospitals around the country had tried everything to break the trance, or whatever controlled the minds of the cultists taken alive. They'd gone way outside the ethical bounds of practice, even confronting several with their spouses, parents, or children. None of it worked.

It was as though the cultists had never seen their loved ones before. They simply would not, or perhaps could not, break character. Several cultists in the best physical condition had been flown to an agency black site in northern Colorado this very afternoon where *enhanced interrogation techniques* were administered. Nothing worked.

Indeed, it seemed likely this was no character or facade, but a real cognitive state of psychosis. It seemed that who these people were now—raving, keening, febrile zealots—were fully dedicated in body and mind to what was still a mysterious ideology and its leader.

The collective nature of it, the behavioral similarities shared between all the cultists who'd been taken alive thus far, was baffling and bone-chilling to behold.

Some things had been clarified. The 41 cultists killed and 19 taken alive, as well as all of the 288 bloodless, dead victims the task force had found over the last four days below the ranch on Fort Peck Lake, in the Christmas light–tinted storage containers at the second location, and in the chicken farm this morning, were all among the list of missing persons from the counties throughout northern Montana. This was the list the task force had been briefed on at the SAC headquarters in Langley, but that list had grown from 591 to 782 in the twelve days since. Most were from Montana, but it now included others from Wyoming, Idaho, and the Dakotas.

This fact forced everyone to engage in the quiet, grim arithmetic of surmising the total number of those still unaccounted for, who all assumed were either already dead at this point, or dying slowly in the same terrifying way.

They'd also done a large profile analysis to assess any characteristics that might influence whether one ended up a victim, or a branded cultist. It seemed there actually were selection criteria. Overall, the branded cultists generally had dispositive criminal records that involved victimization of another; theft, burglary, assault, domestic violence, crimes like that. Those slated for execution generally did not. Likewise, only three people with a clean record and a history of public service were cultists; all the rest were bled to death. There were a decent number of people in both groups whose qualifications for membership were not clear, but the trends were statistically unignorable.

Two of the deceased were twenty-two-year-old women who'd been best friends since kindergarten and had worked together at an assisted living facility almost every day since graduating high school. The one who was killed by exsanguination spent her weekends and free time volunteering or taking the elderly residents to movies or ice cream, while the one who'd ended up a cultist had been stealing from those same people for at least three years. The majority of backgrounds told the same story. These findings were, ultimately, somewhat predictable based on existing profile modeling on cults, terrorist groups, or other criminal organizations; those with an intelligible propensity for crime or harming others ended up cultists, while those without such inclinations didn't make the cut.

None of this helped. At least, it didn't help any of the exhausted, filthy people on the task force rationalize any of the savagery or motivations of this adversary.

The briefing finally ended, a great mercy to all in attendance. Jacobson excused everyone present in the command tent, instructing them to get more food from the mess if they were still hungry, as well as some much-needed rest. No information at all on when or where they'd be making their next move had been shared. They were all just given the vague instruction to stay ready to spin up and dust off at a moment's notice. This was a static directive that virtually all the operators on this task force had developed a deep familiarity with throughout long careers of serving on quick-reaction forces in war zones, global response teams for the CIA, and an array of other crisis and emergency response units.

Deputy Director Benson and his staff exchanged a few words and handshakes with Jacobson and Bishop before they departed from the large tent, appearing as exhausted and disturbed as anyone else. The smattering of nameless, formally attired, and perpetually silent staffers from other intelligence agencies and the White House—a clutch of visibly uncomfortable people that grew larger by the day—avoided any contact with the dirty bodies and piercing gazes of the operators as they awkwardly made their way outside.

The leadership cadre looked from face to face as everyone stood, stretched shoulders or backs, then began quietly shuffling toward the large tent's exit. They saw exhaustion and frustration in the features of most of these people they'd so often shared exhaustion and frustration with over the years, but none saw anything concerning enough to warrant an immediate check-in.

When it came to game warden Clark Rickert, however, none had any baseline to operate from. When it came to this man, their keen eyes told them nothing.

They all looked at Clark, sitting near the entrance to the command tent, leaning back in a folding chair with fingers in the pockets of his jeans and one knee resting over the other, staring at some point on the ground ahead of him. Something about his demeanor, plus their own exhaustion, froze them all in place as everyone else left the command tent.

They hadn't even known this guy for two full weeks, but since the moment they'd met him, he'd been by their side every single minute as they went about their profession. Their profession, unlike his, was the aggressive application of precise, terminal, and extreme violence against those deemed to be enemies of the United States and thus unprotected by due process or any other tenets of the criminal justice system or the Constitution.

Clark, unlike them, was a state law enforcement officer. Someone who went to work every single day under the constant, ambient threat of political or legal liability for any action or behavior deemed excessive. Likewise, he'd never once used violence or discharged a firearm while on the job without a subsequent investigation, mandatory administrative leave, and often state-ordered trauma counseling.

Since the raid on the Brookings ranch, the members of the task force had killed forty-one Americans and taken nineteen prisoners. There were no formal murder or kidnapping investigations going on, none of the procedures that would normally follow any other use of deadly force by government employees. There was no mandatory post-shooting administrative leave or therapy, as had been forced upon Clark a dozen times over the last two decades. There were no arraignments or criminal proceedings initiated for the cultists, or even a whisper of any of this in the press, and so long as everything went according to plan, there never would be.

On top of all that, they'd been shoulder to shoulder with him while encountering the most barbarous, mortifying violence visited upon innocent people that any of them had ever witnessed, let alone at such a large and sickeningly coordinated scale. Even more, these were innocent *Americans*. Clark's fellow Montanans. Montanan *children*, even.

Indeed, since the task force had returned from the raid on the chicken farm, all five of them, and several others, had caught themselves openly staring at Clark as though he were naked. In their exhaustion, his apparent calm, focus, and countenance of well-rested ease stood out so starkly among the rest of the task force that, for a few of them, it actually felt abrasive, like a strobe light or a car alarm.

A minute passed after the last person had left, but the leadership remained seated.

Despite all five of them staring directly at Clark as he spoke, there was something startling about the way his words cut through the heavy, silent air of the tent. He spoke with neither eye contact nor any of his inflection normally found at the end of a question.

"Seems like it's time to have a little chat."

CHAPTER 27

OVER THE LAST few days, it had become increasingly clear to Clark that these five people could tell he was losing his mind.

Clark was not particularly skilled at reading others' emotions or thoughts, but he'd seen them watching him like he was a rabid dog. Their concern was plainly visible.

He could see it in the way they stared at him during meals in the mess tent, during briefings, or as he walked around the FOB or target areas. He figured they saw what he felt, how close he was to a mental breakdown, collapsing into a state of pants-shitting, snarling madness.

He figured if they hadn't already discussed getting him off the task force—contacting Price or Albee to coordinate some kind of mental health intervention—it wouldn't be long until they did. Given the sensitive nature of the operation, he was anxious they'd use their own gray-area resources to have him institutionalized somewhere secure, and uniquely shitty.

But they hadn't yet. Their collective desire to confront him quietly had become clear over the last few hours, so he figured he needed to act now, or he'd never have the chance.

He'd also been hoping to have a private conversation with these particular people, but for very different reasons. Before they kicked him out or put him in a straitjacket, he needed information.

This operation would have only been approved if the brass upstairs knew considerably more about Red Castle, its leader, and its goals than he or any ground-level members of the task force.

He needed that information, because Clark Rickert was losing his mind.

He'd spent the better part of the last week in a state of panic. He'd been fighting against fear, a real, bone-deep fear that he'd never known, and he felt the gate starting to splinter.

What was worse than the delusions he'd been suffering from was his growing confidence that something within the corpus of classified information underlying this operation would explain it all. He prayed every day now that his paranoid delusions could be explained by late-onset schizophrenia or some other condition.

Deep down, he felt these delusions or visions were not actually pathological, but something far more sinister. Something felt natural about them, more memories than dreams. Nothing about them felt intrusive or uninvited. Whenever they came—despite the bolts of fiery, breathtaking anxiety they rode—they also carried the essence of a puzzle piece snapping into place. That familiarity and warmth, how right they felt, was what made them so terrifying.

Clark knew he'd been through a lot. He'd never met his father, was neglected by his mother, and spent most of his adolescence as an orphan. He'd held the dead bodies of his son and his wife. He harbored a secret history as a prolific criminal. He'd killed four different men while close enough to see the eye color of all four. Twice as many people had tried to kill him, and he'd injured or caused great physical and emotional pain to many more than that. He'd been covered in the blood of another man he'd led into danger. He'd done a poor job of comforting that man as he wept and then died. He expeditiously avoided relationships, never took vacations, did not have family, and the handful of people he considered friends enjoyed their mutual silence as much as he did. He did not examine, explore, discuss, or off-load his experiences, baggage, or trauma to any person or even a journal.

All of this is to say that Clark knew well, without any question, that he was a glowing candidate for a mental breakdown. Truth be told, he'd quietly been awaiting one, confident of its approach, for years.

As such, Clark was on an entirely separate operation from everyone else on this task force. Clark was now on a crusade to corroborate his own insanity, a desperate, private mission to substantiate insanity as the provenance of the strange things happening to his mind. He felt, very deeply, that the survival of the entire world depended upon his own madness.

If Clark was not losing his mind, then his condition had a different, horrifying genesis story. Terrified by his own growing certainty that was the case, he clung to the desperate, masochistic hope that plain old insanity was the culprit.

The clarity of purpose deep in his soul that this was the hunt of his life, *the reason he was born*, was something he not only still felt, but that had steadily increased. Like some dark, shameful fetish, he forced that feeling down whenever it crept up. He felt that acquiescing to the instinct—that this operation was his life's calling—represented an unconditional surrender to a terrifying reality.

If insanity did not explain what he'd seen and learned from his visions—if all of this delusional chaos was real—then every living thing on this planet was about to fall under the control of a monster capable of inflicting pain incomprehensible under the limits of human perception.

Consequently, for Clark, mission success now required confirming that *he had not* been chosen to serve on this task force for some deeper reason. If he could do that, he'd be able to relax comfortably into the warmth of his own mental breakdown.

If any such evidence existed, then Jacobson, Bishop, and Benson were the most likely stewards of it. He needed one of them to confirm that the entire body of classified intelligence was completely devoid of anything that could explain his visions. He needed someone privy to that information to dispel his crippling dread—this pulsing cyst of fierce panic that what was going on in his mind was real.

Clark knew what he was good at, and what he was not. Developing platonic relationships, graceful and low-impact navigation of social dynamics, and subtlety were not areas where he excelled. As such, persuading them to disclose classified information was hopeless. He couldn't steal the information; he could barely operate basic software. He couldn't just ask for it, either, because there was no way to articulate any of this without sounding completely, egregiously fucking insane. Ironically, complete, egregious fucking insanity is all Clark wanted to confirm.

Keeping his cool while others lost theirs is one thing he was very good at. So all he could think to do now was get them to turn on one another, or make one of them angry enough to do something reckless. He had no idea how that would play out, but it was the only tactic he'd ever found success with when it came to situations where he needed something from others whom he didn't trust, and who didn't trust him. Rile them up and take advantage when they lost composure.

It was not a deft or intelligent course of action, just the only one he could see. Being honest with himself, it wasn't a course of action at all. He was just scared, angry, confident his time here was running out, and ready to wing it.

When he saw the leadership remaining behind, staring at him, he figured now was as good a time as he'd get, and so made his comment about *having a little chat.*

DuBroux and Reichman just looked vaguely surprised when Clark made the comment, while Jacobson and Nowell looked at Bishop, watching her until she responded, fatigue and a hint of ridicule in her voice.

"A chat about what, exactly, Captain Rickert?"

Clark didn't move as the silence stretched on. Jacobson glanced at Bishop, a bit frustrated by her apparent expectation that Clark would voluntarily fill the lengthening silence. Such an expectation felt preposterous, even for someone who'd only known him for a week and a half, so he spoke instead.

"Well, with the exception of Benson and Malcolm Thorn, the five of us here do comprise the command element, so . . . is there anything you, Rickert, or anyone else feels we ought to discuss outside the ears of those two and the rest of the task force?"

Clark didn't move, while the others looked among one another, all confused at what was happening, but also aware of their own desire to dig into this guy's mind a bit. Jacobson, grasping the collective desire, spoke.

"Captain Rickert, at the Brookings ranch you found something we may have never caught at all. You also seemed to surmise those tracks had been left by a leader of this cult. On top of that, I watched you spend three minutes in that room under the ranch on Fort Peck Lake and diagnose what had happened there, how they'd done it, and the cult's operational structure. Char here told us about your statement regarding where their leader has, and has never physically been. You're a detective, obviously a good one, and we're working on your turf. As we all know, we've been spinning our wheels here, trying to find this asshole and surmise his actual objective or motivation. So, do you have any insight here, anything you haven't shared yet?"

Clark nodded slowly. He spoke the next words just above a whisper.

"*His actual objective or motivation . . .*"

Charlotte glanced at her boss with an expression that—in the silent language they'd developed over the last six years of working ninety-hour weeks together—conveyed her pessimism about the usefulness of whatever would happen next. Clark figured every word Harry had just said was a cover, his way of placating him and stimulating a conversation wherein they could conduct their own psychiatric diagnosis of his insanity, but knew this was his only opportunity to get more out of them, so he'd stay his course.

"Ya see, that's just it, Harry. I think—well, *I damn well know*—that you . . ."

He'd taken a hand from his pocket to point an index finger at Harry, and then aimed it at Charlotte.

"And that *you*, Miss Bishop, know a good deal more about what their objective is than anyone here. Matter of fact, I reckon y'all got read in on some shit that would knock the socks off the rest of us. At the briefing in Langley, agency director Mike Flood callin' this the *greatest national security threat this country's ever faced*. The Joint Chiefs, SecDef, and the president approving domestic DOD deployment and military action against American citizens, keepin' it all from the public. None a' that shit happens without *you two* gettin' a pretty decent understanding of what's really goin' on here, who these crazy fuckers are, and who their leader is. And you want my insight? How about you share a bit a' yours, otherwise what the hell are we doing right now?"

DuBroux placed his hands on the back of a chair and looked down with raised eyebrows, while Nowell looked back at Jacobson and Bishop with an expression that said: *He's got a point*.

Both men had long and prolific careers as gunfighters of the federal government, much accustomed to carrying out orders with the understanding they *were not* aware of the full intelligence package. Even so, the current operation was profoundly different. That difference was enough for them to start pondering what lay within this particular backstory. Charlotte spoke.

"Captain Rickert, what we're doing here is simply seeking your input. Since you found the leader's first steps at the Brookings ranch, we've been several behind. Our wheels are spinning when it comes to getting ahead of this cult leader. You've made observations over this last week that betray a keen intuition regarding this organization and its leader, confirming things at a glance that take us several hours. Whether it's supporting or destroying insurgencies, sabotaging infrastructure, or eliminating high-value targets, our purview at the SOG is unconventional warfare. As such, one of our most critical *tactics, techniques, and procedures* is actually not having rigid TTPs at all. Being open. Actually listening to local assets with specialized expertise, like you and yours. So, Captain, *what the hell we're doing right now* is asking whether you've seen any of this organization's blind spots that we haven't. If not, then say so, and let's all get some goddamn sleep."

Clark thought this was bullshit, and looked quickly among the faces of the others for any signs they felt the same. He saw what appeared to be reluctant but sincere curiosity in all their faces, but he couldn't trust it. Unless a situation was violent or about to be, he'd always been terrible at reading others. He'd expected a mental health intervention, not this effort to pick his madness-addled brain. It overwhelmed him, but he didn't fail to notice this woman's refusal to address his request for all that mattered now: his request for information that might explain what was happening to him. He took a deep breath.

"I just asked for more access to the intelligence package behind an operation I know you have. I will not let you ignore that request, so please consider this me asking for it a second time. And for the love a' Christ, please spare me some lecture on why that ain't possible or proper. I respect you guys, I really do, but I ain't a soldier. I don't like bein' told I ain't allowed to ask questions. I also ain't the kinda guy to go blindly into a breach with a heart fulla trust that the brass, comfy and safe and miles away, ordered me into it for a good reason. What I know is this: I was brought here for a specific purpose. You two possess information that would improve my ability to achieve it, and the ability of these three commandos here to carry out theirs. *Fuckin' period.* I know that, and you know that. So, Harry, Miss Charlotte—other than some clearance and classification rubric I assume you've got laminated and taped onto your office wall, or some stupid-ass devotion to custom and protocol—what reason could you possibly have not to share more information on what's really fuckin' goin' on here?"

A career warrior, Jacobson tensed at Clark's comment about blindly going into a breach, and figured it might be interpreted as an insult by Nowell, DuBroux, and Reichman, as well. Clark, quite uncharacteristically, went on speaking in his dry, loud cadence without being prompted to do so.

"And speakin' a' questions . . ."

Clark looked over to Reichman and wagged an index finger.

"I got one for you, Captain Reichman."

Reichman looked away from Clark and up toward the others as he snorted in amusement, one he might've made watching a drunk moron get kicked out of a bar.

"Eyes on me, Sporty Spice."

Both Nowell and Jacobson had to stifle a laugh. There was something undeniably amusing about this sinewy, unshaven, grizzled mountain man getting sassy with a guy ten years younger, forty pounds heavier, and who shamelessly put more time, effort, and product into his hair than anyone within a hundred miles. Reichman looked back at the older man, cold hostility having replaced any trace of amusement. Clark went on.

"On the morning of the raid on the Brookings ranch, I saw you and your boys haulin' somethin' outta the house. Somethin' big covered in a tarp y'all loaded into an MRAP. Tell me, what was that thing?"

Reichman opened his mouth as though he were about to speak, then closed it. He glanced at the floor, then toward Jacobson and Bishop, shrugging and making some painfully unconvincing expression of annoyance as though the question were ridiculous.

Charlotte let out a quiet groan only Jacobson could hear. He shared her disappointment. Reichman, while a great combat operator and even better leader of them, was obviously lacking in the tradecraft of deceit, a native language to CIA field officers like themselves. They also knew someone like Clark—a skilled domestic law enforcement investigator who'd been on the job since Reichman was barely out of middle school—would see right through his pensive demeanor and anxious glances with even more clarity and speed than they could. Clark immediately confirmed as much.

"Don't be lookin' to Mom and Pop, Tuck. *I asked you* what it was you hauled outta the Brookings house under that tarp. Either tell me, or tell me *you ain't gonna tell me*. Go on ahead and skip any of the bullshit you're tryin' to think up right now."

DuBroux and Nowell had no idea what Clark was referring to, but could clearly see Reichman did. Both looked at Jacobson and Bishop and saw they did too. Jacobson let out a long exhale as he leaned back in his chair. Charlotte bit her lip, knowing she was watching this redneck asshole take full control of the exchange.

Reichman settled a cold, calm gaze onto Clark, all nervousness gone. He'd treat this dipshit as the outsider he was. Stonewall him in the same way he'd stonewalled reporters creeping around Bagram, JBAD, Al Asad, or Baghdad's Green Zone. He spoke in a slow, flat monotone.

"After the Brookings's house was secured, my team pursued a secondary objective of locating, securing, and extracting a certain classified object from the basement of the—"

Clark clapped his hands with so much speed and noise it made everyone flinch.

"Already told ya, *Boy Scout*. Give it to me straight or keep that pretty little dick-sucker shut, 'cause I don't swim in that bullshit."

Reichman stood up so fast his chair flew into the others behind it. From a ranch outside Lubbock, he'd learned how to kick an older man's ass by sixteen, long before he was the six-foot-four-inch, 230-pound chiseled warrior he was now. He'd never raise a hand against a fellow member of the armed forces, but felt confident he could deal with this shit-heel *deer cop* without any serious repercussions. As he stalked toward Clark, after the last ten days of chaos and stomping these infuriatingly mindless cultists, he realized how badly he wanted to hurt someone who could actually feel pain and fear.

The shouting behind him was drowned out by the adrenaline dump churning through his face. Rage-fueled heartbeats hammered, jaw clenched, peripheral vision obscured by a pulsing shadow of black and blood. But when he was only six paces from where Clark remained seated and unmoving, something stopped him in his tracks. Something crashed brutally against all the physiological churning of imminent violence, checking him like a stone wall.

Clark's eyes.

His gray-green eyes. The mocking smirk he'd seen just seconds earlier was gone. Looking at him now, Reichman knew the smirk had never been real. It had been a deception. Like cracked corn to bring in turkey or a gut pile to bring in coyotes, his words and smirk had been the bait. What he saw now was the trap: a wire snare that would constrict his airway, the steel jaws of a foothold that would snap through skin, tendon, and bone.

The man's face itself was empty. It was like looking at a rock slide that, centuries earlier, had slipped and raged down the slope it now rested upon. His eyes, though. His eyes made a promise that terrible, impossible things would happen if Tucker took another step.

Reichman saw it all in a second. By the time Nowell and DuBroux had him by the shoulders and wrists, his body had relaxed, his rage gone, staring as he might at a street magician who'd just done something good, creepy good.

"That's *enough*."

Jacobson snarled the words in a hiss and strode toward Clark, who still hadn't moved.

"You are here, Captain Rickert, for two reasons. *First*, you have a specialized skill set that we suspected would be valuable to the task force, and I'll be the first to say it has been. Second, your status as a local law enforcement officer provides liability insulation with respect to sidestepping the judicial interpretation of the Posse Comitatus Act. I know you're new, but on operations like this, intelligence is *compartmentalized*. There are many reasons for that, but on an administrative level, we simply do not enjoy the luxury of time or bandwidth to brief everyone on everything. There are simply certain aspects of this operation that cannot, and *must not*, be made available to the public. One such aspect is what you've just asked Captain Reichman about. As I said earlier today, if you have a problem with that, *you can fucking walk*."

After a long moment, Clark exhaled and leaned forward to rest his elbows on his knees. Jacobson put his hands on his hips, frustrated by this man's wholesale ignorance with respect to the overall operational benefits of intelligence compartmentalization, and his absolute, exhausted disinterest in lecturing him on it. He shook his head as he began choosing his words.

"Captain Rickert, on this issue, you're simply *flat-out wrong*. There is nothing within the massive exposition of this operation's intelligence foundation that would help with the specific skills and tasks we brought you here to carry out. We're not hiding anything from you that would materially improve your ability to—"

Clark shot to his feet so quickly Jacobson instinctively rotated into his fighting stance.

"Y'all gave Reichman some secret *secondary objective* that Nowell here's lookin' awfully fuckin' surprised by, then stand there with a straight face and say there ain't any additional intelligence you could share that we'd benefit from? Y'all didn't see any reason to share that little tidbit of intelligence with *the officer in charge* of the ground element? With the ground commander of the entire goddamned assault? Explain that to me, Harry. How in Christ's kingdom would that information not improve Nowell's ability to perform his job? What operational benefit comes from keeping that coffin a secret from him?"

Jacobson's lips cracked open just barely as his eyes narrowed. Charlotte did not bother, or think, to mask her expression of surprise. Nowell and DuBroux looked between the leaders of the task force and the game warden in confusion. Jacobson locked eyes with Nowell—who nodded after a long moment, acknowledging what he knew to be a silent promise they'd discuss this later—then looked at Clark and spoke each word slowly.

"How did you know it was a coffin, Captain?"

Clark felt a blossom of rage and rubbed his left eye with a palm.

He could not tell these people he knew it was a coffin because he'd seen it in a vision, or how he knew precisely what was carved into that coffin. The sense of dread and feral panic had only increased when he realized the carvings in that coffin were words written in Coptic Greek, and even more a day after that, when he *knew exactly what the words meant.* Clark hadn't even known such a language existed two weeks earlier, let alone how to read it.

As is the case for many men who've stowed away unresolved trauma somewhere deep within their souls to avoid confronting it, Clark had a gift for quickly and efficiently rendering down any sensation of panic, anxiety, and emotional confusion into rage. Rage provided the option of focusing on an external target, instead of looking inward.

Clark looked up into Jacobson's eyes, then around at the others. Bishop stared at him with Jacobson's same mixture of mistrust and curiosity. Nowell, DuBroux, and Reichman ripped gazes between their team leads and Clark in perplexed anticipation.

This entire effort had gone to shit, Clark knew. He felt his muscles coil in preparation to turn and leave the tent, just as the unfamiliar voice punched across the large tent from behind the group.

"Impressive deductions, Captain Rickert."

CHAPTER 28

FOR THE FIRST time, Clark was actually pleased to see the sinister, pudgy little man. He respected all five others in this room. He'd feigned most of the animosity, hoping it would help get at more information. But this guy was a worthy target. Jacobson let his head drop when he saw who the speaker was, while Bishop looked up toward the ceiling and exhaled slowly.

Clark's eyes narrowed and a smile spread across his face with such a vicious, murderous essence it prompted Nowell and DuBroux to tense and shift their weight, preparing to intercept him. When Clark spoke, his words came cold and slow.

"Haven't caught your name yet, friend."

The small man removed the glasses from his face, pulled out a handkerchief from the inside pocket of his blazer, then used it to clean the lenses. He looked back up at Clark with a smile as he began to speak.

"My name's Malcolm Thorn, Captain Rickert."

His East Coast accent was almost theatrical, dropping the *R*s entirely from the ends of the words *Thorn* and *Rickert*. The man spoke again, and betrayed having listened in on this conversation since the beginning.

"I think Mr. Jacobson's explanation as to why we cannot read you in on more of the intelligence behind this Red Castle and its leader was adequate and comprehensive, and one you should accept as more than sufficient. I also suspect, Captain, that *you yourself* have surmised more about what's going on here than you've shared with your counterparts. Such as your deduction regarding the good Captain Reichman here extracting a coffin from the Brookings residence. What else? I wonder. What intel are *you* in possession of that would benefit the rest of this operation, sir?"

Everyone stared at Clark. Over the last few minutes, Clark realized he'd been wrong about these five having plainly seen his cracking sanity. His confidence the others had seen him becoming unstable was based entirely on how they'd been looking at him over the last week. He'd misread those looks, he now knew. Malcolm Thorn was another matter. Thorn's eyes didn't suggest a general concern for Clark's mental stability, as the others' had. Thorn's piercing eyes suggested he knew about the storms of fragmented, opaque awareness that welled up like a long-forgotten memory seizing Clark's mind and senses, *and what they meant.*

Clark felt he could almost see the information he needed dancing in Thorn's eyes. Unfortunately, what he saw was not the confirmation of his own insanity he so desperately craved. It was a vindictive, cruel affirmation in Thorn's smirk that his visions were connected to everything happening. Clark sniffed loudly, then spoke.

"Let me get somethin' straight. You heard me ask for better access to this operation's intelligence package, or some straight, unfucked answer regarding why that wouldn't be possible. You not only duck and sidestep both requests, but the *first thing* that comes to mind is to suggest *I'm actually the one with critical intel*? Your first instinct—as a career intelligence stooge—is to clumsily flip my request *back on me*, a state employee without any access or intel whatsoever? *Really?* The limp-dicked, window-lickin' kindergartener *no, you* technique? *I'll be damned.* Look, I get tryin' to skirt a question you don't wanna answer, anyone'll do that, but *come on, buddy.* For everyone else's sake, at least try doin' it without this awkward, panicky fat-kid routine. Practice in the mirror or somethin'. Nobody wants to watch a grown man squirm like this."

DuBroux and Jacobson had begun to speak, but Nowell's voice cut straight through theirs and punched hard and deep.

"*Rickert*, that's enough. Fuckin' cool it. Talk about embarrassing schoolyard bullshit, fuck me."

Clark was pleased to see the slight physical reaction Malcolm had to the ridicule, and the smirk on his face waver. Thorn took his glasses off and fiddled with them anxiously, opening and closing his mouth a few times as he searched for words that never came. Clark felt deep in his bones that the man knew something about whatever he was going through, and that felt profoundly invasive and wrong. He wanted to hold him down and rip his teeth out one by one until he wept out an answer. He clocked the others saying something to him but none of the words. He turned from Thorn to face Bishop and Jacobson as he spoke.

"*Look*, I'm just askin' you to share more information that could really benefit the rest of us, increase the chances of us bringing all this chaos to an end. You say, *No, you can't have it*. I'm sure you can rattle off ten different reasons you can't share more intelligence, in addition to the shitty ones you've already mentioned. Point remains, we're better at our jobs and this task force improves the more we know. *Period*. So either go ahead and keep any shitty argument to the contrary to yourselves, or tell us more about this cult, its leader, what they want, and what's really going on here."

Bishop rolled her eyes, uttering, "*This fucking guy*," loud enough for everyone to hear. Nowell hung his head and put his hands on his hips. Reichman crossed his arms and looked toward the ceiling with closed eyes. DuBroux rubbed his temples. Jacobson groaned in exasperation as he leaned forward to place both hands on the back of a chair, unsure how or even whether to respond to such bullheaded ignorance.

None of them would argue that Clark's general point was inherently unreasonable, but none of them would argue with a toddler insisting the sky was blue either. In their professional world, someone demanding access to information classified under the most restrictive Sensitive Compartmented Information controls and Special Access Programs that exist was just patently ridiculous. A complete nonstarter. It would be like someone in Clark's world strolling up with a shotgun, demanding participation in a midnight no-knock raid on some militia den of meth-head poachers because he *loves bears and wants to protect them*. It's just something that's not going to happen.

Bishop spoke softly in French to Jacobson, but with no intention of being unheard. They'd developed the practice of speaking rapid French, German, or Arabic to talk shit about people within earshot they knew didn't speak the language.

"Il est vraiment un putain d'idiot, non?"

Jacobson nodded, agreeing that he was indeed a fucking idiot, and responded in German without looking up.

". . . einer, der keine Ahnung hat, wie sehr dieses Geheimdienstpaket seinen Verstand zerfetzen würde."

Clark's words rolled back fast, clipped, but with a subtle accent that was not American.

"Je pourrais être un putain d'idiot, mais . . ."

Jacobson ripped his gaze up from the floor and found Clark's own, and his words were just as cold and violent.

"There ain't a damn thing you could say that'd *shred my mind*. This world's been tryin' real fuckin' hard to do that for a long, *long time*."

Surprise narrowed Jacobson's eyes while widening Bishop's. DuBroux and Reichman looked at each other with raised eyebrows, and Nowell snorted in amusement. Thorn looked up at Clark. A mischievous grin formed as he began to speak.

"*Très bien, Monsieur Rickert*. But seriously, how'd you know it was a coffin?"

This question took Clark by surprise. It was a frustrating pivot, and Clark knew it was an effective one because he felt his control over the conversation slipping away. He shrugged, crossed his arms, and forced himself to grin right back.

"*I fuckin' didn't*, but it seems like I guessed right."

Thorn looked amused, searching for something in Clark's face. After a few seconds, as though he'd found it, he began to slowly nod, his grin becoming a warm, approving smile. He turned and looked at Bishop, then cocked his head and a thumb in Clark's direction as he spoke.

"He's a cocky asshole, not nearly as smart as he thinks he is, physically past his prime, and emotionally, well . . . the bastard's just a fuckin' mess, a real case a' *bruised fruit*. Even so, I gotta hand it to ya, Charlie. He might just be *exactly* who we needed for this role. He checks almost all the boxes, and we'll have to see, but I got a *damn good feeling* he'll end up checking the last one too. We sure are lucky you stumbled across his file, eh?"

This strange man's counterpunch at Clark had enough unexpected humor and bite that smiles cracked on the faces of DuBroux, Nowell, and Jacobson while Reichman laughed out loud. It had no effect on Charlotte. She'd been the only one to see Thorn wink at her as he mentioned her "luck" in finding Rickert's file.

She'd "stumbled across" the man's file when she walked into her office around five in the morning and found it sitting on top of her keyboard, only a few hours after the man who'd just winked at her had tasked her with finding a local law enforcement liaison for the task force. Thorn turned and began strolling toward the small side entrance to the tent. Charlotte silently closed the case on how that file had gotten there as she stared at his back, her mind conjuring the image of him placing the file on her desk and sauntering out of her office and down the hall with the same gait he used now.

It was immediately clear to Clark that he'd underestimated Thorn and, yet again, overestimated himself. This guy had done something no one else had in a very long time. With only words, he'd stung, shamed, and thrown Clark entirely off balance. Clark could feel himself on the verge of cracking, so he raised his eyebrows, shrugged, then nodded a few times. He was relieved as this attempt at conveying some humor and loser's grace worked, disarming Nowell and DuBroux enough to even laugh. Nowell said something like *you had that one comin', brother*, but it didn't quite register in Clark's mind, where a tempest of anxiety thrashed against the inside of his skull.

He'd never studied French or German, and had certainly never spoken either, but both languages came as naturally as the only one he'd ever known—the only one he'd known until this last week, at least. After each of his visions, it seemed he was fluent in another three or four.

As Thorn approached the exit, Clark was gripped by a desperate need to maintain a dialogue and keep him talking. He had only a few seconds to think up something to say, but his mind was choked by strange words and phrases.

Words and phrases he didn't understand, in more languages he'd never actually heard. Time stopped as they churned behind his eyes and began changing into something more than mere thoughts. The words shrieked out their warnings as they escaped the constraints of a mere thought and emerged as something more, something desperate, something he could feel and hear inside the confines of his mind.

The new moon. To néo fengári. Nocte neomeniae fiet. Luna nueva. *Do not let him ascend.* Az újhol. Arrêtez-le avant la nouvelle lune. *He'll drink the blood of the world.* Lass ihn nicht aufsteigen. *Find him.* Stamatíste ton í skotóste ton. STOP HIM. OPORTET VOS PROHIBERE SANGUINEM RITUM. KILL HIM. PROHIBERE RITUM SANGUINIS.

"*Thorn.*"

No one noticed the state of psychosis burning through Clark's mind; they'd just seen him pinch the bridge of his nose as though he were trying to remember a forgotten name. So when he shouted the man's name far more loudly than necessary, it startled them all. He didn't mean to shout, but as soon as he did, the snarling tumult in his mind disappeared without a trace.

Thorn stopped walking, remained still for a moment, then turned to face Clark. To Charlotte, Thorn looked back at Clark with what seemed like encouragement in his expression. Clark tried to speak, but all he got out was an "it's" and then a "what," before taking a deep breath and barking out the only thing that came to mind.

"*Who the hell* are these cultists? *What the hell* is this operation? *What the fuck* is really going on here?"

Thorn did not move or break eye contact with Clark for several long moments. Questions just like these, specifically that last one—as shallow and laughably vague as it may be—had been shouted at Thorn by the president of the United States a couple of weeks earlier. He'd answered it, too, without looking away from the president's famously intimidating gaze. A gaze similar to that of many others on this task force, one that carried a guarantee of the willingness and ability to apply relentless, calculated, world-shaking power, with a promise to never quit.

Looking into Clark's eyes—eyes awaiting an answer to the *exact same* question the president had asked him weeks earlier—Thorn saw something different. It was a feral, menacing patience. Clark's gaze guaranteed relentless pursuit. Thorn would give this game warden a response, but it would not be the one he gave the president.

Of course, the same questions Clark just asked had been burning through the minds of many on this task force. At this very moment, though none of the seven people in the large tent knew it, these questions were being asked in the minds of a dozen others within a few hundred meters of where they stood.

Ava Pomorski was in her cot in the trailer she shared with several other tactical analysts, asking herself this question as she quietly wept. Former MARSOC operator Chris Harrison, one of the Ground Branch paramilitary officers, asked himself the same from the turret of an MRAP chain-smoking cigarettes with shaky hands. Javier Mendez, a FLIR thermal reconnaissance drone pilot, sat in a toilet stall, thumbing through the beads of his rosary with sweaty hands as he asked God this question.

The question itself—*what the fuck is really going on here?*—came as no surprise to Thorn. He'd figured it was likely someone on the task force would eventually break and demand an answer. He was pleased to be confronting this inevitability here and now, where the only witnesses were the task force leadership cadre. He hadn't rehearsed an answer yet, but he didn't need to. He knew he'd be able to gin one up on the fly, one specially tailored to satisfy whoever happened to be within earshot when the question came, and went about doing that now.

"Captain Rickert, we've gone up against terrorist organizations that peddle an ideology, and cartels that peddle a product: weapons, drugs, or people. Sometimes terrorists sell a bit of dope, and sometimes cartels push a bit of ideology, but neither ever specializes in both. When it comes to a self-proclaimed caliphate imposing their theocratic ethos, *we know what that idea is*, quite well. It's ancient, it's written down, there's no mystery there. When it comes to a cartel that's pushing a product, *they're after money*. We know their product, their margins, their goals, and their market, very well. *There's no mystery there either.*"

Thorn began walking back toward the group, delicately and precisely increasing the volume, tone, and passion of his words as he went on.

"This Red Castle organization, however, seems to be an equal combination of both. Truth be told, they're our first real *twofer*, and boy, they are doing it with gusto, peddling an ideology strong enough to mind-fuck its members with shocking, unseen power, and peddling the lifeblood of American citizens, *on American soil*. Problem is, *we don't know* what the hell their ideology is. Likewise, we know their product is blood, but we don't know who their buyer is, or *why in the hell anyone wants to buy it*. So, we know how to crush theocratic terrorists, and we know how to crush capitalistic cartels, *but both combined into one*, that's something new, Captain Rickert. So that symbol of theirs, *whatever it really means*, heralds something very, *very fucking dangerous* that we do *not fucking understand*."

Clark saw DuBroux straighten his back. Nowell and Reichman began to nod. None of these three men knew who Thorn was or what agency he worked for, but they knew significant authority had been bestowed upon him by the government of the United States. This authority, while mysterious, was made clear and undeniable by Benson, Jacobson, and Bishop's apparent deference toward him. He'd been playing the role of a quiet, strange man on the fringes of the group, but he was becoming a leader before their eyes as the zeal and confidence of his words increased.

"I don't know what they want or why they want it, but they're here, Captain. Here in our own goddamned yard, doing unspeakable shit to our own goddamned people, so *what I do know* is that they need to be crushed. Annihilated. *Smothered in their fucking crib*. You wanna help us do that? *Please fucking do*. You only wanna help if we take time out of our insanely busy schedule to bring you up to speed on the latest nuanced, wildly complicated intelligence? Then *you can fuck right off*. We'll do it without you, and we can certainly find another state law enforcement contingent to provide us requisite constitutional authority and cover. Your call, Captain. You decide whether you're here to hunt and destroy monsters, or whether you want to go back to a career of ticketing unlicensed hunters and fishermen occasionally punctuated by a gunfight with some tweaker asshole. There's no room or fucking time for fence-sitting state-level investigators in a task force like this. *Your call*, but it's one you need to make *before that sun fucking rises.*"

Thorn had been pointing his stubby finger up into Clark's face by the end, which he let drop as he spun on his heel and stormed out of the large tent. This time, no one interrupted his departure. The small man's objective reasonableness was compelling on its own, but the unexpected fire and electricity in his character left them floored.

All five others looked at Clark now. He could feel how the infectious zeal in Thorn's words steeled their nerves, recharged their conviction and focus, and completely depleted their patience for his concerns. He saw in their postures and set of their jaws that Thorn's invective was all the fuel and motivation necessary for them to maintain a relentless grind against this mysterious blood-harvesting cult, this enemy of the United States. *They've done more on less*, Clark assumed.

He couldn't stop himself from softly chuckling as he realized they'd all just witnessed someone working at the level of a real master. A truly rare thing to behold. Thorn had baited Clark into the exchange as Clark had baited Reichman. Unlike Clark's attempt, however, Thorn had sprung his trap and immediately turned the entire room against him. All Clark had achieved was coaxing Nowell and DuBroux into casting a few *he's got a good point* glances at Bishop and Jacobson, surprising them all with familiarity with French and German, and provoking an air force commando into violence.

In effect, Clark had achieved nothing, and would've spent the last half hour more productively sitting alone in his truck. Thorn, on the other hand, had watched the exchange from the shadows, identified which game Clark was playing, then mercilessly beaten him at it. Spanked him like a child.

Clark had taken his opening shot in this exchange by ridiculing Thorn's clumsy attempt to sidestep questions he didn't want to answer. Not only did the guy respond by openly sidestepping Clark's question *again*, but his closing salvo had viciously ridiculed Clark for *even asking the ques-*

tion at all. As a cherry on top, he threw in an impassioned sermon aimed directly at the value systems, priorities, and spirits of everyone else in this tent. Everyone except for Clark.

He took in a deep breath. Bone-deep fatigue filled him. He rubbed his eyes and turned to look into the faces of the others as he spoke.

"Well, I apologize. I suppose I thoroughly derailed things."

Charlotte crossed her arms as she stepped toward Clark, looked at his boots for a moment, appeared to shake some uninvited thought from her mind, and then spoke.

"We're good, Captain. I've been running teams of emotionally fragile *tough guys* for a long time now. I'm no stranger to all the ass-sniffing, neurotic machismo bullshit, daddy issues, and other baggage you meatheads bring along."

The exhausted, slap-happy men eagerly laughed at Bishop's comment, Clark included, but her icy expression did not change as she went on.

"I feel comfortable concluding that Mr. Jacobson's suspicion was misplaced. His hope was that you, Mr. Rickert, might have some insight we've failed to consider that might prove fruitful, illuminating, or otherwise beneficial to this operation. However, I now feel confident no such insight exists. I'm glad we discussed it, though, as embarrassing and directionless as that exchange may have been. If we hadn't, we might've continued thinking you had some uniquely astute investigative aptitude, something that exceeds what, I must admit, is your *true knack for spotting footprints in sand*. As it is, it would seem that you're actually the one most severely frustrated by foggy understanding and informational blind spots. *That*, at least, boosts my own confidence a bit. *Good night, gentlemen.*"

Bishop collected her things and walked through the group toward the end of her comment, so that her *good night* was issued over her shoulder. If Thorn's rhetorical devastation of Clark had been a jab, she'd just given him the cross. Everyone felt the bite of her words. Jacobson stared at Bishop's back for a long moment, then turned and spoke to the others. Jacobson, appreciating his deputy chief more in this moment than he had in a long time, cut the silence.

"I'd hope we're all on the same page now, gentlemen?"

He stared directly at Clark, who did not fail to spot the subtle notes of pity and apology in the faces of the others. He just nodded.

All four men made the effort of saying good night to him, and even a small trace of embarrassment or guilt for having just seen Thorn and

Bishop verbally sodomize the poor guy. However, they forgot about it soon after Clark peeled away from the group. It was comforting to knock someone off a pedestal he had no business occupying.

Clark's mind reeled from his failure. This meant, he knew, the only path left to access the information he needed was through action. Something big and wildly sufficient to mandate his inclusion within the inner circle.

He still clung to the possibility of relaxing into the warmth and comfort of a real mental breakdown, disproving the compelling promise within his visions that the world was facing something immeasurably catastrophic he alone could prevent.

He wasn't at all sure about what that *wild act* would be, but felt confident he'd know it when he saw it.

CHAPTER 29

CLARK STOOD SIPPING from a thermos of coffee in the back of the large command tent. The jets of UH-60s made the ground shake.

He felt a jittery anxiety boiling up from his gut, one that he'd come to recognize over the last weeks as the vanguard of his goddamned *visions*. He could feel he was getting used to them in a way, knowing they came and went in the span of a single blink, no matter how long they *felt*. He had the presence of mind to set the thermos of coffee on the ground, unsure whether he'd drop it or not while in the grips of the experience, then leaned back in his chair.

As always, the vision buried every other thought like an avalanche of wet snow, hijacking all of his senses.

He saw him. The leader. The *barefooted man*. He saw his thick head of black hair, his lean musculature visible under his suede button-down and black jeans. He watched him from behind, his ostrich-skin roper boots clicking as he walked lazily down a familiar-looking street, arms spread wide, face to the evening sky. A reel of time-jumbled moments began turning through Clark's mind—all seeming to be from the perspective of something always shadowing the barefooted man, taking care not to be seen.

He saw him from the back of an old chapel, standing up on the pulpit, laughing warmly at the pews filled with his shuddering, moaning followers staring at him through tears of euphoric joy. He saw him bend over to smell geraniums planted in an old mining cart. Clark saw him from the back of the church again, still up on the pulpit but his back to the pews now, staring down at the church's old pastor, whose throat was torn away, exposing a mess of neck gristle and blood-pinkened vertebrae from chest to chin. He saw him now from inside a small, dark house, through the propped-open screen door to where he sat on the porch in an old rocking chair. He rocked and blew softly into a child's windmill toy, then waved it at a passing delivery truck.

He saw him in the church again, much closer now, from somewhere among the cheering, fevered cultists who formed a ring around their leader. He had the pastor's white-and-gold stole draped over his neck; blood covered the lower half of his smiling face, stomping on the dead pastor's knees, splintering bone and jellying tendons. Clark knew he did this to simplify folding and stuffing the body into the chest where he'd found the pastor's vestments. He saw him on the street again, staring up at a massive Douglas fir tree, gently patting its enormous trunk then sipping blood from a crystal flask.

The span of a blink had elapsed, Clark's eyes began to open, and the vision ended as they always seemed to—in a blast of light and noise as his senses and thoughts returned.

He felt a surprising jolt of excitement, as though he'd just caught someone in a lie, but it was outweighed by titanic disgust.

CHAPTER
30

THIS ADVERSARY IS weak. *The organization at large is on the cusp of wholesale collapse. It's filled with nitwits whose fanaticism is rivaled only by their laughable stupidity. The Red Castle organization at large is nothing more than a vulnerable house of cards. Even more, the task force has been doling outlandishly one-sided ass-kickings upon them, one after another. No one, no organization, could withstand much more of this.*

Disparagement of the cult and a congratulatory review of the task force's conduct thus far had been the most distinct, conspicuous takeaways from this morning's mission briefing. Clark had spent the entire drive thus far retracing the course of the briefing in his mind, which would've been easier had he paid better attention.

Clark had been forced to testify at many criminal trials of those he'd arrested over the years, but he'd never really understood why. He knew why a prosecutor or defense counsel *thought* his direct or cross-examination testimony might help their case; he knew that's why he'd gotten the subpoena. Still, Clark never had, nor ever would say anything in court that wasn't already in the body of evidence, case files, reports, and sworn affidavits he'd created, organized, and already given to the prosecution and defense. He'd built a case and caught the poacher, and had never done so without solid, admissible records. He'd done his part. The trial was someone else's problem now. Someone else's ball to drop. If they got convicted, *cool*. If they got off but never went back to poaching, *great*. If they got off and did go back to poaching, *whatever*. He'd catch them again. That's how shit goes.

Sitting in the briefing early that morning, Clark felt exactly as he always had while at the witness stand. Once again, Clark's superiors had deemed it necessary that he sit quietly in a particular place at a particular time, so he did. However, he'd spent all those hours sitting around instead of being out in the field, tracking and hunting poachers. As such, there was no one alive who could convince Clark Rickert that those criminal trials or these task force briefings had been the best use of his time.

Unlike anyone else in this eight-vehicle convoy, Clark didn't need more than muscle memory plus an occasional glance outside to know precisely where he was.

Some automated instinct, one cooked into him over two decades of enforcing Montana's fishing and hunting laws, suggested he quickly eyeball the river he knew was coming up. When the chaos of spring snowmelt in Montana's rivers began to ebb in early summer—when the tumult of mud-hued white water calmed into a harmonious, glacial flow—fishing season truly began. This is when wealthy, Patagonia-clad fly anglers began flocking to Montana from all around the world. They came to these rivers and streams in droves to pursue the big, wild, beautiful trout Montana was famous for. Most would spook hundreds for every one they actually brought to hand. They came to escape boring jobs, drink, fish, and, with truly shocking regularity, violate angling regulations.

Without thinking of any of that, Clark adjusted the rifle resting between his left leg and the car door, then looked through the rear driver's-side window of the up-armored Suburban. His subconscious navigation system knew they'd just passed through Libby, Montana, so he knew they were about to cross the Kootenai River. He glanced down at the water through the dark tint of the thick ballistic glass.

He liked this river. More than others. It had always felt wild and feral to him. A river mad at the world. As if anger, instead of gravity, motivated it to hack canyons and carve valleys into the landscape.

He went back to scrutinizing each moment of the morning briefing, hoping to flag anything of utility. Unlike the mountain men who ran the first traplines for beaver up this same valley two hundred years earlier, Clark found nothing of any real value.

The tone of the tires' hum changed when the convoy drove off the bridge, which then turned off MT 37 onto Pipe Creek Road. They'd stay on this one as it wound a thirty-two-mile course through mountainous national forest before hitting Yaak, Montana.

Clark had tuned out the banter of the three men in the vehicle with him, though he'd not failed to notice how casual and upbeat they sounded. This positive tone was a notable deviation from the fatigued, disturbed air that had settled among the task force over the last week. Clark assumed it had to do with this morning's briefing, and was genuinely impressed by it. The rhetorical tactic Thorn had used a few nights earlier to solidify the resolve of the leadership they in turn had used this morning to steel the nerves of the others.

During the first half of the briefing, the details of the actual mission of the day had been covered in exacting detail. But an equal amount of time had been spent ridiculing the Red Castle organization and celebrating the task force's violent cloudburst of victories against the cult's strongholds, one after another.

The latter was undeniable as well. Under every metric he could imagine to assess a combat operation, the task force had performed brilliantly. It had been nothing but flawless tactical precision, a showcase of the stunning speed and violence that sets America's Tier-1 combat operators apart within global military history. The task force had also been maintaining a truly relentless operational tempo, burning and turning through kinetic operations that consistently involved abnormally high levels of shooting, killing, and exposure to heinous shit.

The leadership praised the fire-baptized strength and unstoppable will of everyone there. Each of them also made it a point to belittle their adversary with phrases like *asymmetric force profile* and *static, localized, and marginal threat* to describe the weakness of the cult.

This theme, and the tone in which it was delivered, felt contrived to Clark. He'd looked around the room watching for subtle hints in faces and bodies suggesting others found it as canned and patronizing as he did. To his surprise, he saw the opposite. It seemed to be working to lift their collective energy and spirit. Maybe, when well-timed, this kind of pump-up routine is precisely what warriors heading into violence need to hear from their leaders.

That was easy to accept for Clark. He'd found one overarching truth over the last few days, and saw its validity as beyond question; whatever methods were employed by the leaders and operators among this task force, they fucking worked. Terrifyingly well.

In two weeks, Clark had watched it happen four times, start to finish, and each was more stunning than the last. The task force was given a location they'd never seen or heard of—one guarded by a band of armed, deranged cultists with zero apprehension about trying to kill them—and within an hour they'd worked out a plan of how to absolutely dominate every inch of the operational area. Several different plans, in fact, and each with its own branch of operational contingencies. Even more unbelievable was how, only hours after contriving them, these plans were carried out on the ground with shocking speed, ferocious violence, breathtaking precision, and, always, comprehensive mission success.

Consequently, Clark willingly accepted this shit-talking, chest-beating routine as one more element in their professional calculus he just didn't understand. Another broadband frequency flowing between the conductors and the band in this symphony of precise violence, one he couldn't tune in to.

The missing person reports had dropped. So, while there were hundreds of victims still suffering or already dead, the cult seemed to have ceased its kidnapping spree. On top of that, the task force had maintained an almost daily binge of destruction, crushing their adversary in every instance of contact, without suffering any material losses at all.

Clark stared into the impenetrable stem-locked forest rushing by on the west side of the road as all this, once again, passed through his mind. He understood why the successes thus far were worthy of praise, at least under military standards. He understood why the cultists' defense of four separate rural strongholds had been hopeless, pathetic, and worthy of ridicule. He even understood why the leadership would harp on these things to improve morale during this morning's briefing of the current operation. He would concede it all.

Even so, no one knew what this enemy was really up to or trying to achieve, and he was astounded anyone was capable of harboring optimism without that knowledge. It pulsed in Clark's mind, and it got worse the farther up this valley the convoy went, closing in on the target location of their fifth raid and assault.

Jacobson, Bishop, and Benson had laid out the plan that morning. Around three dozen assaulters broken into four ground teams would be using vehicles, in the open, on public roads, to approach this day's target location. This cult stronghold was located on a rural, forested property north of the Yaak River, in the wild, remote sliver of northwestern Montana wedged between Idaho and Canada.

Three additional ground teams—who had stalked into staging and overwatch positions in steep, forested terrain north of the target property— would exploit the cult's response to the convoy. Hours earlier, the human eyes of those on these ground teams in position confirmed what the drones already had; this was, indeed, another cult stronghold. With the positive ID on the target, the convoy would now serve its purpose as a contact patrol along the way, intentionally drawing fire and resistance from any cultists defending their mountain property or any others along the route of approach. At the same time, the three teams already in position would crash in from the other side. Everyone in the vehicles knew they'd be initiating the upcoming gunfight, a fight none doubted these maniacal cultists would enthusiastically commit their bodies and souls to.

Driving headfirst into a real scrap where bad guys were effectively guaranteed to not only shoot, but shoot first, brought a calm excitement to men like the ones who filled these eight vehicles. So many instances of combat followed hours or days of uncertainty and ratcheting tension. The magnificent release of stress and anxiety when the rules of engagement were finally satisfied, the glorious moment a gunfight finally just fucking started, always seemed to follow an insufferable span of time and grueling evolution of complex events. Something about the promise of the cultists' immediate initiation of violence provided a clarity of mind. It was just so neat and tidy when everyone accepted the old rules of violence. This was just regular gameplay, and they were all grateful for it.

Everyone but Clark. He'd never shied away from violence and was entirely unconcerned by his own growing fondness for the eradication of these particular monsters. On several occasions over the years, he'd even felt a pang of relief and gratitude as evil men went for a gun they'd try to kill him with—society's formal charter that one may, *now*, kill another. Even so, he just wasn't like these men. The kind of life experience that carves heuristics into the brain, automating an association between a deadly fight and their own dopamine, clarity, and focus, was something he did not have.

Clark also thought that this convoy tactic—sent right up the middle, in the open, in order to corroborate the existence of lookouts and spotters—contradicted the central message from the briefing, which had been how stupid these cultists were. If the cult's response to the convoy did betray their having lookouts along the access route, then these assholes were not, in fact, as vulnerable and unsophisticated as had been suggested.

"Looking pretty deep in thought back there, game warden."

The operator driving this Suburban, Gavin Moorhouse, glanced quickly up at Clark through the rearview mirror, grinning as he spoke.

"This little mountain hamlet we're about to pass through, *Ward*, you said you'd been here before. I know we don't have any turns, but is there anywhere along our route where two or more people would usually be hanging out?"

Clark looked into the rearview mirror at Gavin, staring at the road through wraparound Oakley sunglasses. He could see a gnarled scar that began on the man's right cheek, disappeared behind the shades, then bisected his eyebrow as it snaked its way into his scalp. A little keepsake, Clark assumed, from the guy's tenure with the Regimental Reconnaissance Company of the 75th Rangers, his former unit that he'd mentioned over dinner in the mess tent the night before, yet another elite war band Clark had never heard of.

"No lights, no stop signs. Might be a crosswalk or yield sign in front of the old general store, which'll be on our right—can't remember, though. There's a post office a street to the west of Main Street, and a little fire station a hundred meters or so past the end of town, so the general store's the only real establishment we'll pass. Usually a few locals hangin' out there on the porch, maybe a few tourists this time of year."

Neither Gavin nor either of the two other men in the vehicle gave any indication of having heard what Clark said. They just scanned the wild country around them in the same way these guys seemed to always take in the world: assessing every detail with a hawkish, unyielding scrutiny while appearing entirely relaxed.

Zach Moritz, the leader of the team Clark was attached to for this mission, sat in the front passenger seat. The operator sitting behind Moritz to Clark's right, a former SEAL everyone called *Mako*, was a tall, muscular guy with a mess of sandy hair and one of the only clean-shaven Ground Branch operators. He had perpetual laughing eyes, a kind of face that always seemed on the verge of smiling.

"You mentioned earlier the town is kinda funky, right? People there just fuckin' weird or what?"

Clark had made a passing reference to the town being a bit strange, and its people a bit peculiar. It wasn't *that* unique, however. Throughout the Rockies from New Mexico to Canada, the Sierras, the Cascades, the Badlands, dozens of old mining towns like it can be found. Towns that sprouted up like weeds in the 1860s. They'd usually appear along a creek, which those first settlers would inevitably name after something terribly mundane within view, like *horse* or *elk* or *trout* or *pine*. As often, they'd name the creek after a native who'd once called the area home but was now, *at best*, unwelcome there. Entire towns grew like a fungus within months—saloons, brothels, assay offices, jails, tack and supply shops, all cobbled together with live-edge logs, canvas, and mud. The alpine aroma replaced by a blend of shit and cooking smoke. Towns where thousands of roughnecked prospectors had flocked to cram in together during the nation's collective hunt for gold. By 1900, when veins had long pinched out, most of these boomtowns' populations had dropped to less than twenty percent of what they'd been at the peak of the gold rush. Today, most are nothing more than a curious name on a map along a county road or in some stretch of national forest. Some still exist.

Of those few that do maintain municipal status, a rare few that ended up being convenient railroad stops are big towns most Americans would recognize by name, but most are just one-store villages that a couple dozen to a couple hundred folks still call home. Ward was one such town. In 1867, it had a population of over 2,500 people. Today, only around 120 year-round residents comprised the little mountain town. Benson had asked Clark if he'd ever been through it during the briefing, then to describe it. He'd explained how the town was at the base of the valley, how the houses rose up on steep slopes to both sides and ahead as one passed through it, how the speed limit dropped down to fifteen for the five hundred meters where the state highway turned into its Main Street. He called it a strange town with peculiar folks, but had done so mostly because he just assumed these kinds of people would be unfamiliar with such places.

"I guess they're a little offbeat. Nothin' *that* weird. It's grizzly country, so most people walk around armed, and compared to most cities I guess it's got a statistically high density of little indoor weed grows or meth kitchens. You'll also see right away that there's some silent town ordinance requiring a broken-down car in front of every house. Its population of sovereign-citizen types is likely higher than most places, but really nothin' all that out of the ordinary for country like this."

The three men acknowledged Clark with a nod or a quiet "Check." In minutes, the lead vehicle passed the Reduce Speed Ahead sign, and half a minute later it passed the bullet-riddled sign for Ward, Montana.

Clark heard faint chatter coming from the radio speakers in the ear protection mounted to the helmet in his lap, so he put it on to listen. The other three hadn't removed or even unbuckled their helmets since they'd loaded into the helicopters that morning, whereas Clark had removed his the second he'd gotten off the chopper at the national forest annex where these up-armored Suburbans had been staged. The window tints effectively blacked out the interiors, but he'd still feel ridiculous wearing one while driving through the towns and country he'd spent his entire life in without one.

Team leaders and 2ICs in each vehicle were flagging the locations of people they saw walking or loitering within view of the rather steep Main Street they drove up through the center of the little town. Someone in the lead vehicle noted two MAMs sitting on the steps of the old white Lutheran church on the hill up ahead on the left side of the street. He'd never heard anyone refer to Montanans as *military-aged males* until that moment. Someone in the vehicle ahead of Clark's noted several more MAMs and an older lady on the porch of the general store up ahead on the right.

The general store. Geraniums planted in mining carts. The small chapel on the hill.

The realization that his vision from earlier that morning had been set right here hit Clark like a wrecking ball. His eyes went wide as he looked frantically around at all the landmarks.

Maybe it was the coiled, poised tension these guys always maintained, maybe it was the military lingo, maybe it was seeing Mako and Moritz casually tighten grips on the carbines resting on their laps or next to their legs, but Clark's heart thundered.

He had a sudden urge to clamp down on his radio's PTT button and scream into the mic boom mounted to his helmet. He needed to tell everyone to *fucking drive*, to *get the hell out of here*. He actually began reaching up toward the PTT button clipped to his plate carrier. A pathetic noise escaped his mouth as he tried to swallow and take a breath to calm himself down, loud enough for Mako to hear and look over at him.

"Whassup, Warden?"

Clark's throat felt swollen by panic. Luckily, there was no need to respond. Urgent shouting came through the radio, prompting all three operators in the SUV to lean forward, scanning for threats. Clark followed suit, despite not hearing what was specifically being shouted over the radios.

Then he saw it. A monstrous old-growth Douglas fir tree up Main Street beyond the general store. It had slowly begun to fall.

Since sprouting from the earth 317 years earlier, it had grown over 160 feet tall, its trunk over 15 feet around. It had survived gale-force winds, heavy spring blizzards, lightning strikes, and sweltering droughts, and bore their scars still. It had been spared by the savage caprice of wildfires, and by the affection of a young girl named Sonya, daughter of the first homesteader here. Sonya was married under the tree she'd convinced her father to let live, as were both her sons, who grew old on that land as their mother had. They sold off parcels as the town grew around them, but never the tract with that tree. Over the years, twelve other weddings had been held, eight babies had been born, and four men had been murdered within its shadow's reach. The giant sentinel continued to grow as the mining town grew around it, and as that town began to wither and die, it just kept on growing.

Until today, and in this final moment of the titan's life, *it roared*.

Hundreds of tons of wood shrieked and groaned as tension built. Deep, hollow cracks echoed across the valley as the base of its trunk began to rip and buckle, turning into a screaming peal of musketry when it began to splinter.

The lead vehicle in the convoy sped up to escape being crushed, disappearing beyond the jumping, tangled mass of dark green limbs and boughs as the tree crashed into the road and straight through the asphalt. The second vehicle—directly in front of Clark's—slammed on its brakes. The trunk of the tree fell directly onto the roof of a house on the west side of Main Street, and the old carriage house–turned-garage along the alley behind Main. Both structures appeared to simply vanish. An explosion of dust and splinters was visible for a moment, but quickly smothered by the mass of tree limbs.

The shouts coming from the guys in the car with him and over the radio dulled to murmurs in Clark's mind. The group of four or five people on the elevated patio in front of the general store had his complete attention. None of them turned toward the earsplitting sound of the falling tree, or the screeching rubber of the SUVs, or even the explosion of noise as the tree crashed into the road and crushed an entire home. They just stared into the row of vehicles like mannequins.

A new noise, behind him, snapped through Clark's paralytic state of confusion and dread. It was an explosion.

All four guys in the car whipped around to look out the back window to find they were staring directly into the sunroof of the last Suburban in the convoy, a bloom of smoke and dust behind it. An IED had been detonated between its rear axle and bumper, rocking the back of the vehicle up into the sky. They watched, numb, as the SUV's momentum stalled and it sat there suspended, vertically, grille to the road. After a moment, it crashed back down onto all four wheels, a few ribbons of burning rubber all that remained of the tires.

The next noise was quite clear, as well. It was a single word. Moritz was turned, looking into the rear of the vehicle, rage and focus balanced in his eyes. He screamed it at them.

"Ambush!"

CHAPTER 31

IT SOUNDED LIKE the inside of an industrial blender filled with nails and marbles. All the windows on the right side of the Suburban seemed to go white at the same time. For a split second, Clark thought someone was throwing paint on the car, then his mind, eyes, and ears caught up with one another. Dozens of bullets were shearing into the bulletproof glass and armored paneling. Each bullet sent a spiderweb of white cracks out from its point of impact.

"Dismount. Off the X. Get off the fucking X."

Like some cognitive relay terminal had gone offline, Clark registered the words but not their meaning.

Five bullets stitched a line up the front windshield. If it were made of anything less than Level 8 bulletproof glass, the rounds would have zippered open Gavin's torso.

By the time Clark's mind clocked the mass surging through the periphery on his right, Mako had already crashed into him. The large man reached around Clark and yanked on the door handle as soon as they connected. Both men, tangled together, fell from the rear of the SUV onto the ground.

The wind blasted from Clark's lungs as they crashed into the cracked asphalt of Main Street. It felt like all 280 pounds of the Ground Branch operator and his combat load-out crunched directly into his solar plexus. Clark hadn't buckled his helmet, but it stayed on just long enough to protect the back of his skull as it smacked into the road. It shot off his head upon impact and stars burst into his vision.

Something about having the air knocked out of him then getting rocked in the head anchored Clark. He'd felt this sensation before. Quite a few times. It was something familiar, a handhold to grasp amid chaos.

When he felt Mako scramble off him, he rolled onto all fours, coughing and hacking, trying to blink vision back into his eyes.

The roaring, piercing din of battle smashed into his ears all at once like an aux cable getting yanked out of an old speaker. An unbroken, furious curtain of sound he could feel in his throat and the roots of his molars. Some noises punched through it, crisp and distinct. Guns blazed all around him. Men were screaming. Bullets punched and tore into metal, glass, wood, and stone. A lattice of hot lead shredding the sound barrier fell over everything. The air itself boiled with snaps and whip cracks.

Clark lifted his head and found Gavin only a few feet to his left. He was crouched low, shooting a consistent pattern of single shots with his suppressed carbine to the west, left of the convoy. Zach Moritz was a few feet ahead, crouched behind the front of their SUV, leaning out to fire quick bursts across Main Street. Bullets ripped into the tire he knelt beside, scouring him with compressed air, dust, gravel, and flecks of rubber. He didn't seem to notice, appearing alarmingly calm as he pressed the PTT button, spoke into his helmet's mic, then changed his magazine. Operators ahead and behind Clark continued shouting over the noise.

"Contact front. Contact right. Contact rear of convoy. Contact left, rear left. Contact general store, upper windows."

Operators shouted out locations of cultists over one another. Clark briefly wondered what the tactical jargon was for *we're fucking surrounded*.

Mako sailed in from Clark's periphery, shooting as he moved. Hot brass spun from his carbine, clinking and skittering around Clark, who planted a palm on one. The hornet sting burn helped him focus. He pushed himself up, turning toward the Suburban, and felt relieved to find his rifle on the ground just below the open door. Mako took controlled shots over the roof of the SUV toward the general store across Main, and used his left hand to slap Clark's shoulder, screaming at him to "get up" and "get ready to move." Clark did not rise, so Mako knelt to change his magazine then slap the game warden, who he assumed was in a state of paralyzed shock. He screamed Clark's name as he turned a snarling face toward him, but whatever else he was going to say died behind his lips.

Mako found Clark up on one knee, brass-checking the rifle he had slung over his shoulder, then looking up at the former SEAL. After a second of eye contact, Mako cracked a huge, exhilarated smile like a boy in a firework store. Clark leaned away from the large operator, looking as though he'd just seen a dog start talking. Mako's genuine smile was something impossibly alien to Clark amid this fray of fire and chaos.

This dude's actually enjoying himself, Clark thought. *It's just another day in the office for these crazy assholes.*

Mako, like all the Ground Branch guys, was unnaturally collected in this kind of environment, but that's not why he smiled now. Since Mako was a boy, every time he'd made first contact with any new thing that felt bone-chilling and fatal, smiling was his organic reaction. He'd smiled in his mother's arms as his family watched a wildfire burn his home, then his entire cul-de-sac, to the ground. He'd smiled while spearfishing as he locked eyes with a tiger shark for the first time. He'd smiled at the first older, bigger man who wanted to fight him for no real reason. He'd smiled the first time an RPG screamed by his head. First encounters with things like that—like whatever was roiling within this game warden's irises—they just made him smile. He leaned forward and shouted over the raging gunfire into the space between Clark's eye and ear.

"Time to kick some tires and start some fires, bro—*be ready to move.*"

He slapped Clark's back then stood into a crouch, firing as soon as his rifle's muzzle cleared the vehicle. Moritz wheeled from the front of the SUV and the pair fell into wraithlike movements toward the front yard to their west. As Clark got onto his feet, he got his first decent view down Main Street and forgot all about following Mako.

Twenty-two seconds had passed since the old tree had crashed across the road.

A cloud of dust, gravel, glass, and metal fragments showered from and around each vehicle, all being shredded by a squall of rifle bullets, slugs, and 00 buckshot. The panels and windows of the Suburbans had met the extreme threshold of their ballistic armor ratings and were starting to crumple, shatter, and implode.

An automatic light machine gun fired down Main Street from inside the double doors of the church on the small rise up ahead. It spat arcs of 7.62mm bullets and tracers into the line of stopped vehicles. The searing, blood-orange flares of the tracers made the weapon's maelstrom of bullets look like a solid jet of molten steel. Someone shouted "covering" and an eruption of suppressed gunfire began behind him, then he flinched as two operators went sprinting by him toward the fallen tree and their isolated teammates beyond.

When they passed between Clark's vehicle and the next, a burst of rifle fire from the other side of the street stitched up one of the operator's sides. The first shot shattered his knee, and the next shots slammed into his ribs, armpit, and shoulder.

Before he'd even finished his collapse, an eruption of return fire from what sounded like hundreds of guns tore across Main Street into the front of the general store. Four cultists had burst from the front doors onto the general store's elevated patio, all shooting wildly down into the road. They surged right into the covering fire being laid down to protect the two operators' maneuver toward the front of the convoy, thoughtlessly exchanging their lives for a chance to cut one operator down. As soon as Clark turned and saw them, they were being torn apart by an enfilade of accurate shots.

The two in front went limp and fell straight down in bloody heaps. One fell back into a seated position against the old storefront. His shirt, shoulders, arms, and head whipped and twitched as bullets ripped into him, blood and tissue jetting and spurting onto the whitewashed barn wood. The fourth cultist, already dead but still moving forward, pitched over the low railing of the elevated patio. His face was the first point of impact with the road below, crunching his lifeless body into a sickening scorpion pose as his legs bent and his boot soles smacked into the back of his head.

Guys from other assault teams sprinted up to drag their motionless teammate toward the houses on the west side of Main Street, away from the bullet magnet Suburbans and the buildings on the east side, where it seemed most of the cultists were firing from. Clark watched a bullet zip through one of these men's right calf and out the front of his pant leg. It must have missed the bone, as the man said nothing, made no sound, just gritted his teeth and kept dragging his buddy to safety.

Twenty-nine seconds had passed since the old tree had crashed across the road.

Clark glanced behind him, down the row of vehicles, and saw the two dozen other operators. One was limp, being dragged by another into the area between two houses on the west side of Main. Two others followed close behind, one hopping along on one foot while the other acted as his crutch. All the rest were fighting. They crouched and moved as they took shots, bounding between their destroyed SUVs and any cover they could find among front yards and driveways.

Bullets shattered pots and window baskets filled with flowers, ferns, and hostas. Envelopes blasted into the air from a mailbox ruptured by a shotgun slug. Faded white picket fences jumped and splintered. Rocking chairs and glider benches on front porches rocked casually back and forth after rounds thumped into them. A cloud of seeds burst from an exploding bird feeder. A bullet shattered a brittle wooden flagpole mounted on a front porch, then a weather-beaten Gadsden flag fluttered down to a front yard.

Clark was momentarily stunned as he watched, in the exact same instant, all the operators within view fall into a collective, orchestrated movement. They moved like a flock of starlings. Hips and bodies turned, and first steps were taken toward the west, away from the vehicles. Clark then felt like an idiot, realizing everyone on the task force was in contact with one another via the radio comms in their helmet-mounted ear protection.

Everyone except for Clark, the outsider, ignorant to all communications, just standing there gawking like an idiot while suffering what would likely be permanent hearing damage. He glanced down to where his helmet had popped off his head, desperate to find it now. In the second that followed, several voices screaming the word *displace* punched through the roar of battle, and a hand grabbed him by the shoulder strap of his plate carrier and ripped him away from the vehicle.

Then he was running, trying to keep up with Moritz, Mako, and several others ahead of them. They weaved like a pack of wolves among Adirondack chairs, grills, clothes lines, and tarp-covered snowmobiles strewn between two old homes.

Bullets cracked into the structures on both sides of him. They tore away trim and faucets and roof shingles, thumped through walls, shattered single-pane windows, and twanged like gongs on wood-burning stoves.

When he reached the backyards and the dirt alley behind the houses on the west side of Main, Clark saw dozens of operators streaming into the area, falling into positions behind cover, and shooting in different directions. Some helped others hop and limp along; some carried the large duffel bags of weapons, ammunition, breaching explosives, and other equipment they'd loaded into each vehicle that morning. Clark looked up the alley to the north just as four cultists came sprinting down it, all of whom were cut down by accurate shots as soon as they appeared. Clark slid into a rusted old snowplow beside Moritz, who was shooting over it to the north.

His mind calmed enough to begin putting names to faces of those around him. Nowell was there, a few meters away screaming into his radio and the face of a Tactical Air Control operator from the 24th STS crouched next to him and screaming into his own radio. He saw guys packing gauze into lacerations and securing tourniquets to their own or their teammates' legs and arms.

One operator Clark didn't know by name was giving chest compressions to one he did: Mike, who appeared well beyond death. One of the actual medics was looking at the back of an operator named Denton who didn't appear to have a scratch on him but lay on his side facing Clark, knees to his chest, coughing and gasping. He looked for someone to help, but everyone wounded had at least one other performing first aid on them. All these guys had live tissue training and years of advanced schooling in combat medicine. Literally everyone present, except for Clark, was an overqualified battlefield medic.

Fifty-one seconds had passed since the old tree had crashed across the road.

A loud burst of unsuppressed gunfire, much closer than any of the rest, erupted behind Clark. He pushed himself away from the snowplow, shouldering his rifle as he spun toward the threat.

A cluster of five cultists—two men and three women, all appearing to be in their twenties—surged forward along the same route Clark had taken only seconds earlier: the junk-strewn causeway of dead grass and hard-packed dirt between the two houses behind him. Three of them were barefooted. Two of them, a man and a woman, were completely naked from the waist up. All of them shrieked as they came, mouths as wide as they could open. The one in front stumbled. The next didn't even glance down as he stepped on her back and launched over her. They seemed to be in a race to be the first to touch the closest operator. They held cheap AR-15s and AK variants at their hips or awkwardly out in front of them, shooting wildly as they heaved forward, directly toward Clark.

He welcomed the familiar distortion of time that always fell into place when he needed to defend himself, the sense that everything on earth was immediately bogged down into slow motion—everything except for him.

He aimed his rifle at the guy leading the group. As soon as his optic's circle-dot reticle settled onto the man's chest, Clark took a single shot. The 5.56mm bullet splintered the shrieking guy's sternum, tore through his right atrium, then shattered his D4 vertebrae on its way out. Like a puppet getting its strings cut, all emotion left the cultist's youthful face as he slammed onto the hard, dusty ground.

But Clark didn't see any of that.

As the guy went limp, he'd already adjusted his illuminated reticle to a spot right between the exposed breasts of the next sprinting, screaming, drooling cultist in the group. She dropped her gun and fell when Clark's bullet tore through her heart, momentum carrying her body so that she slid forward on her face almost three meters, like a lifeless baseball player stealing second base. Before she'd come to rest, Clark squeezed off a shot at the next cultist, who'd just hurdled over her body with form any high school track coach would commend. This third bullet struck the screaming guy just below his right nostril, whipping his head back with neck-breaking force. A smog of his hair and misted blood hung aloft in the warm sunlight that obscured the remaining two cultists, but Clark could see their outlines as they sprinted into it. He put a shot directly in the Adam's apple. Both collapsed upon the bodies of the first three.

He'd taken five shots in just over three seconds.

He took his eye from his optic, scanning for threats in the area beyond the five bodies. He couldn't see the general store or other houses on the far side of Main Street but heard the roar of dozens of guns still being fired from there. He noticed Mako off to his right, crouched behind a rusted bathtub, staring back at him. He was grinning that smile again, eyes wide with boyish wonder, pumping a thumbs-up in Clark's direction as he shouted in his goofy surfer dialect.

"*Fuckin' right on, game warden. That was some eagle-eyed, surgical shit right there.*"

Clark didn't respond. He turned back to the snowplow and noticed another operator a few meters behind Mako staring at him with narrow eyes, grinning and nodding his head. Clark knew this one; they'd chatted a few times over the last few days. Chris Burton was his name. Former Ranger and Green Beret. He'd grown up in Maine. Clark did not acknowledge Burton, either, just scooted back to the snowplow and team leader Zach Moritz, who still knelt behind it. He glanced at Moritz as he fell in beside him and found the man staring into his face. He had an expression of bland, curious appraisal, as though just seeing Clark for the first time and wondering where on earth he'd come from. Nowell's voice cut through the gunfire.

"Rosco, Dean, get an XM250 and 40-mike-mikes on that church until that LMG is *shut the fuck down.*"

Clark was still processing what Nowell had ordered when he heard and felt in his gut a succession of deep *thwunk*s. He looked north up the alley where two operators had run ahead, one shooting what looked like a riot control gun with large, revolving cylinders. Explosions cracked to the north several seconds after each shot. The other operator had dropped the bipod of a light machine gun onto the hood of a rusted-out 1948 Ford F1 that had lost all its windows and tires long before today. He squeezed off controlled bursts of 6.8x51mm bullets into what Clark could not see but assumed was the smoke and flames of the grenade explosions he could hear splintering the entrance of the old chapel.

After the last grenade popped, there was a notable absence of the distinct, thundering machine-gun fire that had been nearly constant since the ambush kicked off. Clark felt tension uncoil from his shoulders and jaw, which he hadn't realized was there until it faded—the unique, ass-clenching anxiety that's cooked into anyone under the hammering fire of a tracer-laced machine gun. Nowell began shouting more commands.

"Nomad Five, secure defensive perimeter and suppress to the south, what's left of Nomad Four and TACP, you're on their six to clear and secure the stone house for casualty triage. All teams, *that's rally point alpha*."

The commander shouted while pointing south down the alley toward a large, old stone home that sat in the middle of a big lot. Before Clark could even think, half the task force was moving. Nowell yelled out another rapid stream of commands.

"Nomad One, displace south one lot and secure defensive perimeter and suppress east. Jake, leave two guys to support Nomad One, take the rest of Nomad Three to secure defensive perimeter and suppress to the west. Nomad Two, on me."

Everyone broke from positions at sprinting pace to follow the commands. Nothing happening was clear to Clark, still being cut off from radio communications, so he'd just stay right on the heels of his team leader, Moritz, now peeling away from the cover they shared to follow Nowell. The two operators who'd silenced the terrifying machine gun sprinted past them to the south, and then Clark could see the small chapel on the rise ahead. The entire face of the structure had been annihilated. The only things visible within the exposed bowels of the dark building were flames licking up from the pews and old wooden floorboards.

Two minutes and six seconds had passed since the tree had been dropped across the road.

They made their way north up the sloping alley in the direction of the church and the lead vehicle that had been cut off from the rest of the convoy. Clark could hear suppressed rifle shots up ahead, distinct from the pealing roar of the operators' suppressing fire behind them.

The six men Clark followed moved fast and shot fast. They did not slow at all as they methodically gunned down the half dozen cultists who'd come sprinting or stumbling by ones or twos from between houses and sheds into the alley ahead of them.

One of them was a young man carrying a Springfield M1A he appeared to have never shot or even held until today. He wore a black hoodie but was completely ass-naked from the waist down. Another was a sixty-something woman dressed in expensive hiking attire shooting a lever-action 30-30 from the hip. She'd been shot in the stomach at some point before she appeared, as a dark slick of blood ran from the wound down to her La Sportiva hiking boots. The next was a middle-aged bald guy with a long goatee in a mechanic's jumpsuit. Unlike most of the other cultists, this guy held and shot a Colt AR-15 with what looked like real experience. His last shot only missed Nowell's head by a few inches, but before he could get off another, Nowell methodically stitched him up with bullets from his groin to his neck.

Whoever they were, whatever they wore, none of them seemed interested in taking cover or avoiding death. They all *screamed* as they rushed the operators. A ghastly, inhuman noise so uniform it sounded rehearsed, equal parts shriek, moan, and cackling laughter. They came with eyes and mouths wide, drool and snot pouring down their faces, shooting wildly with their eclectic assortment of guns. Whenever they passed by a downed cultist, the closest operator would take security shots, putting two or three shots into their head, never slowing or giving the body more than a glance.

The team wheeled back east toward Main, moving along the north side of the enormous tree and the splintered wreckage of the carriage house and entire home smothered under its mass. They could now see the lead vehicle of the convoy for the first time since the old tree had crashed across the road two minutes and fifty-three seconds earlier.

The four operators in the lead Suburban had displaced from the area around the vehicle to the space ahead of them, between the wall of a tree to their south and another cabin to their north. The bodies of eleven cultists were visible between their smoking, destroyed vehicle and the hasty defensive position they'd dug into. One of the operators was on his back, his head completely gone from the nose up. The other three had all been hit in multiple places, but one—based on his heavy eyelids, ashen skin, and the abundant blood covering his gear—seemed worse than the other two.

Clark and Gavin went straight to this one and took him up under each arm. Nowell and Moritz each put a shoulder under the arm of one of the other two survivors, while Mako hefted the dead operator in a fireman carry. The other two operators from Nomad 2—Chris Burton and another Clark was pretty sure was named Phil—provided security, one ahead, one behind, rifles scanning every blind spot as the group moved south, back down the alley. The roar of battle ahead of them continued as the operators banged it out against the cultists dug into every room of every house on the east side of Main Street.

They followed a slick of dirt-caked blood up old wooden stairs that led to the porch of the big stone house at the end of the alley. Several operators fired from windows while others treated the wounded who'd been laid in a row on the living room floor. Clark and Gavin carried the guy through the room and laid him on the dining room table. Clark tried to remember the acronym listing priority of critical wound intervention he'd learned during EMT training a decade earlier. The first, he was pretty sure, was *massive hemorrhage*. He didn't bother with the rest of the list because that's immediately what he found. The guy was bleeding badly from where a bullet had snuck into the side of his belly right outside his front ballistic plate. Clark compressed an entire roll of gauze into it. He was still patting around his chest rig for medical shears he knew were stuffed into it somewhere when Gavin ripped open his teammate's vest and cut through the guy's shirt with his own shears. Another operator everyone called *Chewy* forcefully shouldered Clark aside and took over treating his wounded teammate. Clark just stared at Chewy's and Gavin's backs as they launched into a lightning-fast triage of their casualty.

He wiped his bloody hands on his jeans and walked toward the dining room in the front of the house. He flinched away from the wall, shielding his face with his arm and dropping to his belly as bullets strafed the stone exterior of the house right next to his head. He crawled ahead then rose to a knee when he could aim his rifle out a window. He glanced at the operator to his left, then did a double take. His name was Sean, and Clark had eaten dinner at the same table with him several times.

He was propped up against a leather reading chair below a window. He had two tourniquets cinched tight above his knee, a few inches above the stump of muscle, meat, and exposed bone where the rest of his leg had been minutes earlier. He talked into his helmet's radio mic as he worked with unsettling calm and focus to remove some kind of IV bag and tubing from its packaging. Clark had begun crawling over to help insert it into his arm when he tossed it toward the opening into the living room. Another operator caught it, then turned back to an unconscious man Clark knew was named Jimmy. He must've been in worse condition, although Clark could not see a single scratch on him. It looked like he was just sleeping.

The 24th STS operator and lead tactical-air controller fired his rifle from the front door with one blood-soaked hand and held a large radio with another. He kept glancing back at Nowell, who was dressing an exit wound on the shoulder of a large, heavily bearded operator who appeared entirely unaware of his wound as he fired bursts from his XM250 through the crack of a door that opened onto a little side patio. Clark, still radio-less and deaf to the task force's communications, could only guess what was being communicated between the controller and Nowell through their glances. He considered pulling out the actual radio itself from the pouch on his vest, turning it on loud and holding the damn thing to his ear, but he knew he still wouldn't be able to hear shit over all the shooting. This was the first time since joining the task force he actually longed for that heavy, godforsaken helmet with all its fancy bells and whistles.

He watched Nowell mouth the words *wait one* at the controller before clicking a channel selector then pressing down on his PTT button. He took in a deep breath, let it out, then spoke into his mic. Clark watched Nowell hold an expression of dire, grave focus as he waited for whoever to respond to *whatever* he'd just said. Some response must've come through the command channel, because all the operators in the room, even the wounded, looked up at Nowell with burning eyes.

Nowell nodded at the controller, who held his gaze for a long moment then nodded back and began shouting into his large radio unit. Clark was much closer to this guy, but all he could hear was a jumble of confusing military radio protocol.

"*CAS, grid Charlie tango, heading, offset left, target location, for effect.*"

Clark was about to scream at someone to tell him what the hell was happening when the air force commando turned and jogged from the front door into the living room. He held the mic boom mounted to his helmet, screaming into it, and Clark could hear him clearly now.

"*Incoming. Cover, cover, cover.*"

As one, the operators dove on top of the most severely wounded on the ground, shrouding bodies with their own. A strong hand yanked Clark to the ground. He turned to see it was Moritz, who gestured for Clark to plug his ears and open his mouth. Clark did both things a split second before a thundering blast shook his lungs and eyes.

The glass facings of the old built-in cabinets above Clark blew out. A cloud of dust belched up from the floor and down from the ceiling at the same time.

Then another blast struck. Then another. After the fourth explosion, the operators rose as one. Moritz slapped Clark's shoulder and gestured toward the door with his head, silently ordering the game warden to follow him.

It seemed like every operator was converging on the alley between the large stone house and the houses that ran along Main. Everyone moved deliberately. Clark saw one of the team leaders, Jake, a thin trickle of blood running from his ears, kneeling over one of their duffel bags, throwing loaded rifle magazines to everyone nearby. Clark saw Kyle Brown, an operator from Michigan, use his left hand to put a large pinch of Copenhagen in his lip, while using his right to keep his rifle shouldered and aimed at the side yard he covered.

Looking across the alley, beyond the backs of the houses on their side of Main Street, Clark stopped in his tracks. The expression he'd seen on Nowell's face, and the gravity of his decision, struck home.

The United States military had just conducted an air strike against Americans, on American soil.

The entire east side of Main Street, from the general store to the south, was gone. A few burning studs among the smoke and flames were all that remained. An MQ-9 Reaper drone had just fired AGM-114 Hellfire missiles to level a dozen charming, historic little homes on Main Street.

Moritz barked a few orders at the guys nearby then looked at Clark as he pointed south down the alley.

"Rickert, you hold security here; you're our rear guard, our only eyes on this south approach. You've got other guys holding security behind you to the west, north, and east, and obviously in the house, but you're our south sector. So, *you will fucking kill* anything that comes up that direction, *how copy*?"

Clark nodded, looked back at the destruction the missiles had wrought, then shouted his question at Moritz's back.

"What's happening now? What're you guys, what're we doing?"

Moritz looked back with a wicked, merciless grin and shouted his response.

"We're pushin' the fight, bro. House-by-house clearance. Time to root out every last one of these dickheads."

Moritz turned, and Clark watched as the operators splintered into their three- or four-man teams and began snaking their way around the small town. They all had their brothers' blood on them. They had never been hit this hard out of nowhere, not in Iraq, Afghanistan, Syria, Pakistan, anywhere they'd ever been sent. He was seeing bloodlust in these men for the first time. It was in their eyes. In their shoulders and posture. They were revving in the red, and it was terrifying to behold.

A berserk state of relentless, society-destroying ferocity surged through all of them, right below the skin. It raged and thrashed against the hardened veil of discipline and unshakable focus that set these paramilitary operators apart from any special operations soldiers who've ever existed. As they disappeared, Clark settled in behind the rifle he'd rested across the hood of the truck.

If someone told him how much time had passed since the old tree had been dropped across the road, Clark would readily agree it had been the longest eight minutes and fifty seconds he'd ever lived through.

CHAPTER 32

THE FIRST CASEVAC helicopter had dropped off a six-man quick reaction force plus Harry Jacobson himself, then taken away the most critically injured members of the ground force. Clark had been relieved from his security position to help ferry them from the large stone house to the aircraft. A second helicopter arrived minutes later with an additional QRF element to assist in clearing the small town, structure by structure. Nowell made a call to send more wounded back instead of the bodies of their four KIA, which would remain in the house until the next bird. Clark saw in the faces of Nowell and others that something about this decision was grim. They wanted their fallen taken care of, far away from the hellish place where they'd died.

The cult force had not only identified and implemented almost every available tactical advantage while planning and staging this ambush, but then they'd actually employed them with devastating effect. With some half-decent training in basic infantry and unconventional warfare tactics, many can reliably achieve that first step. Of those, only a rare few are capable of achieving that second step with any reliable effect.

The chaotic flux of combat will shred most plans to shit and tatters, and fast. Once bullets start flying and people start dying, step two of an ambush often dies with them. That is, unless the right people are in charge. Really nailing step two requires formidable skill in leadership, combat tactics, and contingency-based planning. It requires someone at the helm with the kind of field-trialed, nimble decision-making one can only reliably gain through years of trial, error, and experience in combat leadership. It's something chiseled and honed by time and blood.

Those in the task force knew all of this. They'd all watched as the cult had inflicted catastrophic blows from their initial ambush sites, maintained choke point control, utilized the high ground, concealment, and both primary and secondary flanking and enfilade positions. They'd underestimated an adversary's skill, and had been burned and maimed as a result, physically and mentally. What they'd confronted here today, for the first time, was the cult working together subject to the directives of a plan, an undeniably good one.

Far and away the most haunting thing about today was the collective realization that their real target and enemy—the faceless leader of this deranged little army—was something even worse than the monster they'd all built in their minds. He was still a monster, but one with an unexpected fluency in the language of *their own trade*, and his skill had a certain flavor to it that suggested a provenance in guerrilla warfare was likely.

This new condition notwithstanding, they were now slaughtering the cultists. They'd all seen plenty of them make terrible, abjectly suicidal decisions that got them swiftly killed. None of them individually betrayed some new prowess in combat. Nothing had reduced their fevered, fanatical zeal, and the operators had butchered them for it. On top of that, the task force had combat leaders on the ground with unrivaled mastery over the battle-hewn skill of insulating men and planning against the liability of panic.

They also had a few tactical advantages of their own, ones the cult did not: experience and resolve. The Ground Branch operators present had a near-complete immunity to combat-induced panic. Their ability to remain calm and ruthlessly calculated under threat of immediate, painful death was nearly unrivaled, globally or historically. They also possessed a resolve to win a fight that punched right back against the deluded, masochistic fanaticism of the cultists, and rage at being ambushed and seeing friends killed cranked this resolve into a honed and primally terrifying force of destruction.

They also had air superiority. In the fifty minutes that had passed since the air strike had leveled the east side of Main Street, the ground teams had methodically outmaneuvered and ripped apart the cultist positions. Now, only pockets of cult resistance remained in a few cabins and barns on the northern and western fringes of town.

The occasional deep cracks from an enemy's pistol or rifle would roll through the empty streets, sounding dismal and hopeless as they were smothered by a shredding fusillade of gunfire from the operators' suppressed rifles and light machine guns. The occasional eruption of a vicious storm of wispy snaps marked the progress of the enraged, vengeful operators as they hunted the remaining shooters like rats.

Clark sat in a bullet-pocked rocking chair on the porch of one of the little houses along the west side of Main Street. He stared at the smoking, skeletal remains of the houses that'd been slagged by high explosive missiles on the other side of the road.

There were at least three dead cultists at the bottom of a fairly intact set of stairs leading down from what had been a front porch. Maybe four, Clark thought. Just looking at the heaped tangle of meat, shredded clothing, and exposed bone, it wasn't easy to discern a total head count with any confidence.

All eight of the armored Suburbans were burned, shredded husks, hissing and popping quietly as they cooled.

A single arm lay in the street just ten feet from the porch where Clark sat. Where it'd been severed around the shoulder was obscured within its former owner's flannel shirt. The sleeve was still cuffed neatly halfway down the forearm.

A Montana state flag fluttered from its pole, mounted above the doors to the general store, peppered with holes and small burns from bullets and shrapnel.

A half dozen crows stood on the bodies of three dead cultists in the street below the general store's elevated porch, pecking at the exit wounds in their backs, chests, or necks. The occasional bursts of gunfire from the other side of town made the crows jump a few feet into the air, flap their wings once or twice, then drop back down onto the bodies.

Clark gazed up at the sizzling remains of the charming little church up the hill, then lit a cigarette.

A noise across the street brought his attention back to the detritus before him. It was a rhythmic thumping noise, human in its steadiness. Clark rose quickly and flipped the safety on his rifle, then shouldered it and moved to stand behind the post to the right of the porch stairs. Movement caught his attention from a little cellar window of the second house north of the general store. It jumped in its frame at each *thump*. Clark flipped the magnifier down behind his holographic sight. Two *thump*s later, the shatterproof window, bent and mangled, popped out of its frame, followed by two legs. Someone was down there and using both feet to kick it out. Clark's heart rate spiked as he put pressure on the trigger.

Has to be a local who's been hiding out since the cult took the town over, Clark guessed.

As the person shimmied out of the small window frame, however, he saw the distinct symbol of the Red Castle on their inner forearm. It was a filthy young man in his twenties, in flip-flops, khaki shorts, and a hooded athletic shirt with some fly shop's logo. Blood, mostly dried now, caked his face and neck from cuts on his forehead and scalp. He crouched in the gravel outside the window, then winced and jerked his head in the direction of a sudden surge of gunfire along the northern edge of town.

Clark's heart began to pound as he glanced quickly up and down Main Street, making sure there were no task force personnel within view.

What he was about to do, or what he hoped he was about to do, was not something that would benefit from witnesses.

Clark reckoned that if any cultists survived, and if they tried to escape instead of hurling themselves into gunfire, they'd likely try to make that escape by heading east. The eastern wall of the mountain valley rose up only thirty feet behind the properties on Main Street. That's how he'd escape this town on foot if he were one of them. So, fifteen minutes earlier he'd plopped himself down in the rocking chair. All he could do was wait and see.

It seemed now that he'd made the right call. He spoke to himself as he watched the twitchy cultist's eyes flick between the sounds of gunfire and the densely forested mountain behind him.

Run, you fuck. Do it. Make a break for it. Come on, shit for brains. Go. Run.

And he did. Directly east, into the forest and up the mountain. Clark cracked a smile as he jogged between the destroyed vehicles in the street, checking again to make sure he was alone.

The guy either did not know how to move quietly through the forest, or didn't care to. Whichever the case, he would've been easy to track for almost anyone. For Clark Rickert, this guy's escape was an impossibility. He followed him a few hundred meters up the mountain to where he saw the grade of an old mining or logging road cut across its face. It was wildly overgrown with saplings and berry bushes, but it was a much flatter grade. Clark was almost positive the cultist would take it once he reached it, instead of just continuing straight up the mountain. And he was right.

Clark began a real stalk now. A bow hunter's stalk.

It didn't take long for him to close to within around fifty meters of the shuffling, wheezing, mumbling cultist. When he got to around thirty meters, he stood and aimed his rifle. He needed to shoot for bone to really stop him. This was always a risk when it came to nicking an artery, but one certainly worth taking now. He exhaled slowly as he took his shot. The bullet slapped into the sweaty pit of the cultist's left knee. It sounded just like the wet, hollow smack of an arrow's broadhead hitting an elk. Clark supposed the impact might've been just as loud as the suppressed subsonic bullet itself.

Neither sound really mattered, though, because neither would be as loud as the cultist's demented screaming, which Clark assumed would begin within seconds of getting shot. That's why he'd launched into a sprint as soon as he'd pulled the trigger.

He fell upon the cultist just as he'd sucked in a pathetic gasp of shock and pain, clapping a big palm over the guy's mouth. Clark drove into him so that his entire forearm smothered his mouth and pinned him into the forest floor. He held the man in place as he belted out a muffled version of the same jittery, possessed shrieking he'd heard from dozens of other cultists that day. Clark glanced down the forested slope toward Main Street, confident the smothered screaming would not carry that far. He searched the cultist and was surprised to find he still had a wallet.

His name was Trent Vickers, from Bozeman, twenty-three. He had an expired Montana State ID suggesting he'd graduated a year earlier. After a minute he could feel this Trent Vickers running out of breath and calming down a bit, so he leaned into his face and spoke as clearly as he could.

"Trent Vickers. You need to stop screaming. I'm going to take my arm off your mouth, and you're going to talk quietly, do you understand?"

He could see the guy's pupils dilate. A cannibalistic rage was still obvious in his features, but his breathing slowed, his muscles relaxed, and Clark lifted slowly off the smaller man. He crouched next to him, silently, staring into his eyes. Since this hypothesis had come to him several days earlier, he wasn't sure whether any conversation would be necessary. But now, actually staring at one of these cultists eye to eye, he realized this little experiment really would require a bit of foreplay to be worth anything.

Clark also realized in that moment that if he was about to do what he thought he was about to do, it would represent his first real-life action associated with the delusional visions he'd been having. The outcome would prove one of two things. Either that his visions had some reality-shattering, real-world importance, or that he had indeed lost his mind and was now dangerously fucking psychotic. He really hoped to walk away from this interaction shrouded in the relief of the latter.

The man did not scream, just took deep, slow breaths as he glared up at him, lips pulled back over bared teeth, eyes narrowed to slits. Clark considered his words, then cocked his head at the man's left knee.

"That's a lotta blood."

The man said nothing.

"You, your buddies, your boss, y'all seem to *really like blood.*"

The man did not speak, but his eyes and lips turned upward, morphing his expression into a grotesque clown smile.

"Does he have enough blood for the ritual yet?"

Clark had no real idea what that question meant, or what an answer to it would really mean. However, he'd felt strongly for several days now that it was a question he'd really appreciate one of these monsters answering honestly. He couldn't explain what the ritual was, but he knew what it meant. Flecks of spittle spouted from the cultist's mouth when he snarled out a slow response.

"He will soon."

Clark tried, and failed, to stifle a shudder.

"How much's he got so far?"

The man began to giggle softly as he spoke.

"The sweet nectar of the lamb grows deep, *hunter.* I've personally carried out the bloodletting of *nine lambs since his awakening* with my own blade. But I am just *one of many.* After tonight's harvest, he'll need not more than five score and two more."

Clark clenched his hand into a fist to stop it from shaking. Somehow, he knew the amount of blood needed for the ritual wasn't actually a liquid volume, but rather all the blood taken from a specific number of bodies. *The blood from 616 lambs.* So, if this maniac was being honest about only needing blood from 102 more people—and if his own schizophrenic delusions held any validity—it meant the cult had killed and bled 514 people already, based on the total he somehow knew was needed for the ritual. The task force had only found 288 of them so far.

While this fact of how many people they'd failed to save was chilling, it was not as shocking to Clark as what now seemed to be an undeniable connection between whatever was going on in his mind and the chaos burning through the minds of the cultists.

Clark stood, breathing deep to try to control himself. He felt tears well up in his eyes. The cultist began to giggle again, this man who'd just spoken with shuddering ecstasy about kidnapping then murdering nine people with his one blade. It infuriated Clark, sending a storm of rage into his bones. Trent Vickers spoke in a wet hiss.

"He who Keeps the Chains and the Final Word, Devourer of Names, Tearer of Veils, Patron of Silent Screams, our Lord of the Blood Maw and the Hungering Shade has told us all about you and your noxious corruption, Sentinel. He's taught us your smell, he who stands with the lambs out of fear of the wolf. He's taught us how you sound, he who clutches the dying ember. We've howled in rapture as he whispered your names into the weeping mouths of the dying. He's promised us the sacred hymn of your screams and splintering nails as he drags you through the Reliquary of the Flayed to the Altar of the Riven Womb, Sentinel. We'll moan in rapture as he makes his bleeding cuts, we'll howl his names as he rids creation of your ruinous blood, and your last wretched drop boils away, we'll dance with him in the Orchard of Screaming Bone."

Clark wiped his forearm across his mouth and stared down at the young man. His eyelids were getting heavy, skin growing pale. This guy's demeanor and the heavy subject matter at hand had actually made Clark forget he'd shot him. He glanced at the exit wound in the front of the guy's annihilated knee and saw clearly he was bleeding to death, and that time was running out.

He looked back into the man's eyes as he pulled the fixed-blade knife from his belt. He'd had this knife for twenty-four years. The blade had shrunk a full inch in that time, as he ran it on the whetstone almost every evening. It never held anything less than a hair-splitting edge. He'd used it to gut and skin hundreds of animals. Maybe over a thousand. Deer, elk, antelope, moose, grizzly, black bear, lions, wolves, rams, mountain goats, buffalo, cattle, pigs, even a few llamas. Postmortem investigation of a dead animal is a big part of the job for a game warden, and he was certainly no stranger to butchery during his poaching days.

"Look here, Trent. I got this hunch that's been eatin' away at me. So, you and I are gonna try a little somethin' here, *comprende*?"

The guy said nothing, just ground his teeth and smiled back.

Clark pulled a roll of electrical tape from the drop pouch of his chest rig then his large bandana from his back pocket. He wiped the back of his neck with it, then dropped his left knee into his captive's chest as he stuffed the bandana into his mouth. He wrapped the tape around Trent's head until the gag was held firmly in place. The cultist shrieked into the gag and struggled as Clark did this. He kicked and bucked his hips, pounded fists into Clark's chest and shoulders, and wrenched against his hands and thumbs.

Clark didn't notice. Even if he weren't dying from blood loss, Clark would've been able to head and heel this guy like a steer, blindfolded.

He gripped Trent's right wrist in the calloused vise of his large hand and slammed his arm into the pine needles out to his side. He planted his right knee into the pit of his elbow, then bent the man's forearm up so he could see his Red Castle brand. Clark flicked the sinister symbol, then turned and tapped the flat of his blade on Trent's nose a few times.

"Now, I got this feelin' that symbol there is awfully special to ya."

The man's kicking and writhing ceased immediately. Eyes still narrowed in rage, but darting now between Clark's and the brand on the inside of his forearm.

"I've been dyin' to find out just how special that brand is to the folks murderin' their way across this great state. Now I've finally got me one. Ya see, Trent, I know he's the one who gives it to his followers, so I gotta think y'all see it as a gift. Almost like he shared a part of himself with ya, am I right?"

The man's eyes were wide now, locked on Clark's. Tears brimmed then spilled down both temples as he began to tremble. He started mumbling desperate, indecipherable babble into the makeshift gag, wrenching his arm, trying to free it from where this mountain of a man was pinning it to the forest floor. Trent bucked his pelvis into the air, using all his strength to try to turn over, but nothing worked.

Clark smiled at Trent's terror and hysteria. It always felt good seeing the first shred of evidence corroborate one's own hypothesis, despite the reality-bending implications of being right in this instance.

Clark scooched his knee up past Trent's elbow so the only part of his arm that moved was his wrist and fingers. Clark pinched the skin of the forearm, yanked it hard an inch from the muscle, and made his first cut. He'd never skinned a human before but found it pretty similar to most anything else, minus the hide. The cultist coughed and wailed and wept into the gag harder and harder as the neat little patch was carved away. Within ten seconds, only a little strand of skin connected the symbol to the man's body.

When Clark swiped his blade through that final strand of skin, several things happened in the span of a single second.

Trent's eyes blasted open freakishly wide, and he took in a tormented gasp of air like he'd just been pulled from a frozen lake. Hundreds of birds within earshot exploded into hysterical, blind flight, tearing through the forest at top speed, slamming into one another or beak-first into tree trunks. Clark dropped his knife and the bloody coaster of skin, clapping a hand to his chest as the earth fell away under him, his vision blurred, and he went into complete free fall; his stomach lurched upward, his ears popped, and his throat seemed to close. As soon as Trent's gasp ended, his body went completely limp, and Clark's sensation of free fall vanished the instant Trent's head thumped into the pine needles. The forest around them went still again.

A pine siskin and a mountain chickadee lay nearby, wings open and little bodies paralyzed, the siskin raking a single foot against the air.

Clark breathed heavily for a few moments, then looked down, and remembered where he was. He threw himself off Trent's body, grabbed his knife, and frantically cut away at the tape around the unconscious man's head. Trent came to as Clark yanked the bandana from his mouth. He coughed and gagged then opened his eyes, eventually focusing on Clark. He flinched in startled shock, then started trying to scoot backward as he stumbled over frantic words.

"Who the fuck, who . . . who the fuck are you? The hell is this? Where am I? What the fuck is—"

Clark gently but firmly held him in place.

"*Hey, hey, hey.* Whoa. *Easy now*, Trent. Settle down. I'm not going to hurt you."

Clark could see Trent's pupils dilate the instant the pain of his destroyed knee finished its journey up the nervous system and into his brain. Clark lunged forward and covered Trent's mouth with his slab of a palm just as Trent screamed into it. Clark leaned in, forcing Trent to look into his eyes.

"Trent Vickers, I am Captain Clark Rickert, a law enforcement officer with the Montana FWP, all right? I need you to tell me where you've been these last three or four weeks. You need to answer that question *right now*, Trent. Answer it *right now*."

His eyes darted from side to side, and he began to shake as the answer to that question, or lack thereof, hammered his mind. He began crying as he spoke.

"I don't know. I mean, I was fishing this morning, I was just out fishing, just a couple hours ago. I . . . I was just fishing, and then I met . . . I met . . ."

Trent's eyes unfocused as his words died away. Clark tightened his grip on Trent's shoulder and growled into Trent's face.

"Who'd you meet, Trent? *Who did you meet?*"

His crying elevated into terrified, childish weeping now.

"*Him*, that fucking . . . *him*, it was *him*. I was fishing a few hours ago, this morning on the Gallatin, and he came up and started talking to me. That's the last thing I remember, that . . . *fucking man coming up to me*."

His eyes rolled into his head, and he began to vomit. He had gone sheet white. Clark sat him up a bit, but the adjustment obviously sent a raging torrent of pain up from his knee, and Clark covered his mouth until the scream died away. He patted Trent's back lightly as he threw up a bit more. After a few moments, Trent mumbled in a lazy, quivering voice.

"Wha . . . what the fuck happened *to my leg, man? What is going on?*"

Clark could feel Trent's body beginning to lose tension and fall limp. He glanced at Trent's knee. It looked like *gallons* of blood had puddled under the catastrophic wound, and Clark assumed adrenaline was the only thing still keeping his heart pumping. He laid Trent back down and stared into his confused, hazy eyes. He took one of Trent's hands into one of his own and put another on the side of his face as gently as he could. Clark let out a long, slow breath before speaking.

"You're about to die, Trent."

The younger man blinked hard a few times. The words jolted his mind, summoning his body's very last ration of energy for one final, hopeless struggle against the end. He tried to sit up suddenly, but Clark held him down with soft but immovable force. There was real, indignant strength in Trent's first few words, but those that followed dripped with exhausted despair.

"Wait, wait, wait. *Fucking wait.* Hold on. *What?* No, man. *No. Please. Please, no.*"

Clark gripped his hand tighter and stroked his large thumb across Trent's pale, dirty cheek.

"I'm here with ya, bud. I'm right here with ya."

Trent Vickers died about twenty seconds later. Not for the first time, Clark could feel the precise instant the last wisp of life left a body he held in his arms.

That candle of life, the one that's lit somewhere behind the eyes as one leaves the womb—the one that burns, jumps, and flickers through all the happiness, heartbreak, and pain of existence—snuffed out in an instant. A braid of thin smoke cooks from that candlewick for a few minutes, while warmth leaves skin and muscles and joints begin to stiffen. Then, all's quiet.

He scooted away from Trent's body until his back was against a tree. He rested his elbows on his knees as he sat there in shock until, for the first time in a very long time, Clark began to cry.

CHAPTER 33

CLARK HEARD SEVERAL helicopters come in and out of Ward in the twenty minutes since he began his pursuit of the man who was once Trent Vickers. He'd trudged down the steep mountainside back toward town in a daze, but focus returned once he heard the hum and bustle of men and diesel engines. When he could see the back of the general store, he took a knee and scanned Main Street.

Smoke still cooked up from the row of homes that had been shredded into hot scree by the first AGM-114 Hellfire missiles ever fired in combat on American soil. Men moved among the destroyed convoy, using a large truck that must've recently arrived to winch the Suburbans to one side of the street. There was an even larger group of people in front of the general store, mostly obscured from view.

Clark didn't want to be seen coming out of the forest, given what he'd left behind up the mountain above town. He side-hilled through the trees, then dropped down behind one of the houses north of the general store. He checked if anyone was nearby, then strolled into Main Street with the detached confidence of someone who's grown bored with a place.

He slowed a bit as he rounded the enormous stump of the tree that had initiated the ambush. He was unsurprised by the sloppy horizontal, sloping, and back cuts that'd been used to drop it across the road. Once around it, he could see the crowd and activity in front of the general store. A mess of new personnel had arrived, easily identifiable by their lack of combat kit and load-out. A row of surviving cultists, cuffed and restrained, were lined up on the west side of the road as medics treated their wounds. Clark saw Dave Benson on the patio of the general store with Jacobson and Nowell and other support personnel. A UH-60 helicopter roared low up the valley then banked hard before a descent, landing where the others had near the makeshift hospital and rally point in the big stone house.

"Where've you been, game warden? Command's been looking for you."

The voice came from Clark's right. He stopped walking but did not look at the speaker as he pulled out his pack of Marlboro Golds and lit one. He put the pack away as he spoke, cigarette in the corner of his mouth, gaze fixed down Main Street.

"You get the last of 'em?"

He looked at Charlotte Bishop as she responded.

"All of those still in the town, but we assume some ran."

She was leaning against the front door of one of the small homes on the west side of Main. She wore a Georgetown soccer T-shirt tucked into synthetic hiking pants, hair in a ponytail, no makeup, with a radio and a Glock 19 holstered on her belt. She appeared exhausted to Clark. Yet, perhaps amplified in contrast to the wreckage of this place, also beautiful. Her expression suggested she knew she'd surprised him, and enjoyed that. She pushed herself up and walked down the porch steps. She raised her eyebrows at his cigarette and held her hand out. He gave her the pack and his lighter. They both leaned against the back bumper of one of their destroyed Suburbans, smoking together in silence until she spoke.

"DuBroux went ahead with the assault on the compound, despite this ambush. One hundred sixteen victims on-site, all dead and bloodless, no sign of the blood itself. They killed thirteen cultists, took eight alive, no casualties."

Clark nodded, let his last drag out through his nose, then flicked his cigarette butt toward the charred Suburban he'd been inside when the ambush began.

"What's the butcher's bill?"

Charlotte exhaled before responding.

"Five of ours KIA. Eleven wounded, with two of those red-tagged category one: Roddell and Locke. They're in bad shape, definitely fifty-fifty, but both are in surgery. Five are cat-two, wounds they'll recover from, but most are career enders for sure. The other four are NSI, but most of those will stay with the task force. You all killed sixty-seven of them, took ten alive, but two of those will probably be dead before sunset."

Sixty-eight, actually, Clark thought. He could feel her look over at him, her gaze sharpening as an electric tension buzzed into the space between them.

"Mako and a few others back there said you let your hair down today. Made it sound like you're some old Western gunfighter."

He side-eyed her, then looked ahead again. He didn't do anything they hadn't done, or easily could have, but knew they'd been amused seeing a non-SOF operator carry himself as he had.

Charlotte touched his arm gently, making his heart flutter a bit.

"Has he been here? The leader. Has he been in this town?"

He hadn't expected her question. He was overtaken by a very foreign, unfamiliar urge, an almost excited need to share something with someone else. He wanted to tell Charlotte about what he'd just done up on the mountain, about how removing the cultists' brands seemed to cut away hypnotic insanity and un-fuck their rage-shaken minds. He suppressed the urge.

He could not let himself trust this woman. Thorn, Benson, this shot caller from the Special Activities Center, her boss Jacobson, and likely quite a few others up the ladder knew a good deal about what was really going on here, and thus maybe even what was really going on inside himself. He couldn't just go sharing everything he somehow seemed to know, hoping they'd meet him halfway. Besides, he had no idea how he'd even begin to articulate such nonsense without sounding insane. He did not look at her as he finally responded.

"*Yep.*"

Charlotte stepped away from the bumper and faced him. She crossed her arms, expression unchanged.

"*How the hell* can you know . . ."

She looked up at the sky, took a deep breath, then looked at the ground. She was one of the only people alive who knew what they were going up against, and one of the only people alive who knew the strange circumstances of Clark's file being put on her desk. She was sure at this point Thorn had put it there, and so knew this game warden had some significant utility. She didn't know what that utility was, only that it existed, and this pissed her off. She looked back up at him and spoke in a cold, measured tone.

"Any ideas on *when* he was here, or where he went?"

Clark stared at the dirt between his boots for a long moment, then he shot his head up and looked at her. Something in his fiery gray-green eyes made her take an involuntary step back. She'd never seen such desperate vulnerability and fear, or such a terrifying resolve, let alone in the same face at the same time. Clark's words were just above a whisper, but came like magma rolling over a glacier.

"Why was I selected for this task force, Charlotte?"

At this point, Clark felt he actually knew the answer to this question. Or, rather, he could feel it. It was simple and hadn't changed.

He'd been born for this. He'd been born to hunt this barefooted man.

Despite how deep he felt this in his soul and bones, and what he'd just learned from poor young Trent up the mountain, he still desired a third party to substantiate the primal instinct coursing through his dreams and nervous system. He couldn't deny it any longer, but was stubborn, and wouldn't just end his resistance and surrender to it, not until external confirmation.

Charlotte took a deep breath, steeling herself. Her mind had been plagued by this handsome, mysterious, insufferably vague asshole since she'd met him. She was here to kill or capture an adversary, something she'd done many times before, despite how disturbingly different this particular operation was. She'd never had her grasp of the world turned upside down as she had a few weeks earlier when getting briefed on this situation. She'd never gone toe-to-toe against someone, *something* that neither psych profilers nor the entire academies of history and science could explain. *But fuck that*, she thought, *I'll still win*. The unshakable will that made Charlotte Bishop who she was flowed through her, eyes narrowing as she spoke.

"I don't know why you're here. That's the honest truth. *What I do know*, Captain, is that I'm good at one thing, and it's stopping bad people from doing bad things. If you want to help me do that, *then help me do that*. You want to have some emotional crisis about your purpose in life, *do that shit at home*."

She moved slowly closer to Clark as she went on, an edge hardening her words.

"All I know is that you, *of all the stubborn assholes I've gotta deal with*, have at least once displayed a knack for discerning the tracks of this cult's leader. So far as I'm concerned, *that's* the only reason you're here. We've got innocent people to save and evil men to kill. That's my mission; that's the *only thing* important to me. I don't care about *you*, what you know or feel or think, or your mountain tracker bullshit persona. I only care about *stopping him*. So, if you care about the same, then lock your shit up, share what you know, be a team player, or *fuck off*."

Charlotte stared up at him with icy focus in her eyes, her face now less than a foot from Clark's. His mouth was agape, eyes wide. He'd been overwhelmed by how beautiful she was every time they'd interacted, but looking at her now was like staring into the blade of a screaming chop saw. He saw the same startling, immovable resolve in her face that she'd seen in his only moments before.

But then other things came to his mind. Memories.

Trent Vickers's vicious rage and hatred, then his anguish, fear, and pain. The visions that told him what would happen if he cut that brand off an arm, and then what happened when he actually did. The cult leader sipping blood from a crystal flask, his smile of ecstatic delight as he smashed the joints of the old pastor in the back of the now-sizzling chapel. His infallible instinct that this woman, or her boss, or her boss's boss—*someone* in her federal apparatus—knew something about what was happening in his mind. And that person or those people had been keeping it from him, and until that changed, he was still on his own here. Malcolm Thorn's beady, knowing gaze cutting into him. The excruciating humiliation of having begged Thorn, almost screaming, to just tell him what was happening.

It all pulsed through his mind and steeled him with anger. He took a deep breath. As he exhaled, Charlotte watched his features relax into what seemed to be his baseline resting expression of calm, menacing indifference. He slowly leaned toward Charlotte, their faces now only six inches apart.

"I didn't ask about your motivations. I asked a straight question. When you've got yourself a straight answer to it, we can have ourselves a *nice little chat* about what each other knows. Till then, *sweet pea*."

She stared back with a cold, unamused glower. Clark leaned away from her then pushed himself up from the bumper, spine and knees cracking like windfall. Before he could walk around her, she snatched the pack of cigarettes and the lighter from the pouch on his plate carrier with snakelike speed. She lit another cigarette as she walked backward away from him, an expression of lukewarm disappointment on her face as though he'd just told a shitty joke. She shouted over her shoulder as she turned toward the general store.

"Let's go. Command element's going up to the target property—that includes you."

He followed her slowly until he saw her fall in with the rest of the task force leadership assembled in front of the general store. He saw Thorn was nearby, leaning against a burned, blood-flecked fence on the other side of the street, staring back at him. The little man grinned and cocked his eyebrows up in greeting.

An unexpected rage jolted through Clark as he continued by and bounded up the stairs to the general store's patio, then inside, feeling Thorn's grin irk him like a sour aftertaste.

Glass, bullet casings, splinters, potato chips, candy, blood, beer, wine, and liquid from a dozen soft drinks covered the floor of the large, open room. It was a strange sight to behold, having stopped here a number of times over the years for lunch or coffee. A half dozen surveillance, SIGINT, and cryptography specialists worked busily over maps, radios, and ruggedized laptops covering a long butcher-block table set against the back wall.

His boots crunched noisily on the mess as he walked toward a cluster of small tables and chairs near the sandwich and coffee bar. He brushed debris from the counter, leaned an elbow on it, then stared around the room with placid curiosity as though waiting for a tuna melt.

Clark could feel him here, the cult leader. It was his stain, the furrows left behind by the curdled elemental slurry he excreted whenever excited and aroused. Clark assessed it as he would a game trail, looking for any hint as to where the beast might be now. He found one, one he could never articulate but only feel. Several of the support personnel watched the strange game warden as he stepped away from the counter and turned in a slow circle until he was facing away from them, and stopped. They began glancing at one another with raised eyebrows as he remained motionless, staring into the front-left corner of the store.

In the last half hour, Clark had confronted what had become the most crippling fear he'd ever known, the nauseating reality that it had not been delusions assailing his mind and senses, but something else with dire real-world significance. Additional implications, far more specific and terrifying, followed necessarily from that reality, as well. Primarily, the understanding that an impossibly wicked and devastating force posed an imminent threat to all of humanity, and that he played some critical role in thwarting it. He had zero clue what that role was. These visions or whatever afflicted his mind had an infuriating lack of fundamental detail.

When it came to equipping Clark with knowledge he found useless and catastrophically fucking boring, no detail was spared. He could plot seasonal courses he'd never used through the Alps, Ural, and Atlas Mountains, recite ancient literature he'd never read, describe how to navigate oceans using a southern celestial hemisphere he'd never seen, and do it all in Maltese, Arabic, and even a few languages he was pretty sure had never been written down. Once the pulsing fog of panic and dread cleared after every vision, he found another tome of this useless dog shit.

The people staring at Clark's back as he stood motionless, staring into the bullet-shredded corner of an old general store, didn't know about any of that. Clark wasn't thinking about any of it, either, surprisingly.

He was looking to the southeast, the direction the barefooted man's faint trail of spectral rot suggested he'd gone. Clark figured he'd likely have altered course by now, but that's the direction he'd gone from here. Clark Rickert was learning how to track this beast, how to read his sign, and it felt good.

Jacobson saw the tech specialists as he entered, one of whom shrugged and gestured toward the man he was looking for.

"*Captain Rickert*, we're spinning up for the target property now. Let's go."

Jacobson's voice axed through Clark's focus, cutting his bizarre sensory grip on the mélange of trace and spoor the cult leader had left in his path. He kept his eyes to the southeast as he walked backward a few steps, then turned and nodded at Harry as he gestured outside.

"*After you.*"

CHAPTER 34

HE SLOWED DOWN abruptly, then stopped and turned to look behind him, to the northwest. His eye began to twitch, and he ground his teeth.

He's on my trail.

Feeling the Sentinel *see him*, without being able to *see back*, made his skin crawl and blood turn to mud in his veins. He could feel the Sentinel's pleasure at finding his trail. He could feel his resolve. It was terrifying, but far more enraging.

He knew Clark could sense him clenching his trembling, impossibly strong hands into fists. He set upon one of his own disciples in a frenzy of blind, murderous fury. He wept in rage and howled at the Sentinel's connection to him.

He shattered bones in the cultist's hands and face. He tore belts and ribbons of skin from his chest, shoulders, and back with the fingernails he felt growing. He felt the cultist's sense of joy at the righteous, immaculate sanctity of being chosen for this moment of blood, pain, and rapture. This only drove up his rage until he roared down into his disciple's crying, smiling, bleeding face. Skin on his nose and cheeks blistered under the rippling heat blasted from his glowing furnace of a mouth. A euphoric smile spread across the disciple's face as he stared back into the eyes of his master, the eyes of the *thing* beating and flaying him to death.

When it was over, he felt weak. He was still on his knees, leaning forward and breathing heavily as he rested his face and forearms within the remains of his disciple's torso, a broth of ribs, spine, blood, and pulped organs. He began to weep, then lifted his blood-covered face and began to laugh.

Feel me, Sentinel. Feel this.

He licked the blood from his lips as he pushed himself to his feet. He ignored the other dozen cultists who mumbled their prayers to him. He nodded at them, and they dropped upon the corpse. They growled and shrieked as they began to feed.

He had a trick to pull, this go-round. It'd been so hard, before. He could always reach his retinue of blood knights, the seventy-two perpetually bound to him, *his* path, and this realm. Despite what had largely been their uselessness to his efforts in past chapters, it had still always been the only inherently fair part of this wretched deal, each getting their own court of heralds, forever equal, forever here. He'd always been able to blow his war horn in their dreams, but to infuriatingly little effect.

This time, however, the world had grown so small. Travel, so easy. Maybe, this time, with these resources, he could summon some to stir up trouble, use as surprises. He gave it a try, and felt them, and felt them *feel him. Well, now,* he thought, *this time, with them, things could get deliciously chaotic.*

He stared into the northwest, still breathing heavily, and began to laugh. Tufts of wheatgrass and bluebell flowers around his feet began to wither as though they were in a microwave.

It didn't matter this time, Sentinel.

He laughed harder as he harnessed his resolve.

This time, you are going to fail.

CHAPTER 35

BENSON, JACOBSON, BISHOP, and Thorn had taken a hop to the target property on a UH-60. Clark watched their helicopter scream over them as they took an old bridge over the Yaak River. He'd set off about fifteen minutes earlier with Reichman, Nowell, and one of his operators driving another up-armored Suburban that'd been brought up after the ambush. It was a short drive, and no one spoke.

The property was nestled at the foot of the last American stretch of the Purcell Mountains, which rose steeply behind it and ran only about ten miles before crashing through the Canadian border.

There was a large stone-and-log cabin in the center of two clear acres surrounded by dense forest. Several barns and outbuildings pocked the cleared area, as did an equal number of government vehicles and a small MH-6 Little Bird helicopter. Most of the windows of the cabin were shot away, and a dark slick of blood stood out on the flagstone steps leading down from the porch.

Thin ropes of smoke danced up from the husk of what had been a 1998 Ford F-250. Six or seven dead, rotting goats the cultists had shot were in a cluster between the house and the barn, while two living goats grazed on the summer-browned grass between the bloating corpses. Body bags were lined up in the weed-strewn gravel driveway beside the cabin, not far from where eight prisoners were seated, hands and ankles flex-cuffed, all staring absently or mumbling to themselves.

Clark felt his first pang of guilt, seeing them. Knowing they were curable, imagining their old selves as prisoners, thrashing against the walls of the small, dark box that held them somewhere deep behind their eyes. He'd deal with that eventually. He wasn't sure how or when to reveal what he'd learned on that front, but knew the feds took decent care of them, physically at least, so could bide his time a bit longer.

He saw DuBroux greet the others then gesture up the bloodstained steps to the cabin. He, Reichman, and Nowell piled out of the SUV and joined them on the porch. Clark brushed past Charlotte, where she leaned a shoulder on the balustrade and rolled her eyes when she felt him pluck his pack of cigarettes from her back pocket. Clark glanced through the shattered windows, finding the house completely torn to shreds inside. It had seemingly eaten thousands of rifle rounds.

Benson dropped his sport coat over the back of an old rocking chair, then loosened his tie and began rolling up his sleeves as he sat. Jacobson sat in the chair across from him. Thorn leaned back on the railing on the far side of the porch. The rest stood. Everyone looked around the cabin or out toward the trees, their resolve fighting against the bone-deep exhaustion and shock in all their eyes. Harry spoke first.

"Well, all our assets at this location as well as those back in Ward will exfil to the FOB as soon as battle damage assessments and site exploitations are wrapped up at both AOs. So, DDO, what do you got for us?"

Benson leaned forward, resting his elbows on his knees, and stared at his linked fingers as he spoke.

"I've ordered a suite of new assets to replace and bolster all task force contingents across the board. More UAV teams, tech and field surveillance specialists, and a few more logistics officers. You need anything or anyone else, I'll make it happen. The director's sending us another hefty combat arms contingent. He re-tasked the eleven Ground Branch guys you had running a workup down at Bragg plus a couple of two-man GRS teams. He also tapped Admiral Rourke at JSOC, who's sending us a full DEVGRU troop from Nowell's old Red Squad. They're all inbound to the FOB now, and I want them all falling right into Nowell's ground command just to keep things simple. Makes sense to me to have the GRS guys buttress the QRF and recon elements, our own SOG operators backfill established ground teams, and to keep the Team Six guys modular, use them as full assault teams or to augment others, as needed. But that's your call to make with Nowell and Bishop, Harry, so structure it however you think's best."

No one responded, but Bishop and Nowell looked at each other in surprise, then at Harry who crossed his arms and leaned back in his chair and looked between them both with raised eyebrows that said *holy shit*. All three of them knew what a uniquely dire situation this had become after today, but this addition to the task force brought the reality home.

Clark put a cigarette in his mouth then held an open hand toward Charlotte, who stared at it for a second before taking his lighter from her pocket and throwing it to him. A full minute passed as the group sat in silence, cigarette smoke winding up through the mildewed log ceiling of the porch. Everyone looked up as a large Steller's jay landed on the railing of the porch. It sat for a moment, then seemed shocked to find the others there and blasted back into the air. The crew chief of the MH-6 helicopter ratcheted on something near one of the helicopter's skids, the *click*s echoing around the forest. DuBroux nodded at Benson as he broke their quiet spell.

"What's our cover and concealment protocol for *this one*, DDO? Having a hard time imagining any after-action OpSec strategy that could keep the operation shrouded from the public and press after the chaos in Ward."

Benson leaned back in his chair, rested one leg over the other, then flicked a few glass shards from the sole of his custom Italian dress shoe.

"Nonissue. I've got it covered."

DuBroux glanced at Jacobson, who nodded, leaned forward slowly, and rested his elbows on the dirty, weather-stained table.

"I know this is your wheelhouse, Dave, but like Special Agent DuBroux here, I am curious what our plan is to keep an engagement of this severity and noise under wraps."

Benson did not take his eyes from some indistinct spot across the porch as he responded in a slow, detached voice.

"Catastrophic wildfire . . ."

The others began looking at one another as the silence stretched on, then Benson continued.

"It's a real threat here in the Rocky Mountain West, *especially* during a hot, dry summer following a dry winter, such as this one. Nowell's patrols have been monitoring a grass fire that kicked up in the shooting on the west side of town. Rained a bit last night, high dew point and relative humidity this morning, so it's moving slow, but I bet it starts creeping up that side of the valley as the day heats up."

Bishop looked at Jacobson, silently conveying her failure to grasp what the hell Benson was talking about. DuBroux raised his eyebrows and crossed his arms. Nowell and Reichman glanced at each other. Before anyone could ask, Benson went on in a somewhat whimsical, distant tone.

"*A fierce, dry lightning storm* settled right above Ward an hour before our convoy arrived. An hour from now, all optical and thermal sat imagery, radar playbacks, smoke dispersion models, and autonomous weather gauge reports available online will confirm as much . . ."

Everyone was silent, the implications of Benson's words beginning to dawn on them all as he continued.

"An hour ago, I cut the NSA eggheads at Fort Meade loose to start tweaking weather data archived by NOAA, NWS, commercial weather services, local news stations, even private hobbyists. PAG's propo, media, and covert influence teams back at the SAC are shoring up the narrative now. The president himself has already briefed the governor, and should be briefing the USFS's district forester right now, ensuring the story's kept straight regarding ignition sources. We've got forty-three positive IDs of the sixty-seven cultists killed in Ward today. Forty of those are locals, with social security, VA records, vehicle and voter registrations, and tax IDs, all linked to homes in Ward. Before we came inside I tasked teams to start dumping thirty of their bodies in or near their respective homes, and the other ten in their vehicles, which'll be arranged to reflect a harrowing but unsuccessful effort to flee the conflagration. All will be found burned down to brittle bone, and the governor's selected state detectives and coroners will make sure that's what's reported."

He looked up at DuBroux.

"It's also no secret that little towns like this always have some prepper types with stockpiles of ammo and Tannerite. Several such stockpiles will be confirmed shortly by the particular federal incident commander I've ensured will be leading the wildfire response. This sufficiently explains whatever some errant hiker might've *thought* they heard over the last few hours, the state police roadblocks in and out of town the governor's already set in place, and the ferocious speed and behavior of the tragic wildfire itself."

Benson looked at Jacobson square in the eye.

"More simply, Harry, in about forty minutes we're burning that valley, that town, and everything in it *to fucking ash*, then blaming it on the weather and a tragically avoidable lack of fire mitigation efforts."

Jacobson and Bishop looked at each other, both appearing downright impressed with this cover story. Nowell, DuBroux, and Reichman nodded, surprise and approval on their faces as well. Since joining the task force, all Clark had seen in Benson was angst, impatience, poor leadership, and an insufferable deficit in social intelligence. He'd taken him for a politician. A sycophantic bureaucrat. And perhaps Benson was all those things. But now, for the first time, Clark saw Benson's capacity for shrewd, ruthless calculation, his aptitude for lightning-fast problem solving, and his frightening devotion to mission success. He should've known to assume these traits were minimum qualifications for anyone who held his job. Confronted by how shallow and incomplete his assessment of the man had been, Clark felt stupid.

Jacobson looked around at the others.

"Well, we should get rolling; we've already got a lead on another target package. I know it's a stiff turnaround, but we'll likely be OTM early tomorrow, if not tonight. So, anyone got anything else?"

Clark knew none of these people would complain or question the outlandish notion of going straight back into the chaos. So, despite how alarming and abusive he found the idea, he wouldn't either. Then Thorn's unexpected, nasally voice grabbed everyone's attention.

"Eight days, I think? Yeah. Around eight days until the night of the new moon."

Jacobson's eyes narrowed, Bishop's widened, both expressions portraying exasperated annoyance at Thorn's strange comment. Benson closed his eyes and sighed. The others stared at Thorn, blinking slowly in confusion. Clark, however, felt adrenaline numb his limbs.

The new moon.

Over the last week, this phrase and concept had bruised the interior of Clark's skull, repeating over and over in thirty different languages that all hissed it in the same dreadful voice. The night of the new moon was something sacred, critical, and imperative to the barefooted man. Thorn nodded slowly at him, his sly, knowing eyes locked on his. Nowell began to ask what the hell he was talking about, but Thorn interrupted him.

"The new moon is when it's the darkest in its monthlong cycle, the lunar dichotomy of a full moon. *Full moons* get all the glory. Folklore, horror, romance, fantasy, every genre *obsesses* over them. It's gone stale, though, am I right? The *darkest night of the month*, now that's exhilarating. You've got to think the night of a new moon is when the truly wild things of the world see some opportunity, and become the most dangerous versions of themselves."

Thorn spoke casually, as though he were at a bar bullshitting with buddies from high school, entirely unconcerned by how ridiculous he sounded. Someone, maybe Nowell, asked something in a frustrated, fatigued tone, but Clark didn't hear what was actually said. He just stared back at Thorn, who held his gaze, unflinching.

The others eventually saw Thorn and Clark staring at each other. The tension between them grew into something almost palpable, electric and humid. Clark knew now, without any shadow of a doubt, that Thorn knew about his affliction—his visions. He'd suspected this. Knew it to be the case, almost. But it was official now.

Clark looked away, staring into the house through the shattered windows. A dusty old shoulder mount of a whitetail buck hung above the smoke-blackened stones of the hearth inside. A bullet from the morning's gunfight had torn away its nose. He appraised the score of its rack and tried to guess which county in central or eastern Montana he reckoned it'd been killed in, decades earlier. Thorn's voice betrayed a hint of irritation.

"Captain Rickert . . ."

Clark did not respond. Tension slowed and fattened the silence until Thorn spoke again.

"What do you think about the night of a *new moon*, sir? Do you share my appreciation for its significance?"

DuBroux whispered a chain of profanity heard by all. Reichman turned, planted his palms on the railing of the porch, and shook his head. Nowell tried his question again, demanding Thorn explain "what the fuck" his point was.

Benson, Jacobson, and Bishop, on the other hand, stared at Clark. He saw the pensive apprehension in their expressions—as though sitting on a restaurant patio as a jittery tweaker shuffles by them on the sidewalk, arguing with God. It was enough for Clark to conclude they knew why Thorn asked these cryptic questions, or enough to not find them strange. Clark did not take his eyes from the old, abused taxidermy.

"If there's a new moon in mid- to late September, there's a magic little window right around first light, probably the best chance all year long to trick a big bull elk and catch it in the open. Elk spend most of the day bedded in thick, dark timber, and even when they're moving in the morning and evening they'll still generally avoid leaving cover. But during the rut, when love is in the air, they'll take some chances and mess around in the open a bit. The night of a *full* moon during the rut, they'll bugle and fight and breed all night long, then bed down in the timber real early, exhausted.

Night of a *new* moon during the rut, however, as dark as it is, they won't want to, but they'll stay hunkered safe in the woods, jonesing the whole time. By first light that next mornin', their instincts are just screamin' at 'em to get some. It's a truly special moment. Brief little window when old, monster, bush-wise bulls are so horny they might just do somethin' uncharacteristically dumb and reckless they'd never dream of doing any other day a' the year. So, yes, Malcolm, as a fella fond of trickin' big ol' humdinger bulls into arrow range, I share your appreciation for the significance of a new moon. Shall we move onto heat lightning, maybe the Big Dipper?"

Thorn appeared unamused as he drummed his fingers on the railing. DuBroux and Reichman laughed at Clark's jab as they glared at Thorn with scornful, exhausted, dangerous eyes. Nowell wasn't able to bridle his frustration at this cryptic, veiled exchange.

"*Mother a' Christ*, I can't do this, DDO. I can't handle another minute of this little asshole flirting with Rickert, *not today*. Are we fuckin' done here?"

Thorn spoke before anyone else could, with the same startling authority that had entranced them several nights earlier.

"*Excuse me*, but I can't shake the suspicion that Captain Rickert learned something today that might help us find the man we've been looking for. Captain Rickert, are you able to dispel or expand upon my suspicion?"

Thorn's accusation was naked, made without any support. There was no way someone like Thorn could make such a bizarre accusation after a day like this without Benson, Jacobson, and Bishop demanding the grounds for it. *Unless they knew the grounds already*, Clark thought, and when he found all three staring back at him with reluctant curiosity, he figured they did. He took in a deep breath and nodded as he began to speak with a searing timbre in his voice.

"Make you a deal, Thorn . . ."

Thorn's eyes narrowed and his mouth closed. Only Clark could see his quick, furtive glance at Benson. Clark took a step toward the smaller man, his voice quieter.

"You tell me the real reason I was selected for this task force, and I'll tell you about what I might've learned toda—"

Clark was cut off by DuBroux's loud scoff and the words that followed right on its heels.

"Captain, *read the damn room*. You think you're special? After everything that happened today, can you really think this is all about you?"

Charlotte's first words punched into the air immediately after DuBroux's last.

"Dwight's right. After everything that happened today, you're here bargaining for your selection criteria? *I am the one* who found your IC file while looking for a local law enforcement liaison, all right? Just as I've found a dozen others before. I'm the only reason *you're fucking here.*"

Clark's response was immediate.

"And how exactly did you find my file, *Charlie*?"

Charlotte's eyes darted quickly onto Clark's chin, then back to his eyes. She was floored by hearing this question asked aloud, the question she'd been privately mulling over for weeks. Not only that, but he'd called her *Charlie* for the first time, just as Thorn had in the command tent when he commended her for finding Rickert's file, and winked at her. Only a single second had passed, and she hadn't moved at all, but as though she'd pointed a finger at him and shouted his name, Clark nodded slowly and looked over at Thorn.

Benson launched up from his chair. No one present had ever seen him move that fast. His eyes were narrow, his face a mask of exhausted rage, and his finger, like a loaded and primed dueling pistol, was aimed at Clark's face. An electrical fire coursed through his words.

"*Captain Rickert.* Let me make something *very* clear. The standing interpretation of eighteen USC section 1385 is the *only motherfucking reason you're here*. Federal law authorizes the military to enforce domestic law and policy within the continental United States so long as local law enforcement participates. You can charm the task force with your country bumpkin wit and poise, or even more horseback-riding charades, *all you fucking please*, but you, Captain, are just a *rubber fucking stamp here*. I expect *nothing more* from you, and will tolerate *nothing more* from you. Roll with the ground teams, join the command briefings, kill some cultists, fuck an analyst at the FOB if you want, *I don't give a shit*. But you're an afterthought here, Rickert. A *formality*. Behave as such, *or you're fucking done.*"

Benson pivoted from the conversation with the same breakneck speed he'd stood with. He spun toward the others, seeming to forget Clark altogether, and rattled off a timeline for the next hour. Those here would exfil back to the FOB via helicopter, and the task force personnel in Ward would depart within the hour to rally and debrief at the FOB.

He turned and stormed from the porch toward the group of his and Jacobson's staffers stepping from vehicles that had just arrived. Everyone except for Clark followed after him. Thorn was the only one with the gall to meet Clark's eyes as he crossed the porch. There was a peculiar urgency in his gaze, almost paternal, something between a warning and a plea.

DuBroux peeled away from the others to resume his command over the ground teams still working around the property. Reichman and Nowell went straight toward the SUV they'd driven there. Charlotte, Jacobson, and Thorn followed Benson toward his staff gathering in front of the large cabin.

Clark left the porch and skirted around the group, stopping a few meters from the line of restrained cultists.

He'd just made his final attempt, with spoken word, to gain access to the library of intelligence he needed to understand what was happening to him and expedite his hunt of the barefooted man. DuBroux, Charlotte, and Benson had openly ridiculed his effort, and the others' silence was an endorsement of that ridicule.

They'd just collectively staked a boundary, delineating his status as a barely tolerable outsider. But he'd known this already. He was working among what was effectively America's Pro Bowl of its most chillingly dangerous Tier-1 combat operators, under the command of what was effectively America's Best in Show for ingenious and callous leaders of clandestine capture-kill operations. His status had not changed on that porch; he'd just been reminded of it. Despite the disdain Benson had cooked into that reminder, he felt a sense of relief.

He'd always been an outsider, and had always preferred it that way. Other people talked too much and moved too slowly.

He was not surprised by this outcome, and it simplified things. He'd never been gifted with cunning, social cleverness, or any persuasive agility. He'd tried just asking them why he was here, individually and as a group. He'd tried to reason it out of them. He'd begged them. He'd gone so far as to scream a pitiful plea a few nights earlier that Thorn reveal what was going on, in front of everyone. But the only indignity he felt now was at himself for even trying to rely on things as petty as words and guile. He'd only done so because he'd assumed his only superlative qualities—reckless tenacity and a fierce will—were useless in this effort.

But that's all Clark had left now, so far as he saw things. He needed to act. He needed to stun and shock them. *Scare them.* Merely telling them about how removing the brand served to free the cultists from their hypnosis had endless potential outcomes. It needed to be something far more direct and simple. He needed to do something that would either get him kicked off the task force, or set him apart with such distinction it would mandate his inclusion in the top echelon of shot callers on this operation. He was fully aware his stunt might result in his being detained and then interrogated, but figured those in the top echelon he sought to join would be the ones doing the interrogating. That was a start, and he'd figure something else out from there. No more veiled exchanges. No more discussion. No more fucking words. He needed to act, and they needed to see.

He approached the row of restrained cultists and knelt before one at the far end: a tall, middle-aged man, mumbling to himself with his hands cuffed behind his back. Clark stared curiously into the guy's distant, furious eyes. He reached forward, grasping his right elbow where it jutted out behind his ribs. The man looked up then, expression unchanged. Clark smiled and tapped the branded symbol on his inner forearm.

"Cut the mark off one of y'all about an hour ago."

Clark pinched the skin under the brand, hard, between calloused fingertips.

"As soon as I took it from his arm, it severed the connection like *that*."

Clark snapped the fingers of his free hand inches from the cultist's widening eyes. He pinched the skin under the symbol even harder, then raised his voice to a volume he hoped would allow most of the prisoners to hear him, but no one else. He'd felt something deep in his mind or soul holding these words back for days, patiently awaiting the trust he gave it now.

"I can see him, you know, your dirt-bound apostle of whimpers and worms. I can feel his groveling hunger. The lord of the leech, your shepherd of rot and rats *grows weak*. He knows it's already over, that I'll stop the ritual before the new moon. He can feel his own demise flowing through my veins as dread clots and boils within his own. Your anointed husk shall be banished *yet again* to scream and seethe in the silent dark. *Ipsum nunc audio. Flet et orat et clamat. Scio vos quoque iram suam sentire. Tempus est tibi clamare.*"

After Clark's last word, the reaction was instantaneous. They heard his command, and all of them—even the glassy-eyed one hooked up to an IV and a transfusion at the far end of the row—obeyed it, *and began to scream.*

Their eyes rolled back in their heads. They thrashed against their restraints. Several dislocated their own shoulders in the first seconds. Someone's ulna bone above the wrist cracked audibly, then another's a few seconds later. Tears poured down their cheeks, then blood from their mouths as they bit through their tongues. Several gagged and choked through their screams until they began vomiting down the front of their filthy clothes. Several others fell into what looked like a seizure.

Everyone within view stared in shock and revulsion at the gyrating, shrieking prisoners. After a few seconds of stunned silence, orders were shouted and task force personnel began running in to restrain them.

Clark rose slowly, appraising the row of convulsing cultists. He nodded in approval. He turned toward the task force leadership.

Thorn was several meters ahead of the others, slowly removing his glasses, marveling at the scene with unhidden astonishment. Benson, Jacobson, and Bishop flicked their eyes between the cultists and Clark, confusion evolving into appalled disbelief.

Like a country fair magician politely acknowledging applause, Clark lifted Frank Farrington's old Stetson from his head, held it over his chest as he took a small bow. As he turned back toward his troupe of sobbing, screaming cultists writhing behind him, he began to whistle the tune, Clark's tune, the tune from *High Plains Drifter*.

CHAPTER 36

"I UNDERSTAND, SIR. *As outlined in the report, offers of foreign support were anticipated once the event began, as was their increasing insistence and agitation as the lunar cycle progresses. I've spent as much time conferring with my international counterparts over the last days and weeks as I have with the task force; I've been in contact with London, Rome, Moscow, and Cairo in the last hour. I know the SecDef and others have reviewed all the same offers of guidance and assets, as well, and we've maintained regular contact throughout each day, as you know, and I believe they've independently reached all the same conclusions. I assure you, sir, under these dire circumstances, I would not let something as petty as pride, some notion of regional authority, or even the constraints of national sovereignty prevent my willingness to accept support. As soon as I see any operational value or utility in the assets or intelligence being offered, I'll not hesitate to gratefully accept it . . . Yes, Mr. President. First thing in the morning, as usual . . . Thank you, Mr. President."*

Thorn ended the call on his iridium satellite phone and set it back into the charger next to the other half dozen he used throughout the day. He went to the small sink and washed his hands just as vigorously as he had twice already since he'd arrived back at the FOB. He sat in the chair at the foot of the single bed in the small, containerized living unit he'd been provided. The floor and walls hummed from the air-conditioning unit and the diesel generator powering it. He stared at nothing for a moment, breathing deeply.

He took the glasses from his face, squeezed his eyes shut, pinched the bridge of his nose, and ruminated on what he'd seen Clark Rickert do over the last few days. How he'd appeared fluent in French and German several days earlier. How the man had used a few words to set those cultists at the mountain property into a state of suicidal panic.

His classified position within the federal government of the United States granted him extraordinary, unrestricted, executive-level access to all federally acquired information. It also came with a bottomless pit of dark money, private and secure international travel at the snap of a finger, and the ability to contact any world leader at virtually any time.

However, Malcolm Thorn's actual job description and expected duties were opaque, even to him.

He took out one of the several journals where he'd consolidated what he deemed the most important information about this situation, but then just drummed his fingers on its worn cover. He'd memorized every word inside, a decade ago.

In 2003, Thorn was sworn in as the fifteenth American to hold this position. It granted him access to all seventeen known private libraries around the world focused on archiving records, accounts, studies, and research of this situation. After visiting them all, he'd realized his predecessors had done at least one thing well, and that was making America's library the most comprehensive of those seventeen, even superior to the Vatican's. It had everything available in all the others combined, in their original languages and English translations, most of which Thorn had retranslated himself as his mistrust and disappointment in his predecessors grew.

For almost a century now, the global consensus among the few who'd tracked these occurrences was that, throughout recorded history, there had been twenty-two confirmed events of this particular nature. Problem was, when it came to anything earlier than the event of 1471—known to Thorn and his few living international contemporaries as D-Event XIX— the detail and general usefulness of the records accelerated downhill.

Records prior to that fell behind increasingly thick and obnoxious veils of fable, legend, or other mystical bullshit. This wasn't unique to Thorn's particular canon of research. It's something many historians who comb the annals of pre-Reformation Europe, North Africa, and the Levant were familiar with. Thorn learned how corrosive and toxic theocratic superstition could be to the simple effort of accurate recordkeeping— festooning what should've been just a fact-based, concise description of something with infuriating magical nonsense.

So, when it came to the global compendium of knowledge on this issue, there was only so much to work with.

The official corpus of American records generated by his own office was considerably smaller, composed of whatever had been passed down by the fourteen others who'd held this position since 1783. Their collective record was a barely legible, manic, hand-scrawled mess. Thorn saw it as an increasingly maddening informational snowball that'd been rolling for almost 220 years while being torn, stained, annotated, and unnecessarily fucked with by each of those men along the way. Within their own notes, Thorn could read their flagrant misunderstandings or how they'd misread or just entirely missed important context. Very few people alive had notable experience in robust record investigations or legal discovery at the time those men had been appointed to this position, and their technological constraints were undeniable. However, Thorn did not give them much grace for this. He'd studied writers and academics from his fourteen predecessors' respective lifetimes. Those intellectuals possessed a keen analytical shrewdness that most of his predecessors simply did not have, and he'd spent countless hours damning them for it.

Only one, Thorn's predecessor, had even seen a version of the internet during their tenure, and only two events had taken place since the position had been formed. The first of those, D-Event XXI, had already been thwarted by the Scots before Thorn's predecessor or President Thomas Jefferson had even gotten word it had begun. The second event, 1909's D-Event XXII, was the first to take place on the North American continent, so it was America's first oversight of an event.

Thorn had access to two journals and a six-letter correspondence with the War Department from the man who'd held his position during the event in 1909.

The six letters provided updates and summaries to President Taft and Jacob Dickinson, his secretary of war at the time. They were, unfortunately, more infuriating than enlightening. Each was vague and ended with an assurance that he'd relay more detail—specifically those regarding the Sentinel, the Tormentor, and the ritual—in person at an upcoming meeting, as they'd all previously agreed was the best way to keep the information secure.

The two journals were only marginally more helpful. He'd lacked basic record discipline, going weeks at a time between some entries, but it's all Thorn had, so he'd read them repeatedly. The man had been sixty-two years old in 1909, a Union army veteran who'd lost his arm below the elbow during the Battle of Cold Harbor. He was among the thirteen thousand men who'd been maimed or killed during the infamously suicidal and strategically useless charges ordered by General Grant over three gruesome, humid days. Grant famously never forgave himself for what many described as his *act of mass murder* at Cold Harbor. To Thorn's great frustration, his predecessor hadn't either. The only snippets of useful information hid amid easily fifty times as much furious reflection on General Grant—some of which this miserable son of a bitch had felt compelled to scribble down during the goddamned D-Event XXII itself.

That was really it. That's what Thorn had to work with. He also knew the duties of his position that had been established over time were based upon a nightmarishly arcane puzzle of historic records, correspondence, and fable.

The first duty was to identify and confirm when an event had begun, as it seemed nobody had ever been able to accurately forecast one. This was enabled by the Confluence Protocol, a program fewer than one hundred people knew existed. It's a compartmentalized multinational network of atmospheric, magnetic, seismic, and deep-ocean telemetry nodes, a sensor-fused data network. Each participating scientific unit is funded by benign national grants and believes its focus is narrow and innocuous: monitoring auroral anomalies, EM frequencies, seismic symmetry, migratory disorientation, deep crustal harmonics, hyperspectral satellite noise, and the like. But they are in fact feeding live data into a convergent system whose true function is understood only by its controlling core: to watch for the harmonic pattern preceding an event.

The need for such a thing was based on the cryptic minutiae within the historic records regarding natural observations associated with the beginning of an event. In 1909, rudimentary data compiled by scientists recording auroral, seismic, and barometric activity, as well as some experimenting with transatlantic telegraphy, told a story. However, this story was only noticed by those privy to the sealed libraries focused on the events. Since then, the Confluence Protocol was developed and honed into the watchtower of science it is today. Analysis of the data from 1909 gave those few who stood sentry now a hypothesis of what patterns to look for.

In that time, Malcolm Thorn contributed more to that pattern analysis than most others. So few of Thorn's international contemporaries were surprised when it was he who spotted the pattern several weeks ago. It began with the barometric drop recorded by the British army weather station in the Hindu Kush for that *precise* number of seconds. Then came the seismic and transducer readings, the symmetrical seismic activity and shifts in landlocked water oscillations at those precise equilateral locations. Then the hyperspectral satellite data, the equatorial auroral activity and minute shift in atmospheric Schumann Resonance. The Confluence Protocol had worked perfectly, and when everyone who knew of its existence got Thorn's alert, they were terrified to learn that it had.

Thorn's next duty, once the event was confirmed to be underway and he'd alerted his global counterparts, was to brief the president and executive cabinet. His most critical duties came next—the seminal objective of which was to stop the ritual by way of *finding the weapon*.

After he'd found *the weapon*—referred to most frequently as the *Sentinel*, among dozens of other names—his role was to control and direct his subject. However, there were subsidiary expectations and guidelines. The most critical urged the importance of keeping the identity of this Sentinel and the profound meaning thereof concealed from as many people as possible, *even from the Sentinel himself*.

There were many reasons for this, articulated in many languages over several millennia. The central gist was that as the Sentinel's knowledge increased regarding what he was, so did the enemy's ability to forecast his actions: the character most frequently described as the *Tormentor*. Essentially, when the event began, the Sentinel's only real advantage was a one-sided ability to see or feel or otherwise predict the actions of the Tormentor. As his awareness of who he was and that significance grew, the sensory connection between them equalized. Thus, the Sentinel not only lost his advantage, but the Tormentor gained it.

A pair of Scottish men involved with D-Event XXI in 1803 found their success at stopping the ritual was more swift and effective by merely shadowing him, letting *him* reach conclusions on his own. A Frenchman had written several letters about D-Event XX in 1698, and noted that his efforts to teach the Sentinel about who and what he was actually complicated things to an almost disastrous effect. Thus, he'd included the suggestion for those in the future: *Montrez-lui ses ailes, mais il doit apprendre à voler seul—show him his wings, but he must learn to fly alone.*

This vague and infuriating industry standard—that it was critical to shroud as much substantive backstory as possible from the Sentinel himself—complicated the simultaneous expectation that Thorn control and direct that same man. The flagrantly contradictory expectations had stressed him out for over two decades. Now, it might drive him mad.

There were other tidbits of intelligence that Thorn, like those before him, had flagged as potentially important given the frequency and emphasis of references to them throughout the jumbled, global records of events.

One was referenced dozens of times throughout history, and pertained to the advantage the Sentinel had: the ability to see, feel, or sense the Tormentor in some way. The common thread suggested that the Sentinel, once the event began, would become afflicted by states of delusional mania that were inexplicably associated with the moon. In several records, this affliction was vaguely explained as being related to, or even the conduit of, the Sentinel's ability to see or sense the Tormentor—a power the Sentinel would lose, and the Tormentor would gain, should he become aware of who and what he was.

Greek and Byzantine records referred to this affliction as the Selenomania, while Roman records charted it as Lunamania. Normans and Vikings called it the *Mánagalr*, the *moon rage*. By the time folks started scribbling in Middle English and other early forms of modern languages, it was some contemporary translation of *moon madness*.

However, those ancient fools failed to record the physiological symptoms of moon rage with any real functional utility. This incensed Thorn. Without symptoms, diagnosing such a fantastical cognitive disorder in another turned into a fucking clown show. He'd almost given up.

Then he saw it.

He wasn't certain that's what he was seeing, but then he saw it again. And again. In a blink, the game warden appeared to just *go somewhere else*. He was actually pretty good at hiding the shock when he returned to present reality from wherever his mind had taken him. Not good enough to hide it from Thorn, though.

Within seven of the historic records mentioning this *moon rage*, Thorn found references to *the new moon* within the same excerpt. None of his predecessors had made note of this, unsurprisingly, though on this charge Thorn did not blame them too harshly. Hundreds of these old records were written by tree-worshipping pagans or polytheists who regularly rattled on about celestial and atmospheric nonsense.

One point stood out as the most salient, universally understood bedrock of D-Events themselves. The ritual. The earliest, express reference to it was made in a Roman record from 451 BC. From that anchor point, a timeline was developed that was based on hundreds of other records found in modern-day Libya, Egypt, Israel, Turkey, Iraq, Greece, Russia, and all over Europe from Spain to Norway. All had the same general narrative summary and explanation for this ritual.

The ultimate purpose of Thorn's entire role—perhaps the only reason world powers still bothered tasking people like Thorn to watch, wait, and quietly prepare for these events—was to stop the ritual.

Although, wherever the dire need to stop the ritual was mentioned, it was almost always followed by two other aggravating points. The first was the unanimous, historic consensus that the Sentinel had to be involved in stopping the ritual. Throughout history, this character had either started and led or somehow folded into the existing effort to stop it. The second was the abject lack of any clarity on what the hell the goddamned ritual actually was, what went into it, or why this Tormentor sought to carry it out. There were countless references to the preparation of the ritual, the Tormentor's need to collect all the paraphernalia and all the blood needed to carry it out, but nothing with any reliable detail.

Thorn had memorized every hypothesis, ancient or recent, of what would've happened had the ritual been completed. They were all different, but did seem to agree on one thing: completion of the ritual would imbue the Tormentor with power he'd use to subjugate the world's population into lives of painful, horrifying servility. However, Thorn also knew none of these prognosticating dickheads had any idea what would happen. *Because it never had.* Every single one of the twenty-two known D-Events had ended with the Sentinel either killing the Tormentor before the ritual was prepared, or stopping the ritual from taking place once it had been. There were also countless references to how one could *just feel* the catastrophic nature of the consequences, the closer the new moon came.

Thorn knew he'd nailed the first parts of his job: identify when D-Event XXIII began, notify his counterparts around the world, re-brief the president on what that meant, and then explain what it meant to whomever the president wanted included.

With respect to his second duty, Thorn had been keeping an eye on Clark Rickert for over two years now, ever since the game warden had hunted down and killed Elijah Austin Miles—a man Thorn had been keeping an eye on for quite a bit longer.

Elijah Austin Miles, as well as Thorn could surmise, was *one of the seventy-two*. This was another frustratingly porous legend, but one dispositively associated with and as present in the records as the D-Events and their associated emergence of the Tormentor and the Sentinel. The general idea was that each of these two champions always had a retinue of seventy-two regular, mortal people walking the earth between their periodic reemergence. Thorn had spent years unsure why the hell this legend had been addended to the records, or how these allegedly predestined 144 assholes were relevant to anything. Then it clicked.

Fifteen years earlier, Thorn's Swedish and Norwegian counterparts successfully lobbied to add additional nodes to the Confluence Protocol focused on biometrics, biolinguistics, and cognitive neuroscience. Thorn was unaware how observational data from such fields could possibly be helpful, until about six years ago. This program was aimed at identifying members of the fabled 144. It was profoundly more challenging to find the seventy-two *good ones*, given their conduct being presumptively more benign, and thus less prone to chaos, furor, headlines, or other anomalous conduct. The bad ones, on the other hand, would be easier to track. Medical records of two people, both hospitalized with head trauma at the same time, were flagged by these new human-focused nodes of the Confluence Protocol as potential *high-interest* individuals related to the lore of the two seventy-two-person groups. EEG data showed both had REM spiking in identical frequencies and low-band subharmonics, as well as perfectly synced heartbeat deceleration, spikes in galvanic skin response, and core temperature drops. One—a former officer in the Croatian Defense Council who'd led and enthusiastically engaged in the massacres of Bosniak civilians after the 1992 Battle of Prozor—was in an ICU in Zagreb. The other—a lowlife with sadistic proclivities toward people and animals—was in an ICU in Missoula, where he'd spent a month after getting beaten almost to death in prison.

The Croat died, but Thorn kept an eye on Miles, wondering what, or more specifically, *who*, such a character might bump into. When Clark Rickert had killed Elijah Miles, he'd wondered whether the game warden could be his man. That confidence had grown in the two years since, and then even more since meeting the guy. Despite that, he still wasn't certain, and had long wondered how one obtained conclusive certainty about who the Sentinel really was. Given their prolific role throughout history, he'd figured they'd just let everyone else know. That was until today.

After today, Thorn was as close to certain as he could ever be. He felt it in his bones. Region 4 Captain Clark Rickert *was the Sentinel*.

However, fulfilling this ancient duty had been tragically underwhelming. Thorn had no idea how to even begin directing and guiding this troglodytic, reckless, stupid asshole. Let alone how to do so while keeping the knowledge and significance of who, and what, Clark was from the other leadership here and *from Clark himself.*

Thorn was, yet again, floored by how little he had to work with.

Millennia of recordkeeping. Centuries of covert multinational intelligence collection, communication, and research had preceded America's formal induction into the intergovernmental effort to study, prepare for, and address these events. It had all continued in the almost two and a half centuries since, as well, in conjunction with the profound resource allocation of the United States. He'd read all the journals, notes, records, and findings known to exist, and had learned eight languages just to review original sources. He'd traveled the world, meeting with the others who'd been tasked by their own countries to monitor and prepare for this. He'd devoted his life to it.

But here he was, in Montana, dealing with it alone and with no idea what to do. The irresponsibility, the oversight, the abject failure of his predecessors, his government, and the entire world to properly prepare him for this moment were staggering.

Thorn tapped his foot on the floor of the trailer and felt tears build behind his eyes. The unshakable pessimist in him began to run through all the same questions, yet again.

If they don't care, why should I? If this barefooted Tormentor is really capable of such global destruction, why the hell didn't they prepare properly? If I'm not even supposed to tell Clark what he is or what's going on here, and he's supposed to figure it all out on his own, why am I even still here? Why the fuck was I ever here?

He shook his head clear.

He hadn't failed. *Yet.* He'd executed every step of his duties thus far, and from what he could tell, he'd done it faster and more effectively than any who'd come before. He'd done well. He needed to believe that, at least.

But now what?

Just through the executive insertion of Thorn into the leadership of this task force, and Thorn's own insistence that Clark also be added, it was undeniable that Benson, Jacobson, and Bishop grasped some of what was going on. They were smart, and Thorn knew they'd see some connection running between the president and the imposition of their local law enforcement liaison, Clark Rickert.

He'd hoped these circumstances and their intellect would cue them into the expectation for discretion and tact when it came to interacting with Rickert. He also knew, after he'd briefed them all at the White House, these three had been explicitly ordered by their agency director and the secretary of defense not to ask Thorn a single question. He'd watched the video recording of this meeting, and knew how they'd responded, what they'd asked. From that, he knew they saw him as a *historian*, a useless archivist. He hadn't cared, but sitting here now, it made him hate them.

And since a few hours ago, when those cultists had reacted to whatever Clark had whispered to them as though it were some curse or hex—since realizing he'd finally found the Sentinel—he truly felt useless. The sensation made him hate his predecessors, the president, Clark Rickert, and every other person who'd known about this cyclical, cataclysmic event and not at least taken better goddamned notes.

He frowned as he considered the substance, character, and background of Rickert—the man he'd eagerly given an oath twenty-one years earlier to find, guide, advise, and serve as steward for. He grunted, then smacked the mug off his desk, shattering it against the wall of the trailer.

All those who'd written records throughout history describing the Sentinel were just as full of shit and unhelpful as all the rest, it would seem.

They'd all assured Thorn he would be a wise, courageous polyglot. They'd all described this Sentinel as some contemplative, stoic warrior and artisan. He'd been promised a Templar, a paladin of selfless, Arthurian virtue.

Lucius Quinctius Cincinnatus had described the man Thorn had spent his life looking for as: *he of the light who awaits the darkness, tireless and unseen, to stand against its wrath.*

Thorn got Clark fucking Rickert, a feral, angry, low-IQ, emotional basket case.

But those ancient assholes, Cincinnatus, all the rest, they'd just been lying, Thorn reflected. They'd probably dealt with someone just like Clark. Someone just as bullheaded and brash and fucking moronic. That's what Thorn told himself now, at least.

Tough love, Thorn thought, *this caveman employs, and thus will respond to brutish, crude, simple authority, so if he wants to talk shit like a teenager, that's what I've got to do as well.*

As soon as he heard the knock on his flimsy door, Thorn knew the confrontation he'd been dreading had come.

CHAPTER 37

CLARK HADN'T ENDED up getting detained. Not really, at least. They hadn't disarmed him, although it was obvious someone had instructed at least three operators he'd seen to shadow him until they were back at the FOB. Upon landing in the UH-60 helicopter, before being allowed to shower or head to his truck, he'd been "asked" to join a leadership briefing in the command tent. Once there, two of these operators stood behind his chair, never leaving his blind spots.

He'd only been there for five minutes when Benson, Jacobson, Bishop, and one of Benson's staffers entered the large tent together. Thorn, however, the only one Clark wanted to see, was missing. Benson and Bishop both lanced him with questions while Jacobson remained silent.

How did you do that? How'd you set them off? What did you say to them? Why did they respond that way? How'd you know they'd respond that way?

Clark had answered all of them, somewhat honestly, with some variation of *it was just a hunch.*

He had no plan now. He'd known he had to do something that would knock the socks off the others and get their attention. It seemed he'd succeeded in that respect, but it would have to be all freestyle from here, something he had no real gift for. As each minute went by, watching the frustration, confusion, and exhausted disbelief in their faces, he felt more confident that only Malcolm Thorn knew what he wanted to know. These people looked as confused and disturbed as Clark felt himself. The questions had ebbed, and Jacobson pulled up a chair. The others stood or sat behind him.

Clark, just as perplexed as anyone else at his own ability to send that band of cultists into the fit of crazed insanity, grew impatient. He hadn't said anything in over a minute, and when he violently cleared his throat, it took everyone off guard.

"I'm just lookin' for a straight answer to a straight question, *nothin' more*. At this point, when it comes to my question of why I was selected for this task force, couple things seem clear. First, seems like Thorn can answer that, and y'all probably can't, at least not entirely. Second, I got this feelin' you three *know Thorn has this answer*, even if you don't yourselves. So let's stop wasting time. I know he's within shouting distance, so go round the little asshole up. If he answers my question, I'll tell y'all *all about* my hunches and intuitions. Doubt you'll like what I've gotta tell ya, Lord knows I fuckin' don't, but I'll give it to ya straight."

Clark looked up at Benson as he addressed Harry.

"Let's also not forget the ultimatum Benson laid down back on that porch. I was to fall in line as a quiet, obedient *local law enforcement liaison*, or get booted from the task force. I respect that kinda line in the sand, Benson. I really do. And only minutes after you laid it down, I crossed it. So . . ."

Clark looked from Benson to Jacobson.

"I'm gonna make this *real easy on everyone*. In about sixty seconds, I'm gonna stand up, walk to my truck, and drive outta your lives and back into mine. And I'll do it without a glance or a fuckin' word. That's a call I'm makin' and layin' down right now, one *I will follow through on*. However, I see three alternatives to it. First is you puttin' a bullet in my head, *right fuckin' now*. Second is you and your boys tryin' to restrain me. But if we go down that road, Harry, no matter how many Tasers or jujitsu moves y'all got, I give you my word right now *I will leave you no choice but to fuckin' kill me*. The third alternative is you sendin' someone off in the next forty seconds to fetch Malcolm Thorn."

Everyone stiffened. The operators behind Clark gripped their rifles tighter as they glanced at Jacobson, who shook his head once but did not take his eyes from Clark. No one, including Jacobson, knew how they'd react to Clark trying to leave this place, but they all felt it was a sure thing that he was about to try.

Benson, Bishop, and Jacobson certainly had been jarred by the president's unexplained insistence that the strange Thorn be included at the command level of this task force. Thus, all were now rapt by the increasingly bizarre connection between the shadowy figure Thorn and this mysterious, hectoring game warden. The tension had ratcheted exponentially every second until Benson spoke.

"*Get Thorn.*"

Two minutes later, Benson's staffer ushered Thorn into the tent. When he entered, Benson ordered the two operators and his own staffer to leave. One of the operators hesitated, looking at Jacobson as he shifted his weight from foot to foot. Benson saw this and snarled his command.

"Anyone without clearance for SCI-restricted and SAP-controlled intel will *immediately leave this fucking tent.*"

The operator glanced at Bishop, then Jacobson, then nodded to Benson.

"*Aye-aye*, boss."

Thorn slowed to a stop when he reached a spot to Clark's left. He looked at the ground, removed his glasses, and squinted his eyes shut as he pinched the bridge of his nose. Clark adjusted his ass in the chair to face him a bit, and spoke through an amused expression.

"*Well, howdy*, Malcolm. We were all just wonderin' why—"

The volume and venom in Thorn's voice shocked everyone.

"*Shut your fucking mouth.*"

Thorn hadn't turned or even opened his eyes as he spoke, just shot a finger toward Clark like a parent scolding a child.

Even more unexpected was Clark's immediate response, and the slow, glacial strength in his voice.

"No, sir. If you wanna shut my mouth, you'll have to do it with those little hands a' yours."

Clark's eyes narrowed.

"I'm gonna ask you one question, one time. You don't answer it, I'm gonna walk, or make these fellas fuckin' kill me. Pretty simple shit here, pal. So let's give it one final go: *Why exactly was I selected to be on this task force?*"

Thorn would play hardball. It was worth it, at least one last time. If this asshole cowboy called his bluff, he would eat his pride and tack course, but it was worth one last try. He took a deep breath, put his glasses back on, and shrugged, his East Coast accent as strong as ever.

"*Walk. Go.* Everyone here's frightened, Captain Rickert, but if you're too chickenshit to handle this operation, then scamper off, *cowboy*. Like Benson said earlier, you're just a rubber stamp, a legal requirement. We don't have time for your insecurities."

Benson, Bishop, and Jacobson shifted weight uncomfortably or crossed their arms, looking between Thorn and Clark, unconvinced but no counter-argument coming to mind. Thorn stepped toward Clark.

"Look, Captain, you've obviously got some personal shit to deal with, and we don't have time or room for loose cannons on this task force. Maybe you're still too shaken up about your son Ben's death and Mary's suicide, but—"

Frank Farrington's old Stetson hat flipped from Clark's head as he exploded forward. All the others saw was blurred mass both impossibly dark and unbearably bright. A blast of static, iodized air shunted into the canvas throughout the massive tent. Everyone felt their ears pop and stomachs lurch. Before Frank's hat hit the ground, Clark had the smaller man in both hands.

He gripped Thorn's jacket and shirt collars in one and clamped the lower half of Thorn's face within the other; his palm covered Thorn's mouth, his thumb and fingers sunk deep into the soft skin under his ears. Thorn's eyes bulged as he felt his mandible creak and his front teeth grind together. When Clark growled into his face, he could feel the tears coating his eyes and spit inside his lips begin to actually freeze.

"Say their names again and you'll scream the oldest of mine as I feed you your eyes. A name screamed as I waded through the blood of kingdoms long dust before the oldest now known. A name screamed by kings as I drowned them in the blood of their own sons. I am not your soldier or redeemer; I am slaughter incarnate, butchery manifest. I am the unseen, he who awaits the coming wrath, the lordless blade that makes the night wail. Si profers nomina familiae meae iterum, mundum citius quam tenebrosum principem quem times delebo."

Jacobson was on him, forcing himself between Clark and the smaller man. Clark let go of Thorn's face but kept ahold of his jacket and shirt, which were both starting to tear at their seams. Though over twenty years Clark's senior, Harry was a lifelong student in the grips, pressure points, and the precise tensions necessary to take complete physical control over another man, no matter what they thought about it.

He applied that mastery as he grabbed and tried to wrench Clark away from Thorn, and was stunned. He could feel Clark was not actively resisting against him, but he still felt as though he weighed ten tons. It was like trying to move a bulldozer. Thorn's face went sheet-white as Clark continued screaming into it.

"I might not know what the hell that meant, but I know you do, Thorn. I know you know what that fuckin' meant. Spin all the bullshit you want for the others, but I know you know what's happening to me."

Charlotte stepped abruptly in front of Clark and grabbed him by the chin with a strong hand. She stared into his eyes and spoke in a calm, hard voice.

"Stop, Clark. Stop this. You need to let go of him, take a breath, and relax. Right now."

Clark went quiet and still. His pupils were so dilated his eyes looked black, and she watched them retract to the center of his gray-green irises. She released her grip on his chin but kept her fingers on his cheek. Clark took a deep breath, and finally registered the brutal sensation of his entire body being filled with broken glass. When he exhaled, it all washed away. In that same moment, Harry felt Clark relax and actually looked at the man's arms expecting to see it happening. The rebar-reinforced concrete he'd been fighting against turned back into normal human muscle. Harry spun Clark away, speaking a quiet, firm command into his ear that he "stand down and relax." The words helped Clark bring his mind back under control. He took a few deep breaths then patted Jacobson's elbow.

"I'm cool. I'm cool, Harry. I'm done."

Jacobson cautiously released him.

Clark glanced at Charlotte and Benson, then Thorn standing behind them. All stared back with furtive eyes that suggested they were actually ready to run from him. He turned away from them and walked slowly back toward where he'd been seated.

He picked up his hat, dusted it off, and ran a hand through his thick head of gray-flecked brown hair. His hands shook, his heart pounded, and he could feel the pressure of tears behind his eyes. He half turned toward the others. A fault line of emotion they'd never heard quaked his words.

"I'm done here. I wish you all the best a' luck."

Charlotte stepped toward him and began to speak, but stopped when she felt Jacobson's gentle but immovable grip on her upper arm. She looked to Benson. The DDO shrugged, looking terrified and exhausted. All three looked at Thorn.

He felt the bite of their collective glower. He knew, as well as they did, how unnecessarily cruel he'd just been, and how he'd deserved to get his teeth kicked in for it. He knew his disdain for this game warden had boiled over and that he'd crossed a line bringing up his family. He also acknowledged that Clark had just called his bluff. Staring at Clark's back as he strode toward the exit, he knew it was time to swallow his pride, and did not hesitate.

"Elijah Austin Miles..."

Clark stopped. The others looked from Clark's back to Thorn, who removed his torn blazer and tossed it on the ground, loosened his tie, and spoke with a confident, casual strength that seemed impossible from a guy who'd almost just had his head torn off.

"You knew him as a dope-fiend poacher, but I knew him as something else. Let's just say he was a suspected member of a group that we—those of us tasked with keeping tabs on all this madness—have a particular interest in. So I'd been keeping an eye on Miles for quite some time, waiting to see what a guy like that might get himself into. Or *who a guy like that might bump into*. When you put a bullet in that knuckle dragger's head, that's when I found you, Captain. Now, I'm gonna answer your question, but here's the thing: I cannot provide more context. I cannot answer any follow-up *how*s or *why*s or *when*s, but I'll give you a straight answer based on what I've just disclosed about my job and duties. I give you my word that if this operation's successful, I'll set aside the weeks it'll take to explain *all the rest*."

Thorn's Boston accent was thicker than ever, hacking into his words like an acid, rendering down the final *R* in every word that had one. Thorn took another step toward Clark as he went on, who'd only half turned toward the others and stared at Thorn from the corner of a squinted eye.

"Benson, Jacobson, Bishop, and three dozen other top dogs back east know what this cult leader is, what he's trying to do, and the threat he poses for the world, at least to the extent anyone alive does. My job, *my duty*, was to provide that information to those people when the threat presented itself, so they could address it. Most, even these three here, thought that was the extent of my role. It wasn't."

Clark didn't move as Thorn took another step toward him.

"Other than myself, there are only five people who know a few additional things about what's going on here, and when I'm finished talking, you four will make it a club of nine."

Benson stepped forward with an open palm facing Thorn, who cut him off before he could speak.

"*Fuckin' can it*, Benson, all right? I've got full autonomous disclosure authority. Don't believe me? Call POTUS—*he's in this little club too.* Here, use my phone, *unless you've also got his direct line."*

Benson closed his mouth, let his hand fall, and Thorn turned back to Clark and went on. He spoke in deliberate, clipped words, as though considering the implications of every syllable.

"Those five people were the only ones who knew about the other part of my job, the project I've been working on for over two decades. That project was to find a particular person who would need to be a part of the effort to stop this enemy when he finally emerged. So, Captain Rickert, the real reason you were selected for this task force is because, well . . . *I'm pretty sure you're that particular fucking person."*

Thorn saw the judgment and disbelief in Clark's narrow eyes. He put his hands in his pockets and nodded in acknowledgment of Clark's silent skepticism. His voice quieted, grew more casual.

"It's fair for you to not trust that. *Hell*, I'm not even sure I do. Maybe I only pegged you as the fella I'd been looking for because you're the one who waxed Elijah Miles. I'd put a lot of stock in that, you know. I'd grown confident that—if that asshole got himself killed in a fight—whoever put him in the dirt would be my guy, but I don't know. Spent two decades trying to find a knucklehead in a stack of fuckin' knuckleheads, so maybe I just started seeing what I wanted to see."

He stepped toward Clark and looked at him with fierce eyes, then spoke slowly and deliberately again.

"If I were to tell you anything more, Clark, whatever's happening to you would stop happening to you, and while I don't deserve it, I'm going to ask that you trust me when I say: *We really do not want that to happen.* I will not risk that. So please, *please* do not leave, and I swear on my own life and all I hold dear that I'll explain everything after we see this through."

He looked at Clark until his eyes became tired and distant, his expression falling into the kind someone might have while begging for something they didn't expect or deserve. Clark finally removed his hat and inspected it, flicking away spots of dirt. He did not look up as he spoke.

"Just outta curiosity, which one of his names y'all been usin'? Azrael, Maelgrim, Acheron, Moros? Gideon or Melchior? There's another one, more recent, pretty sure it starts with a *D*, can't remember it though . . . Somethin' new, maybe?"

Benson, Bishop, and Jacobson watched Thorn for a reaction. Renewed focus widened his eyes, but he did not answer. Clark rubbed a calloused palm up the three-day scruff on his neck and chin. It was unnaturally loud in the tense silence. He stared into the empty space between them for a long moment. When he finally spoke, he did so in an uncharacteristic monotone, free of all his usual inflection.

"The writing on the coffin you had removed from the Brookings ranch is in Coptic Greek, vaguely translating to *from the shadows of forgotten sands, I'll rise again, thirst unquenched, hunger unending.* The shit carved into that lady we found at the base of the tree, it's Sumerian, but written poorly and awkwardly, so it'd rhyme when translated into English, something like *every cycle I'll rise anew, from slumber deep my reign renew, beware the night my shadow stir, my thirst the world shall all incur.* I assume the lab tests of the substance found around the victims' mouths at the blood mills was pretty surprising. A genetic anomaly, some hybrid of a modern human and another extinct hominid, Neanderthal maybe. I'm sure you've figured out all those coins they had in their mouths are silver, from just about every Iron Age kingdom close to the Mediterranean. Y'all check the brands on the cultists' arms? The necrosis? Find that little surprise yet?"

Clark looked at the others now, leaving time for this one to be answered, but no one spoke. Eventually, Harry lifted his eyebrows a bit and nodded almost imperceptibly. Clark nodded back and went on.

"Then I reckon that kicked off a whole mess a' tests. Did some spectroscopy and chromatography, I assume, looked at the collagen fiber and cellular morphology? Probably ran it all through a comparative analysis. So I'd imagine there are quite a few folks wondering how it's possible for all those wounds to be thousands of years old."

Charlotte only somewhat successfully stifled a gasp. Benson took a step toward Clark, mouth agape, looking at the game warden as though he'd just teleported into the room. Jacobson remained completely still. All three were as certain as they'd ever been about anything that there wasn't a soul within hundreds of miles, other than them and Thorn, who knew any of what Clark had just said.

Thorn's eyes narrowed, but hope and disbelief gleamed through them in equal measure. His voice quivered a bit as he spoke.

"*Êtes-vous capable de voir à travers ses yeux? Esne connexa? Estne connexio casus, an ad eam faciendam manum extendisti?*"

Benson, Jacobson, and Bishop were all fluent in French and knew the first question had been whether Clark *could see through his eyes.* They also had the education in Latin to cobble together the second and third, asking if they were connected, and if so, whether that was something Clark had control over.

"*Nah*, not through his eyes. It's like I'm followin' him, never too close but somewhere nearby. There's a connection, but it's strange, erratic, never comes through with a clean signal. And yeah, they just . . . *happen*, I guess. Like a dream. Certainly not somethin' I've ever initiated myself."

Thorn's shoulders slumped as he exhaled. He felt a weight that had been growing for decades flow from his body. He closed his eyes and grinned, then laughed a bit. No one spoke. Jacobson and Charlotte looked at each other briefly, then at Benson, who stared at Clark with their same astonishment. Thorn looked up at Clark, appearing relieved, almost grateful. He walked the last few paces to Clark and extended a hand.

Knowing now, without any doubt, whose eyes he finally stared into, he spoke his first two words slowly, and with a reverence that came from the bottom of his heart.

"*Captain Rickert*, I sincerely apologize for what I said earlier about your family, and do so without expectation of your acceptance. It would be hard for you to understand how badly I want to tell you more right now, but I cannot. I really cannot. I'm truly sorry I can't say more at this time, but once we see this through, I vow to you that I will tell you everything I know. For now, you're going to have to, well . . . *try to make your own connections*."

Clark glanced at Thorn's hand with suspicion, mulling over his words, then back into his eyes as he shook it.

"Guess I'll stick around, then. And I suppose I let my temper cook up a bit too. So we're square."

Thorn exhaled through his nose and nodded as he closed his eyes, looking like he'd just received a negative biopsy. Clark let go of Thorn's hand and took a hesitant step toward the other three. He looked at Charlotte. They held each other's gaze as he kneaded his hat. She could see his mind search for something to say. He didn't find anything, so he put the hat on his head, tipped the brim toward her, and walked away.

Thorn glanced over at the others, smiling, uncaring whether they saw the tears in his eyes. Then he stared at the ground. He had finally, at very long last, just shaken the hand of the Sentinel.

CHAPTER 38

CLARK GASPED AND sat up as the loud banging on the side of his truck topper jarred him awake, his hand finding the grip of his Sig 9mm in the same instant. It'd only been ninety minutes since he'd finished his last bourbon and managed to fall asleep, but it felt like he'd been out for days. He heard more noise then: helicopter rotor blades, diesel engines coughing into service, distant shouting.

"*Let's go, Rickert, get your shit in gear, we're Oscar Mike in five.*"

Adrenaline sent him flying out the back of his truck and scrambling into his duty gear. Even after too much bourbon, Clark never failed to arrange his boots, rifle, vest, and pack in a manner conducive to quick action. He stared around the FOB and tried to rub the blur from his eyes, then did a quick gear check. He grabbed a water bottle from the back of his cab, locked his truck, and ran toward the command tent, finishing the thirty-two ounces of water just as he entered.

There were people moving with urgency everywhere. Clark checked his watch. He confirmed again he hadn't even fallen asleep two full hours earlier, not understanding how all these hundreds of people could've stirred into such a frenzy of readiness and speed.

Reichman shouted orders at some of his team from the 24th STS and into a radio as he ran past Clark toward the large briefing table at the far end of the tent. Clark followed. DuBroux, Reichman, Jake, Moritz, and several of the other team leaders and senior Ground Branch and HRT guys Clark knew were staring at Nowell, who rattled off orders and gestured at satellite imagery on the big displays behind him. There were others there, too, whom Clark hadn't ever seen.

One, a bear of a man, stood out first. He had a massive beard and cropped brown hair, nodding as his sharp eyes followed everything Nowell pointed to. A group of five others stood at the large man's flanks with matching combat pants, short-sleeved combat shirts, and plate carriers, all in the same desert MARPAT camo pattern, and some kind of red patch on their chest, sleeve, or both. The large former SEAL, Mako, was among them, his elbow resting on one's shoulder.

Other men in full battle kit glanced at Clark with faces he didn't recognize and more of the piercing, impatient eyes that challenged everything they looked at to a fight, the same eyes that seemed to be a qualification for Ground Branch selection. They obviously wondered why this asshole in jeans, Crispi hiking boots, a dirty old plate carrier, and a Hill People Gear backpack was loitering at the fringes of this group of killers. Nowell picked up on their curiosity.

"*New guys*, this is Captain Rickert, our local law enforcement liaison; he's run with us on every op so far. Clark, no time for intros, these are the new guys, augments from Ground Branch and Team Six. You're with Moritz and his team again; they'll catch you up in the bird."

All quickly nodded and looked back at Nowell, except for the massive SEAL. He narrowed his eyes at Clark.

"Is the cop squared away?"

Mako responded before Nowell could, talking through a smile.

"*Oh yeah*, Bobby. This one's surgical, ice-fuckin'-cold. He put on a clinic yesterday, dusted a whole pile of 'em."

Most of those around the table looked back at Clark, but only Bobby found him staring back. Jackson Nowell had been Bobby's boss when he used to run this same squad within DEVGRU. Nowell snapped the big man's attention back onto him with a quiet, sharp tone that carried an authority earned through time.

"*Wouldn't be here if he weren't.*"

Bobby nodded. Nowell let a full second pass, then fell right back into his lightning-fast mission brief. All Clark could gather was that a few surveillance and recon teams had been inserted into overwatch positions around a target location several hours earlier, just as they had done at every target location preceding an assault. Everything had gone smoothly until about thirteen minutes ago, when their cover had been blown and they were in some serious trouble. A swarm of assault teams were about to load into the choppers screaming outside and crash into the location from every direction. This prospect got Clark's heart pounding.

Clark had excused himself from the briefing the evening before, so now for the first time he scanned the satellite imagery and maps on the monitors behind Nowell. He saw something he recognized, so he went around the group to get a closer look, squinting up at them. Jacobson's voice surprised Clark and many of the others as it unexpectedly cut through and dampened the hum of voices.

"What is it, Captain Rickert?"

Clark looked over and saw him standing across the large tables. His staffers, and most of the operators, looked between the two. Clark pointed at the digital display and cleared his throat.

"This is the Hammond ranch. Where we're headed, I assume? Used to work there."

Jacobson stared back with hot, focused eyes.

"Anything we should know about it?"

Clark shrugged.

"They got a *whole lotta guns*, and they sure hate feds, but I'd guess nothing other than that y'all don't already know."

Some chuckled at the comment, but Jacobson's focus did not shake.

"Anything else?"

Clark stared back at him. The memory of the night before, what Harry had seen, crashed back into his mind. Clark didn't speak, but he held Harry's gaze and shook his head. Harry nodded at this, and gestured to Nowell, who looked between the two for a moment, then finished the briefing.

Less than ten minutes later, Clark was on a UH-60 helicopter at three thousand feet, screaming at 170 mph through the silver-blue haze of early dawn.

Team leader Zach Moritz ran through the basics of the situation. The eight guys who made up the four surveillance and advanced recon teams had infilled to overwatch positions several hours earlier. Just under a half hour ago, for reasons that remained unclear, they'd all had to break cover and go loud, and had remained engaged in a heavy, confusing gunfight. There was considerable distance between their four positions, and it wasn't clear how all four had been discovered at the same time, or what kind of force each faced. All four pairs were ordered to immediately break contact and carry out a fighting withdrawal as they tried to link up. A few minutes after that, linking up was ruled impossible until they had support, so they all fell into escape and evasion procedures. Command ordered the static QRF to stand by as it became clear that the four teams were in fighting retreats away from the target area and one another, and it remained entirely unclear what the enemy force profile was. Instead, the entire assault force was ordered to initiate the assault to try to draw fire by crashing into the target area.

That's all of what Clark was able to gather, at least, as well as the general consensus that this was not fucking good. He tried to picture this chaos happening on a piece of land he knew so well.

The eight-thousand-acre Hammond ranch was one of the most beautiful pieces of property Clark had ever spent time on. It was nestled right into the base of the Crazy Mountains—a steep island range isolated from the rest of the Rockies that blasted into the sky, surrounded by miles of prairie. When Clark was eighteen, the patriarch of the family, Mr. Hammond himself, had hired him to kill coyotes. When those got scarce, he'd asked Clark if he was comfortable illegally killing wolves, cougars, or anything else that messed with his cattle. Clark very much was, and very much had. When Clark's illegal game hunting career started picking up, he went straight to Mr. Hammond, asking if he could take his "clients" to hunt elk, deer, or predators on the western reaches of his ranch and cut him in on the fees he'd charge.

The Hammond ranch was one of several dozen large tracts of private land where Clark had secret pay-to-play arrangements with a foreman, ranch manager, or the owners themselves. Many of these were owned by wealthy doctors, lawyers, or finance dudes from back east or California who'd spend a month or two a year there in $10,000 worth of new silver-and-turquoise embroidered western garb. Clark had truly enjoyed taking other wealthy doctors, lawyers, or finance douchebags from back east or California onto those properties, and ripping their eyes out with laughably extortionary "guiding fees" for the privilege.

America never had a shortage of rich assholes desperate for a grip-and-grin photo with a dead bear, buck, or bull elk, who were also entirely unconcerned about violating some western state's hunting regulations. Clark had been in the game before social media too. That demographic of assholes had only grown since, and, he assumed, so had the market of eager influencers willing to pay obscene guiding fees to some roguish, bush-wise "local guide" who could promise hunt success without any annoying paperwork. Then they'd post the picture to Instagram, along with some fiction about *arduous weeks spent stalking beasts deep in the backcountry*, despite having shot them illegally over an alfalfa bale from the back of a truck on some private ranch.

They were only five minutes out now, and Clark felt anxious at the thought of seeing Mr. Hammond or either of his sons. He wondered if they'd been *turned* and joined the cult, or if they'd been murdered like the owners of the chicken farm or the ranch on Fort Peck Lake. Either way, he'd likely be laying eyes on them shortly, and would not enjoy either version.

Clark leaned forward to get a view when the helicopter started dropping in altitude, and could see the sun starting to kiss the upper granite reaches of Crazy Peak with pink and orange. He could see the six other UH-60s now, dropping fast and hard toward the ranch, still mostly obscured by the fog burning off the mountain. What Clark saw, where he found himself, shook him to his core.

The 160th Special Operations Aviation Regiment, the Night Stalkers, some of the world's most talented pilots—flying almost a half billion dollars' worth of the most advanced stealth-packaged helicopters in existence—ferried forty-two of the most high-speed, dangerous warfighters the world had ever seen, each of whom the government had poured millions of dollars into training, deploying, honing, and arming. All of this, *and Clark*.

He was riding this careening tidal wave of advanced, terrifying technology and death toward that quiet, lovely mountain property where he used to extort rich guys as he drank Steel Reserve and chain-smoked cigarettes. He couldn't help shaking his head at it all.

They dropped low and fast, causing Clark's stomach to do the same. He knew his team would be setting down in the pasture to the southeast of the large ranch house. He gripped a retention strap and tensed every muscle as he swore the pilot was about to smash right into the crowns of the poplars and cottonwoods that lined the long driveway.

Before he knew what was happening, the pilot had brought the aircraft to a perfectly still hover, skids just two feet above the thick, green grass being savaged by the rotor wash, and the team was jumping from the helicopter. When he centered himself after hitting the ground and looked around, all six guys were spread in a skirmish line, rifles shouldered, *sprinting* toward the house. Other helicopters were ripping up from where they'd dropped other teams around the target area. As he ran after his team, and the roar of the helicopters began to fade, he could hear gunfire. Most was suppressed, but quite a bit cracked through the early morning to spill into a roaring echo.

As had been the case during all these wild raids and assaults, he had no hope of trying to monitor or decipher the acronyms and commands blitzing across the radio into his ear. All Clark could do was shadow and mirror the movements of his team leader, and do his best to keep up.

They reached a white split-rail fence that ran around the homestead. He saw his first cultist then, a middle-aged guy in ranch-hand attire, running across the green, landscaped yard around the main house, shooting down the driveway at something to Clark's right. Clark had just begun shouldering his rifle when the guy was cut down by a wall of fire from his own team and the one moving up the driveway. Clark vaguely recognized the guy just as a bullet cracked into his forehead, snapping his head back so violently his beige cattleman hat popped straight up into the air. Long jets of bright blood spit from his back as more bullets ripped through his chest and shoulders. He crumpled onto the grass, his body motionless except for one hand that opened and closed. Opened and closed.

Clark's attention snapped back to the present as his team flowed over the fence and he scrambled after them. Other teams were visible as they surged into the area from other directions. Clark heard a burst of shooting, but when he looked toward the main house, the four shrieking cultists who'd burst from the front door were already tangled into one another and tumbling down the steps from the porch.

One of them, an older man, appeared to try to sit up once they'd crashed into the flagstone landing at the bottom. He didn't get far; five or six bullets punched into his belly, chest, and neck, and he fell onto his back as blood poured from his mouth and nose. Fine, misted blood burst from heads and limbs that jumped and twitched as bullets cranked into the shivering heap of bodies.

He felt a jolt of guilt and shame as Trent Vickers popped into his mind, along with the knowledge that these people could be saved by removing their brand.

A crack from behind him punched through the din and roar of the gunfire, and he heard the jittery, shrieking scream just as he turned toward the noise.

A single cultist had been hiding in a small irrigation pump house only thirty meters behind Clark. She'd kicked the door open and was sprinting straight toward him. She carried a hatchet raised above her head in her right hand, and a massive bowie knife in her left held straight out like a spear. She was in her mid-twenties and had striking blue eyes, wide with rage and madness. Her mane of filthy golden hair trailed out behind her.

As the former Ranger Gavin wheeled around and brought his weapon up toward the woman, he experienced something he'd later reflect had felt like a computer glitch, but in his perception. Without Gavin noticing any passage of time, Clark Rickert went from standing completely still next to him, to sprinting full speed toward the woman. He vaguely registered Clark's open palm slapping the barrel of his M4 toward the ground, but only after he'd felt the rifle buck in his hands. The other assaulters still bringing rifles to bear on the woman checked and dropped their muzzles when they saw Clark go flying into their lines of fire. By the time Moritz, Mako, and several others began screaming profanity at Clark's stupidity, he was on her.

When the woman's bowie knife was one foot from his chest, Clark struck her extended forearm with a vicious, openhanded clap. It whipped her arm out and around her body so hard it dislocated her shoulder and sent the knife spinning into the air farther than anything she'd ever thrown. In the same instant, he'd reached up and caught her wrist below the hatchet arcing down toward his collarbone. He cranked her wrist with a quick movement, caught the hatchet with his free hand, and casually tossed it to the side. In a blur, he grabbed her shoulders as he wheeled around her, then swept a shin into both her calves, booting her legs straight out in front of her. While her body was airborne and parallel with the ground, he cupped the back of her head, put a palm on her chest, and planted her flat into the earth. He'd protected her skull, but the rest of her body impacted violently, blasting the air from her lungs.

It had all gone down so incredibly fast that the operators who'd seen it just stared, silent and blinking, trying to reverse engineer the sequence of events. Although it could've been what Clark was doing now that had frozen them in surprise.

The young woman writhed under Clark's grip, coughing and gagging. Strain and murderous rage bulged the veins in her neck as much as her eyes. Her teeth snapped audibly as she bit at his arms and up toward his face. No one present had ever seen Clark look so shocked by fear. No one alive had. He pinned her to the gravel and shook her by the shoulders. A tremor of panic ran through his voice as he shouted into her face.

"Lucy. Lucy Westerna, look at me. Lucy, it's me. It's me."

CHAPTER 39

CLARK RAISED HIS eyebrows in thanks as Mako passed him some antiseptic wipes, gauze, and athletic tape. He began wiping lazily at the bleeding, feline scratches covering his forearms, chest, neck, and face.

Mako sat on a bucket across from where Clark leaned back against the large doors of the stables. The operators had taken five other cultists alive. With Lucy, all six had been restrained and secured in horse stalls within the stables. They could hear their muffled voices as they giggled, mumbled, and chanted.

Mako had stepped in to separate Clark from the young woman he was trying to calm down as she shrieked and clawed filthy fingernails into his chest and face. It was obvious this cultist had been someone he knew, a terrifying scenario every single member of the task force had considered over the last weeks. Quite a few of the operators had begun to stare at the spectacle in bemused, empathetic revulsion.

Clark did not resist Mako's suggestion that they restrain her with the others. He did insist on carrying her there and restraining her himself, which earned him another lancing of scratches to his face, neck, and arms.

Once Clark was finished, Mako watched him kneel and stare into her big, furious eyes. His muscles coiled when he saw Clark rest his hand on the hilt of the knife sheathed on his belt. When he saw Clark's index finger extend toward the strap button holding the knife in its sheath, Mako dropped a hard, heavy hand onto his shoulder. He squeezed, sinking a thumb into Clark's brachial plexus and pinching his trapezius against his clavicle.

Clark felt the assurance of martial expertise and extreme pain in Mako's hand, promises Clark could feel the former SEAL make through the precise angles, pressure, and casual speed of his grip.

Clark looked up at Mako as he stood slowly, then down again at Lucy as he backed away. Neither man had spoken in the two minutes since. A pair of helicopters landed in the pasture closest to the house to drop off a large group from command. When they lifted back off and he could be heard again, Mako finally spoke.

"Is she family, that one? A friend of yours?"

Clark stared into the morning sky as he ran an antiseptic wipe along one of the nastier scratches on his neck. He threw the wipe to the dirt and ran a forearm across his face.

"*Yeah.*"

Mako nodded, not taking his eyes from Clark's.

"Look, man, I do really believe they'll figure out how to shake the crazy off these cultists. It'll take some time and a *lotta fuckin' therapy*, but I do believe that. I really think they'll figure out a way to, I dunno . . . *break* whatever's got 'em."

Clark finally looked at Mako. He appeared amused by the younger man's optimism, nodded, then looked up at the sky again.

"Yeah, maybe so."

Voices caught their attention as a group moved quickly between the ranch house and the huge stables. Benson and Jacobson were at the head, a half dozen support personnel behind, followed by Bishop, who was maintaining four different conversations between a radio in one hand, a cell phone in the other, and two of her staffers.

Nowell and the DEVGRU commander, Bobby, and a group of their operators were walking fast in another direction, as fast as one can before it becomes a run.

Several dozen others moved in pairs or clusters between the outbuildings. Mako put an ear to his helmet's radio speaker and narrowed his eyes. Clark glanced over toward the area he was fairly certain he'd dropped his helmet while carrying Lucy into the stable, didn't see it, then looked at Mako.

"What's the situation?"

Mako waited for the transmission to end, then cleared his throat.

"We can't find our boys, any of the eight from the four advanced pairs. We haven't made contact with them since we were still on the birds, and all their transponders and IR strobes went dark around the same time. We're hoping they decided to do that intentionally. Anything they'd have seen to motivate doing that cannot be fuckin' good, but that's all we can hope for now."

Clark stared at Mako, saw his anxiety.

"You ain't gotta babysit me. On my son's grave, Mako, I would *never* do anything to hurt that girl in there."

Mako flit his gaze between Clark's right and left eyes, then nodded.

"All right, then."

He stood and jogged after Gavin, Moritz, and the others from this morning's assault team.

Clark took a deep breath. He felt scared, entirely unsure what would happen. What kind of door it might open, or what would be able to come through. But he was pretty sure it was what Thorn had been hinting at the night before, and at this point, there wasn't much left to lose. He wasn't sure how it was done, but it was a sense, a reflex, not something aided by a rule book. So Clark closed his eyes, and, for the first time, *he reached out.*

CHAPTER 40

CLARK FOUND HIM in a meadow.

He recognized the place, even in the flat, early morning light. He'd been here before, seen that horseshoe of rock outcroppings on the other side of the glade. He knew the path that led here, the one that wound through the aspen forest that ended not far behind him.

Clark was where he usually found himself in these moments, off and away, *shadowing him*. Fifteen or so cultists were on their knees between Clark's vague un-position and the man himself. They rocked back and forth. Clark strained to listen to what they were chanting, but quickly gave up as the first whispers of it came through and it made him nauseous.

Clark focused on him, the one he'd reached out to find. He was a few feet beyond the weeping, chanting cultists.

He was dancing.

Clark had seen him dance before. Somewhere in Anatolia, so very long ago. This was not at all the same.

Clark realized he, the cult leader, was actually in the midst of an undeniably flawless honky-tonk stomp. After his last step, he fell gracefully into the electric slide, embellished with sweeping kicks that sent clouds of gravel and dust directly into the faces of his disciples.

The dancing cult leader spun flamboyantly on his heel and crouched low as he mimicked drawing invisible pistols from nonexistent holsters on his belt. He aimed fingers at the operators up ahead of the group as he mouthed the sounds *pew, pew, pew.*

The operators.

Clark couldn't see them until now, as though the provocative little stunt had unshrouded them. All eight of them were there, at the base of the rock outcropping on the other side of the meadow. Five were stripped down to their underwear, while the other three were completely naked. All their clothes, gear, and weapons were in piles at their feet.

The cult leader mimicked the act of blowing smoke from the muzzles of his two pistols as he smiled. He finished the awkward gimmick by spinning the imaginary guns back into his nonexistent holsters. Then he exploded toward the operators at impossible speed, grass and dirt blasting away from where he'd been standing.

He flew across the thirty-meter area in a single bound, and brushed the shoulders of his coat as he began casually strolling down the row of men from Ground Branch and the 24th STS.

He stopped at one near the middle of the row and smiled warmly as he ran the backs of his fingers tenderly down his cheek. Clark wanted to scream, to end this, but found he had no idea how.

The man, whom Clark recognized, snarled hatred and profanities into the beast's smiling face. He patted the furious man on the chest a few times and stared back at his disciples. They began to shake and howl.

His teeth parted as he reached the apex of a smile and began to open his mouth—*but his mouth did not stop opening*.

He tilted his deformed head back and belched a scream made visible by a burst of cinders, smoke, and ash through an impossibly huge mouth lined with hundreds of ivory needles.

He wheeled on the screaming operator and tilted his head to the side as he stared into his eyes. Then he bit, and everything between his chin and his shoulders disappeared into the beast's gaping maw.

The vision ended in a flash of darkness, and Clark woke up.

CHAPTER 41

EVERYONE WITHIN CLARK'S field of view stopped moving as they listened to the bone-chilling transmission.

"Angel 1 for TFL, that's an A-firm, they're all up here. We've got PID on all eight. All presumed KIA, but administering presumptive treatment now."

Nowell and Bobby and a dozen other operators within Clark's view began sprinting to the west, disappearing behind the big house.

Jacobson—who'd been up on the porch of the main house where support staff had set up an impromptu surveillance drone monitor array—began shouting into a radio as he ran after the others. Benson was in the driveway below the porch, surrounded by his staff. He looked down at where Clark sat near the big stables. He turned away after a few moments, hung his head, then spiked the radio he'd been holding into the ground. Several behind him flinched away. Charlotte had been pacing between the trees in the yard to one side of the house, shouting into a radio and a satellite phone. When she'd heard the transmission she stopped pacing. She started to turn toward Clark, but didn't. Instead, she dropped her hands to her sides and screamed, "Fuck," just once.

Mako stared at Clark with wide eyes as he stood slowly and grabbed his helmet from the fence post he'd set it on. He'd been told to make sure Clark stayed there, but in Mako's mind, that duty had ended when the crazy-ass cowboy had been proven right. He started to say something, but stopped. He stared for another moment, then turned and jogged after the rest.

Clark hung his head and sighed, then pushed himself up. It had all started about twenty minutes earlier, when Clark had snapped out of his vision.

He'd come back to reality, or *this* reality, coughing and gasping, and pushed himself to his feet. He started running toward the spot he thought he'd dropped his helmet, then remembered he could just yank the cable that connected to his helmet from the radio and use it normally. He could feel he was panicking. He needed to tell someone. He frantically reached and spun in a circle, trying to reach his radio pouch. Then he saw Mako staring at him as he would at a lunatic who'd started hallucinating bugs infesting his clothes. *Mako is staring at a hallucinating lunatic*, Clark mused as he sprinted toward the big man.

He had Mako hail Nowell, who rushed to their position within a minute. Clark pulled Nowell aside by the elbow, not wanting to explain what he needed to in front of everyone. He squared up with the commander and looked him in the eye as he spoke his question just above a whisper.

"Nowell, do you trust me?"

Nowell narrowed his eyes in confusion but responded immediately.

"*No.* What? Fuck no."

Clark raised his eyebrows, cocked his head a bit, and nodded, silently acknowledging how reasonable that answer was.

Unaware of any reasonable way to explain himself, he launched into what he'd seen in his vision: delusions Nowell had no idea he'd been afflicted with, let alone anything about their significance. He told Nowell to get Jacobson and Bishop over to corroborate what he'd just told him. Nowell had, and Clark watched as he relayed the synopsis of Clark's manic, ridiculous fever dream with impatient rage in his voice. Nowell watched them clench jaws and stare at Clark with some burning mixture of anger and fear, then watched Clark nod at them silently with imploring eyes. Nowell looked between the pair of SOG leaders and Clark, feeling like he was the one starting to lose his mind. He was about to tell them all to fuck themselves and walk away when Jacobson stepped close and looked into his eyes.

"Get a team there, wherever he says they should go. *Right now.*"

Nowell looked at Harry with disbelief, but didn't need more confirmation than the older man's icy glare. He nodded and went about doing it.

Ten minutes later, Clark watched them all surging up the slope into the trees toward where he'd remembered the meadow. He hadn't actually heard the transmission that'd sent them into a frenzied charge up the mountain, but felt a grim certainty it validated what he'd seen.

He walked after the others, not wanting to, but needing to validate it all with his own eyes. He didn't bother looking at Benson or Charlotte, whom he could sense watching him as he passed. He rounded the big, lovely house, then saw the trail the others ahead were taking up into aspen-shrouded slopes that formed an apron around this entire base of the mountain.

He remembered this winding trail now. He'd walked it quite a few times. Before he began to hear it babble and hum through the rustle of aspen leaves, Clark knew he was approaching the small, cold, fast mountain stream that ran through this drainage. The same one that cut through the lovely meadow with the horseshoe of rock outcroppings he'd reach in about eight to ten minutes. The morning sun flared now, igniting the aspens into a neon green so bright it seemed the leaves emitted their own light. A few pairs and small groups of task force personnel ran past him, but he just walked. He'd seen what lay ahead, and he needed to think about Lucy and how to handle what he had to do next.

When he knew he was close, he looked ahead and could see several dozen operators in the clearing through the leaves. When he stepped into the meadow, he saw they formed a large crescent around the base of the ancient rock outcroppings.

One operator was bent at the waist, hands on his knees, vomiting into the tall, yellow grass swaying gently in the morning breeze. Another off to Clark's right sat with his face in his hands on the bank of the stream, while another knelt beside him and patted his back and spoke softly into his ear.

In the center of the pool below those two men, where the stream slowed, Clark saw a small cutthroat trout rise. He saw its white mouth and ruby gill plates as it broke the surface to swallow a morning-hatched caddis fly. The insect had been born only an hour earlier. It had just felt the sun for the first time. It then tried its wings for the first time, and that had not gone well.

A helicopter came roaring in. Clark used his forearm to shield his eyes from the dust and grass it kicked into the air. The aspens whipped and leaned under the jet-powered wind. Some of Reichman's pararescue guys and a task force surgeon leapt the four feet down from the aircraft's skids, then ran in a crouch toward the others. Clark saw movement up the slope to their left: a mule deer doe and her two spotted fawns jumped up from their beds, stared down at the men and their roaring machine, then disappeared in a bound. Clark strolled over to where he'd seen him dancing, laughing as he kicked dirt into the faces of his cultists.

Several exhausted, blood-soaked operators worked to remove the four bodies, each still affixed to a wooden crucifix, trails of coagulating blood running from where the rail spikes had been driven into their wrists and ankles. The wounds on all their throats were visible even from here, torn away entirely from the chin to the chest, their vertebrae peeking out from the dark blood and muscle. Other operators leaned over the four who'd already been taken down—squeezing the bag-valve respirators they pressed over their dead buddies' mouths as protocol dictated they do until specialists arrive—then pushed themselves away from their bodies to make way for those who just had.

Clark saw Nowell at the edge of the group, staring at him, his eyes dark, murderous slits. Clark saw the accusation in the gaze, and felt it, as well. This scene of unspeakable butchery was the result of his failure to warn them in time.

Clark looked away from Nowell, back at the pool in the creek where the trout had just eaten the fly. He thought of the coyotes ripping the calf out of its mother, devouring it alive at her feet in the slush and mud.

He turned and went back to Lucy.

CHAPTER

42

CHARLOTTE AND BENSON were at the stables when Clark had gotten there. From the questions that followed, it was clear someone had briefed them on his and Lucy's interaction from earlier in the morning.

He spent a few minutes answering their questions, explaining who she was and how he knew her. When they were done, Clark stared at them both with narrow eyes for a long, awkward stint of silence. Then he asked them, very slowly, if they'd known she'd been taken. Both swore they hadn't, and given how many hundreds of names had been added to the list of missing in the last few weeks, he believed them. For now.

The awkwardness of what they'd learned about Clark and had seen the night before and over the last hour hung heavily between them. He could feel the blizzard of questions on the verge of cracking their composure. Jacobson arrived a few minutes later, and when he saw those three, he told his staffers to wait outside without even looking at them. His fiery gaze and shaking hands added to the tension of what remained unsaid and unasked.

Clark had to address it eventually. They all would. He knew they needed to know anything potentially important that he did. Specifically, any information related to the situation at hand. So he sat down on a dirty chair outside the doors to the horse stall where he'd put Lucy, and would try to do that.

"I don't know much you all don't. There are a few things, though. I can't confirm any of it as fact, not in the way I came to know somethin' as factual up until a couple of weeks ago—by seeing it with my own eyes."

Charlotte crossed her arms as she spoke.

"Then how can we trust it as actionable information? How can you?"

Clark rested one knee atop the other.

"Not sure either of us really can. What I can tell you is, though I've never touched either, I know how to fieldstrip an 1800 Baker rifle and a French Charleville musket, and I'm a pretty damn good shot with both. I know which local herbs will drop a fever, and which'll kill ya, in ten different places I've never been. I know how to lead a Macedonian cavalry formation, where and how to dig a well in North Africa, how to rig and sail a brigantine, and which sea currents to trust and which to fear from the Aegean to the Bay of Bengal. I know the library in Alexandria was emptied a few days before it burned, and I could draw you a map right now to where most a' them scrolls are still buried. Don't even know how many languages I speak now, but I'll betcha you don't know one I don't."

Benson spoke. His Italian was perfect, but traces of American swam in his Polish and Hebrew that he'd never managed to shake.

"*Questo ti suona familiare? Może ten poznajesz lepiej? Ma da'atcha shen'nase et zeh achshav?*"

Clark responded without looking up from the ground, speaking with faint accents in all three languages, but none Benson had ever heard.

"*La familiarità è scioccante. Nie, ten jest równie znajomy. Anu yecholim lenasot et ze shetirze.*"

Unfamiliar with Polish and Hebrew, Jacobson and Bishop looked at Benson, who took a deep breath, shrugged, then slowly nodded. Clark went on.

"Look, I'm not gonna explain it because I can't. This is just the shit in my brain that I reckon y'all should know. Here's what I got, take it or leave it. First, he needs the blood of six hundred sixteen people. *That's his number.* It ain't about a particular volume, it's all about the number of people, and it's for his ritual. All I know about the ritual is it's why he's here. Don't know what happens once he completes it, but I do know he never has. I can also tell you that he's already got all the blood he needs, and he's got it all wherever he'll be doin' this ritual. No clue where that is, so that's where y'all come in. I know there's lots of people still missin', but that's gotta be the only priority now."

Benson put a hand up toward Clark.

"Wait, *what the hell does that mean?*"

Clark sighed, a sound that epitomized deep exhaustion.

"It means what it fuckin' means, Dave. *You decide.* He's got what he needs, where he needs it. You wanna go around savin' people, go on ahead, but that doesn't matter anymore."

Bishop and Benson asked two different versions of *"are you out of your fucking mind?"* Jacobson roared over them both.

"Those are Americans, Captain. American *prisoners of war*, so far as I see it. If there's even a chance at saving one American from these maniacs, *we're fucking taking it*, do you understand? You don't get to walk in here after your little telekinesis gimmicks and whatever the hell that was last night and start *calling fucking plays*. I don't know what you are or what your role in all this is, but suggesting we—"

Clark slapped his palm on his thigh as he stood and cut Harry off.

"You're fuckin' right, Harry. *You are right.* You don't owe me anything, and I would not presume to ask for anything either. I'm gonna say this again, for the last time: What I'm tellin' you, *I know*. I ain't gonna debate its validity because I've got no fuckin' idea how to defend it. I saw him start killin' your boys up in that meadow, so I told you how and where, then you went and saw I hadn't made it up. I don't wanna be right about this shit, Harry. *I don't wanna see any a' this shit."*

Clark started slamming his finger into his temple as he snarled his final words. He stepped away from Harry, made himself take a deep breath. He tried to steady his words, and did not do well.

"I'm just tellin' you, he's killed six hundred sixteen of those folks, he's got all their blood, and he ain't movin' around anymore. Wherever he's at now, that's where it's all goin' down. I know somethin' else too . . ."

He turned to face them directly.

"He's carrying out the ritual in four days. On Friday, during the new moon, which is a lunar phase, and not something entirely tethered to the measurement of a day we use. Pretty sure the actual new moon phase starts around five in the afternoon on Friday, but it's gotta go down, *for him*, on the night of the new moon. He *awoke* on the darkest night of the lunar cycle, and has one cycle to prep for the ritual that's gotta go down on the next darkest night. So, sometime after sunset on Friday. So, yeah, we've got four days."

All three opened their mouths to speak, but Clark went on.

"It's Monday, so it's more like four and a half days. I got a feelin' he'll be rather punctual, so gotta assume he'll start the ritual the *second* the sun sets, which is 9:15 on Friday evenin', so . . ."

Clark looked at his watch.

"That's what's gonna happen in about one hundred six hours. He can't go far, either, from wherever he's started preparing the ritual, and the closer we get to the new moon, the shorter that chain gets."

He saw anger, anxiety, and skepticism building in all their faces. He turned and strode several steps away from them down the long, center aisle that ran through the stables. Charlotte stepped forward and put her hand up as she closed her eyes, reserving the time to speak once she found her words. When she found them, she looked at Clark's back.

"Details like that, like his having started to prepare, and his inability to stray from the ritual site once he has, I just . . . I'm sorry, *how can you be sure of that?* How can we make operational decisions on that information when there are still hundreds of people missing, and focus on wherever he is instead?"

They all stared at him, having to squint. His features were obscured by the dust swirling in the beam of morning light that cut into the stable from the open doors at the far end. The illusion made it look faintly as though Clark grew as he turned and walked slowly back toward them. The cultists restrained in the stalls started to moan as Clark began to speak, which he did fast, almost too fast to follow.

"Because if he completes it, Charlotte Alice Bishop, a darker malice than any known will rule this world. He will condemn all living things to a fate of exquisite misery beyond our limits to feel. But then he'll teach you how to feel more. He'll bury you in his gardens of rot and bones, water you with blood and bile, nurture the roots of your senses until they've grown to experience brand-new kinds of pain and dread. When you've forgotten the words needed to pray for a death that will never come, when that broth of terror and pain has made it so you do not even remember how to beg . . . he'll remind you how."

The cultists' moaning went silent as soon as he did. The team had recoiled at his fervent intensity and his uncharacteristically poetic speech, and Clark appeared to, as well. He shuddered and coughed and looked at them in embarrassed surprise. He put his hands on his knees and breathed hard, spitting into the dirt.

Clark eventually stood upright again and looked up at them with apologetic, exhausted eyes. He rubbed a palm against his forehead as though trying to erase a filthy, wicked thought. He spoke quietly, with guilt in his voice that made them all feel true pity for him. Charlotte felt anger at the tear she could feel was about to fall from her eye and quickly wiped it with the back of her hand.

"I can't be sure of it, Charlotte. I'm sorry. I'm so sorry. It just pops into my mind, don't even notice that it has, it's just there and I know it. Know it as well as my own damn name."

He looked up at her. She had fear in her eyes, and empathy, like she was watching an old dog die. Benson crossed his arms and squinted at Clark. Jacobson began to say something but stopped himself. Clark spoke softly.

"*There's somethin' else.*"

They all looked at him, already overwhelmed by whatever it would be.

"Last thing I gotta show y'all. I learned it in my visions too. I need you to hear me say: My faith, my knowledge of what I've already told ya, is far deeper and more unshakable than what I'm about to show ya. This is somethin' that *flickered* through my mind, like a leaf on the breeze. That ritual taking place somewhere within a few hundred miles of here in about four days, on the other hand, *that's been burnin' into my mind like molten steel.*"

All three looked back at Clark with nervous, impatient eyes. Benson shook his head as he spoke.

"*Christ, man*, get on with it. The hell are you about to show us?"

Clark nodded and walked toward a horse stall's heavy door. It went all the way to the tall ceiling, turning from barn wood to steel bars about nine feet up. He stared up at it as he patted the door with one hand and reached behind his back with the other, nimbly removing the flex-cuffs he kept on the back of his belt.

"Y'all ain't gonna like the sound. Just know, it won't last more 'n ten seconds, and at the end, you'll be doin' what I'm about to *on an industrial scale.*"

Clark launched himself through the door and slammed it behind him. Before the others had even reacted, he'd secured the inside handle to the jamb with one set of flex-cuffs. By the time Harry was pounding on the door, he'd secured it with another, and was already pinning Lucy to the ground, knife in hand.

"Forgive me for this, Miss Lucy."

When they heard the cultist inside begin shrieking, Harry started throwing his shoulder into the wall. Benson and Charlotte were screaming at Clark. Their staffers outside sprinted into the stables, Mako and several operators just behind them with rifles raised.

When the shrieking abruptly stopped, a burst of wind hit them all in the eyes. Dust jumped from every surface and crack in the large stables as though the structure itself had exhaled. It was like the silence that replaced the cultist's hellish screaming was a weighted blanket, leaving them all stunned.

Mako was the first to recover, quickly moving Harry away from the door before smashing his considerably larger weight into it. The entire wall along that side of the stable shook. He took a few steps back, wiped his mouth, then charged into it again.

The door cracked open as the handle ripped off to dangle from the jamb by the flex-cuffs. Mako, Harry, and two other operators poured into the stall, Benson and Bishop right behind them. As soon as they entered, everyone went still.

Clark was kneeling, an arm around the young woman, rubbing her shoulder gently while clamping a wad of gauze to the inside of her forearm. They watched in disbelief as the young woman reached up and touched his cheek. She looked drunk and dazed as she slowly smiled and tears fell from her eyes. She spoke just above a whisper.

"Cap . . . Captain Rickert?"

Clark smiled at her with more warmth and kindness than anyone alive in this world had ever seen.

He turned to face the others as he grabbed something near his knee and showed it to them. They leaned in, squinting at it, recognizing the symbol first, and then the fact that it was burned into a coaster of pale, dirty human skin. They gasped or swore in unison as they looked between the flap of skin, the spot where Clark held gauze to the young woman's arm, and then her face.

She still smiled up at Clark in mystified wonder, then turned slowly toward the others. She flinched and yelped a bit as she realized they were there, then grasped Clark's hand as she scooted into him.

"Who . . . who the heck are they?"

Clark squeezed her hand and smiled at her again.

"Don't fret, Miss Lucy. These are just some of my friends."

She snorted softly, still appearing dazed and on the verge of passing out, but a nervous grin appeared at the corners of her mouth.

"Come on, now, Cap. We both know you ain't got any friends."

CHAPTER

43

CLARK FOLLOWED HIS son Ben down the trail that wound from the house to the creek that ran through their land. It was after dinner, the summer light lying sideways across the world, shadows reaching as far as shadows did before they ate the last light. Ben was in that stage between two and three, right before a kid stops flailing their arms around as they run. A wake of grasshoppers shot away from his little Crocs as he ran, blasting off into the tall grass before snapping their noisy wings for an extra boost. Clark told Ben to wait up, to slow down a bit. Ben turned, looked back at him with those big blue eyes, smiled, then kept on going. Clark smiled back, trying to tell him to slow down again, but he couldn't hear his voice. Ben shouted something back, but he couldn't hear that either. There was some other noise. It wasn't loud, but it consumed all others. Clark slowed and shaded his eyes as he turned, looking back toward the house and the other side of the valley.

The moon filled half the evening sky. But it was moving, *screaming* toward the earth. Reaching for each horizon as it got closer and closer. Clark tried to move, but he was stuck. He tried to scream for Ben but couldn't breathe. The earth shook. Boulders and cliffs on the valley wall split and burst. The moon filled the entire sky right before it struck.

Clark gasped as he shot up from his rollout bed in the back of his truck. He coughed and wiped his eyes, swearing. It was the same goddamned dream that'd plagued him for decades. He felt around for his Nalgene bottle and drank half the warm water within. He looked at his watch and saw it was almost 10:00 a.m.

Holy shit, Clark thought. He'd been asleep for almost seventeen hours. The realization shot adrenaline into his body, and he leaned forward to wipe away some condensation from the little window of his topper. The

FOB hadn't disappeared; there were a few people carrying something just at the edge of his view. He lay back down and stretched.

Everything that followed that experience in the stables with Lucy had been a blur. He'd asked to talk with her privately, which the others had respected. When she'd confirmed his suspicions, his mouth went dry. He'd then carried her to the CASEVAC helicopter himself. The sixty or so people at the Hammond ranch by that time formed a causeway he walked down toward the helicopter. Operators, leadership, the support staff, everyone stared at her in awe. Some crossed themselves. One even reached out a hand and touched her shoulder with wide eyes. He remembered walking by Nowell, and the look he'd given Clark. It had been a dangerous one, but with Lucy in his arms to protect, Clark had never felt so violent in his life. He'd have burned cities to ash in that moment. Nowell looked away first.

Reichman, and then even Lucy herself, had to break Clark's insistence on going with her. As he watched the helicopter grow smaller, Benson asked what she'd told him back in the stables in their one-on-one conversation. Clark did not respond. Benson accepted that, then made some comment about how she'd be fine. Clark remembered now having responded by leaning in close to Benson and whispering directly into his ear that, *if she weren't, he'd cut his fingers off and shove each one up his asshole*. Clark cringed at this memory, then shrugged it away. He'd said worse things to better men.

He'd gotten back to the FOB by around 2:00 p.m., when he remembered concluding that he'd never been more exhausted in his life. He went straight for his truck. He remembered vaguely hearing DuBroux mention the after-action debrief, and hating him for it. He managed to keep himself awake, but did not participate. It had been a profoundly depressing, anguished space to be in; all those guys who'd not only just had eight of their brothers terribly murdered, but by an adversary who seemed even farther ahead of them now. Clark was too tired to be sad about them now, or even happy about Lucy.

He remembered a group of a dozen or so Ground Branch and Team Six operators who'd been the last to leave the target joining about halfway through. He remembered seeing the big one, Bobby, staring daggers at him as he entered, as Nowell had.

When the AAR finally ended, when he'd left the command tent, he vaguely remembered someone shouting his name, and turning to see Mako, Moritz, and Gavin pushing someone back inside. Whoever it'd been shouted something about *the freak*: why *the freak didn't warn us*, whether *the freak was even on our side*.

Clark grunted, then turned around, too exhausted to even begin contemplating how task force personnel would react to the knowledge of his prophetic affliction. DuBroux and some of his HRT guys asked Clark if he'd join them for chow, which he declined. He also remembered stopping, turning, and declaring that if he woke up under anything other than natural circumstances, he'd *start cutting dicks off and burying motherfuckers alive*. He remembered they'd laughed, but still cringed at himself again.

After running back through this nebulous memory from the day before, he pulled a T-shirt over his head, clambered out of his truck, and froze.

More than half the FOB was just gone. The command tent, all the trailers and housing, well over half the vehicles, all of the aircraft, had just disappeared. There were still some of the pop-up structures and some people moving around, but all of them were packing things up and hauling them to idling trucks. He stood there, barefooted, in athletic shorts and a T-shirt, staring blankly at the scene around him, unable to process it.

"Morning, sleepyhead."

Clark spun around, startled.

Charlotte Bishop was sitting in one of his camping chairs beside his truck. The Glock on her hip contrasted wildly with the dirty white Vans, jeans, and T-shirt she wore. She used a hand to shade her eyes from the bright morning sun, and the other to point at the other chair, where a plastic fork sat atop a foil-wrapped plate of food.

"Saved a plate from the mess tent before they packed it all up."

Clark nodded, grunted his thanks, and sat. He inhaled the instant eggs, bagel, sausage, and fruit in two minutes. He chugged the rest of his water, then eyed Charlotte a bit warily.

"How is—"

Charlotte interrupted him, nodding as she spoke.

"Lucy's fine, in relatively good health. Severe dehydration, anemic, and a couple of broken ribs, but otherwise fine. They'll be bringing her son to the hospital to be with her this afternoon."

Clark nodded but looked no less suspicious. After a moment he looked away, then gestured at the area around them with an open hand.

"So..."

She laughed a bit and pushed a strand of hair behind an ear.

"Standing up a new FOB a little ways outside Big Sky."

Clark raised his eyebrows.

"Not the best spot to keep this whole carnival outta the public eye."

Charlotte shrugged.

"Won't really matter for much longer."

She crossed one leg over the other as Clark stared at her, waiting for her to go on.

"We found him."

Clark's eye twitched, but he didn't move.

"Where?"

Her tone got serious.

"Holed up in a very tacky twenty-four-thousand-square-foot mansion on a fourteen-hundred-acre property a bit outside the Yellowstone Club. Owned by a telecom billionaire no one's heard from in eleven days. Some analysts running through satt-playback flagged it, trucks coming up to the property for the last five days and branded cultists unloading jugs and barrels. At least sixty-five cultists confirmed on-site, roving patrols, static security, even some with spotting scopes on the roof. So, whether he's there right now or not, seems likely the blood is, and if what you told us yesterday in that stable about where to be looking was worth anything, this is our spot. We've already got containment underway, recon and overwatch *in force* this time, and are working on accessing an adjacent property to use as command for the assault. It's got an equally tacky albeit somewhat smaller mansion on it, but good commanding views. Based on your theory about Friday night being the big deadline, our plan is to hit it Thursday night."

Clark nodded, unable to hide his grin.

"Well, I'll be *doggone*. Well done, Miss Bishop."

She shrugged casually, and Clark spoke as he rose from his chair.

"Yellowstone Club, eh? Certainly an upgrade from that chicken farm and that busted ass shit-scrape up in the Breaks."

Charlotte nodded.

"I've actually been there a few times, used to go there on ski trips with my family."

Clark snorted and stretched his arms over his head, speaking quietly through a mocking grin.

"*Yeah, I bet you did, Bishop.*"

She raised an eyebrow, flipped him off, and spoke in a high, haughty accent.

"You prefer trailer-reared women, like yourself? Just perpetually aggrieved and mistrusting of anyone with generational money and higher education?"

Clark chuckled as he went toward the back of his truck.

"Nah, I've known good, kind folks who're also smart and wealthy. *Never one who's a member a' the fuckin' Yellowstone Club, though.*"

Charlotte laughed. Clark came around from the back of his truck, still in his faded T-shirt, but now in jeans, his old flat-toe boots, and Frank Farrington's Stetson. He leaned on the rear driver's-side door and looked at her.

"So, where am I goin'?"

Charlotte sprang up, clapped her hands, grabbed the small pack that was at her feet, and smiled. Clark, once again, was floored by her beauty.

"I've got the location. I can run nav."

He stared at her as she grabbed both camping chairs, folded them closed, and threw them in the back of the truck. She went around and opened the passenger door, then stepped up and leaned over the top of the cab, slapping the roof a few times, talking in a ridiculous accent.

"*Time to hit the trails, partner. Let's go.* Seriously, moving the FOB and standing everything up will take more time than it'll take us to drive there, and I could benefit from detaching for a few hours."

It was an almost four-hour drive, and Charlotte made repeated calls on her satellite phone for the first forty-five minutes as they wound their way toward I-90 on quiet county and BLM roads. When Charlotte finally put the phone down and spoke to him, it surprised Clark.

"So, what, you're like some fuckin' . . . *superhuman?*"

Clark glanced at her from the corner of his eye, then looked ahead again. She leaned over and slapped him on the knee.

"Oh, *come on, man*, I'm just messing with you. I'm probably the only woman alive who runs capture-kill special rendition teams of Tier-1 operators for a living. If anyone here's a superhuman, *it's definitely me.*"

He chuckled at that and glanced over at her. She was staring at him, genuine curiosity in her eyes.

"All the cultists in our custody had their brands removed throughout the last sixteen hours. Some while being monitored with different cameras and sensors. The moment it got cut away was . . . well, they observed some very strange and unexplainable environmental phenomena. The people themselves, none of them remember much about where they've been, what happened. Only little bits and pieces here and there. They all clearly remember meeting *him*, him saying something that intrigued them in some way, and then the world going black."

Clark glanced at her quickly then back at the road.

"Well, good. I guess."

She kept staring at him.

"Did Lucy have any memories of her time under his spell?"

Clark tried not move his hands or eyes at all, then wondered if that was more obvious.

"Nope."

She continued to stare at him, feeling this was likely as good a time as she'd find to finally ask the question she'd been curious about for a while.

"What'd you do before you became a game warden?"

Clark felt a pang of anxiety and glanced at her quickly, grateful when she continued.

"I've read your IC file. There isn't much about you I don't know. Well, not including all these *new things* about you. There's a peculiar professional black hole between 1998 and 2004. I know you bought a nice chunk of land and built a home in that period, got married, had a child, bought a couple of trucks, a tractor, and purchased a rather large and diversified collection of guns. And that you did it all with *whistle-clean money*. What I haven't figured out is just *where that money came from*. You're a terrible fit for most of the criminal profiles given your records and locations during that time, but my leading theory is you smuggled guns and perhaps even a few people over the Canadian border. Tell me, *am I close*?"

He took a deep breath, and the anxiety was gone. In fact, for the first time in his life, after what he'd been through these last two weeks, the criminal career he'd gone to such profound lengths to erase all records of and hide from the world felt quite insignificant.

He glanced at her again. She smiled as the breeze from the cracked window set strands of her hair flowing across her smiling face. Her eyes were stunning, burning gold in the afternoon light. He had no hope of avoiding surrender.

"Well, Char, while I suppose it's part of your job description, I still gotta ask . . . *Can you keep a secret?*"

For the next few hours, for the first time in a very long time, Clark Rickert talked with another person about himself.

CHAPTER 44

AFTER TALKING FOR three straight hours, Clark and Charlotte reached the new FOB outside Big Sky in the last light of day. It was on a big piece of private land tucked up against the north side of the Blaze and Gallatin Mountains. Clark knew this country well. The FOB itself had a main gate and was enclosed within sixteen-foot visual screen fencing, the kind fracking operations use. It looked, to Clark, like a military operation trying very poorly to dress up like a fracking operation.

Charlotte had not had a conversation like that with anyone in twelve years, since she was twenty-two and finishing college. Clark had not had a conversation like that in twenty, when he was twenty-three and his life was about to be ripped apart.

He'd never told a single soul about his criminal career until today, and did not regret doing so. She'd never told a soul about the man she'd killed while working undercover in South Africa, the one who'd sneak into the neighboring apartment to rape his own nieces, and didn't regret doing so either.

When he put his truck in park, both behaved a bit awkwardly, reaching for their things and moving them from one spot to another, looking for nothing at all near their feet or in a cup holder, and then finally just sitting there. They glanced at each other, neither wanting to reach for the door—to leave this and go out into that and all it meant—and then locked eyes. Clark chuckled a bit and shook his head, absolutely no idea what to say. Charlotte opened her mouth to say something, but closed it again, and bit the inside of her lip. Neither knew how hard the other's heart was pounding. Both were catastrophically unconditioned in the nuance of romance. Middle schoolers probably had more aptitude in moments like this, the way they'd been sculpted and conditioned by chaos, solitude, and raging work addictions their entire adult lives. One of the several satellite phones in Charlotte's bag blasted an alert that snapped them out of it. They traded one last look, then both exited the truck at the same time.

Charlotte fell into a busy cascade of duties immediately, while Clark idled around just as he had at the last two FOBs, strolling its perimeter until summoned to the briefing.

They both spent the rest of the day thinking about what might've happened had they just stayed in the truck for five more minutes. They filled each other's thoughts for hours, something astonishingly foreign to both of them.

Clark knew there was a way to distract himself, but was terrified to do it again. He knew he had to, though. He made his way back to his truck and got into the passenger seat. He leaned the chair back and let his mind reach. It was getting different. He wasn't sucked so far away from the present.

The first thing he felt was his teeth chattering. Not Clark's teeth, *his teeth*. Then he saw him from somewhere low, as though he crouched in the dark. It was a large, cavernous space, close to the size of Clark's house. Cobblestone floors and walls, heavy oak beams, actual torch sconces. It was an empty wine cellar, Clark realized: a massive, ridiculous, Yellowstone Club–type douchebag's wine cellar. He saw *him*. He was humming a tune Clark couldn't hear as he stared down and carefully arranged obsidian blades, silver coins, and human fingers and tongues. Then he'd crawl with grotesque, pale limbs with too many joints across the large room to fuss meticulously over smaller arrangements of gems and salt and human scalps.

Clark came out of the vision and bolted up, looking around, checking his watch, then lying back again. Then *he went back.*

On several occasions, Clark watched him pluck a cursed object from one of his sinister designs with his wet spider-leg fingers. He'd sniff it, lick it, kiss it gently, then stare at it in growing disgust before screaming and swiping the entire arrangement into the wall. Then he'd start over. On several occasions he whipped his head around to look behind him, lip quivering, eyes darting around Clark's vantage. His limbs would shorten, face shrink back to normal size and shift back into something far more human in these moments. Clark could feel him sensing his presence somehow, and his anger and fear at his inability to confirm it. Whether he could confirm Clark was there watching or not, he knew Clark was close, and Clark could feel how much it agitated him. Clark knew his presence was what was causing the blisters and oozing boils that pocked along his reptilian spine.

For the first time, Clark chose when to leave a vision, and did. He'd need to go back frequently to study that place, the ritual, the leader himself. All of it. But he needed a break, the last day's briefing was in an hour, and he was starving. So he got out of his truck and walked through the darkening FOB toward the mess tent. He ate alone, ate fast, and did not fail to notice the increased number of eyes on him as he did.

He made the quick stroll to the command tent and stopped before he went inside. He braced himself for the squall of awkward emotion he assumed would accompany seeing Charlotte. He shook his head, steeled himself, and walked in.

All the leadership and a few of their respective team leads were present around the large tables flanked by monitors in the center of the tent. The first one Clark locked eyes with was Nowell, who stared back at him with the same murderous glare he'd given him the day before. The commander passed the tablet he was holding to one of his guys, then strode directly toward Clark.

Nowell did not slow as he closed on the game warden until their faces were inches apart. His words were like the quiet thunder of a hurricane still an hour off the coast.

"Look, Rickert: I don't know shit about your *little issue*, so I'm gonna cut down to it and ask this once, and *you will* respond with a *yes* or a *no*. Yesterday, when you had your fucking . . . *vision*, is there *anything at all* you could've done to prevent that from happening and save my guys?"

Clark responded with a single word.

"No."

Nowell didn't see a lie but searched Clark's eyes for anywhere one might be hiding. After a long moment he took a step away and crossed his arms. The tension of someone prepared and eager to explode into violence relaxed from Nowell's back and shoulders, but his expression remained the same balance of rage and disgust.

"That may be the case, but not many are gonna buy it. Spent the last couple of days wondering *what other fucking tricks* might be up the sleeve of a man who's been hiding a magical ability to see things in his mind. Also been wondering why the hell that man didn't employ that or any other such fucking gifts in a manner that could've saved or even given us the goddamned chance of *potentially saving* the lives of those eight men. *And I sure as hell ain't the only one here who's been wondering about those things*. And you've provided some truly fertile fucking ground for reasonable suspicion to grow regarding your character and dedication to mission success here, Captain Rickert."

Gavin, Jake, Burton, Moritz, and a half dozen other Ground Branch guys Clark had gotten to know stood behind Nowell, staring at him. Clark quickly scanned their faces, which all sported an expression somewhere between mistrust and revulsion. Nowell went on in a louder, more controlled tone, but his eyes remained slits of black ice.

"You went way the fuck off the reservation, Rickert. After the ambush in Ward, hunting that kid down, skinning the brand off his arm, killing him. Not even gonna bother asking how such a concept came to you. But you figure out how to save these people, how to easily undo their brainwashing, and you keep that to your fucking self? You were there when we hit the Hammond ranch yesterday morning, and in possession of an effective, field-tested method of immediately freeing these people from their insanity . . . and you keep that to yourself as you watch us engage and kill them, *kill those fucking Americans*. You didn't say a word, didn't do a *goddamn thing to stop it* when you could've. Then, you only reveal your little trick out of necessity, to protect someone you knew, that girl Lucy. I'm not gonna ask *what kinda man could possibly do that*, because *I know the fucking answer*: a fucking asshole, of a variety I will not tolerate the presence of. Beyond that, just the decision to conceal information of such critical fucking operational relevance to this entire situation, I mean . . . *Holy shit*, Rickert. You're an increasingly severe liability to this operation in every way."

Clark bit the inside of his cheek, looked at the ground, and nodded.

"You're right. Not sharing that info, not tellin' y'all about the effect of removing the brand, that was a shit-for-brains call on my part. Had I shared it that evening after the ambush, maybe some of those branded folks defending the Hammond ranch wouldn't be dead. Maybe we would've gone in there with a commitment to taking them alive. But . . . *maybe fuckin' not*. Those eight fellas a' yours were already in contact, gettin' shot at by the time we spun up, then nonresponsive and fully MIA by the time we jumped off the choppers. So ask yourself, Nowell, all you fellas ask yourselves: How much gumption would y'all have had hittin' that target that mornin'—*to rescue your buddies we knew were already tit-deep in shit*—with nonlethal weapons? How many of y'all would've been *just fine* hitting that target with Tasers, pepper spray, and some riot-control game plan? We're still talkin' about the people who've butchered their way through this state while perpetually keen on shootin' before talkin'. Even with the knowledge we could un-fuck their madness, how many would've been *totally cool* going in there with a commitment *not to kill the people enthusiastically trying to kill you and your buddies*? How about this: Has anyone on this task force ever, *a single time*, gone into hostile territory to rescue brothers under fire with anything less than a commitment to *utterly fuckin' destroy* anybody who *even appears* to be opposing that effort?"

Almost everyone standing around Nowell broke eye contact with Clark. With his eyebrows raised, Jake looked at Moritz, who looked back and actually nodded in acknowledgment of the point. Nowell's expression didn't change, and Clark went on before he could offer a rebuttal.

"*But you're still right.* I should've told y'all about skinning the brand off that fella after the ambush, instead of *showin'* y'all live the next mornin' when necessity arose. I made a shitty call—one that might've prevented some of those folks we tangled with the next mornin' from escaping whatever hell that brand locks 'em into—*but it was a call I had reason to make*. Not sure the bosses want us doin' this here and now, Nowell, *but fuck it*. You know as well as I do that Benson and all the other spook shepherds runnin' this outfit have been spoon-feedin' me, *in particular*, absolute bullshit since day one—to say *nothin'* of the information of *critical fuckin' personal relevance* they've been concealing *from me*. At the top of this exchange you said you didn't know shit about my *little issue*. Well, *neither do fuckin' I, Commander*. You know who does? Your goddamned bosses, *and their goddamned bosses*."

Clark's voice had just started taking on extra volume and edge when Benson and Jacobson began shouting something about both men shutting up and dealing with it later. Everyone within Clark's vision turned toward those voices, except for Nowell. His eyes remained fixed on Clark's. He was about to speak again when his body tensed and he looked to his left.

That was the only warning Clark had before the massive fist hammered into his forehead above the eyebrow. Stars burst in his vision. His hat spun off as his head whipped to the side, but he didn't go down.

He turned in the direction the fist had come from to find the massive DEVGRU leader, Bobby. He stared at Clark with an expression of detached, murderous focus that had been the last thing many men had ever seen. Nowell had both his hands on the larger man's chest, pushing him back, ordering him to cool down. Clark bowed his head toward Bobby and spoke cordially.

"Evenin', Robert."

Bobby faked left, then slapped Nowell's arms down as he surged past him on the right, moving with the explosive fluidity of an NFL defensive end. He brought his hands up as he surged toward Clark. He feinted a jab, then swung a huge right hook at Clark's face, which he skillfully rolled into another huge hook with his left. Clark didn't respond to the feint, then dropped all his weight onto his back foot as he casually weaved under both hooks. Bobby straightened and threw a wildly fast combination for a man of his size: two left jabs then a right cross. All three were aimed at Clark's chin with the force of a train piston. Clark slipped both jabs and the cross without moving his feet, just his head. Bobby kept his hands up but stopped advancing, eyes narrowing as he looked the game warden up and down.

Clark stood there staring back at him, hands at his sides, open and relaxed. Blood from the gash on his forehead ran around both sides of his eye, channeled down his cheek, and dripped from his jaw and chin onto his old T-shirt. When he spoke, it sounded like each word was dragged through hot gravel.

"If you ain't finished, you'll be coughin' up memories of me for a year."

Bobby slowly dropped his hands and relaxed his shoulders, and didn't resist Nowell or the three other DEVGRU guys hauling him back. Clark looked at the faces of the crowd that had rushed toward the melee. They looked at him as though he were a leper who'd just stripped naked and shit on the floor. He saw revulsion, fear, and even pity. It was how Charlotte, Harry, and Benson had looked at him in the stables at the Hammond ranch. He'd readily accepted his status as a strange outsider since joining the task force, but quite a few of those present now had warmed up to him over the last weeks. Whatever ground had been gained had just officially been lost. He was an alien to them all now. A freak.

Clark didn't acknowledge anyone within the crowd that'd rushed in to break up the melee as he picked up Frank Farrington's old Stetson. He walked through the group toward the tables and monitors in the center of the tent. As he went, he removed the bandana from his back pocket, wiped the blood from around his eye, then folded it and pressed it into the cut above his eyebrow.

He looked up when Jacobson stopped him with a hand on his shoulder. Charlotte came up next to him, took the bandana from Clark without comment, then inspected the wound underneath. Both looked concerned, and very tired, as they glanced between his eyes and forehead. Jacobson squeezed his shoulder a bit when he spoke.

"You all right? Sorry about that. Some of the team feel, well . . . What happened yesterday rattled some guys, guys who were already pretty damn rattled. We haven't had the chance to brief everyone on your, uhm . . . *situation*, what you're going through. Once we bring everyone up to speed, I'm sure that—"

Clark cut him off.

"*No.* There's no time, Harry. We've got sixty-some hours left. I'm sure y'all spent all day puttin' together an assault plan. Let's hear the plan and chop it up. Enough a' the fuckin' sideshow."

Clark looked at Charlotte blankly as he took the bandana from her hand and stepped past them both toward the map and schematic-covered tables. Bobby's punch hadn't hurt much, but it'd certainly doused the giddy spark of romance he'd felt dancing in his gut since he and Charlotte left his truck. On the far side of one of the tables stood Thorn, whom Clark hadn't seen since their animated exchange a few days earlier.

Clark had homed in on something while staring at Bobby, and then the faces of the others as Bobby was hauled away. Looking at Thorn now, Clark reached a conclusion. It resolved a quandary he'd been only vaguely aware of, but still somehow felt inevitable.

Thorn stared back at him with a casual, knowing grin. This annoyed Clark, so he flipped the little man off with the middle finger of the hand holding his old hat, then looked away. Clark didn't see it, but Thorn's smile only grew.

CHAPTER 45

IT ONLY TOOK a couple of minutes to calm things down, then Jacobson launched into the briefing without delay.

Blueprints and satellite images covered the dozen large monitors flanking the large tables. The first thing they went over was the complex internal layout to the mansion. The man who'd built the home was the owner's brother. They'd compiled blueprints, surveys, and every public-facing record available. However, they'd also been able to confirm other things. Through the owner's and the builder's expenses for materials, machinery rentals, and labor, the billing timeline, and site inspection materials, it was obvious that considerable un-permitted work had been done. Based on that, the consensus of the specialist analysts was that most of this work was carried out underground. Search history data for the owner and his brother showed some ambient interest in bunkers or shelters, but far more interest in Italian- or Spanish-style wine cellars, dining rooms, and other more benign subterranean construction. So it was possible they'd built some armored bunker down there, but it was far more likely to be some profoundly expensive re-creation of European aesthetic.

On top of that, what was confirmable was that the place was a structural fortress. All steel-reinforced masonry of huge fieldstone, single beams cut from trees, reinforced framing, insulated and reinforced concrete, and double-wall construction from top to bottom. The verandas and patios that surrounded the home were made entirely from massive river- and fieldstone.

DuBroux interjected as soon as the conversation was moving toward assault planning for the raid planned for around three in the morning on Friday, only about fifty-five hours from now.

"Forgive me if the reason is obvious, but why can't we just bomb this place into gravel and ash? We certainly possess the ability to do so many thousands of times over."

Harry and Charlotte looked at Benson and Nowell. Nowell spoke first.

"Believe it or not, there are quite a few reasons. The first is that the president, SecDef, and several Joint Chiefs explicitly forbade such an option. This place is considerably well-built, and guaranteeing atomization of the potentially bunkerized levels underground would require considerable ordnance. I'm talkin' JDAMS, Dwight. A lot of them. That didn't seem like any kinda problem to me personally after these last weeks, so I asked for more explanation, and a considerable fuckin' amount was provided . . ."

Benson clicked a remote and a new array of images were populated on the screens, each headlined with one of the reasons an assault was required. They'd considered this extensively, it seemed. Benson took it from here.

"First and foremost is the need for *controlled neutralization*. The leader's plan hinges on a precise, ritualistic process. A tactical assault allows the operators to precisely disable or remove the components of this system. Bombing would likely destroy vital intelligence leaving America, and the world, vulnerable to similar threats in the future. We're effectively guaranteed not only a similar threat in the future, but this *identical* threat. The days of going into this blind are over. No offense to your esteemed predecessors, Mr. Thorn, but we're not going to let that happen again with a couple of one-hundred-twenty-year-old notebooks to guide us."

Malcolm Thorn put his hands together in prayer and nodded. Benson's voice was sharp and loud.

"I need to make this very clear. This *event* has not yet occurred in a time where those who face it have had access to our suite of technological assets. POTUS and the rest of executive leadership and, from what I've gathered over the last day, the military and political leadership throughout the developed world want the ability to dedicate world-changing resources to undermining this threat. This adversary is like *weather*, in that it's guaranteed to return. When it does, we're going to understand it down to the *molecular fucking level*, is that understood?"

Most of those in the room responded to Benson with a "Yes, sir." He gestured toward another screen.

"Another reason for assault is our need for absolute confirmation of target elimination. More than any other target we've ever pursued, this is one *we cannot* assume to be dead in some rubble. This man is a threat to human existence; a smoking crater *will not cut it*. We need eyes on his corpse, we need to dissect his corpse, then we need to study his corpse for one hundred fucking years. So, we go in, we see it done, and we walk out knowing the world keeps turning tomorrow. Is that understood?"

Everyone in the room responded to Benson with a "Yes, sir," even Clark, to his surprise. Most of those present had never heard him speak in such a quietly violent, calculated, impassioned way. He put his hands on the table, and looked into the eyes of those surrounding it.

"The need for an assault is actually pretty clear. First, we're here to stop a physical, ambulatory activity from taking place. *We're here to stop a ritual . . .*"

Benson, and quite a few others, looked at Clark.

"Unfortunately, our adversary has fortified himself within what is very possibly the residential structure most capable of withstanding ballistic munitions in the Rocky Mountain West. It has deep, well-designed basements and cellars. We also don't know what goes into this ritual. We cannot confirm ceasing such an act if we bury those areas in rubble that would take several days to clear. On top of that, we cannot leave our descendants as abjectly fucking blind *as our ancestors left us*. And if we atomize that ritual, and this adversary, that's precisely what we fucking do. All they left us with was vague theory. *No.* No, we will not be doing that. We will be conducting an assault with the most capable, intelligent, calculated, and ferocious assembly of glass-eating warriors this earth *has ever fucking seen*. A ground assault insulates the future of this world from the liabilities created by this cyclical threat we know will return. It's as simple as that."

Benson looked around the room, as did Jacobson standing behind him, both taking the measure of everyone's resolve. Neither found any lack thereof.

They spent the next two hours brainstorming assault options. Twenty minutes into that, Clark had already grown weary of feigning attention, and irritated by the constant glances in his direction, especially Thorn's. So he moved away from the tables to a chair on the periphery of the gathering and stared at his boots. *Goddamn a man who finds this rude*, he thought. He'd never contributed anything valuable to the previous assault plans. This wasn't his wheelhouse.

Sitting there, Clark was startled by his own growing disdain and frustration at everything around him. All these world-class assets. All the resources, money, effort, and technology. The media, the military, the state government, the Department of Justice, the White House, the entire American government. *Every* fucking government. All this fuss. Clark was surprised to find he felt, more than anything else, embarrassed for them. He'd spent the last weeks feeling like a clueless tourist who'd stumbled into the wrong room. Now, sitting here, he was confronted by the awareness that no one in the tent, or anyone else involved in this struggle, had the faintest idea what the hell was really going on here.

Clark, somehow, felt that he did. Not in a way he could explain. If someone asked him to try, it would be like someone asking him to explain why he liked the Jimi Hendrix *Blues* album. He didn't know, *he just fuckin' did*.

What had been Clark's burning desire to violently interrogate Malcolm Thorn—for more information about what was happening to him and what this all really meant—went dull and flat as he sat there. Eventually, it just evaporated. There wasn't any point. In fact, Clark felt protective of his newfound, inexplicable grasp on the situation, as though any other person's attempt to clarify things could harm it. Human explanations about this chaos, written or spoken, simply wouldn't be able to get there. Any human language would just catastrophically flatten all the context Clark now felt but couldn't articulate. He had no desire to stop or undermine these people's efforts. He didn't feel like they were doing something wrong or wasting time. He just felt like *he was*.

As there would be three or four more op-planning meetings and briefings like this the next day, and again on Thursday before the assault, they adjourned before it got too late. Clark intentionally avoided eye contact with everyone there as he made a quick bolt for the exit, especially Thorn and Charlotte. He went back to his truck, and pulled himself onto his foam mattress. He reached into a corner and took a long pull of bourbon. He'd need it, where he was going.

Clark had some scouting to do. He needed to learn the landscape and the layout of this mansion. This castle of blood.

And he did. It exhausted him.

When he'd come back to himself and felt he'd reached his limit, he quickly fell asleep and began to dream.

In the first dream, Clark saw a sword in his hand, buried up to the hilt in *his* stomach on some rampart in a hot, dry landscape, men screaming and dying all around him. In the next, he saw him on a beach, crawling away from Clark as he wept and begged and drooled. Clark could feel the tip of his spear slide off spine and ribs as he plunged it into his back. In the next, he saw him outside a stone chapel in foggy, green hill country, dead men and women all around him. He was on his knees facing Clark, hands clasped together. He repeated, "Just once, please just once, please just this once." Clark gripped a flintlock pistol in his hand, the muzzle against his forehead, and relished the despair and anguish in *his* face just before Clark pulled the trigger.

He enjoyed these dreams, more than any he could remember.

CHAPTER

46

THE NEXT DAY, they all convened in the large home that sat across the valley from the target mansion, which the task force had requisitioned as its new command for the assault the next day.

Clark looked around the massive living room, with its thirty-foot ceilings and monstrous hearth that must've taken a quarry-load of river rocks to construct. He looked at the men summoned here to run through the operational plan for the assault. Almost all of them gave him a wide berth, which he was fine with. Six Ground Branch assault teams, a fifteen-man troop of DEVGRU operators who'd be split into two additional assault teams, and the FBI HRT's own assault element. In addition to these guys, there were two dozen more in surveillance and overwatch teams creeping around the mountains this very minute, an eight-man QRF on standby, and dozens of others manning drones, satellites, and comms with manned aircraft in static ready patterns, a button away from flattening the entire valley from above.

He'd dwelled on this since it had all begun, the differences between himself and virtually everyone else here. Everyone around him was some kind of warfighter. Many were involved in logistics, analysis, tech operations, transport, but all of them had only ever done so while in support of combat operations or some violent clandestine effort. When it came to the guys on the ground teams, this disparity was even greater. Some of them had occupational specialties associated with hostage rescue, air traffic control, or combat medicine, but they were all, first and foremost, *combat operators*. This was obviously the case for the Ground Branch guys, having all come from JSOC units, but also the FBI HRT operators. All but one of them were former military, and all of them had deployed with JSOC into war zones since joining the HRT ranks.

Clark took them all in. All these guys were just gunfighters. Like Viking raiders or Comanche lancers, their entire profession was to ambush, raid, steal, kidnap, and kill, and to do these things by surprise in places where they were very unwelcome.

Jacobson's voice cut through the hum and buzz of a room full of amped-up men covered in battle gear.

"Command, on me, please."

He was in the sprawling kitchen a few steps above the living room. Clark followed Nowell, DuBroux, Reichman, and the massive Bobby to where Jacobson, Charlotte, and Benson stood around one of the kitchen islands covered in maps and satellite imagery. A cathedral of a dining room was set off the kitchen, where over a dozen comms technicians surrounded a long tortoiseshell table covered in equipment.

The owner of the house hesitantly peeked into the kitchen, then was kindly encouraged onward by some of Benson's staff. Charlotte had provided a brief overview of this man when they'd arrived at the house an hour earlier.

He was a recently widowed shipping magnate who spent most of his year between New York and Copenhagen, but a month or so at this *quaint mountain abode*. He had one fifteen-year-old son at the prestigious Milton Academy in Massachusetts, a Dassault Falcon 8X jet, and around $750 million in assets Bishop could find in the three minutes she'd spent looking into him.

She'd also explained how he'd attempted to call his attorneys as soon as they'd arrived, how Benson had gently taken the phone from him as he sat him down, explained how he was effectively a federal prisoner for the next couple of days and how he would be justly compensated for all his time, loss, and inconvenience, all while a security and IT team scoured every inch of the house. Within twelve minutes, the team had full control over the entire electrical system and the internet, and everything connected to either. They'd deployed cellular and satellite jamming devices, and had disabled all four cars, both motorcycles, and even the six bicycles on the property.

The owner was, perhaps justly, a nervous-looking man around Clark's own age and, like Clark, was fit and lean. Unlike Clark, he was clean-shaven, his hair was immaculately slicked back, and he wore pointy black leather shoes, black slacks, and a thin black sweater. His apparent anxiety seemed strangely at odds with the religious physical fitness regimen he obviously maintained. He also had on a flashy watch that jumped out.

Clark saw an obnoxiously fussy thing with exposed innards and cogs taking up more of its face than the actual timepiece, while Benson and Bishop saw a Bovet Fleurier Tourbillon Limited Edition they both knew cost around $100,000.

Jacobson introduced the man, who waved awkwardly and could not hide his shock at all the large, heavily armed men in his living room.

"Everyone, this is our host, Matthew Kabath."

He nodded as he tried to make eye contact with those around his kitchen island. Benson spoke next.

"Mr. Kabath here mentioned there might be some additional spots to the south where a clear line of sight can be established into the neighboring property. If you wouldn't mind, Mr. Kabath, we'd appreciate if you could point those out on the plat map so Mr. DuBroux here can go have a look at them. We've got about three hundred degrees of overwatch control, and we need to close that circle by finding some spots here along the downslope side of your property."

Kabath seemed startled by Benson's reminder, and anxiously began tracing shaky fingers over the map. He picked up one of the satellite images to compare it to the plat, and pointed to a spot along a tree line a few hundred meters down the gentle slope from the house.

"I . . . I think one of them would be here, although . . ."

He looked closer at the satellite image, then back at the plat.

"Yes, I believe one of them is here, and, wait . . ."

He glanced out the wall of windows facing down the slope as though it might help him orient himself, then back at the satellite image. He awkwardly muttered apologies as the others looked around at one another. DuBroux spoke in his gravelly, predatory, and somehow still classically formal voice.

"Not to worry, Mr. Kabath. Jacobson, my guys and I can scout the area later on and likely ID these spots from the ground; it's not an issue at all."

Jacobson looked at his watch, then quickly at Kabath before looking back at DuBroux.

"I'd like overwatch snugged in and a new shift set by eighteen hundred hours, so maybe do that now, before we kick off the briefing."

DuBroux nodded and began turning from the island as Kabath spoke.

"I could come along, if you'd like? I can certainly point out the spots on the ground, I just can't really tell with these maps."

DuBroux looked at Benson, who nodded at him, then back at Kabath.

"That would be kind of you, Mr. Kabath. I'll assemble my guys and we'll get going here."

Clark caught Charlotte staring at him and felt as awkward as she must've when she looked away quickly. Benson and Jacobson began rattling off technical jargon about breach contingencies. Reichman and Bobby leaned in to look at one of the maps and blocked Clark's view. He really didn't want to be here, and spoke as soon as he was moving.

"I'm gonna go with DuBroux, get some fresh air."

Jacobson held his gaze for a moment and nodded.

Clark went out onto the huge back deck off the kitchen and trotted down the stairs after DuBroux, three of his HRT snipers, and Matthew Kabath, who walked ahead of them with his long fingers linked together behind his back. There was a vague trail leading from the porch into the meadow that sloped down toward the wall of trees, and it was obvious neither this guy, nor his prep-school-imprisoned son, spent much time messing around outside. As they got closer to the trees, Clark could now see why DuBroux wanted to find clear lines of sight from here: the castle across the valley was not easy to see from the bottom floors of the new FOB, and it was a view they'd want.

They stopped at a few spots Kabath had suggested, quickly inspected the shooting lanes they provided, and wrote them off. They'd been strolling along the sloping tree line for about six minutes when the transmission came through.

DuBroux and his guys had their helmets on, while Clark only had the small earpiece he ran from his radio. When he heard it crackle to life, he could tell it was Jacobson's voice.

"Do not react to this transmission. I repeat, do not physically or verbally react to this transmission."

Clark slowed and began to snug the earpiece tighter into his ear, but stopped himself and kept walking, unable to prevent himself from glancing at the others. They'd slowed a bit when they'd heard Jacobson's voice, as well, then also just kept walking.

"We've got you guys on EO/IR and another thermal drone."

There was a quick break in the transmission.

"Kabath does not have any heat signature. I repeat, homeowner Kabath is showing up entirely cold, no heat signature."

CHAPTER 47

CLARK, DUBROUX, AND the three snipers flicked their eyes between one another then glared into the fancy man's back, fifteen feet ahead of them.

"*Apprehend Kabath. I repeat, immediately apprehend Kabath.*"

The two snipers closest to Kabath began leaning forward. DuBroux had done the same and reached for the flex-cuffs he kept in the webbing on the back of his plate carrier.

Then Kabath stopped.

Something about it, the way he planted his feet and let his hands fall to rest at his sides, froze the other five men in place.

The HRT snipers glanced at DuBroux, then brought their rifles up and spread out to the flanks. DuBroux and Clark aimed their rifles at the tall man's back, as well. When DuBroux was about to demand that he raise his hands, Kabath spoke. He just stared ahead at the trees, and while he spoke in a calm, soft tone, his voice felt impossibly close.

"I must say..."

He put his hands on his hips and squinted up for a moment, then wagged a finger into the sky.

"All these new gadgets, they *sure do make it tricky* to pull a fast one."

DuBroux shouted first.

"*Hands, hands up, straight up above your head.*"

His three guys joined the chorus immediately with shouts for him to put his hands in the air. Kabath looked down at his palms.

"Hands..."

He turned slowly, a childish, excited smile on his face. His hands were up, but only as high as his face, palms toward the shouting men. *His voice*. It sounded like he was whispering in each man's ear as he began to speak.

"Here's the church..."

He brought his hands together slowly, linking his fingers, smile growing wider as he began to giggle.

"Here's the steeple. Open the doors, and..."

His face fell into a mocking, operatic sad face, his voice roared like a bellowing furnace, and he flipped his hands over to expose twelve-inch-long fingers, new knuckles sprouting along their lengths as he began to wiggle them.

"See alllll the people."

Kabath moved in a streak of black toward the closest FBI sniper. He grabbed him by his ankles, spun low, then stood as he swung the man over his head like a felling axe. The man died instantly as his ribs, sternum, spine, collarbones, and every bone in his face splintered.

He was already on the next man before the others could track him with their rifles. He grabbed an elbow, raised his arm up, then cranked a snake-fast uppercut into his armpit. The man's arm and entire shoulder were cleaved away from his body by the blow. He tossed the bleeding haunch into the trunk of a nearby spruce, the explosion of gore shaking the entire tree. He gingerly grasped the back of the stunned man's head then landed a precise *pop* onto his forehead with an open palm—skull shattered, turning the brain to a hash of fat and bone.

In a bound, he flew into the third sniper between DuBroux and Clark. The gut-flipping force and air displacement blew them back several feet, and DuBroux's head whipped hard against a rock.

The sniper got a shot off, but not until what had been Matthew Kabath was already inside his rifle's muzzle. Kabath punched both fists straight into his chest and gripped the insides of both scapulae with his freakishly long fingers. He kissed the man's nose, then wrenched outward with explosive force. Ribs and clavicle cracked away from the spine as his upper body splayed open. Tissue and blood vented all over the laughing *thing* that tore the man apart, and his arms sloughed to the ground before the rest of his body.

The beast wheeled back toward the two surviving men. He struck a grotesque pose for a moment, his full, blood-caked upper body turned toward the sky. He brought his hands to his face, palms up, then flexed and wiggled his long fingers as he began to sniff them, and then lick them. His head snapped down and he popped a finger from his puckered lips, then pointed it at the stunned, blinking DuBroux as he began to walk toward him.

Clark got up and stumbled between the two, caught himself with a palm to the dirt, then rose, trying to catch his breath.

The former Mr. Kabath stopped, let his head drop to one side, and stared at Clark through what had become jet-black eyes. He *tsked*, then spoke, his voice a wet warble.

"Not your turn yet, soldier boy."

Clark felt something when he locked eyes with the man, who'd somehow grown two feet taller. Something he hadn't felt since he'd gazed down the barefooted trail leading away from the Brookings ranch. It came upon him in a flooding rush. It was a ferocious calm. A tenacious relaxation. Somehow, incredibly, it was only in this moment that Clark realized he was staring *at him*, the one he'd been hunting.

Something in Clark's eyes must've betrayed his revelation, because Kabath surged forward, his face a blood-caked mask of annoyed disgust. A cocky smirk showed through the gore as he balled his fist, wound his arm back, and threw a massive haymaker at Clark's face.

Back at the house, all those staring at the large monitor showing the drone's high-resolution live feed stopped breathing as the giant punch sailed toward Clark's face. The same preternatural fist that had just punched straight through torsos, crushed skulls to pulp, and torn three men into shredded meat. Jacobson and Nowell gripped the backs of chairs with white knuckles. Benson screamed into the radio for Clark to get the hell out of there. Charlotte gasped and covered her mouth with both hands, eyes wide. Time slowed as they awaited what they knew would be a decapitating blow.

Clark didn't do anything. He couldn't have if he'd wanted to. The punch was just too damn fast. He'd been here before, quite a few times: that instant you realize you're about to get hit, but there's nothing you can do about it other than eat the punch and hope it doesn't hit the off switch.

The fist cracked into Clark's left cheekbone. His head snapped to the side. He scrunched his nose, blinked a few times, then looked back into the black eyes, now wide. They narrowed as he let out a glottal, feline snarl and rolled straight into a monstrous left hook.

Clark fell into the comfortable boxing stance he'd either trained, sparred, or fought from every single week since he was fourteen.

All his weight went to his back foot, left hand came up, and he weaved with and dropped under the hook. As the fist whistled over his scalp, he cranked his back foot, pistoned his body, and threw a left hook from his hips. It cracked into the freakish man below the bottom rib. Clark didn't pause, being only halfway through the single continuous motion. He let momentum carry him, rolled with his shoulder and hips, shifted his weight to his front foot, and by the time his left hand came back to his face, his entire body was cranking a right uppercut into Kabath's kidney.

The first hit connected so hard it knocked the huge man to the side several inches as a wet thud echoed down the valley. The second hit actually lifted both the man's feet an inch off the ground. All the air blasted from Kabath's lungs in a shriek that sputtered into a gargling groan. He doubled over at the impact, almost lost his feet, then shuffled away from the game warden, drool and snot dripping down his chin, black eyes wide with real terror as he gasped hideously for breath.

Clark relaxed his shoulders and let his hands fall to his sides. What he saw, and what he felt, was something he'd never forget.

What he was looking at was something sacrosanct. It was pure. The fear he saw in his adversary's eyes, the pain, the blood he spilled, it was a communion for Clark. The destruction of this beast was something clean, honest, and righteous. The annihilation of *this thing* was a sacred deliverance.

He could not explain it, but didn't need to. He could feel it all now. This is what Clark was.

Matthew Kabath, Azrael, Maelgrim, Acheron, Moros, Gideon, Melchior, this *stain* of a thousand names, began to quiver. Tears spilled from his eyes and dripped onto his trembling, blood-caked jaw. He spoke with a tremor.

"It's you."

Clark pulled the knife from his belt in the same instant he exploded forward, moving faster than he ever had.

The beast pulled in the darkness from the valley around him. He summoned it to him in waves, beams, and single drops, from wherever a shadow was to be found. A blast of empty, inverted color blew Clark's hair back as he drove the knife into nothing.

Like those *pops* in his ankles or knees when he stood from a chair, the rage crackling through Clark dissipated.

It was no matter. He knew where he'd gone, and knew he couldn't go anywhere now. The sun was setting, and the new moon would be upon him in a few days. He was chained to the site of his wicked blood rites. More importantly, Clark knew this was over. He could feel him materialize back in the castle across the valley, fall to his knees, and shriek into closed fists.

Clark smiled as his enemy screamed, and screamed, and screamed.

He sheathed his knife and went to DuBroux, who was kneeling now, rubbing the back of his head and staring at him through squinted, defensive eyes.

Bobby and a dozen of his DEVGRU guys—who'd come sprinting down the mountain as soon as they'd grasped what was happening from the drone feed—crested over the rise above them, shouting commands at one another, rifles aimed in every direction.

Clark knelt in front of DuBroux, pointing at his head.

"You good?"

DuBroux raised his eyebrows and gestured with his forehead over Clark's shoulder.

"What in Christ's *bloody fucking kingdom* did I just see?"

Clark snorted a laugh through a weak smile, then looked up the hill toward the Team Six guys.

"Reckon we just saw how that asshole disappeared off the top a' that mountain."

DuBroux snorted out a dry laugh. Clark nodded, took a deep breath, then rose and held a hand out.

"Let's see to your boys."

Everyone in the dining room up the mountain had been staring at the screen in silence until Nowell spoke in a quiet voice.

"Did y'all see that?"

Ground Branch operator Chris Burton, standing over his shoulder, responded, his words slow and clipped.

"*Uhhh*, you mean, did I just see that dude . . . *fucking teleport?*"

Nowell shrugged in acknowledgment. He pointed at one of the drone operators sitting at the dining table.

"Well, that part was strange, but no. Hey, play that back."

The young guy didn't move, he just stared at his screen, mouth hanging open. Nowell popped him on the shoulder with the back of his hand

and repeated himself. The guy flinched like Nowell had thrown a glass of water on him, then grabbed the mouse and started clicking, muttering, "Sorry," as he worked.

Everyone leaned in to the screens as the operator rewound the feed, Benson removing his glasses and standing inches from the display. Charlotte still had not taken her hands from her mouth. Jacobson pointed at the screen.

"*There, stop it there*, and slow it down to twenty-five percent."

They watched Clark get punched in the face again, but that's not what they all wanted to see. They watched the left haymaker flying toward his other cheek, watched him weave under the punch, and then they saw it.

As soon as Clark threw the left hook, a boiling black heat signature pulsed. A ring of it formed and spread from his feet. A ball of it grew around his fist, surging brighter, hotter, until the punch connected, and the heat flashed away. They watched it happen again a second later when he threw his right uppercut, except even hotter, and a burning heat mark was left over the other man's kidney, where Clark had landed the punch.

When Clark's shoulders relaxed and his hands went to his sides, another boiling-black heat signature grew below him, and kept growing. They could see Kabath's lips move, the second word obviously being *you*, and watched the heat grow as Clark pulled his knife. As he surged toward Kabath, a blast of heat exploded below Clark, arcing away in a shock wave from where he'd launched forward. The grass blew back ten feet in every direction. DuBroux winced and shielded his eyes.

They all stood there staring at the large monitor, trying to digest what they'd witnessed, until the young drone operator broke the spell of silence. He slowly spun his chair around to look at Benson, then at Jacobson, and then spoke with a pitiful tremor in his voice.

"What, what did your guy just . . . *What the hell is he?*"

None of the task force leaders present tried to obfuscate, misdirect, or respond in some way that would help maintain this guy's operational focus, as they normally would have. None even looked at him. They were asking themselves the same question, and after what they'd just seen, none of them had any idea what the hell Captain Clark Rickert was.

CHAPTER 48

THEY FOUND THE real Matthew Kabath only thirty minutes after the thing posing as him killed three FBI HRT operators with its bare hands. He was dead, stuffed into the bathroom of his private jet parked at Bozeman Yellowstone International.

Around that same time, Clark and DuBroux walked back into the mansion after their confrontation with the late Matthew Kabath's impostor. Clark could see the disbelief and fear in every face staring back at him, and felt the abrasive weight of the attention.

Benson, Jacobson, Bishop, and the team leaders had managed to compartmentalize and refocus the task force after the chaos at the Hammond ranch a few days earlier, but just barely. The innate sense that they opposed something consequentially, extraordinarily evil had already been growing within every member of the task force. Each encounter with this enemy or their brutalized victims had been another whiplash, another bloody gouge flayed into their emotional stability. As such, their ability to maintain operational focus after the events at the Hammond ranch had been remarkable.

Over a dozen operators and support personnel had watched Clark Rickert frantically rave at Commander Nowell about some prophetic delusion he'd just awoken from, and his unhinged explanation of how he knew the precise location of their crucified team members. It didn't take long for everyone present at that AO to hear about the game warden's embarrassing, panicky spectacle. It also hadn't taken long for them all to see, with their own eyes, that every gruesome detail of that impossible vision was true.

Shortly thereafter, most present had heard how this same madman had broken the maniacal, violent spell infecting the cult members by removing the symbol branded onto their arms. Then they'd watched him carry the exhausted, confused, and terrified young woman—who'd been a deranged, shrieking cultist only minutes earlier—to the evacuation point. Despite all the questions, demands, and dread these events filled the task force with, the leadership had managed to refocus them all, albeit with repeated assurances that more would be disclosed at the operation's conclusion.

Now, doing so felt impossible after what'd just happened. Both men were unsurprised by the severe expressions and body language of those staring at Clark when he walked back into that large house. Several dozen people present had just seen—in real time—that frail, squeamish billionaire morph into something with inhuman speed and strength. They'd watched this impossible *thing* butcher three of their teammates in seconds, and carry itself with a grotesque, bestial savagery so exquisitely *wrong* it'd made most of them gag, and several vomit. Seconds later, they'd seen the quiet game warden confront this new horrifying, sanity-shaking enemy, and then watched him reveal an even more jarring capacity for speed and ferocious violence.

Clark Rickert had been an unknown, unpredictable, and increasingly unmanageable variable since the start. Now he was one apparently capable of catastrophic harm to those around him. Such a variable was like a virus to sensitive and meticulously conditional kinetic operations like this, one with an unacceptably high mortality rate. Benson and Jacobson recognized this, and both knew they could not run this complex team of assets, or carry out this dynamic final operation, without vaccinating against such a virus. And so they did, and without any concern regarding what Thorn, their superiors, the secretary of defense, or the president himself might have to say about it. They glanced at each other, silently conveying their acknowledgment of what needed to be done. Mission success was their supreme mandate, and nothing that jeopardized operational control— like Clark Rickert's newly revealed *abilities*—was even remotely acceptable. Bishop also saw all of this for what it was. When Jacobson turned toward her, she was already whispering into his ear.

"Get him out of here and isolated, right now."

Jacobson and one of his staffers ushered Clark from the mansion and into the three-car garage under the large Swiss chalet–style guesthouse of this strange, garish FOB. There were no vehicles parked in there, making it feel huge. Jacobson asked Clark to stay there for the time being while they dealt with the deaths of the three FBI HRT agents, their impact on the overall assault plan, and all the other issues that'd stem from what had just gone down. He added a comment that he thought it best that Clark remain separated from the rest of the task force, just for the time being. As he said this, both men watched Jacobson's staffer remove wiring from all three of the oversized garage doors' motorized openers, retrofitting this place into a jail. Clark turned toward Jacobson, who was grateful for the sympathy he saw in Clark's face as he nodded in acknowledgment, removed his hat, and set it on a workbench built into the garage wall. Clark did not fail to hear them lock the door leading from the garage into the mudroom at the base of the stairs, his final way out.

Clark knew there were two rooms entered only through the garage: a single half bathroom and a utility vault for the suite upstairs. After checking those, Clark spent an hour poking around the storage shelves and cabinets, then moved onto the well-provisioned workbenches. There were almost enough high-quality tools in there to run a professional carpentry, mechanic, and landscaping operation. There was also probably $80,000 worth of welding equipment in one corner, much of which was still boxed. Clark decided there was a significant probability the real Matthew Kabath had hired someone to *stock it with anything a man living in the mountains might ever need*. And they certainly had, without sparing expense.

A few hours in, one of Benson's staffers brought him a sandwich and a bag of chips. Clark nodded at the visibly terrified guy who behaved as though he were bringing the shitty lunch into a tiger cage. The only company Clark had was the hum and bustle of a busy communications and surveillance team that'd set up their equipment in the guesthouse above the garage.

About three hours later, when the next visitor arrived, he was staring down at a Stihl MS 881 Magnum chain saw he'd disassembled and spread atop one of the workbenches. He'd wanted one of these saws, but was neither a professional logger nor a wealthy man, so couldn't justify the necessity. Clark could tell from the cleanliness of the machine that the real Matthew Kabath hadn't used it once while alive, and certainly wouldn't now.

Charlotte could only see his back as she stepped into the garage, and the duty belt, plate carrier, backpack, helmet, and rifle he'd piled on the ground next to the stool where he sat. She hadn't been sure why she'd come here, but she had. She stared at Clark's back for a moment, wondering who, or *what*, she was looking at. She thought back on first meeting him at Langley, what felt like years ago. How she felt she'd seen something ruthless, uncompromising, and ancient in his eyes. How frightened she'd been of him. How shaky she felt, not being able to read, assess, and categorize him.

None of that had really changed.

She walked up to him, increasingly anxious and uncertain of what she'd say. When he heard her and turned and stood from the stool, her uncertainty had evolved into a complete flatline of social and creative grace, but Clark's mind jammed up even worse. So they just stared at each other. It went on long enough that it grew past awkwardness, both just quietly comfortable in their own and each other's lack for words.

Charlotte felt, eventually, something simple would suffice. Something honest and plain. She put a few fingers on his chest as she rose onto her toes and kissed him on the cheek. She kept looking at him as she dropped back down.

He caught her hand. As soon as he began to step toward her, she closed the distance between them. Their lips met gently, but deepened with slow, synchronized passion. She reached up and slid fingers through his hair and traced the line of his jaw. He ran his fingers around the back of her neck then pulled her body into his with an arm around her waist. Every passing second of the kiss felt deliberate, each with its own delicate intensity. When their lips finally parted, their foreheads rested against each other. They kissed again, less passionately, but looking into each other's eyes, both making sure it was real. She put her arms around his neck and her cheek against his and he pulled her into his body again.

Clark squeezed her tight for a few more seconds, then they stepped apart. They stared at each other, still unsure what to say. Charlotte's mind cleared a bit, and she looked at the ground between them as she began preparing her explanation as to why he'd been separated from the rest of the task force and how the plan for the assault had developed. She'd rehearsed this before coming to the garage, as well as the justification for their decision that Clark would remain behind. There was simply no reasonable basis for folding someone or *something* like him into such a dynamic, complex assault plan. They'd half lied to Thorn about this decision, assuming he'd go ballistic if his special ward was excluded from the final confrontation. They told him they'd keep Rickert separated from the others for everyone's peace of mind just for now, then, once final preparations and staging for the raid began, fold him into a ground team as they had on all the raids before. In reality, they'd decided to keep him confined until the assault was mostly concluded and the main and upper levels of the mansion were cleared and secure. They'd do this whether he liked it or not, and all assumed he certainly would fucking not. But she wouldn't lie to Clark about that decision, not now, and felt some vague hope he'd actually understand it.

When she looked back up into his face, something in Clark's eyes said he did understand, and that he wasn't interested in such things now. He squeezed her hand as though assuring her of this, and she'd never felt so grateful. She brought his hand up to her mouth, kissed his fingers, then turned and left.

Clark didn't have any clue what she'd come there to tell him, and certainly hadn't intended to convey any silent assurances. He was happy she'd come, and his heart had skipped a beat when he saw her enter the garage. He'd thought about her all day. When their lips met, he experienced a kind of boyish excitement he'd forgotten existed, and as much relief at having her validate the affection he'd felt burning through him.

Watching her leave the garage, however, Clark wondered if romantic affection is really why she'd come to visit him. He wondered if she'd come because, somehow, she knew.

CHAPTER 49

IT WAS A certain thing now. A wordless import they could all feel. The terrible weight of the coming raid, and what its outcome meant for the world. Something grinding and noxious undulated silently from the cult's final stronghold down the valley. It was a subtle gnaw, like a dog whistle hitting an eardrum. This putrid, harassing effect was manifestly worse if staring directly at the mansion. This was felt by personnel in overwatch positions on the ground around the valley staring at it through optics or with naked eyes. Yet it was felt just as distinctly by drone pilots and sensor operators staring at it through digital monitors at Creech Air Force Base in Nevada and Holloman Air Force Base in New Mexico. It made mouths water, ears ring, and even a few noses bleed.

For Harry Jacobson, this feeling churned up an emotional recollection of sorts, a memory of this same sensation.

Several decades earlier, Harry had found himself on the deck of a forty-seven-foot Beneteau Oceanis about 120 miles east of Cuba. He'd just sailed into the calm and ominously pleasant eye at the center of a hurricane, mostly by accident. It was an almost paralytic juxtaposition, so sudden and dramatic was the change in conditions. He stared at the sun on his hands, feeling like this was some cruel trick. When he realized where he was, and what this was, he figured that was a pretty fucking fair way to describe getting shat into the eye of a hurricane: the illusion of hope within a veneer of sanctuary. Having long ago mastered the acceptance of imminent death, Harry shrugged and went about making repairs. He was working against a state of sickening exhaustion, but also against time, which seemed to be functioning again. Throughout the relentless thrashing he'd somehow just survived, it felt like time itself had been brutalized as violently as he and this stolen sailboat had. Ten hours had been bent, warped, and stretched into ten years. As he'd stared into the gunmetal-and-bruise-hued storm wall pulsing with lightning and closing back in around him—and felt the storm's vow that the thrashing to come would be far, far worse—he'd felt much as he did now, staring at that mansion.

However, reflecting on this, Harry realized he was not actually reencountering a sensation he'd felt before. This one was new. Though both similarly imbued with a silent promise that he'd die screaming through broken teeth, that hurricane had been a ruthlessly dispassionate thing. It hadn't felt vengeful. It hadn't wanted him to beg.

It hadn't felt hungry.

When the head of the task force's surveillance wing began speaking, Harry's thoughts were yanked back to the new issue at hand, to the newest link in the chain of infuriatingly inexplicable headaches and fuckups he felt beginning to define this entire operation.

"We'll maintain constant scrutiny of the manned, UAV, ground, and satellite ISR spectrum we've already got on station. We've got thermal and IR, high-res optical, Lidar, multi- and hyperspectral satellite imaging, synthetic aperture radar, EM, RF, and SIGINT scoping tech, the best MASINT tools that exist, all plugged into fusion overlays subject to constant AI and human monitoring. We'll have any anomalous blip of radiation, seismic, acoustic, or magnetic activity within one hundred miles flagged and located instantly. We've got the best persistent, multisource intel collection suite ever deployed by man, right here, right now. I'm sorry, but there's . . . there's just no tech left to employ here, DDO. Everything we've got is already online."

Harry, the head of task force's surveillance wing, and all the others in the room, cringed inwardly in anticipation of the question Benson had screamed some version of fifteen times over the last nine hours: *Then how the hell haven't we found him yet?*

Benson did not repeat his demands regarding the escape, and excused the head of task force's surveillance wing with an impatient hand gesture. However, without it having to be stated, as the surveillance chief left the room, all of them—even Thorn—knew the attention bandwidth and time available to expend on this new and unfortunate issue had officially just run out.

Even if they had found any indication of where Clark had gone, at this point they'd still have to assign new assets from off-site to pursue. Jacobson and Bishop would pass along a target profile and contingencies to another state and federal unit, but a missing local law enforcement liaison was someone else's problem now. And only if they survived the coming fight, which they all felt markedly less certain about as the sun rose and marked the celestial countdown to the final assault. Besides, this development had kept them all mostly sleepless throughout the night.

Final contact had been made by an operator who'd been sent into the impromptu brig in the garage with a sleeping bag, pillow, and a meal around half till midnight. Just under four hours later, another operator was sent in to make a status check. This is when, about nine hours ago, they'd realized he and much of his duty gear were gone, though he'd left behind his plate carrier and helmet.

They'd flipped the place quickly. Starting with the half bathroom only accessed through the garage, they scoured the structure for any hiding place or breach large enough for him to have escaped through. There was only one regular door in and out of the garage, which opened into the mudroom at the base of the stairs leading up to the guest suite. Other than that, there were the three copper-trimmed wooden garage doors themselves. Guards had been watching these entrances since shortly after he'd been brought in there, and both who'd been there since final contact were certain none had opened. This was confirmed by the security cameras covering every entrance of the residence, air-gapped by the cybersecurity and IT specialists when they set up this FOB, but still keeping a footage archive.

As soon as they'd finished reviewing that footage over the shoulders of the tech specialists, DuBroux turned abruptly and stormed toward the front door. Benson, Jacobson, Nowell, Charlotte, and several others followed. DuBroux spoke to them over his shoulder as he made his way outside and toward the garage and guesthouse.

"They matched the house's stone wainscoting along the front and sides, the parts visible from the driveway and the main house. They didn't bother with the backside, the side facing into the timber and slope that no one can see."

DuBroux stopped at the door that opened to the mudroom at the bottom of the stairs, pointing at the masonry along the base of the garage.

Benson shrugged.

"I hadn't noticed."

DuBroux held his gaze as he opened the door.

"Well, the guy you locked in here sure as hell had."

They all followed DuBroux into the garage, then stopped to watch him slowly walk along the length of the long workbenches and tool racks, scanning everything. He stopped at one point, staring at all the tools mounted to the equipment paneling above the LED-lit work surface. He began checking the drawers nearby, then knelt to look through all the hard cases stowed underneath the bench. After opening the last one, he turned quickly, scanning the entire garage until his gaze locked onto a massive Snap-On roll cab tool cabinet. He went to it quickly, stopped, and grabbed something sitting on the padded work surface on top of it. He turned and held the stud finder up so they could see it, smiling and shaking his head. Before they could ask anything about its significance, he knelt at one end of the tool cab, slammed the wheel lock down, then started heaving the massive chest away from the wall. The others drew up behind him as he knelt next to the newly exposed wall. He exhaled noisily, shook his head, then turned toward them. Seeing that they didn't yet grasp what they were looking at, he stood and slammed a boot into the drywall above the baseboard, dislodging a big square of it. He knelt and picked it up, ran his finger along the edge and turned it over, then held it up to show them the little strap handle that'd been stapled to the inside. He set it aside, pulled a tac-light from his vest, and leaned into the hole. He came back out with a large bundle of dusty microfiber cloth, then held it up to the others as he spoke.

"Used this for the mess he made cutting through the drywall. He used the oscillating multitool that's missing from the wall over there, and probably the compass and wallboard saws missing from that unused set in the drawer. Probably used them to get through the insulation and vapor barrier too. Looks like he used wire snips to cut through the stucco mesh after that, then some combo of handsaw, blade, and elbow grease to rip through the stucco siding itself. Slapped that little handle on that square of drywall, plus some kind of clear adhesive to snug it back into place from the other side. Seemed to work well enough, at least to pass at a glance by someone rushing a search."

As he spoke that last sentence, he'd glanced over and cocked his head at one of the special agents on his HRT team, Rick Porter, the one who'd helped with the initial sweep of the garage once they'd found it empty of life. Rick felt the sting of this criticism from his boss, and acknowledged it by pursing his lips and nodding. DuBroux looked back at the hole as he rose to his feet. A smile spread across his face as he spoke mostly to himself.

"Damn fine work. Simple, quick, and effective."

He looked at the others now.

"I'd wager he took other tools with him, as well. Porter, go get Fisk, Durst, and Lucas. We're going to comb the place, put this puzzle together."

Since then, the task force had taken advantage of what was effectively the most robust technological surveillance package on earth to find him. They'd also employed the profound collective skill set of this particular task force regarding this particular situation—finding someone who did not want to be found. To maintain focus on the impending assault, the leadership decided to keep most personnel in the dark regarding the missing person. They wanted to avoid burdening as many people as possible with yet another sinister, unexplainable circumstance they'd neither foreseen nor prevented. Besides, the cover story was conveniently simple: *finding a cultist somewhere in the area and capturing them alive without alerting any others would provide critical intelligence prior to the raid, and doing so while exercising the most extreme levels of restraint against the employment of lethal measures unless absolutely necessary.*

It was just a manhunt, and one with a very broad net, as their target was essentially any living person located within the area. They were all masters at this. They just didn't know they were hunting Clark Rickert.

Unfortunately, neither their technological assets nor the human tradecraft worked. The game warden seemed to have vanished. Everyone aware of this development knew how significant a strategic threat it posed to operational security, and it was also just fucking infuriating. This was a crescendo of the suspicions that had already grown hot regarding Clark's motives, abilities, and who or what he even was. But they simply didn't have the time to dwell on all the tactical implications of him turning on them. They made some adjustments to the version of the assault plan Clark had last seen, but that's all the operational security they could spare. The timing had to remain the same. This was it. It was the eleventh hour, and everyone in the valley knew it.

Throughout the night, they'd engaged in debate over why Clark had left. DuBroux and Jacobson both proposed the theory that Clark went off to see this through by himself, and thus maintained the objective of stopping the ritual. It fit the man's character, to an extent. However, the theory didn't hold much water. They all felt many things about Clark, but none took him for an idiot. They knew beyond any doubt that trying to infiltrate and take down that stronghold would be abjectly suicidal even for any six-man Ground Branch assault team, let alone one man. There were at least seventy-five confirmed cultists defending the mansion. It was highly likely that the deadliest group of gunfighters and martial artists on earth was assembled here and now, and not a single one of them would consider it remotely possible to survive such a one-man effort.

Nowell, Bobby, Reichman, and Benson seemed to share the belief that Clark's mind, will, or both had finally broken. He'd just had enough, couldn't take it, and lit out. He wasn't a career combat operator, after all, and none could confidently proclaim that he was even on their side anymore, let alone what the hell he really was. Thorn didn't suggest any potential motive, despite Benson and others repeatedly lancing into him regarding the motives of Thorn's *fucking freak-show pet*. Thorn had seemed as surprised by Clark's disappearance as the rest, and as the hours ticked on he'd grown angsty, and then seemed genuinely afraid. This was uncomfortable to be around, representative as it was of some version of the fear they all now felt growing.

Charlotte hadn't opined on Clark's motive. Indeed, she'd ended the discussions of it when she'd interrupted Nowell, Bobby, and DuBroux's latest exchange on the matter with a barbed suggestion that they *hold further pontification on his fucking motive until we establish the vaguest clue regarding his fucking location.*

Charlotte did wonder, though. She wondered where he was right now, and what could have possibly drawn him away from this team and this purpose. His decision to just up and leave was infuriating. But at this point, to a certain extent, the game warden had given all he had to give. The task force was staged, set to assault, and they had an enemy cornered. She, like all the rest here, knew what they had to do, and what was at stake if they didn't, and that did not leave much bandwidth for dwelling on the motives of a strange man she'd kissed the night before.

Around midday, one of the Ground Branch K9 teams—Reggie and his handler, Quinn, who'd worked closely with Clark following that barefooted trail into the mountains after the first assault—did end up finding a spot Clark had certainly been at some point since escaping the garage. It was the first time all day any of the K9s had indicated a positive identification, so the full leadership cadre had gathered to watch on digital monitors as a ground team followed the tracking dog, streaming live via helmet and gun cams. The team was on the other side of the steep ridge across the valley, several miles from the FOB. The dog lost the scent in a small glade under a rock outcropping. Items taken from the garage were found there while the K9 team ran growing laps around the spot, but that scent trail ended right there, just as the barefooted man's had.

It became increasingly clear that this was where Clark Rickert had apparently undertaken a concerning little project. There were bits and pieces of paracord, zip ties, landscaping jute netting, safety wire, HVAC barrier foil, three empty cans of spray paint, a half dozen spent tubes of Gorilla Glue, and strips of some kind of thick cloth. One of the operators on the scene was holding a larger piece of the cloth up to one of the cameras, trying to describe the consistency. DuBroux interrupted him with a growled "Son of a bitch," then turned away from the screens. Everyone stared at his back, watching him shake his head and stare out the huge windows toward the large mountains reaching up beyond the far ridge of the valley, waiting for him to explain himself. He chuckled softly before he turned back to look at the others, all staring back at him. For the second time that day, the career investigator realized he'd need to bring the others up to speed.

"The only thing in the garbage can in the garage was the packaging for two six-by-eight-foot welding blankets . . ."

DuBroux looked between them expectantly, eyebrows raised as though waiting for them to get a joke.

Benson and Nowell swore almost simultaneously when, it seemed, they finally did. Jacobson, Bishop, and a few of the sensor technicians all groaned a second later—the kind of groan made by someone realizing, mid-flight, they'd forgotten something very fucking important. DuBroux chuckled again as he turned away from the others, back toward the stunning view of rolling mountains streaked in the gray of granite, the dark green of firs, and the light green of aspens.

"Damn fine work. Simple, quick, and effective."

CHAPTER 50

THEY HAD NEVER met before, but they hadn't needed to. They hadn't even exchanged names when they'd assembled several days earlier, or at any point during the travel and preparation since. They'd barely even talked at all.

They hadn't known it, but they'd been born for this. They'd realized this over the last weeks when he'd reached them in their dreams, the holy patron they'd been created to serve.

One was a sixty-four-year-old man, a middle school teacher from Madison, Wisconsin. One was a homeless forty-six-year-old man from Las Vegas, blind in one eye. One was a thirty-six-year-old woman from Broomfield, Colorado, still on maternity leave after giving birth to her second child three months earlier. One was a twenty-five-year-old man from New Orleans who'd never held a real job but had risen high in the ranks of his gang and survived well beyond the life expectancy of a pimp and drug dealer. The last to join the group was a nineteen-year-old woman from Portland, Oregon, who'd been living between the streets and her mother's home, violently addicted to heroin and on hour thirty-six without any. She'd been shaking with chills and vomiting in the back of the old van since they passed through Evanston, Wyoming, yet still religiously focused on what was to come.

They all were.

The pilgrimage was clear; every last detail shared to them by their blessed father in their dreams over the last several nights.

They knew exactly where to leave the van, exactly where to start hiking and the precise route to get them close to the mansion above his holy temple of blood, and exactly where to arrange themselves to initiate the attack on the wretched enemy's headquarters.

They all had semiautomatic rifles and handguns. They all had a clear vision of what was expected of them. They were all desperate to spill the enemy's blood. That wretched woman's blood, in particular. The one their master had told them his nemesis harbored a kindling love for. That was the one they'd try to kill, and in doing so, bring that center of operations to a halt.

And they were getting very, very close.

CHAPTER 51

THE FIRST FLAT shade of a day's light was still hours away. Darkness reigned. As such, the sparks that sizzled from the rockets cut distinct trails through the air.

A minute earlier, the order had been issued for the sniper teams to engage. Nineteen rifles shattered the quiet mountain dawn. The opening salvo of 7.62x51mm, .300 Win-Mag, and .50-caliber bullets killed nine cultists outright, and dropped four more who'd bleed to death in the coming minutes. The sniper fire continued to crackle and bark around the valley over the next minute as the assaulters with MAAWS and M141 rocket launchers pushed forward into firing positions. The sniper fire continued once those started getting fired, but it was much harder to hear.

Rockets screamed through the air into entrances of the mansion in staggered volleys from every direction. Four FGM-148 Javelin missiles were launched into the top story of the mansion from firing positions farther away, and their cracking roar elevated the level of auditory chaos considerably.

The massive fieldstone exterior cracked, burst, and ruptured. On occasion, entire stones from the upper stories would go spinning into the valley, a foxtail of smoke and dust following them to where they crashed into boulders and snapped tree trunks with almost as much noise as the rockets themselves.

Many of the rockets were detonating against the stone-and-heavy-timber exterior of the structure. This had been intended, for these rockets were being used as a breaching mechanism to clear any booby traps or IEDs set to tear apart breaching parties. On several of these entrances, the cultists had indeed rigged explosive traps, and the assaulters grinned wolfishly as the sound and light of their sympathetic detonations could be seen flaring as they cracked off.

The four MH-6 Little Bird helicopters eventually maneuvered in to drop the two assault teams onto the top floor. It looked as though the Javelins had vesicated the upper level, but overwatch had confirmed the fire-suppression system was active, fire risk tolerable, so they were going in.

The explosives fell silent, and while a good amount of shooting from inside the place could still be heard, none of the assaulters felt fear right now. It was time for them to breach and raid. It was time for them to kill.

The energy was electric with fearless, vengeful, excited rage. It could be seen in their bodies, their hungry eyes, and their grinding teeth. This enemy had hurt them very badly.

It was an ancient thing, this energy possessing the group of warriors. One that stretched back to the earliest written history. A sieging force is one that suffers. They're the ones far from home, afflicted with malnutrition, starvation, dysentery, lice, roaches, rats, and infuriating boredom. They go through all this while freezing to death, or being wet for so long they watch their own skin slough away, or baking under relentless sun and dust, or slopping through hot mud, festering with the shit and decay of rotting animals and men. They're killed, maimed, and brutalized for maddening stretches of time by a significantly smaller number of defenders, and endure this without any real ability to hit back.

The culmination, in a way, was even worse. After months of bombardment, trenching, and mining, a breach is *finally* made in the wall. And there is no more horrifying and bloody a place in warfare than a breach. The stinking, starving, and sick men of the besieging force are sent into a confined space where the very air boils with fire, steel, and screams. *Again and again and again.* Struggling up literal causeways of shredded bodies. They'd suffered and toiled all those months just to charge blindly into this pinched funnel of death and shrieking terror.

Then, however, everything can change.

The moment the defenders finally retreat from the breach—the first glimpse an assaulter has of an open route into the city or castle—the suffering and misery of the siege immediately transform into one of the most astonishingly destructive forces of rage, cruelty, and barbarism humanity has ever known.

The sieges of Jerusalem, Constantinople, Béziers, Limoges, Antwerp,

Drogheda, Magdeburg, Badajoz. The moment those sick, hungry, terrified men finally got inside, a bloodlust was awoken within them so severe it led to instances of wanton butchery that have haunted the world for centuries.

These men of the task force had not been besieging the walls of this castle for months or years, starving and freezing. These were not the same circumstances of a traditional siege. However, what they had been fighting against was something more purely evil than any of those who've stormed a breach before. That might just be enough to awaken that same cursed fiend incubating within all men. The one that has hatched at the top of so many breaches throughout history, seized the mind of its host, *and screamed.*

As the assault teams fell upon the balconies off the top floor via helicopter insertions, others began moving toward their own breaches. Moritz's team was slated to make entry over the large veranda into the cavernous living room. They rose together from their final staging position, picking up speed as they went. Mako, Moritz, Gavin, Burton, they all craved the opportunity to spill blood in a way they never had. Two other teams snaked fast and silent toward the castle on their right, and another up ahead to the left.

Everyone in every assault team felt it now. A rage, but unlike any they'd ever felt. A fury that was not entirely organic. It felt synthetic, like it came from somewhere or something outside themselves. The desire to inflict pain and kill hit like mainlined amphetamines.

They surged up the stairs onto the veranda as three cultists came out through the wreckage of the massive French doors.

The sight of them, alone, made everyone on the assault teams begin to howl and shriek. The cultists only got a few shots off, all of which cracked white gouges into the pink flagstone of the veranda, before everyone was killing them. No one slowed as they shot, and all of them pumped bullets into their bodies as they hurdled over them and into the breach. They barely noticed the meat-colored robes the cultists were wearing, secured with gold rope and their symbol emblazoned in gold on their breast.

The rockets had shredded the imported furniture, chandeliers, and finery throughout the entire living room.

A group of four cultists ran from left to right a few meters into the room, and had barely started to turn when they were T-boned by the assaulters. Gavin squeezed off a burst point-blank into one's face. Moritz speared one in the ribs with his suppressor, shooting upon impact, more as the cultist fell, and then into the middle-aged woman's face when she was on her back, long past death. Mako let his rifle hang on its sling and form-tackled one like a defensive end. The cultist's ribs cracked audibly as Mako smashed him into the marble floor, and so did other bones as Mako began stomping on his neck. Burton shot one in the head, killing him instantly, but shot him eight more times until his body was motionless. All were in the same flesh-red robes.

They could hear the sounds of voices coming from their radios, but they didn't care about those.

More jittery screaming of cultists came from the right, and the team turned to see another group surging into the massive living room toward them, but they'd only made it a few steps before a second assault team, led by Jake, crushed into them from the side. They'd unleashed a wall of fire just before connecting with the bullet-riddled group, but most of them hadn't fallen yet, so Jake and his guys fell upon them with their hands, their bodies, and the same frenzied rage.

Shooting and screaming came from the grand entryway as more cultists poured down the massive staircase. When Moritz and his group got within view of the wide breezeways above on the second floor, they all began shooting at cultists running down it, straight through the ornately carved white-and-gold railings and balustrades, bursting knees and shattering ankles.

The robed body of a woman, out of nowhere, came flying down to the marble floor of the entry from above. She landed almost flat on her feet. Her ankles, knees, and femurs all buckle-fractured in a sickening crunch as everything below her pelvis was pulped.

When they'd gone farther into the entry, Moritz looked up into the atrium that went all the way to the third floor. One of the teams from the roof insertion had pushed their way to the third-story breezeway where they'd trapped a group of cultists. Two more of the robed bodies were hurled from up there. One belly flopped into the marble floor beyond the stairs and the wet smack echoed up through the atrium. The second connected with the stairs coming down from the second floor. His ankles, knees, and forearms shattered on impact, and then he went rolling down the stairs, arms and legs flopping unnaturally as though each had grown a second elbow or knee below the ones they'd been born with. Moritz and Mako both shot the tumbling, shrieking, broken cultist at least five times from the side of the massive staircase.

Most of the operators, again, could hear a voice being shouted into their ears, but had no time or care for such things. Some of them felt a desire to listen, to respond, some strange urge to *stop* their teammates from going any deeper into whatever this was they all felt taking them over, but none did.

A roar that had not been heard since the days of Danish sea raiders came from up ahead. Bobby and his DEVGRU team came tearing down the long hall that led to the massive oak front doors. A group of cultists had just hit the park-sized landing on the stairs between the first and second floors as the SEALs got to the base. The Navy men did not slow as they flew up toward the landing and crashed into the cultists. They moved like a desert flash flood crashing through a slot canyon. Moritz saw one of the SEALs get shot directly in the throat, but he didn't slow, he just continued bounding up the stairs as torrents of blood gushed down his tactical gear through gargled wheezes until he collapsed onto all fours. The SEALs had shot most of the cultists by the time the assaulters blitzed into them.

Moritz saw Bobby shoot two of them point-blank in the face then drop his rifle to grab a third by the collar and start smashing the forehead of his ballistic helmet into their face, shattering the young man's nose, cheeks, and orbital bones and covering Bobby's roaring, bearded face in blood. Another cultist was tackled to the ground by a SEAL who drove his thumbs into his eyes as far as they could go, not seeming to notice the small revolver being emptied into the side of his stomach.

Moritz spun and began running down the long hallway to the right, moving on memory from the blueprints and 3D models they'd all studied for days, the rest of the team on his heels. They saw another group of operators crash into the hallway ahead of them. It was Nowell's team. His eyes were wild, his helmet gone, and a distinct, bloody imprint of a row of teeth in his forehead indicating he, like his Red Squad brother Bobby, had also been headbutting cultists. One of his guys straight-kicked a shrieking young woman wielding a fire axe to the ground. Another picked up the axe and slammed it down, cutting her left arm off at the elbow, and then her right, and then started on her ankles.

DuBroux and his HRT team came flying into view toward Moritz, moving like felines, low and smooth. DuBroux had just glanced over at

Nowell when a cultist came sprinting out of a room behind him and his small FBI team: a short, academic-looking middle-aged man, wielding an actual sword. No one in Moritz's or Nowell's team at this end of the hall could risk taking a shot, but DuBroux immediately made it clear he was just fine.

He weaved under the decapitating swing of the sword and popped back up to his full height before the cultist had even finished the stroke. With the power of a Clydesdale, he planted a boot into the man's chest. It sent him flying backward into the wall of the hallway. With the speed of a shark, DuBroux pulled the fixed blade from the sheath on the front of his plate carrier and flew inside the man's guard. He stabbed the knife up under the man's chin, twisted it ninety degrees, and ripped it free. He stepped aside just in time to let the man fall face-first into the floor.

They heard the voices screaming and roaring into their ears, but they also didn't. They felt something wordlessly screaming at them to listen, to get control, but whatever it was was weak. Those voices did not matter now. The breach was taken, the black flag was raised, and all that mattered now or ever had was this slaughter.

They heard the mumbles and shrieks of cultists in the large drawing room they knew to be at the end of the hall, and all of their heads whipped in that direction. Then, without orders or a word, all three teams were moving like wolves. As they crashed into the large double doors, all of them were already roaring battle cries. The room was filled with cultists digging through chests, trunks, and duffels for weapons. One, already armed with an AR-15, began emptying his magazine toward the operators. Most of the shots went into the groin and stomach of a guy on Nowell's team, who collapsed as his pelvis and lower spine were shattered, but it was already far, far too late. The operators spread through the room like fire.

Back at the FOB, Benson gave up screaming into his mic and slammed his headset into the wall under the monitor he'd been following Nowell's team on.

Jacobson still hissed urgent commands into his mic as he ripped his gaze between a half dozen monitors arrayed before him.

Charlotte had leaned back into a chair, staring up blankly at all sixteen monitors covering one side of the living room of what was once Matthew Kabath's mansion, each screen switching between live feeds from cameras attached to helmets and weapons of the operators, a seizure-inducing, live-action mosaic of unbridled butchery.

When Moritz's, Nowell's, and DuBroux's teams set upon the fifteen or so unprepared cultists, all thirty people within view of that sixteen-monitor array in the tactical operation center fell completely silent. Even Jacobson gave up trying to hail the team leads and stepped back to behold the spectacle of absolute savagery.

On one screen, an operator had a cultist pinned to the floor with a boot on his head and appeared to be trying to pull her arm from her body at the shoulder. On another, an operator was stomping on the head of a cultist who'd died ten or twelve stomps earlier. On another, a cultist was on her knees staring straight up into the camera with bulging eyes as an operator gripped her hair with one hand, and forced his other down her throat almost to the elbow.

Not a single one of the operators had spoken an English word in over three minutes. All they heard now was their inhuman snarls and shrieks as they hunted cultists throughout the mansion and killed them in horrible, terrible ways.

There was no order. No control. No humanity.

Every single one of the operators had lost their minds.

Jacobson stepped toward a control terminal, stared at the screens for another few moments, then turned the volume down.

CHAPTER
52

THE TORMENTOR—AT ALMOST the same moment Harry turned the volume down—looked up at the oaken-beamed ceiling of the large subterranean area, closed his eyes, and smiled. He'd been worried, at first. The siege began earlier than he'd anticipated. He still had around sixteen hours until he could see it all through.

However, he knew the five blood knights of his perpetual earthly retinue—those he'd been able to reach and instruct by dream—would soon be springing their little surprise upon the enemy leaders in the mansion up the valley. He'd wanted more, but of his seventy-two, those five were the only ones capable of getting here in time. There were more than twice that many here on this continent, but one was still too young, and the wicked sheep in this new vile country had incarcerated the rest. These five would do, however. They were working with vision and foresight that those they hunted didn't know existed, and his blood nights would make them pay for that ignorance in pain. That would buy him some more time, in addition to the surprises waiting for the bestial warriors upstairs. When he heard them, when he heard the music of their new *affliction*, he calmed, and his optimism returned.

This was one of his rare, special tricks he seldom got to play with. It was one of the only things left in this repulsive realm that he remained somewhat unfamiliar with. It had only ever worked a few times, only in these final hours, and only on men who'd spent lives at war. *The warrior's blood rage*. He hadn't been certain it would be here, waiting to consume them. But as this final day and countdown to the sacred moonrise began earlier that night, he could feel it, smell it, and taste it as it began to seep from this place of the ritual. His final defense mechanism, one could say. A heavy musk of vile, cursed disease only he knew was there, and one they'd have to run right into.

He could hear its paradoxical effect on the men clearly in their roaring and snarling. The tenor of exquisite pleasure only felt when surrendering to a berserker's mania, and the alto of a good man's life-changing horror at what he was doing to someone's body, and how amazing it felt. The way those two sounds struggled against each other made him tear up and giggle. He wished he could suck on those sounds, pop and gnash them between his teeth, then swallow them and feel them in his body. He could also clearly distinguish the difference between a scream of blood rage and a scream of pain. When they overlapped and oscillated that metallic way loud sounds can, such music had always made his heart flutter. But to hear it here, and now, was something truly divine.

His canines and outer incisors throbbed with warm, entirely erotic thrums, something he'd only ever felt a few times before, only when he was close. But he'd never, ever come this close. One of the few disciples he'd had remain below slinked up to his side and spoke as he glanced nervously at the ceiling.

"My patron father, dearest shepherd of screams, shall we add more fortification to the entry?"

The Tormentor shook his head, then looked down at the pathetic wretch.

"No . . . no, no. They'll be busy a good, long while. I left treats for them. I made sure to leave them extra meat. Several of your brothers and sisters are locked in places *very, very tricky* to access, confined in *certain positions* to ensure your dear, sweet siblings are unable to go too long without whimpering or writhing, and certainly unable to sleep. Those monsters above will not be able to resist hunting *them* down like truffle pigs."

He'd been basking in the sounds of the seven sacred pain chants coming from the ceremonial room. *The hymns of final remonstration.* He'd carved the glyphs and runes into the seven disciples he needed present for the final rites several hours ago, when the final solar rotation began to mark the last day before the last, darkest night. First, he'd carved away parts of them to ensure their blessed liturgies were tinged by genuine pain. Then, he'd wired them through muscles and between bones and staked them into postures to venerate the seven numinous virtues, and of course to ensure they didn't disturb the sacred ritual arrangements. He'd forgotten about their hymnals, so aroused had he been by the muffled melody of butchery above.

He'd forgotten them, until they went silent.

He whipped around and surged down the hall until he reached the doors to the wine cellar. He'd already begun screaming in a forgotten tongue as he wheeled into the dank, candlelit room.

Then he stopped.

His disciples were silent because they were all dead, prematurely leaking their putrid, yet-unsanctified fluids into his sacred arrangements. *That* he barely noticed.

All he noticed was the man standing in the center of the ritual focal point, staring into his eyes. The room was dark. Low, warm light from dozens of candle clusters danced erratically on the old stone and oak of the walls, floor, and ceiling, but dark shadows danced in the room as well and outweighed the candlelight. Even so, he didn't need light to know who it was. He could *feel* who it was. His closeness made his skin sting and the sores on his spine rupture and ooze. Rage and terror battled in his churning gut, and his heart froze.

It was the Sentinel.

It was not over, though. *This could not mean it was already over.* He would still carry it out. It could be done, though. He was already crying, but then began to laugh. It would take great, ancient magic to repair the hexes and rites at this late stage, now that these seven were dead and defiling his venerated ritual arrangements. He laughed harder as he realized this, and harder still at the Sentinel's ignorance, his belief that killing them would end this. His laughter grew into a screaming shriek of triumph as he realized this wretched cur would be here, *in this righteous place*, to behold his ascendance with his own wretched eyes. It could not be more deliciously perfect.

All he needed to do now was beat him.

There was no one else here. No other blood; he'd have smelled as much. This newest Sentinel *came all by himself*. He would enjoy no assistance from an army of pagans or Christlings, the hordes of feral sheep he always seemed to bring along with him in the past to despoil everything. He'd finally, *finally* come to the confrontation alone. He took this as a sign, a blessed one, that the world, now, today, was finally ready for his ascendance. This Sentinel of the light's time had ended, and his was to begin. His laughter grew into a raging bellow he could see blowing the hair on the Sentinel's head and making him squint against its heat.

This time, *it would be just them, and that was just fine.*

CHAPTER 53

THE CASTLE OF blood. *The day of the new moon.*

When Clark had reached that glade, he'd been running for forty-two minutes. Mostly at a jog, given mountainous terrain, but never walking. The darkness certainly didn't make it easy either. New-moon darkness. He was pretty sure he'd gone just over four miles. Either way, this spot would do well enough for some work under the red light of his headlamp, given the overhang and position of the dark rock outcropping looming up against the stars. It was vaguely near where he planned to make his first stop, anyway. The purpose of this spot of course depended on whether he was correct in assuming he still had an hour or so left before they sent someone in to check on him and find an empty garage, an hour or so left until the dogs, drones, professional man hunters, and Christ knew what else was cut loose to track him down. Besides, he knew if this part of his plan wasn't handled by then, and done very well, he was toast anyway, so he had to get to work. He could also hear the small creek a few meters away, and that he would need.

It was a miracle he'd gotten that far. He'd heard the operator who'd brought him lunch well enough to push the tool cab back against the wall and continue his feigned inspection of the chain saw by the time he came in. Charlotte, though, that woman moved quietly. She'd almost caught him, and would have if it hadn't been for that ridiculous, heavy outer door closing behind her. He'd finished the hole over an hour before the operator came in with the pillow, blanket, and dinner, but wanted that final check to go well to buy him the most time. He waited five minutes after that guy had left, and got to work. He'd cut himself in several places ferrying all his gear and then squeezing himself through, but he'd done it. He'd pulled the heavy tool bench back into place with the paracord tether he'd tied, then reached back through to clamp the wheel lock and secure the drywall into place. He'd hidden where he could see the two operators watching the three garage doors and the regular entrance to the guest suite for five minutes, then started to run.

When he got there, he opened his pack and the small nylon duffel he'd stolen to carry the extra gear he'd also stolen. He unfurled the two welding blankets, then the stack of HVAC barrier tape he'd already cut into nearly one hundred irregular shingles he hoped would help shatter any outline of his body's heat signature. He superglued these onto one of the blankets, then laid the jute netting over them which he fastened into place with several dozen zip ties and safety wire. He secured this larger cloak onto the outside of his pack. He added a few paracord lanyards in the upper corners so he could pull it down around his head, and a few in the middle of each side he could tie into his pack straps if he needed to move quickly without drag. He cut the second welding blanket into strips he secured around his legs and ankles, forearms and wrists, and neck. He cut another, smaller veil-sized patch he secured to the carry handle of his pack that he could pull over his head as additional cover.

He started the actual camouflaging by streaking the tan welding blankets with green and brown spray paint. Then, he scrambled down to the little stream and began removing rocks from the bed under the frigid, clear water. Once he found good, dark mud, he began ferrying load after load to his cloak and rubbing the dark, wet sediment all over every square inch. Finally, he started zip-tying bunches of beargrass, wheatgrass, fescue, lichen, small boughs from aspens and firs, and light branches from serviceberry and chokecherry bushes. This was the most time-consuming, especially working from dim red light, but once done, he made quick work of securing them to the jute netting on his cloaks.

He stood and inspected the entire mess, and was more pleased than he'd thought he would be. This thermal and IR cloak would be his only chance of evading the drone surveillance. This was his only hope, and despite that pressure, he reckoned it might actually work.

The cloak didn't resemble clothing, or even a welding blanket. It looked like a landslide frozen mid-roll. Clark knew the value of good camouflage better than most living men, and thus knew deceiving the eye looking for you isn't actually all about the camouflage itself. This getup, on the other hand, was designed to deceive everything a machine looked for in a man.

He heaved it all onto himself and made some practice movements, made a few adjustments, then began his stalk toward the mansion, where he could feel the ritual being prepared.

He had his decoy: the assault itself. He knew what would happen, or could feel what was to come. He knew what would happen to those men once they got inside. He also knew he'd likely need that distraction, that final bit of cover should he need some noise to cover his movements. He felt guilt, knowing what was about to happen to their minds and souls, but the stakes were too high now, and they were tough fellas, and not in as tragic a condition as any of the cultists they would be punishing soon. He had his decoy, and now his camouflage.

All that was left to close on this prey was his stalk, and that's what he was better at than anything he'd ever tried.

He kept low to the slope, letting the wind find him first. He'd long known the futility of fighting the mountain; it's the only witness, and it gets a say in where you go and how you get there. Now he'd listen to it again.

He hadn't felt this alive in years. Not since the days when silence was his language and patience his best weapon. There were no radios now. No drone and sniper overwatch. No night vision. Just a man, his wit, and the oldest kind of quiet. To the task force's eyes, he'd vanished. But this was no trick. No magic, as he assumed some probably thought. This was just mastery. Mastery of terrain, time, and how to become the thing that doesn't get seen or noticed until it's already taken its first shot.

He moved like he used to in the old days, when he was nameless. Faceless. When Clark Rickert was a wraith no one could catch. The days before the badge when every breath was a decision, and every step could mean ruin. Each sound he made was accounted for. Each shift of weight, each breath, every flex of muscle was deliberate. It wasn't movement. It was unmaking, ceasing, carving himself out of the world until nothing unnecessary remained. It wasn't sneaking either. Sneaking is for those who think they can outwit noise. He passed through a place the way shadows crawl when no one's watching—patient, certain, and inevitable. There's a logic to natural thresholds too: tree line to clearing, snowpack to rock, silence to wind. Cross them wrong and it's over. He'd spent a life learning where the thresholds really were. This was not infiltration. This was a resurrection of who he'd once been. He felt no anger, hate, fear, angst, or confidence. He felt the line. The one he'd always known how to ride, barefooted and blindfolded.

He'd never forgotten the way the old game wardens, staties, sheriffs, and feds who'd chased him through these mountains had moved: the cadence of their sweeps, how they'd talk to themselves or their horse or their dog when they thought they were alone. He knew those men looking for him now were predators of an entirely different caliber from those who'd pursued him as a poacher. But he also knew they'd never hunted anyone, or anything, like him.

He chewed pine sap and packed his boots with wet moss. He knew how dogs smelled the world, and how to poison the shape of his scent like an artist with a brush. He hung oil rags he'd taken from the garage soaked in pine sap and creek mud from low-hanging branches, or smears of blood from the cuts he'd gotten shimmying out of the hole in the garage wall, on willow boughs at staggered intervals behind him. He knew what such things did to a dog's mind. When the dogs came, their noses lifted, and thus so did the trail, up and up, until it got lost in the air and had them retracing their steps, showing less confidence, thereby making their handlers less confident. Wasting their time.

The world's most advanced sensors were clawing for him, as well. Drones, scopes, signals, the works. Yet still nothing. Clark understood the simple truth that you can't catch the wind, and you can't track what moves more slowly than thought. He knew drones saw heat signatures, but he also knew what they *really saw* was panic. They saw heat when someone failed to obscure it. He moved beneath their gaze like a rumor: never still, never fast, never sure enough to lock on. He could hear the ground teams all around the valley. He knew they were on his trail, but he didn't flinch. That was hours ago. That was who they were chasing, the old him, the one he wanted them to chase. He was someone else now. Something else.

He used the streams that trickled through the valley a few months a year. Whenever he'd come upon one, he'd go upstream two to three hundred meters, only stepping on submerged stones, until he found a dry rock slab to climb out of it, never forgetting to toss silt and duff atop his trail of dripping water. At one point he pressed a bloodied rag into a game trail and dragged it with a branch toward a ravine. Then he crossed back upstream barefooted, in reverse, leaving a dozen false readings for the dogs and infuriating questions for their handlers.

At one point he'd been within nineteen meters of a trio of patrolling operators. They passed below his concealed position close enough that he heard the plastic buckles click on one of their chest rigs. He watched their foot placement, the rhythm of their breathing. He saw the way the younger one kept looking uphill, like he didn't trust the quiet. That was good. *He shouldn't.*

On five or six other occasions he'd been within one hundred meters of others. That was fine. There was no planned path; there was just a silent, controlled, meandering tumble through the eyes and ears of those trying to find him. They were trained to pursue men with urges, plans, and objectives, but he was no such thing today. Staying on the good side of the wind was the only hard rule in this game, he knew, and he was a master of that.

Finding a shallow creek bed just before dusk, Clark stripped, waded up the icy current for nearly three hundred meters, then pressed his entire outfit—cloak, gear, and all—into the creek's silt and algae. When he emerged onto dry land at twilight, he moved like a slug, just three meters a minute under the thick canopy. From both sky and ground, he looked like fallen detritus in a shadow seam. A drone flew directly over him at one point and kept going, as they had all day.

When evening had finally settled in and the sun began to set, he was comfortably concealed within the tree line, about 130 meters behind the back veranda of the mansion. He left his rifle here, at the base of a tree, and went forward to close the final distance.

It took him over three hours to cover ninety-two of those meters, moving inch by inch.

He moved with the patience of erosion, shifting just enough to blur the baseline of stillness. He crawled like the ground itself had weight, dragging his elbows a fraction of an inch at a time, knees never rising, every inch earned by the stillness of everything else. The secret wasn't stealth—it was discipline, the kind that made each movement smaller than a heartbeat.

He saw or heard or smelled the cultist guards on the back veranda and elsewhere. They clearly were not operating pursuant to any set patrol or security protocols. They mumbled their wicked incantations and gibberish as they stalked or loitered around, waiting for something to hurt.

He still spent another forty minutes studying them as he snaked closer. They were irregular and aimless, but that, too, was a pattern. Most of them didn't look up. Fewer still looked behind them. None of them looked for something like him. He studied the architecture of the mansion with his own eyes for the first time this close.

The build was modern, all sealed concrete bases and rain-screen stonework. But nothing is immune to the mountains' flex and temper, and men had built this place, and Clark knew men—how they cut corners, trusted tools too much, and always forgot the seams they themselves had hidden. The spot he chose wasn't a weakness in the structure. It was a mistake in the landscaping. A small utility access behind a gas line cutoff box, almost invisible behind a decorative boulder at the base of the veranda. He'd seen it in the structure's schematics, but it'd been ruled out as a breaching access point because of how narrow it was, and with how loud the assault was planned to be, stealth options were not prioritized. From the front, it looked sealed. From the side, the paint hid a warped rivet. He pushed it a bit to close the final twenty or so meters to the base of the veranda, holding the tag ends so his cloak didn't drag. When he reached the base, he crouched and waited a minute before slinking down the wall toward his target. When he reached it, he took out his multitool and began the slow process of quietly teasing the panel loose.

The panel started to give, and he opened the tool's blade to cut a line through the paint still holding it to the opening. He eased it away, and peered in to find it led to a maintenance corridor—crawling height, full of PVC, copper, and insulation wrap. No motion detectors, no cameras, and no people. He pulled himself in, dragging his IR cloak behind him, and resealed the panel from the inside using two micro bungee cords and a tack of putty he'd brought from the garage. It was hot inside the walls, and narrow. He quietly snipped the zip ties holding the cloak to his pack, then moved slow enough that not even the mice scurried.

Eventually, after only one bend, it opened into the residence's huge, master utility vault. He knew that would be the case from the blueprints, but hadn't been entirely sure whether the access would be straightforward. He'd left his helmet behind in the garage, but only after removing one of the night vision tubes from the mount on his helmet. He took it from his pocket, turned it on, and did a quick scan. The floor was concrete, and overhead copper and PEX lines crisscrossed in ordered chaos. Within the room, he saw two water heaters, HVAC manifolds, the largest furnace he'd ever seen, breaker panels, glycol pumps, a water softener, and more.

He clocked a door, and moved toward it taking quick glances through the night vision monocular. When he got there, he could hear faint chanting, low and arrhythmic. He scanned around again and saw a large industrial humidifier, the kind installed to keep the corks stowing millions of dollars of wine nice and safe. He moved to it and found a duct leading from the humidifier into a low service hatch, which he figured he had no choice but to believe and trust at this point must lead to some damn place within the wine cellar. Once there, he'd know exactly where to go. He'd been there before several times. In a way, at least. He chugged some water and ditched his pack, taking only the few things he'd need, then climbed into the service shaft under the ducting, which made him feel claustrophobic for the first real time in his life.

It was a slow, arduous thirty meters of slithering to get to a vented panel he could barely see through, but just enough to tell it opened into one of the several outer cloisters of the ridiculous monastery-modeled wine cellar. The panel was hinged on one side, and secured on the other with two small Phillips-head screws, heads facing the wine cellar. He wedged the small pry bar he'd taken from the garage under the hatch, flexed the board until the screw stems bowed. Then, using a socket head taped backward to a driver, he gripped the exposed threads and twisted slowly. The wood's own tension did the work—one squeaking turn at a time.

It took a while to get the hatch open, but fifty minutes still remained until his particularly noisy decoy and diversion would arrive, if they still planned on kicking the raid off around three in the morning.

As it was, both Clark and his nemesis, within shouting distance of each other, awaited the opportunities that would arise once the assaulters fell victim to the blood rage. Clark, however, wasn't certain what blood rage was; he just had some dreamlike awareness that it was coming, and knew it would be loud, fast, and sickeningly fucking terrifying when it arrived. Waiting for that wave of demon-spurred butchery to crash into this mansion, and for the structure he was in to get rocked by explosive ordnance—while crammed horizontally into a hot service shaft—created a kind of anxiety that was new to Clark Rickert. He didn't try to find calm through meditation; he just clenched his fists and ground his teeth until it finally came.

When the first explosive went off, he felt it in his molars as much as he heard it. He did not have to wait long for the next one, and as a cluster of bursts tore through the structure above him, he cranked open the hatch and dropped into the room. It was not the primary wine cellar, but one of the side chambers with a few racks of Spanish whites, an antique coffee table, and a few reading chairs atop a Persian rug. He closed the hatch quickly and dropped to a knee behind the end of one of the rows of albariño. He knew the route through the dark, stone-cobbled bunker to the large primary wine cellar, but not who or what he'd encounter along the way. He urged himself to move, but his mind and muscles fought him. He'd never been within a building suffering literal artillery fire before, and it was a hell of a thing. He felt every explosion as the pressure wash thrummed in his gut, his throat, and the roots of his molars. The giant oak beams and stonework groaned and squealed as dust would kick and spurt from the ceiling at each blast. He knew, however, that as soon as it ended, the assault teams would flood this place, and from there he'd have little time.

When fifteen seconds passed since the last explosion, he made his move. He crept low, fast, and silently. He knew the ritual room was up ahead on the left, and that there was one room he'd never seen inside on his telepathic visits here coming up on his right.

He'd almost made it to the door of that room on the right when it began to open. He froze in a shadow at the base of the wall. A rather short cultist carrying a chamberstick with a burning red candle backed slowly into the hallway, already pulling on the knob of the large door shutting it behind them. Clark knew he had to act, and did. This cultist was slow, and Clark was very, very fast.

He gripped the chin with one hand and yanked up, then buried his knife into the side of the cultist's neck, aiming for the Adam's apple. When he felt the blade strike the spine, he used his free hand to grasp the chamberstick to prevent it from being dropped, and wrenched the blade side to side. A shocking torrent of blood released in a gush onto the floor at their feet. When Clark felt their muscles go slack, he began lowering them to the ground. As he did, he noticed it was a very old woman, at least eighty years old. The breath caught in his throat when he saw the look of shock and pain that'd frozen on her wrinkled, starch-white face in her final moment of life. He checked her arm, confirming she was a cultist, but this did not offer him any consolation.

He quietly dragged her into the darkness within the room she'd come from, then shut it. Sounds of gunfire and screaming were coming from the upper floors now. Adrenaline was coursing now and drove Clark into a bounding jog toward the large double doors into the primary wine cellar, the ritual room.

When Clark heard the snarling rage begin upstairs, he could also feel *him* begin to bask in the choir of slaughter. He didn't know where he was, precisely, but whatever connection existed between them told him he was farther down the corridor, and not within the room he was about to enter. He was so confident in this new sense he entered the room quickly, far faster than he would've without such a primal awareness.

When he closed the doors and put his back against them—when he looked upon the ritual space with his own eyes for the first time—he winced and gasped aloud.

The ritual arrangements were as he'd seen them in his mind, but he had not expected the seven naked people at equal points around its perimeter. The presence of others is not what surprised him, but their condition took his breath away. They'd been wired, chained, and staked into grotesque, impossible positions. They moaned some hideous chant in unison as they rocked against their restraints in their repulsive postures. All appeared close to death and all were missing at least one limb; fresh stumps he could see had been cauterized with some kind of pitch or tar. He steeled himself as he started to approach one, crouching a bit to inspect their restraints. It looked as though they'd been trussed into place with hundreds of meters of wire that entered and exited their bodies in countless places in every limb, throughout their torsos, and even their faces.

One of them suddenly ripped her head up toward him, snarling through bloody foam. He flinched and swore and staggered away. Her eyes were jet black. The other six slowly rolled their heads in his direction, their eyes onyx pits as well, and their chanting began to grow in volume. Clark gagged and swallowed bile as he felt the sounds weave into him. His teeth started chattering audibly, and his hands began shaking so bad he could barely pull the knife from his sheath. He closed his eyes, forced himself to take a deep breath, and summoned the indomitable strength and righteous purpose he'd felt the day before seeing fear in the eyes of his nemesis. When he opened his eyes, all seven hissed like cats.

He felt a brief pang of hesitation, then told himself these ones were too far gone. Physically, they may never recover, brand or no brand, but there was something dark in them now. His stain. When he felt that, he went about the grim business of putting them down.

He could feel something leave the first when he cut his throat; nothing he could see, but he could somehow sense the smoky, reptilian form, feel how wicked and terrified it was by his blade. He felt dark *things* leave each of the others as they died, as well. All seven had their own distinct form and impression that collectively began to ring some bell, pull at some thread of memory he couldn't access, and didn't really care to. The process of exposing some part of them where a single, lethal stab or cut could be made was difficult for several of the rest, given the rigid positions they'd been forced into.

This experience was so jarring and repulsive he failed to notice the absolute silence that would replace the guttural chanting until it finally came. When it did, Clark cursed his stupidity. Then he took a deep breath. He hadn't switched mindsets yet, and it was time. He hadn't ended his stalk. He'd spent the last almost twenty-eight hours trying to entirely remove himself from this world, to turn into shadow and silence.

He rolled his shoulders and stretched his neck as he stepped into the middle of the ritual arrangement, shaking away the tension and strain of the last two sleepless days. He had to switch mindsets, and do it now, because Clark could feel him again, *and he was coming.*

CHAPTER 54

THE TORMENTOR'S LAUGHTER began to wane. Finding the Sentinel here, now, *alone*—it was just too perfect. He had the urge to sing a song, an ancient song he knew had once meant a great deal to the Sentinel many lifetimes ago. He wondered whether it would stir any pain in him, if this one was capable of remembering what it'd meant, or the people he'd loved who'd sung it so often. He wondered if the harmony could remind this new Sentinel, make him see or even just sense any of the children, wives, or friends he'd taken from this ignorant despoiler over the millennia. That would be a glorious gift in this moment, and he wanted to find out.

He spread his arms wide, took in a deep breath, and then stopped abruptly.

The Sentinel had started to whistle. It was a strange, foreign tune, but the desolate loneliness it carried could still be felt all the same. The Tormentor's jaw began to quiver, and his eye began to twitch. An intoxicatingly raw hate boiled through him. *He knew exactly what he was doing with such a tune.*

Clark didn't, but he'd had a hunch. He had some vague awareness that this *thing* disliked being interrupted, but knew very well that the loneliness of the dark he'd been banished back to so many times was his greatest torture, and escaping it his greatest motivation. Clark had lived most his life as a lonely man, but knew the reason the melody from *High Plains Drifter* seemed always close to mind was because, for him, it was a celebration of loneliness.

Clark smiled when he saw this discomfort in the monstrous features of his nemesis.

He stood at least two feet taller than Clark, and would be two feet more if his back weren't so hideously hunched so that his head jutted out.

He wore the same meat-colored robe he seemed to have put all his minions in for this final day, but it was far too small and didn't cover much of him. His arms had grown enough so that his twelve-inch fingers with their extra knuckles twitched next to his knees. His feet were massive. His toe knuckles arched up so there was a gap of empty space between the balls of his feet and where his long, hooked toes clicked against the stone floor. His ribs barreled outward in front of him at his chest. His head had elongated, but his ashen skin had not accommodated it well; it stretched tight over his skull, split in several places. His nose and eyes had stretched into slits, while his mouth had actually grown to reach from ear to ear. Clark could see his massive, pearl-white upper canines jutting from his maw of at least sixty needle-thin teeth that clicked and snapped as his rage made him shake.

At the end of the melody, Clark saw and heard this thing inhale and shift his posture, preparing to speak. Clark interrupted him with loud, sharp words.

"*Nah*. Just keep that filthy fuckin' screamer shut. Ain't a damn thing that needs sayin' between you and me."

Every muscle in Clark's body was ready to draw his 10mm Glock and pump all sixteen hollow-point slugs into this monster's grotesque chest, but he had a deep, immovable desire for his opponent to make the first move. So he'd try to make him.

Clark ran his foot in a large arc through all the meticulously arranged ritual items he stood in the middle of. It sent a wave of fingers, scalps, stones, teeth, wedding bands, feathers, salt, bonemeal, and bird skulls showering to the side. The monster winced and groaned as he did it, then balled his giant fists and growled. But he didn't move. Clark did it again, kicking up another, even larger wave of the disgusting paraphernalia.

He winced and growled again through clenched teeth, drool and froth pouring from its cracked, gray lips. Its entire body shook, then went completely still. It smiled and bowed its head.

Just then a group of its shrieking cultists broke around both sides of it in a full sprint, heading directly for Clark. He was shocked, but did not hesitate. He drew the Glock 20, fell into his shooting stance, and started shooting, plugging them one by one, every shot to the chest.

He shot two on the right first, who crumpled and slowed the others behind them. He shot one on the left, then another on the right jumping over the first two. He switched back to the left side and fired as fast as he could into the group of three only feet in front of him now. He switched back to the right and dumped his last two shots directly into the face of the large, bearded cultist roaring just a foot away.

His violence-primed mind had clocked that there was still one cultist who'd swarmed around the monster at the entrance to the room whom he hadn't shot yet. When the bearded man fell forward toward him, Clark saw she was right there behind him, already halfway through a double-handed swing, the machete just about ten inches above his forehead. He ducked to the side and brought his shoulder low to avoid the cut. When he knew he'd avoided the machete and was now inside her guard, he rose quickly and shoulder checked her in the neck and chin, meeting her wild momentum with his own. The blow connected so hard the back of her head smacked into the stone floor while her feet were still in the air. He'd ejected the spent magazine and had begun reaching for another in the mag holster on his left hip before her body came to rest.

Before he found the magazine, a dagger of ice, fire, and pure pain ripped through his left arm somewhere between the elbow and wrist. He turned and saw he was on him, the Tormentor himself, gripping Clark's left arm in his massive hand with all five of its inch-long fingernails entirely sunk into his muscle. Clark swung the heavy Glock 20 handgun in a hatchet strike toward its face, but it backhanded Clark's right arm and sent the pistol flying. Before Clark prepared another strike, it pulled him toward its face and roared. The sound was so loud that sound just ceased to be. An exhaust of embers and ash from its mouth burned the skin on Clark's face.

He gave up trying to wrench his arm from the grip and pivoted on his left foot, sending a fierce leg kick into the inside of the beast's right knee. Clark had a moment of satisfaction as he felt the force of his boot connect and the bone crunch underneath, but then he was in the air. He vaguely registered being sideways before crashing back-first into the wall, four feet above the ground. The air blasted from his lungs before he fell, and he only partially succeeded in catching himself so he didn't smash his face into the floor.

He scanned around himself frantically to locate his opponent, whom he found half limping and half hopping toward him, one hand on the knee he'd cracked, screaming in rage so violently Clark's vision shook. He pushed himself up and tried to gain some distance, but the Tormentor was on him again.

It gripped Clark by the calf this time, and he felt the same white-hot, nauseating pain as its blades of fingernails tore through skin and muscle. It spun and threw Clark bodily back into the center of the room. Clark landed on his ass this time, and tried again to scramble away from the beast coming right at him.

He shot a straight kick at its bad knee, not connecting well, but enough to stagger it and buy himself enough time to get to his feet. By the time he had, the beast was swinging a massive, clawed hand toward his face. He weaved under it, almost fell when the pain in his leg made his eyes water, but still rose with his left uppercut he snapped out with his hips and shoulder. It hit the beast right under his protruded sternum, cracking ribs. The monster doubled over, as Clark had gambled on. His right cross buried itself into the jowls under its jaw. It reeled away from Clark, who followed in pursuit despite the seething pain and cranked an overhanded cross down toward its kidney. The blow connected, sending electric pain through the beast, but as he reeled in pain he exploded into the smaller man and both went tumbling through the cellar, tangled together like they'd been ejected from a car crash.

The Tormentor scrambled atop Clark at the end of their slide and brought an open palm down on his face, but was stopped short with an eruption of pain. Clark had drawn the blade sheathed crosswise on the back of his belt during the tumble, then stabbed it through the massive palm before it crushed his face. The beast saw two inches of blade sticking through the top of his hand just as Clark began to torque it violently side to side. The Tormentor wailed in pain and swatted at Clark's face with its free hand, but Clark had already surged up, abandoning the knife to wrap both arms around its neck and bring himself in closer. Both beings only had a split second of eye contact before Clark began slamming his forehead into the remnants of the Tormentor's nose and mouth, driving forward so he ended up on top, head slamming down relentlessly the entire time, and then his elbows. The monster bucked frantically until his freakish feet were planted in Clark's pelvis, then flipped the smaller man off him. They both ended up on their knees, eyes locked, and surged toward each other in the same instant.

Then, the Tormentor stopped. It was something he'd felt. Something tragic and terrible. A part of himself being lost. He put his hand over his chest and let out an anguished wail toward the ceiling.

As it did, it could feel this vile Sentinel had felt it, through him, and that he also knew precisely what this had been. Somehow, through their connection, he could feel that it was *he* who'd done this. It was the Sentinel who'd manufactured this treachery. He looked down at him, shaking with rage.

And Clark Rickert smiled back.

CHAPTER
55

THE FIVE BLOOD knights had spent the last hour of the drive blessing their lord through the venerated chants and hymnals he'd taught them. They were so close to their rapture now. So close to the blood. They couldn't have talked if they'd wanted to, with their jaws clamped shut, breathing noisily through their teeth.

They all knew the way, precisely where he'd told them to leave the van, arm themselves, and begin their slow, quiet hike into the positions where they'd initiate their attack and begin this most sacred harvest of blood. When they rounded the last bend on the mountainous Green Drake Road, one ridge away from where the task force had established their FOB, they all started rocking back and forth. When they could see the parking spot in the headlights, the one he'd carved into their dreaming minds, they started squealing and growling through clenched teeth. When the oldest of them slowed the vehicle, put it in park, and turned off the engine, they all fell silent.

They needed to focus now. They needed to center themselves for the task ahead. They turned toward one another, all sporting expressions of febrile dedication and reverence for the holy work to come. The oldest, the one their lord had found first, nodded at each of them, just once, then unbuckled his seat belt.

As he did, every window on the 2006 Honda Odyssey shattered. Two of the occupants of the vehicle died in that same instant. Two more died between two and six seconds later. The youngest of the blood knights managed to get the sliding door open and collapse onto the mountain road. She fell onto her side and vomited onto the glass-covered asphalt. This was partly induced by the severe heroin withdrawals she was still very much afflicted with, but also a physiological reaction brought on by the trauma and pain caused by the four 5.56 bullets that'd just shredded through her left lung, stomach, and intestines.

She rolled onto her hands, pushed herself onto her knees, and began crawling around the vehicle. All she could see was the enemy headquarters, and the face of Charlotte Bishop, the one whose blood she craved so badly.

A fifth and final 5.56 bullet entered her body through the crown of her skull, and killed her. Five babies would be born around the world exactly eleven minutes and six seconds after each of the five who'd just been killed. Until then, the Tormentor's earthly retinue of blood knights had shrunk to sixty-seven, none of whom were close enough to heed his call.

Leonard Price brought the rifle optic from his eye, then pulsed his weapon light three times, squinting into the darkness to the side of the van where he knew his other three teammates were concealed. A light pulsed three times in response, and he started moving cautiously toward the van. The other three reached it first, and used their own weapon lights to check that all the occupants had been killed. Price nudged the young woman he'd just shot in the head with the muzzle of his rifle, then checked her pulse. Feeling no sign of life, he hissed at the others, just above a whisper.

"Status?"

The closest member of this impromptu team whispered back.

"All dead, confirmed."

Price rose on crackling knees and nodded, feeling overwhelmed at what he was looking at, what he'd just done, what it all meant, but not letting himself lose focus. He took a deep breath.

"All right, we know the plan. You two, get the tow truck. We needa get this rig back to Rickert's property as soon as fuckin' possible, and we've got a decent drive ahead. We'll stay here and clean the shards from the windows and tape over the bullet holes. We'll be done by the time you're back, and have the bodies all wrapped, but will need your help loadin' 'em up into the FWP cruiser. I'll follow you all the way back, right on your ass, and call off any attention we might draw. You, uh . . . you sure you gotta good spot to bury this thing?"

Price could see the outline of Pete's head, nodding in the darkness, but it was his brother who spoke.

"Don't worry about that, sir. This ain't the first secret Montana will take to the grave for ol' Clarky."

Price nodded at the peculiar statement, then watched Clark's oldest friends, Pete and Hank—as identical today as they'd been when Clark had met them as boys—hustle down the road to where they'd stashed their truck. He took another deep, shuddering breath. A hand gripped his shoulder, then patted it softly a few times.

He looked over at Liz Lobdell—the agency's head legal counsel, whom Clark himself had taught to shoot the AR-15 she carried now as though she'd been in the infantry her entire life. She smiled at him.

"Don't fret, big guy. If Clark Rickert said these were rotten folks who just had to go, you know as well as I do, *these were some rotten fuckin' folks who definitely had to fuckin' go.*"

Price did know that. He took another deep breath, then nodded toward the body at his feet.

"Well let's get to work, counselor."

CHAPTER 56

THE TORMENTOR HELD the Sentinel's gaze as he ripped the blade from his destroyed palm, gasping at the pain as he did. He would end this now. He'd eat this human's innards and make him watch, then force him to share the meal. Throughout all the thousands of years of this conflict, he'd never known such rage toward his opponent. He rose and lunged at the smaller man, but then he froze.

Clark had finally drawn the Sig P365 compact 9mm he'd had holstered inside his waistband, after what felt like a lifetime spent trying to do so.

The torn and bleeding Sentinel pushed himself to his feet with his broken, shredded left arm. Wincing in pain, yet still smiling, he shot a hollow-point 9mm into the demon's remaining good knee, bursting it in a small puff of rotten bone and blood. He collapsed to his knees, both of which were now catastrophically fractured, and shrieked at the pain. Before he'd run out of breath, another shot slammed into the inside of his left elbow, which he instinctively gripped in his massive right hand, and he shrieked again, looking at the Sentinel with incredulity, as though this treatment was offensive and unwarranted. The Sentinel's smile just grew in response. He let his pistol drop a bit, a move that oozed with infuriating confidence. He knew this man would not miss. He began the effort of begging, and was interrupted again.

"*No.* Not this time. Not sure how those last versions a' me handled things, but I ain't gonna let ya beg. Much as I wanna see ya squirm, it's just too fuckin' pathetic."

Clark stepped toward the massive, pitiful, broken thing at his feet. He looked up and saw the smaller man's strength, despite his wounds. He saw the Sentinel's victory, and he began to scream.

He screamed in the way only an ancient soul can. The way only one who's been tortured and abused through centuries of suffering can scream. And he screamed the way a father does when holding the body of his murdered child, still warm with life, but whom he'd not been close enough to save yet still close enough to see die. He also screamed like an exhausted three-year-old boy in the peak fits of a tantrum. He kicked and drooled and thrashed and wept until he began to cough and gag on his own pain.

Clark Rickert, the Sentinel, leaned into his face. His eyes were weary with blood loss and pain, but he looked entirely comfortable with that. Just as he felt the inevitability of his own loss, the Sentinel hissed words into the Tormentor's face, words he understood in a language he'd spoken for a long time.

"*In tenebras te reiciam, ibique supplicare poteris.*"

I will cast you into the darkness, and there you will be able to beg.

The Tormentor was about to buck and writhe, but the Sentinel spoke again. This Sentinel, in particular, had seemed more removed and detached from his ancient line than any ever had, until he spoke.

"We move on. You don't. That's why you always fuckin' lose. You were never a god, ol' buddy. Just a leech too proud to rot. I own you, Drac, and I always fuckin' have."

The pair stared into each other's eyes for one moment, and then the world erupted in flames.

CHAPTER 57

THE BEEPING HAD woken Clark. When he saw Thorn's face, he tried to move for the first time in four hours.

The man looked older as he leaned close, putting a gentle palm on Clark's chest and lowering him back down onto the stretcher. Clark lifted his hands and saw the catheters stuck into his wrists, the bandages all over both arms, then lay back and closed his eyes. Thorn's accent was the first thing he heard in this new life.

"You know, Rickert, the doc says your survival was a miracle. After they pulled you outta the rubble, the SSE team reckoned you were under five tons of stone and debris. Also said you should've suffered full organ failure, that you'd lost almost two full pints of blood *beyond* the current world record for blood loss. Can you believe that? You're gonna be in the Guinness fuckin' book."

Clark used the little strength he had to raise a hand and beckon the man closer, who obliged. Clark whispered, the loudest he could speak.

"Pr . . . Price. I need to talk to Leonard Price, what's the—"

Thorn squeezed his hand and smiled.

"Don't worry, pal. Price, Liz, the twins, they're all fine. Everything went smooth. I also didn't really have a choice but to tell Benson, Jacobson, and Bishop about that little sideshow, but don't worry about that. They owe ya; *we all fuckin' do, kid.*"

Clark stared at Thorn, seeing no ruse, and let his muscles relax. The night Clark had arrived at this new FOB—the night Bobby had attacked him—Clark had told Thorn about his telepathic interception of the Tormentor's sinister plans regarding the five members of his earthly retinue, their plan, and their location. Thorn, having no real desire or choice but to trust the Sentinel, agreed to help him arrange the ambush. Clark had given

Thorn the names of those he'd already contacted about it, and Thorn handled the rest, largely letting the group carry out their existing plan, but employing his considerable assets to ensure Clark's four friends saw it through without hassle or delay.

Clark looked around again, realizing he was in a large bedroom he figured was likely back at the FOB based on the lack of burns or bullet holes. He looked back at Thorn, who must've seen some hint of Clark's mind catching back up to him, as he squeezed Clark's hand and smiled.

"Let me catch you up to speed, eh?"

He did, and Clark listened.

Jacobson had apparently seen enough of the insanity and ordered a pilot to ferry him straight to the target mansion. When he arrived, the operators had already begun to calm a bit; some were even found weeping at what they'd just done. He went about getting the guys back under control and establishing some semblance of order. As this was going on, the teams heard a profound racket coming from beneath their feet and assembled breaching teams to begin clearing the route to the large subterranean level. Once they'd cleared their way down there, they found the clamor of violence was coming from the big wine cellar. The large double doors—behind which some biblical fight was heard taking place—were smoking, their copper bracing glowing red-hot.

A second before they breached the door, however, came the experiential glimmer—a flash of recollection, however, was of the best moments of their lives.

For Jackson Nowell, it was when he brought his parents into the delivery room to meet his new son. For Tucker Reichman, it was the moment he walked out of the lender's office after paying off his father's ranch. For Dwight DuBroux, it was the look in his daughter's eye the day he surprised her at a soccer game after getting home from a deployment. For David Benson, it was the body-trembling relief and happiness in his wife's face when the surgeon told them how well her operation had gone. For Harry Jacobson, it was the night he'd returned from Vietnam and sat on the porch with his father drinking cold beer, listening to insects die in a bug zapper, without either of them saying a word to each other.

For Charlotte Bishop, it was a day in the eighth grade, biking around her neighborhood with her twin sister. The best friend she'd ever had, or ever would. The only person she thought about every day when she woke up, and when she'd been in bed trying to fall asleep. The person she'd missed so terribly every day for the last fifteen years since she'd died on the same bike she had been riding that *perfect day*.

For Malcolm Thorn, it was a moment from several nights earlier, the pinnacle of his career, his life's work: shaking hands with Clark Rickert—his ward, *the Sentinel*. Even in this life-changing moment of euphoric relief, Thorn had the presence of mind to check his watch, making sure to stamp the exact time in his memory. He was excited to comb through any EMF, seismograph, magnetometer, or IR satellite data available for this location at this moment. He assumed the expulsion of force and energy would appear similar to that which he'd observed over the Brookings ranch, exactly one lunar month earlier, which told him this D-Event had begun. Once they all shook the effect of this sensation, they detonated the breaching charges and blew the entrance.

"What they found was *you*, kid. You, about a dozen dead cultists, and bits and pieces of their lord and savior. They traced blood, fingernails, hair, teeth, and tissue back to the profile they'd developed from the FOB based on things the impostor Matthew Kabath had worn or held."

Clark only nodded, barely following, and vaguely registered some of the frenzied medics over the next twenty minutes who'd come to run vitals and checks upon his waking up. He knew he was back at the FOB, in one of the sixteen bedrooms of the mansion. Even in his diminished state, he figured pretending to be asleep would be the best course of action. When he'd heard things settle down for long enough, he turned over toward where Thorn had been sitting and cracked an eye open.

There he remained, grinning at him as though he knew he'd been faking it. Clark beckoned him over with a finger.

When he leaned in, Clark whispered his question.

"Why were you followin' Elijah Austin Miles?"

Thorn's eyes went wide, and he pursed his lips, staring at Clark as he considered his words.

"I'll tell you more about it soon, but for now I'll tell ya this: he's one of the *seventy-two*. Really, he's one of the one hundred forty-four, but they're split, half good, half evil. They are those things in this world that are, well . . . *from another place*, you could say. They're not as wicked and powerful as your buddy we've been chasing, nowhere fuckin' close. They're just worth keeping an eye on. Watchin' out for *who they might bump into*."

Clark took a deep breath before his next whisper.

"So you spent years watchin' that asshole, just to see if he bumped into me?"

Thorn looked down, smiled, then leaned toward Clark.

"Son, I spent years watchin' *thousands of assholes just to see if they bumped into you.*"

Clark laughed, then coughed, then coughed more.

A few minutes later, he waved Thorn close again. He hadn't finished preparing his words, and waited another minute, settled on the simplest version of the message he was trying to convey, then hissed them out.

"I don't think he's dead."

Thorn raised his eyebrows and leaned back in his chair, nodding slowly.

"Yeah, didn't really think so either. But doesn't matter now. See, once the ritual's stopped, so far as I understand it, he's just a normal asshole like the rest of us. *Threat's over.*"

Clark stared at him for a long time, not feeling the truth in what Thorn said, but not finding any reason to challenge it. He could feel it was over. This feeling was indescribable, but as clear as feeling the hot sun or pouring rain. The threat was gone. He had won.

Thorn leaned in again.

"Look, kid, you've only got one job now, and it's healin' up. I made you a promise I intend to keep. As soon as you're fit to travel, I'm flyin' you out to DC and takin' a much-needed vacation to bring you all the way up to speed. You understand? You need to heal, and sleep, and hydrate, and sleep more."

Clark tried to smile and nod, and a few minutes later, Thorn was gone.

Clark slept for the next two hours, and awoke with a decent amount of his strength back. DuBroux and Nowell stopped by, both laughing and insisting on shaking his hand. DuBroux had not lost faith in him, apparently, and Nowell had, based on his apology. Benson and Jacobson were next. Clark had fallen asleep again, and hadn't awoken again for two more hours.

When Clark slowly awoke and blinked light and context back into his eyes, he found Charlotte Bishop sitting in the room, watching him. She leaned forward, appeared to consider her words for a moment, then spoke.

"How are you feeling? The gashes on your arm and leg all right?"

Clark nodded and held out a hand, which she took. When she did,

Clark felt an almost startling amount of strength return to his body. He sat up slowly, despite Charlotte's protests, then swung his legs over the side of the bed. He rolled his ankles, not feeling much pain in the calf that monster had ripped open. Then he raised his hand up to his face, squeezed a fist, then flexed his forearm: even less pain, despite his wounds from only about six hours earlier. He squinted at the bandages covering them when Charlotte spoke.

"Not sure there's an easy way to explain this, but your, uhm . . . your wounds are healing at an impossibly rapid rate. They've already been taking blood and tissue samples to assess the anomaly, just so you know."

They looked at each other for a moment. She looked down, then spoke again.

"So, given the resolution of this operation, you're technically free to go. Our medical team is insisting you go to Bozeman for further physical evaluation, but once we had the leader's DNA and blood all over that cellar, this task force was effectively dissolved, at least with respect to non-DOD contractors, such as yourself."

Clark nodded, unsure what to say. She sat next to him on the bed, still holding his hand, and told him about how his gear and truck were already being ferried to the Region 4 FWP headquarters, and that there was an ambulance here waiting to take him to the hospital for those additional scans. Clark felt strange, the dissolution of this task force being so abrupt. He supposed this kind of modular framework and their usual operational tempo made it normal for them, and just shrugged.

Clark held out an arm, which Charlotte took.

"Well, guess I'll head to the doc, then—no reason to keep those ambulance folks waiting."

She put an arm through his and helped guide him through the house. He let her do this, despite feeling as though he could navigate surprisingly well on his own. Everyone they passed stopped their after-action tasks to stare at him. They made their way out into the large roundabout driveway, where a paramedic emerged from the passenger seat of the ambulance idling outside the garage doors. Clark silently asked him for a minute with a single finger.

He turned toward Charlotte and took one of her hands in his. They stood there for a moment, silently, until she stepped toward him, and he pulled her in. When their lips finally parted, their bodies did not. She ran her fingers along his jaw and around his neck, and he held her around her waist and tucked a strand of hair behind her ear. He cocked his head toward the house.

"So how long's it take to wrap a job like this up? Your little outfit hasn't exactly been the leave-no-trace kinda camper around here."

She smiled at that.

"Oh, couple more days. We've gotten quite a bit of damage control underway already. Besides, my job is to *make the messes*. We've got a *whole other department* to clean them up."

Clark grinned.

"So straight back east, huh? They send you somewhere this great from somewhere so shitty, and won't let you hang out here for a while? Even after a gig like this one?"

She smiled, then looked at him shyly.

"I mean—*other than the Yellowstone Club*, of course—I can't say what else there is around these mountains for me."

Clark let her go, but kept ahold of her hands. He stared at the ground, then looked back up at her.

"*I sure as hell can.*"

She bit the inside of her cheek and looked up at him.

"So . . . *what*, I just come hang out with you at your ranch for a while? *Just drink beer and shoot shit* until you get home from work?"

He snorted out a laugh and smiled.

"Be careful, now. I'm gonna fall in love with you if you keep talkin' like that."

She laughed at that harder than he'd heard her laugh. It was a sound he very much wanted to hear again, and often. He squeezed her hands.

"I've got enough sick and vacay days stacked to disappear for a year if I wanted to. Reckon I could cash a few in if you wanted to swing by for a bit."

She was more serious now, looking between both his eyes. She saw whatever she'd been looking for, and nodded, speaking just above a whisper.

"All right."

Clark smiled.

"All right."

She reached up, put her hands on his cheeks, and kissed him.

"Well, *Captain*, I suppose I'll see you pretty soon, then."

He wrapped his arms around her waist.

"Porch light'll be on till you get there."

EPILOGUE

IN A LATE-NIGHT moment of half lucidity, Clark had wondered if what he felt was similar to what a Pacific steelhead felt. He wondered if this whim was similar to the one they felt, the one that told them it was time.

A steelhead, born in some gravel bed in a small creek in the mountains of Idaho, would fight and tumble its way downstream until it found a larger creek. It would fight onward from there, toward a larger river, then from there toward the mighty Columbia River, and then, eventually, if it was one of the lucky few, it would finally taste the salt of the Pacific. Months or even years later, dodging seals and sharks somewhere off the coast of Russian, Japan, or Alaska, it would begin to *sense something*. A transceiver of sorts, somewhere in its tiny brain, would pick up on a probe signal that blinked to life with a dull, magnetic pulse. This signal came from the cold, clear waters of that mountain stream where it was born. The beacon would begin to blink, and with a flick of its spotted tail it would turn and begin its journey home—and not merely *home* to that particular tributary of the Columbia, but all the way to that exact same damn stretch of little mountain creek where it was born.

This connection, or *homing ability*, continues to perplex the international academy of sciences to this day. Some say they use magnetoreception, subconsciously flagging magnetic north and using the position of the sun to find their way home. Some say they're imprinted by the unique chemical profile of the water they're born in. It's been studied in Russia's Kamchatka Peninsula and coastal rivers of Alaska, Canada, Washington, Oregon, all the way down to the Santa Margarita River, just forty-five miles from the Mexican border, but none have actually figured it out.

Over the last days, a beacon in Clark's mind had begun a dull, magnetic pulse, as well. One he was quite sure would prove equally mysterious and perplexing to scientists.

Until recently, Clark had spent a lifetime treating whims as he treated ticks: combing himself over, hunting them down with diligent routine, and killing any found before it could burrow its diseased little carapace into his skin. Hunches were different from whims, to Clark. Both were uninvited suggestions that boiled up from somewhere deep in the mind, but a hunch was the by-product of experience-honed intuition, something worthy of trust. A whim, on the other hand, was impulsive and brash, something that could only be justified after the fact.

However, based on the recent changes to himself—and his understanding of the world—he'd realized that whims were things he needed to trust more. Like a firefly pulsing rhythmically in a hardwood forest on the night of a new moon, they were things worthy of being followed. Cautiously, to be sure, but deserving of attention.

So, when Clark felt the whim to walk out of his office that afternoon and make the five-hour drive to the little roadhouse outside Miles City, Montana, he did. He'd almost turned around several times, but forced himself to trust the whim, and surrendered to it.

Not entirely, though. This was not an unconditional surrender. He had gotten into his truck, driven all 330 miles to Miles City, and he would certainly go into the little cantina. That, however, is when he would ignore the whim so he could see what he needed to see and feel what he needed to feel before doing what this instinct implored him to.

He'd been to this roadhouse before. Quite a few times.

Sitting at the bar, feeling his anxiety grow, he heard the bell over the door jingle, and forced his mind clear.

He caught a look at the man who entered in the mirror over the bar.

The man scanned the small establishment. He saw there were only two other patrons. One sat at the bar wearing an old black Stetson. The other, an old drunk—who'd likely been judicially relegated to the cheap mountain bike leaning against the wall outside after repeated DUIs—sat in the far corner of the bar, barely keeping his head up while clutching his Coors Banquet in both hands. John Prine's "Pretty Good" was playing on the overhead speakers, a song he'd only heard for the first time recently, and had thoroughly enjoyed. Accepting the song and the relative emptiness of the dive as good signs, he figured this would do just fine, and sat four stools down from Clark.

As soon as he did, Clark grabbed both the beers and the bourbons he'd ordered two minutes earlier, got up, and sat down next to the newcomer.

When they locked eyes, every muscle in the newcomer's body froze. Clark wasn't sure what was going to happen, but he figured the best first move would be to slide him a beer and a shot. The man eyed the drinks suspiciously, then Clark held his bourbon up.

"So, what do I call ya?"

The man squinted back at him for a moment, then broke out laughing. It was a tired laugh, but a real one. He hung his head, shook it, then grabbed the bourbon, and clinked it against Clark's.

"You didn't like *Matthew Kabath*?"

Clark shook his head.

"Not so much."

They both downed the shots, and the chubby, bored-looking bartender emerged from the kitchen to promptly pour them two more, without asking for permission or making eye contact. The two men stared at each other for several long moments, until the newcomer spoke.

"Well, then, you can call me by *any old name you'd like*, amigo."

Clark squinted past him. He spoke with the accents of a thousand languages, yet wove and braided every dialect of contemporary American parlance Clark had ever heard into his words.

"What was your last one, in 1909?"

He grinned, and Clark caught the first glimmer of what he'd come here looking for.

"I was Teddy, last time."

Clark nodded.

"And who was I?"

The guy chuckled a bit and slapped his hand lightly on the bar.

"My dearest chap, I forget how you just don't . . . *remember a thing*. Sometimes you recall a *little*, but these last few, *merde*. You've been completely witless. *No idea* what's going on until I show up."

Clark heard one hundred different accents coiled into the man's voice, some from languages that hadn't been spoken in millennia. He ignored this, then cocked his eyebrows and his head in acknowledgment, and grinned up at him.

"Still ended up comin' out on top, though, didn't I?"

He smiled at Clark's reply, but not before Clark saw the briefest flash of anger twitch through his face. It was a resentful anger, coated with ancient, familial hatreds.

"As we've discussed before, *you get a lifetime*, while I only get a month. Not exactly even odds there, *mein bruder im kampf*. You're not the one who pops out of a box and has mere *weeks* to catch up with *literally everything*. This time, in particular, *santa mierda*. The weapons, vehicles, the food, microwaves, the *governments*? And *good God*, man, *what the hell* happened to Europe? Several complete structural remodels, monarchies just *gone* like dust? These telephones, *cell phones*, air travel, blasted *space travel*? Don't even get me started on the internet, *dulce madre de Cristo*. It's never been this big of a jump. Never even close. Can you empathize with me here, even a little?"

Clark took a pull from his beer.

"You sure talk normal. Minus a few words or phrases here or there, you'd pass as a local—a local to this *time* at least, so it seems you're a quick enough learner."

He rolled his eyes.

"Come on, *dude*. Observe, assess, reiterate local parlance and dialect? Takes an hour to get down, *tops*. That's the easy part, but imagine bumping into your first Wi-Fi router, or your first drone. *Miserere mei fratris*."

Clark tapped a finger on the bar top and then pointed it at him.

"Fair points, but I'm goin' into this blind. None of it started comin' back to me until *after* you'd already *been awakened* or whatever. So, to an extent, I was catchin' up with about as much wild bullshit as you were those few weeks."

He took a deep breath through his nose and looked at Clark through the corner of his eye a bit conspiratorially.

"You really don't remember any of it? Any of our old times?"

An encouraging, knowing grin spread on his face. Clark shrugged and shook his head.

"*Nah*, already said, didn't know who the shit you were till you were already kickin' around brainwashin' folks. I still don't have any memories from before, at least nothing with a date or any context. Images or moments pop up every once and again, but they're more like dreams than memories."

The man shook his head at Clark, sincere commiseration in his expression.

"That's truly a shame. *C'est dommage, mon frère*. We're cursed with this eternal duel, but only I can enjoy the momentary thrill of looking back upon our all history, *all the moments of chaos we've shared*, with no compatriot to enjoy it with. *C'est une tragédie.*"

Clark just shrugged.

"I dunno. Seems like a lotta baggage."

The man bobbed his head from side to side then spoke with growing animation.

"For you, yes, I suppose it might be. All the parents, wives, children, grandchildren, and all the rest. I concede, that's not something I'd have to deal with. But, *mein bruder*, believe me, there are some things you'd want to have in the archive. I saw you *lead an army* in Gaul when *we were on the same team*. You were friends with Cincinnatus *and* Alexander, like . . . real, true friends. You don't have any memory of that? And the *Battle of Breadfield* in Transylvania? *Kenyérmezei csata*? 1479? You cut down one hundred four Ottomans *in three hours*. *Nghidlek it-truch. I shit you not*, as they say these days. I counted their bodies myself."

Clark noted with mild, almost subconscious interest his own fluency in Hungarian and Maltese, two more languages he hadn't encountered until this moment. Even so, this guy could be making all these anecdotes up entirely, or they could be true. He'd never know, so he just shrugged.

The grumpy, disenchanted-looking bartender emerged again and poured them another round of shots. Clark nodded at the barkeep, steeling himself a bit as he decided now would be a good time to ask the question. The only one he came here to ask.

"So what now, for you? What do you do now?"

The man shrugged as he met Clark's eyes then glanced around, *almost* effectively shrouding the discomfort the question made him feel.

"*Quando le cose vanno male, prendi la vita con filosofia*. Same thing I've done before when you ruin the party but don't kill me, I suppose. Just *go about the rest of life* starting as a guy in his forties. Travel. Pick up a new hobby maybe."

Clark knew the old Italian expression, somehow, about *taking life with philosophy when things go wrong*, but did not dwell on it, he just nodded and looked away as his heart began to race. He took a breath and exhaled, taking great care to make it smooth and free from any shuddering.

He'd *felt* there had been moments in their *past lives* together when this man had survived despite the ritual being interrupted. He knew and felt, like the sensation of the sun on his skin, that this man's powers died with the ritual: his impossible strength and speed, along with his wicked schemes, doused in the catacombs under that castle of blood.

However, in the last weeks, he'd been plagued by the quandary of whether the evil itself had died with the ritual, *or* whether it could only die with the man. He'd been hoping the former, and his desire for it had grown every day.

However, he'd felt a grating, electric sensation in his soul. A flicker of this man's evil remained somewhere in the world. Like the steelhead jolted with the knowledge that *it was time* to return to the little mountain stream it was born in, he felt the presence of that flicker of evil out there, looking for an opportunity, and even if devoid of his power, still capable of terrible things.

Clark tried to keep his voice steady and unconcerned as he spoke.

"So that's it, we're just done? We can forget about all this and go about our lives? Throw me a bone here."

The man looked at him then, genuine surprise in his eyes. A smile began to spread on his face, slowly, and Clark saw a glimmer of vindictive malice touch the corners of his eyes. In that moment, Clark saw it. He saw *exactly* what he'd come here looking for. He leaned closer to Clark's face, studying both of his eyes.

"You really don't know, do you?"

Clark looked around the room, shrugging.

"Know *fuckin' what*?"

The man looked tired, disappointed almost.

"Well, I can't let any of those other cretins get a leg up, so, *I guess I've got to tell you.*"

He put his drink down on the bar, leaned an elbow on it, and turned on his stool to face Clark directly. The excited mockery in his eyes bled into his words.

"I'm just the *first of the four who cometh*. Doesn't that sound familiar, tough guy? *He who stands unseen* to banish the wrath of the darkness, *blah, blah, blah*. Yes, my dear chap—*you and me*, that's all finished now. *Me?* I'm worthless, a sack of bones and meat like all the rest. *But you, frater meus,* are about to have a *very wild few years.*"

Clark couldn't hide his anxiety at this comment, the titanic, bone-chilling dread it sent crashing through him. But he hadn't come here to talk about that particular hunch or whim, whichever it was. He nodded and stared at the bar, then looked up at the man with as much feigned innocent curiosity as he could muster.

"All right, you can bitch about all the leaps in technology you want, I get it. I've only ever lived this life, so I'll give you that as something I can't understand. But answer me this . . . *How about the music these days?*"

The man pursed his lips and grinned a bit. He shook his head, reluctant to admit it, then he smiled at Clark through the sides of his eyes.

"*I will admit,* this *honky-tonk* genre, Waylon Jennings and that Hank Williams fella, that's some good stuff. And these country line dances, I must say."

Clark loved both musicians this man just mentioned, but hated line dancing, something he'd hidden from Mary—who'd loved it—until the day she'd died. He'd come to hate it even more after watching this abomination do country dances at the feet of the men he'd crucified. He hid this hatred now just as he'd hidden it from Mary, and wagged a finger as he got up, smiling and cocking his head toward the jukebox.

"Follow me. *Wait till you hear this.*"

Clark strolled over to the jukebox and started flipping through the pages. The man grabbed his beer and followed him. He shook his head in disgust as he glared at the drunk old-timer across the pool table, now fully asleep, head and shoulders crumpled into the corner wall and audibly snoring. Clark tapped on the glass window of the jukebox when he'd found it.

"This, right here. It ain't honky-tonk, but this guy's name is *Jimi Hendrix*, best guitar player to ever live. This song you're about to hear is called 'Born Under a Bad Sign,' from his album *Blues*. If you don't love this, I'll let you have the ritual next time around, all right?"

That got a real smile out of him. Clark, again, saw the evil slithering underneath it.

He thumbed in a few quarters, punched in the code, and the bass line started coming through the old speakers. Clark stood there, unmoving, until the guitar came in about ten seconds later, then pointed up at the speaker.

"*Listen to this.* I'm getting us more bourbon."

The guy shrugged and nodded, an amused smile on his face. Clark walked up to the bar and knocked loudly on it a few times.

Clark's heart was pounding in his ears. Adrenaline numbed his hands and face. He took a few deep breaths and thought back on all the vicious, carnal evil he'd seen orchestrated by this man's caprice.

He thought about the ambush in Ward, the preacher in that church. He thought about the eight men he'd crucified, then danced in front of. He thought of the three FBI HRT agents he'd torn apart with his bare hands. He thought about all the people, young and old, drained of their blood and chained to chairs in those terrifying places. He thought about the look he'd just seen in his eye, the look he'd seen so many times. The lies. The deception. *The evil.*

Clark thought about Lucy Westerna.

The slouched, disenchanted bartender appeared and splashed more Four Roses into both glasses.

Clark took the glasses back toward the man, who was flipping through the pages of the jukebox. He set the glasses quietly on the scuffed, beer-stained long rail of the pool table. Without looking, he slowly grabbed the broken pool cue he'd snapped over his knee then set there ten minutes before *he* got to the bar.

One of his favorite songs was playing loudly from the old speakers. He knew by heart that almost a minute and a half had passed since he'd started it, and that he couldn't wait any longer.

Clark closed the distance to where the man stood, his back to Clark, in a halo of warm, yellow light cast from the jukebox.

He grabbed this monster under the chin, yanked his head back, and drove the sharp end of the broken pool cue through his back left ribs. Blood spurted a few times then *sprayed* onto the glass of the jukebox as the blade of wood punched out the front of his chest. Clark knew, with what felt like thousands of years of experience, it had gone directly through his heart. The man dropped his beer, bottle shattering at their feet, and grasped at the hands and face of the man who'd killed him so many times before.

Clark whispered into his ear.

"*Ego sum qui obicio tenebras,* ya *fuckin' asshole.*"

He had a Glock 9mm pistol holstered inside his waistband, knives in two different pockets, and a rifle in his car. Even so, he just couldn't resist the urge to shove a wooden stake through this monster's heart, and when he felt him die, he was very happy he'd done so.

He didn't know why, and would never think on it again, but he'd felt no other method would've been appropriate.

He let the limp body fall.

After a few seconds, the bartender walked out from behind the bar and stood next to Clark, a bottle of beer in one hand and a bar towel in the other. The drunk, who'd been snoring in the corner, pushed the brim of his hat up with a finger, scanned the scene, then sat up straight on the bar stool. He grabbed his beer and trundled over to stand on Clark's other side. The three men stared at the body for a minute, none speaking.

The bartender, and the drunk from the corner, took sips from their beers in the same instant, then wiped their mouths with the backs of their hands. Clark spoke without looking away from the body.

"Thanks again, fellas."

Pete slung the bar towel over his shoulder. Hank clapped Clark on the back. Both Pete and Hank spoke the same four words in unison.

"Don't mention it, bud."

ACKNOWLEDGMENTS

WE WANT TO acknowledge the incredible support and guidance of our representatives Scott Glassgold, Liz Parker, and Anthony Mattero—without whom we would be rudderless. We would especially like to acknowledge the singular kindness, wisdom, taste, and vision of our editor Emily Bestler—whose partnership has been an invaluable and essential part of telling the stories we have wanted to tell.